"Acclaimed novelist Dave Eggers returns with a road-tripping tribute to self-discovery in the forty-ninth state. . . . Eggers uses the trio's escapades and the characters they encounter to explore and make provocative commentary on wide-ranging themes: the American identity, our society's relationship (or lack thereof) with nature, and the United States' astounding appetite for violence. . . . [But] at its heart *Heroes of the Frontier* is a story about adventure—and the personal growth that can come from it."

—Kelley McMillan, *National Geographic*

"Thorough, detail-driven and well-paced. . . . Read *Heroes of the Frontier*. It's an engaging, picaresque adventure with contemporary themes."   —D. Grant Black, *Toronto Star*

"A story of adventure and daring. . . . Eggers makes the case that there is meaning in movement, however blind or misguided it might appear from the outset, a claim with which all the world's daring adventurers throughout history would surely agree."   —Leilani Clark, KQED

"*Heroes of the Frontier* shows us what happens to a family when chaos is embraced deliberately; when the order of suburban life is replaced by the anarchy of a road trip. . . . It gleefully defies classification but in returning again and again to the complex, overpowering love between guardian and child, feels like classic Eggers."

—Melissa Katsoulis, *The Times* (London)

"Eggers is going big in this book, tackling a topic no less broad than America itself. . . . Sweeping, self-aware."
—Michael Melgaard, *National Post*

"One of the best things about *Heroes* is Josie herself. She runs counter to the traditional travel/escape narrative by the mere fact of her gender and her being a mom with kids in tow. She wins our respect through her grit, her admirable way of interacting with her two energetic and intelligent children, her confidence and her resolve. . . . The children—wise-beyond-his-years Paul and wild, red-haired, accident-prone Ana—are sketched with a sensitive ear for their peculiarities."
—Claude Peck, *Minneapolis Star Tribune*

"Dave Eggers has proven time and again that his novels are worth the read. . . . From start to finish, *Heroes of the Frontier* is a joy—one that relishes in its absurd humor while digging at deeper truths about life and family in modern America."
—Bill Jones, *The A.V. Club*

"Count on Eggers for clear-eyed wisdom, a wry sense of humor and a tonal agility, bouncing effortlessly from humor to tragedy and back again. . . . Remarkably brave and resonant."
—*USA Today*

"Eggers's language is its own frontier: bracingly bitter and funny and real."
—*Entertainment Weekly*

"Captivating. . . . Part adventure, part social critique, the book is occasionally harrowing and often very funny. . . . As Eggers takes Josie through wildfires, avalanches, lightning strikes and narrow escapes from the long arm of the law, he suggests there's something a little heroic in all of us."

—Georgia Rowe, *San Jose Mercury News*

"[Eggers's] latest, *Heroes of the Frontier*, is by far his most fun work of fiction, and maybe also his most substantial— expressing something of the bone-deep moral and cultural exhaustion that might drive a middle-aged American lib- eral to flee the country. . . . This gentle, forceful novel might equally serve as a reminder that the frontier spirit still guides the loftiest American ideals, as well as the betrayed, disfigured and debased."

—Stephen Phelan, *Sunday Herald* (UK)

"Extraordinary. . . . It is impossible not to be impressed by a writer so ready to remake himself. . . . Sharp and often funny. . . . Unforgettable."

—Claire Lowdon, *The Times* (London)

"Dave Eggers has become the most acute chronicler of our chaotic era. . . . His remarkable spate of recent fiction has shown him engaged, in a vigorous literary midperiod, with nothing less than the state of the American nation."

—Robert Collins, *The Sunday Times* (London)

DAVE EGGERS

HEROES OF THE FRONTIER

Dave Eggers grew up near Chicago and graduated from the University of Illinois at Urbana-Champaign. He is the founder of McSweeney's, an independent publishing house in San Francisco that produces books, a quarterly journal of new writing (*Timothy McSweeney's Quarterly Concern*), and a monthly magazine (*The Believer*). McSweeney's also published Voice of Witness, a nonprofit book series that uses oral history to illuminate human rights crises around the world. In 2002, he cofounded 826 Valencia, a nonprofit youth writing and tutoring center in San Francisco's Mission District. Sister centers have since opened in seven other American cities under the umbrella of 826 National, and like-minded centers have opened in Dublin, London, Copenhagen, Stockholm, and St. Paul/Minneapolis, among other locations. His work has been nominated for the National Book Award, the Pulitzer Prize, and the National Book Critics Circle Award and has won the Dayton Literary Peace Prize, France's Prix Médicis, Germany's Albatross Prize, the National Magazine Award, and the American Book Award. Eggers lives in Northern California with his family.

www.mcsweeneys.net

Also by Dave Eggers

FICTION

Your Fathers, Where Are They? And the Prophets, Do They Live Forever?
The Circle
A Hologram for the King
What Is the What
How We Are Hungry
You Shall Know Our Velocity!

NONFICTION

Understanding the Sky
Zeitoun

FOR YOUNG READERS

The Wild Things

MEMOIR

A Heartbreaking Work of Staggering Genius

AS EDITOR

Surviving Justice: America's Wrongfully Convicted and Exonerated
The Voice of Witness Reader: Ten Years of Amplifying Unheard Voices
Teachers Have It Easy: The Big Sacrifices and Small Salaries of America's Teachers
The Better of McSweeney's

PICTURE BOOK

This Bridge Will Not Be Gray

HEROES OF THE FRONTIER

HEROES
OF THE
FRONTIER

a novel

DAVE EGGERS

VINTAGE BOOKS
A Division of Penguin Random House LLC
New York

FIRST VINTAGE BOOKS EDITION, JUNE 2017

Copyright © 2016 by Dave Eggers

All rights reserved. Published in the United States by Vintage Books, a division
of Penguin Random House LLC, New York, and in Canada by Random House
of Canada, a division of Penguin Random House Canada Limited, Toronto.
Originally published in hardcover in the United States by Alfred A. Knopf,
a division of Penguin Random House LLC, New York, in 2016.

Vintage and colophon are registered trademarks of
Penguin Random House LLC.

A portion of this work first appeared in *The New Yorker* (www.newyorker.com) as
"The Alaska of Giants and Gods" on November 17, 2014.

The Cataloging-in-Publication Data is on file at the Library of Congress.

Vintage Books Trade Paperback ISBN: 978-1-101-97463-6
eBook ISBN: 978-0-451-49381-1

Book design by Claudia Martinez

www.vintagebooks.com

Printed in the United States of America
10 9 8 7 6 5 4 3 2 1

HEROES OF THE FRONTIER

HEROES OF PROGRESS LIFE

I.

THERE IS PROUD HAPPINESS, happiness born of doing good work in the light of day, years of worthwhile labor, and afterward being tired, and content, and surrounded by family and friends, bathed in satisfaction and ready for a deserved rest—sleep or death, it would not matter.

Then there is the happiness of one's personal slum. The happiness of being alone, and tipsy on red wine, in the passenger seat of an ancient recreational vehicle parked somewhere in Alaska's deep south, staring into a scribble of black trees, afraid to go to sleep for fear that at any moment someone will get past the toy lock on the RV door and murder you and your two small children sleeping above.

Josie squinted into the low light of a long summer evening at a rest stop in southern Alaska. She was happy this night, with her pinot, in this RV in the dark, surrounded by unknown woods, and became less afraid with every new sip from her yellow plastic cup. She was content, though she knew this was a fleeting and artificial contentment, she knew this was all wrong—she should not be in Alaska, not like this. She had been a dentist and was no longer a dentist. The father of her children, an invertebrate, a loose-boweled man named Carl, a man who had told Josie marriage-by-documentation was a sham, the paper superfluous and reductive, had, eighteen months after he'd moved out, found a different woman to marry him. He'd met and now was, improbably, impossibly, marrying some other person, a person from Florida. It was happening in September, and Josie was fully justified in leaving, in disappearing until it was all over. Carl had no idea she had taken the children out of Ohio. Almost out of North America. And he could not know. And what could better grant her invisibility than this, a rolling home, no fixed address, a white RV in a state with a million other wayward travelers, all of them in white RVs? No one could ever find her. She'd contemplated leaving the country altogether, but Ana didn't have a passport and Carl was needed to get one, so that option was out. Alaska was at once the same country but another country, was almost Russia, was almost oblivion, and if Josie left her phone and used only cash—she'd brought three thousand dollars in the kind of velvet bag meant to hold gold coins or magic beans—she was untraceable, untrackable. And she'd been a Girl Scout. She could tie a knot, gut a fish, start a fire. Alaska did not daunt her.

* * *

She and the kids had landed in Anchorage earlier that day, a grey day without promise or beauty, but the moment she'd stepped off the plane she found herself inspired. "Okay guys!" she'd said to her exhausted, hungry children. They had never expressed any interest in Alaska, and now here they were. "Here we are!" she'd said, and she'd done a celebratory little march. Neither child smiled.

She'd piled them into this rented RV and had driven off, no plan in mind. The manufacturers called the vehicle the Chateau, but that was thirty years ago, and now it was broken-down and dangerous to its passengers and all who shared the highway with it. But after a day on the road, her kids were fine. They were strange. There was Paul, eight years old, with the cold caring eyes of an ice priest, a gentle, slow-moving boy who was far more reasonable and kind and wise than his mother. And there was Ana, only five, a constant threat to the social contract. She was a green-eyed animal with a burst of irrationally red hair and a knack for assessing the most breakable object in any room and then breaking it with incredible alacrity.

Josie, hearing the roar of a truck passing through on the nearby highway, poured herself a second cup. This is allowed, she told herself, and closed her eyes.

But where was the Alaska of magic and clarity? This place was choked with the haze of a dozen forest fires, spread around the state like a prison break, and it was not majestic, no, not yet. All they'd seen so far was cluttered and tough.

They'd seen seaplanes. They'd seen hundreds of homes for sale. They'd seen a roadside ad for a tree farm looking for a buyer. They'd seen another RV, not unlike theirs, parked on the side of the road, under a high sheer mountain wall. The mother of the family was squatting on the side of the road. They'd seen lacquered log cabin homes. They'd seen in a convenience store also made of lacquered logs, a T-shirt that said *Don't blame me. I voted for the American.*

So where were the heroes? All she knew where she had come from were cowards. No, there was one brave man, and she'd helped to get him killed. One courageous man now dead. Everyone took everything and Jeremy was dead. Find me someone bold, she asked the dark trees before her. Find me someone of substance, she demanded of the mountains beyond.

Alaska had been on her mind only a few weeks before she'd decided to leave Ohio. She had a stepsister, Sam, up in Homer, a stepsister who was not quite a stepsister, and who she hadn't seen in years but who had held great mystique because she lived in Alaska, and owned her own business, and piloted a boat or ship of some kind, and had raised two daughters largely alone, her husband a fisherman gone for months at a time. To hear Sam tell it he was no prize and his absences no great loss.

Josie had never been to Alaska and outside of Homer had no idea where to go or what to do there. But she wrote to

Sam, telling her she was coming, and Sam wrote her back, saying that was fine. Josie took this as a good sign, that her stepsister who she hadn't seen in five years just said "fine" and did no kind of beseeching or encouraging. Sam was an Alaskan now, and that meant, Josie was sure, a plainspoken and linear existence centered around work and trees and sky, and this kind of disposition was what Josie craved in others and herself. She wanted no more of the useless drama of life. If theatrics were necessary, fine. If a human were ascending a mountain, and on that ascent there were storms and avalanches and bolts of lightning from angry skies, then she could accept drama, participate in drama. But suburban drama was so tiresome, so absurd on its face, that she could no longer be around anyone who thought it real or worthwhile.

So they flew up and found their baggage and then found Stan. He owned the recreational vehicle she had rented—the Chateau—and he was standing outside baggage claim, holding a sign with Josie's name on it. He was as she imagined him—a retired man in his seventies, hearty and with a way of swinging his hands, as if they were heavy things, bunches of bananas, he was delivering. They loaded their luggage into the vehicle and were off. Josie turned around to look at her children. They looked tired and unclean. "Cool, huh guys?" she asked, indicating the Chateau's environs, a patchwork of plaids and wood veneers. Stan was white-haired and wore ironed jeans and clean powder-blue sneakers. Josie sat in the front seat, the children in a banquette in back, as they drove the ten miles from the airport to Stan's house, where the paperwork for the Chateau would be done. Ana was soon asleep against the horizontal blinds. Paul smiled wanly and closed his ice-priest eyes. Stan adjusted his rearview mirror to see them, and seeing them through Stan's eyes, Josie knew they did not look like her children. They were mismatched to her and to each other. Josie's hair was black, Paul's khaki, Ana's red. Josie's eyes were brown and small, Paul's enormous and blue, Ana's green and shaped like paisleys.

When they arrived in Stan's driveway, he parked the Chateau and the kids were invited to play in the yard. Ana immediately went to a large tree with a hole in the trunk and stuck her hand in. "Look, I got a baby!" she yelled, holding an invisible baby.

"Sorry," Josie said.

Stan nodded gravely, as if Josie had said *My child is demented and incurable.* He got out the owner's manual and went through the functions of the RV with the seriousness of someone explaining the dismantling of a bomb. There was the oven, the speedometer, odometer, bathroom, cleanout, electrical hookup, various levers and cushions and hidden compartments.

"You've operated a recreational vehicle before," he said, as if there could be no other answer.

"Of course. Many times," Josie said. "And I used to drive a bus."

She'd never done either, but sensed that Stan took the Chateau seriously but not so much Josie. She had to instill in him some confidence that she wouldn't drive the Chateau off a cliff. He led her around the vehicle, noting the pre-existing damage on a clipboard, and as he did, Josie saw a boy of about six in the bay window of Stan's home, staring out at them. The room where he stood seemed to be entirely white—white walls, white wall-to-wall carpet, a white lamp on a white table. Soon a grandmotherly woman, likely Stan's wife, arrived behind the boy, put her hands on his shoulders, turned him around and guided him back into the depths of the house.

Josie expected, after the inspection, that she and the kids would be invited into the home, but they were not.

"See you in three weeks," Stan said, for that was the duration they'd agreed on. Josie thought the trip might be extended, for a month or indefinitely, and figured she'd call Stan when that became clearer.

"Okay," Josie said, and got into the driver's seat. She pulled the long arm, extending from the steering wheel like an antler, down to Reverse, unable to shake the sense that the plan had been to invite her and the kids inside, but something had convinced Stan to keep them away from his pristine white house and grandson.

"Drive safe now," he said, waving his banana hands.

They had three days to kill before Sam was back from one of her tours. She was taking a group of French executives into the woods to look at birds and bears, and wouldn't be back till Sunday. Josie planned to spend a day or two in Anchorage, but when she drove through the city, the Chateau creaking and shuddering, she saw a street fair, and thousands of people in bright tanktops and sandals, and she wanted to flee. They left the metropolis, going south, and soon encountered signs for an animal park of some kind. *Most popular attraction in Alaska* was the claim. Just when Josie was sure they would pass the attraction without Ana being made aware, Paul spoke.

"Animal park," he said to Ana.

His ability to read had greatly complicated their family.

The kids wanted badly to go, and Josie wanted badly to speed past the attraction, but the signs had mentioned bears and bison and moose, and the idea that they could cross all these mammals from their list in the first few hours held some appeal.

They pulled over.

"You need your jacket," Paul said to Ana, who was already at the Chateau door. Paul held it out to her like a butler would. "Hold your sleeves so they don't bunch," he said. Ana held her shirt-sleeves and slipped her arms into the jacket. Josie watched all this, feeling superfluous.

Inside a log-cabin office, Josie paid a criminal amount, sixty-six dollars for the three of them. There were usually guides and carts that would drive guests around the premises, but everyone was gone or vacationing, so Josie and the kids were alone in what seemed to be a zoo after an apocalypse. She thought of the Iraqi zoo after the coalition's bombings, the lions and cheetahs roaming free but starving, looking for cats and dogs to eat, and finding neither.

This was not so bad. But it was sad like any zoo is sad, a place where no one really wants to be. The humans feel guilty about being there at all, crushed by thoughts of capture and captivity and bad food and drugs and fences. And the animals barely move. They saw a pair of moose, and their new calf, none of them stirring. They saw a single sleeping bison, its coat threadbare, its eyes half-open and furious. They saw an antelope, spindly and stupid; it walked a few feet before stopping to look forlornly into the grey mountains beyond. Its eyes said, *Take me, Lord. I am now broken.*

They returned to the log cabin for refreshments. "Check it out," a tour guide said to Josie's kids as they drank lemonade. He pointed to a mountain range nearby, where, he said, there was a rare thing: a small group of bighorn sheep, cutting a horizontal line across the ridge, east to west. "Use the binoculars," he said, and Paul and Ana raced to a stationary set, anchored to the deck.

"I see them," Paul said. As Paul ceded the binoculars to Ana, Josie squinted into the distance, finding the group, a smattering of vague white dots against the mountainside. It was a baffling thing, seeing twelve or fifteen animals standing comfortably on what seemed to be a clean vertical wall. Josie took a turn at the binoculars, found the sheep and in the sky saw a dark shadow slashing across their path. She assumed it was a hawk of some kind, so she swung the binoculars around but found nothing. She returned to the sheep, finding one in particular that seemed to be looking right back at her. The sheep looked very pleased with its life, hadn't a care in the world, even though it was standing on a quarter-inch of shelf, two thousand feet up. Josie adjusted the focus a bit, now seeing the sheep even more clearly, and as she locked into a wonderfully clear view of the animal, two things happened in rapid succession.

First, the clouds above the sheep seemed to break, parting as if to allow a narrow ray of godlight to shine on the animal's downy head. Josie could see the animal's bright grey eyes, its feathery cotton-white hair, and as Josie was staring at the sheep, and the sheep at Josie, as it was showing Josie what unadulterated bliss was, revealing the secrets of its uncomplicated life high above everything—as this was happening, a dark shape entered Josie's view. A dark wing. This was a predatory bird, enormous, its wingspan wide and opaque like a black umbrella. And then the bird dropped down and its talons took the sheep by the shoulders, lifted it just a few inches up and away from the cliff, and released it. The sheep fell from view. Josie stood, and with her naked eyes watched the sheep as it descended from the mountain, oblivious and unstruggling, like a ragdoll steadily falling to an unseeable place of rest.

"Eagle," the guide said, then whistled appreciatively. "Wonderful, wonderful." He explained that this was a common but rarely seen method eagles used to kill large prey: an eagle would lift and drop an animal from great heights, allowing the prey to fall a few hundred feet to its death on the rocks below, breaking every bone. Then the eagle would sail down, grab the dead animal in whole or in pieces, and bring its flesh back to its children for consumption. "Why did you want us to see that?" Josie asked the guide, knowing it would haunt her thoughts, would scar her children, but the guide was gone.

"What happened, Mama?" Ana asked. Paul had heard and understood the guide's narration, and Josie was sorry he knew the treachery of every level of the animal world, but was grateful that Ana was free, for now, from such knowledge.

"Nothing," Josie said. "Let's go."

It was best, she told the kids, to get out of the Anchorage area, to really leave, to strike out and make their own path. So they stopped at a grocery store and loaded up. The store was twenty acres, it did not end; it sold stereos, lawn furniture, wigs, guns, gasoline. It was full of truckers, some large families, some people who seemed of Native blood, some weathered Caucasians, everyone looking very tired. Josie bought enough groceries for a week, stored them as best she could in the Chateau's particle-board cabinets, and left.

The speed limit on most highways in Alaska seemed to be sixty-five, but the Chateau would not exceed forty-eight. It took inordinately long to get to forty, and ten minutes of asthmatic heaving to get from forty to forty-seven, and after that the whole assembly seemed ready to pull apart like an exploding star. So for the first few hours Josie drove at forty-eight, while the traffic around her was going twenty miles faster. On two-lane roads, there were usually four or six cars behind her, honking and cursing until Josie could find a wide shoulder where she could pull over, allow them all to pass and then get back on the road, knowing in five minutes she would accumulate another line of angry followers. Stan had said nothing about any of this.

She'd made the kids sandwiches, and served them on actual plates, and now they were finished and wanted to know where to put the plates. She told them to put them on the counter, and at the next stoplight the plates fell to the ground, breaking and sending the remnants of lunch to every Chateau nook and cranny. The trip had begun.

Josie knew nothing about Seward but it was somewhere near Homer so she decided that would be their destination for the day. They drove an hour or so, and found some brutally gorgeous bay, the water a hard mirror, white mountains rising beyond like a wall of dead presidents. Josie pulled over, just for a picture or two, but already everything inside the vehicle was filthy—the floor was muddy, there were clothes and wrappers strewn about, and most of Ana's chips were on the floor. Josie felt a sudden exhaustion come over her. She pulled the blinds, let the kids watch *Tom and Jerry*—in Spanish, it was the only DVD they'd brought, leaving in a hurry as they did—and on their little machine they watched the cartoons as trucks hammered past them, each giving the Chateau a gentle rocking. Twenty minutes later the children were asleep and she was still awake.

She moved into the passenger seat, opened a twist-off pinot, poured herself a cup, and settled in with a copy of *Old West* magazine. Stan had left five copies in the Chateau—a forty-year-old magazine offering TRUE TALES OF THE OLD WEST. In it there was a column called "Trails Grown Dim," where readers would send in requests for information about long-lost kin.

"In the Republic of Texas census of 1840," read one, "is word of Thomas Clifton of Austin County with the statement that he owned 349 acres of land. I would like to hear from any of his descendants." That was signed by one Reginald Hayes. Josie considered Mr. Hayes, feeling for him, imagining the fascinating legal battles he had in store when he tried to reclaim those 349 Austin County acres.

"Perhaps someone could help us locate my mother's sisters," the next entry read, "the daughters of Walter Loomis and Mary Snell. My mother Bess was the oldest. She last saw her sisters in Arkansas in 1926. There was Rose, Mavis and Lorna. My mother, a wanderer, didn't write and has never heard from them since. We would love to hear from anyone knowing about them. They would be in their fifties now, I believe."

The rest of the page was filled with half-told stories of abandonment and distress, and the occasional hint of larceny or homicide.

"David Arnold died in Colorado in 1912 and was buried in McPherson, Kansas," read the page's last item. "A wife and four children survived him. Two daughters are now living, I believe. Would like a copy of his obituary for family records or would like to know where he died and if murder was ever proved. Also, was it ever proved that the deaths of his two sons in 1913 were tied in with his murder? He was my great-uncle."

Josie filled her cup again. She put the magazine down and looked out the window. A smile spread across her lips. Being so far from Carl and his crimes made her smile. She and Carl had parted ways a few years into his phase of heavy urination. Extraordinary, unprecedented frequency. He had been a healthy man! Maybe not a man who could carry her across the threshold—he was thin, she was not so thin—but still an active non-consumptive man with two arms, two legs, a flat stomach. So why did he piss all night and all day? The image of Carl that came to mind, now eighteen months after their split, was of him standing, a wide stance, at the toilet, the door open, waiting to piss. Or actually pissing. Or shaking after pissing. Unzipping before or after pissing. Changing his plaid housepants because he didn't shake well enough after pissing and had dribbled on them and they now smelled like piss. Pissing twice in the early morning. Pissing six or seven times after dinner. Pissing all day. Getting out of bed three times every night to piss.

It's your prostate, Josie told him.

You're a dentist, he told her.

16

It wasn't his prostate, his proctologist said. But the proctologist had no idea what it was, either. No one had any idea what it was. Carl shat all the time, too. You could count his daily shits but why would you?

At least six. Starting with his first cup of coffee. First sip. Again Josie pictured his back, saw him standing at the kitchen counter in front of his single-serve coffeemaker. Wearing his plaid housepants. The plaid housepants, made of wool, were too short, too thick, and were spattered with white paint—he'd painted the kids' bathroom and had done a terrible job. And he wore these paint-spattered pants why? To remind himself and the world that he was a man of action. A man who could paint (poorly) a child's bathroom. So he would stand there, waiting for the machine to fill his little blue cup. Finally his little blue cup would get filled, and he would take it, lean against the counter, look out in the yard, and then, at the first sip, as if that first drop had liquidated his innards, loosened all that was stuck, he would rush to the bathroom, the one near the garage, and begin his day of shitting. Eight, ten shits a day. Why was she thinking about this?

Then he'd come out, bragging to the kids about how he *did some good work in there,* or that he *did the job like a man should do.* He knew he shat a lot and tried to make it funny. Josie committed a fatal mistake early in their union, allowing him to think he was funny, giggling along with him when he giggled at his own jokes—then she had to keep laughing. Years of strained laughter. But how could a person keep laughing under conditions like that? The kids barely saw him away from the toilet. He would have discussions with them while on the toilet. He once fixed Paul's walkie-talkie while sitting on that toilet—as Carl laid down the batteries, the machinery of his bowels was grinding wetly below. And then they tested the walkie-talkies! While he continued to shit, or try to shit. Carl sitting there, Paul in another room. "Breaker 1-9," Carl said, then: "Breaker B-M!"

It was an abomination. She took to leaving the house before it began. It was like Schrödinger's cat. She knew the shitting would happen, but if she was gone, out the door before his first sip of coffee, would the shitting actually happen? Yes and no. Josie tried to put a stop to it, but he countered. *What,* he said, *you'd rather have an anal-retentive?* He was serious. She took a long pull on her pinot. It cooled her, opened her.

Early on they decided not to tell people Carl had been a patient when they'd met. Explaining it all rendered it all too pedestrian—he was looking to get his teeth cleaned and looked online for local dentists. Her office was the only one with a last-minute opening. For any feeling human, would that qualify as romantic? She barely noticed him during the exam. Then, a few weeks later, she was at Foot Locker, looking for socks, when a man, a customer sitting below her, one hand in a shoe, looked up and said hello. She had no idea who he was. But he was handsome, with alabaster skin, green eyes and long lashes.

"I'm Carl," he said, removing his hand from the shoe and offering it to her. "From the dentist's office."

He laughed a long while, as if the idea of a job at Foot Locker, for anyone, was the greatest joke. "No. No, I don't work here," he said.

He was four years younger than Josie and had the energy of a housebound puppy. For a year it was fun. She was a year into her own practice, and he helped out, ran errands, hung pictures in the waiting room, kept everything manic and light. He liked to ride bikes. To get ice cream. To play kick-ball. He ate chocolate power bars from crinkly gold wrappers. His libido was unstoppable, his control nonexistent. She was dating a twelve-year-old.

But he was twenty-seven. He was not gainfully employed then, and had never had a steady job before or since. His father owned some immeasurable stretch of Costa Rica, which he'd clear-cut to make room for cows destined to be eaten by American and Japanese carnivores, and so any occupation involving a scale less grand somehow did not quite suit Carl.

"We've raised a dilettante," Luisa, his mother, said. She was Chilean by birth, raised in Santiago, her mother a doctor, her father a diplomat, also a depressive. She'd met Carl's red-haired American father, Lou, in Mexico City, when she was a graduate student. She'd had Carl and his two brothers while Lou, raised in an oil family, bought land in Costa Rica, razed forests, raised cows, built an empire. He'd asked for a divorce ten years before to marry the ex-wife of a well-known and dead Chiapan narco. Luisa and Lou had an improbably good relationship. "He's so much better from a distance," Luisa said.

Now she was a wizened, beautiful woman of sixty, living on her own terms in Key West, with a group of sunburned, day-drinking friends. When they met, Josie loved everything about her—her candor, her grim wit, her insights into Carl. "He inherited his father's short attention span, but not his father's vision."

Carl had collected a dozen or so licenses and skills. He was a realtor for a few years, though he sold nothing. He'd dabbled in furniture design, fashion, sport fishing. He had a closet full of photography equipment. Though Josie and Luisa were both obliged to love Carl, the tragedy was that they liked each other far more than either liked him.

"Last year he had me videotape him," Luisa said in her raspy voice. "He's still discovering his relationship to the world," she said, "discovering his own body, you know. One day he asked me to film him walking—from the front, the back and the side. He said he wanted to be sure he walked the way he thought he walked. So I filmed my son, this grown man, walking up and down the street. He seemed satisfied with the results."

"He's prettier than you." That's what Sam said when she met Carl. "That can't be good." He could be fun. Cowards are often fantastically charming. But could anything begun at a Foot Locker become grand? Josie had never married Carl, and that was a story, a series of interconnected stories, episodes, decisions and reversals, both she and Carl culpable. Finally, with her strong endorsement, he'd left. At the time she was happy for it. Coward. Coward coward, she thought—it was the basic building block of his DNA, cowardice and whatever mutation had produced his gripless bowels. On so many levels he was a coward, but she had not anticipated the way he would disappear after he moved out. What had she wanted? She'd wanted general involvement, a monthly visit maybe, a father who would take the kids for a weekend. He was good enough with children—harmless around Ana, benign with Paul. He seemed to like children, really, thought he could make them laugh, and his juvenile outlook on life seemed to sync perfectly with theirs.

He was, years after they met, still a child, still discovering his relationship to the world, discovering his own body. One day he asked Josie to film him walking, too. Josie was shocked, but didn't let on she knew Luisa had done the same thing. "I think I know how I walk, but I've never seen it objectively," he said. "I want to make sure I walk the way I think I walk." So Josie filmed this grown man walking up and down the street. But then, six months later, he was gone. He saw the kids twice the year he left, once the year after.

Josie turned on the radio, heard Sam Cooke singing some simple song, and thought that only writers of pop songs and singers of pop music really knew how to live. Write a song—how long could it take? Minutes? Maybe an hour,

21

maybe a day. Then sing the song to people who will love you for it. Who will love the music. Bring renewable joy to millions. Or just thousands. Or just hundreds. Does it matter? The music does not die. Sam Cooke, long gone, only dust now, was still with us, was now vibrating through Josie and was carving new neural pathways in her children's minds, his voice so clear, a magnificent songbird coming through the radio and alighting on her shoulder, even here, even now, at nine o'clock, in this broken RV, somewhere between Anchorage and Homer. Though dead too soon, Sam Cooke knew how to live. Did he *know* he knew how to live?

Josie, rearranging herself in the Chateau, poured herself another cup. Three would be it. She rolled down the window and took in the acrid air. The fires were a hundred miles away, she'd been told, but the air everywhere was burned and predatory. Her throat fought her, her lungs petitioned for relief. She rolled the window up and through the glass she thought she saw a deer but realized it was an old sawhorse. She swished the wine in her mouth, gargled briefly, swallowed. Occasionally a gust would push the Chateau to a tilt and the dishes in the cupboards would rattle gently.

She flipped through her *Old West,* then threw it onto the dashboard. Even the plaintive searches of "Trails Grown Dim" made her sad, jealous. She had been born a blank. Her parents were blanks. All her relatives were blanks, though many were addicts, and she had a cousin who identified as an anarchist, but otherwise Josie's people were blanks. They were from nowhere. To be American is to be blank, and a true American is truly blank. Thus, all in all, Josie was a truly great American.

Still, she heard occasional and vague references to Denmark. Once or twice she heard her parents mention some connection to Finland. Her parents knew nothing about these cultures, these nationalities. They cooked no national dishes, they taught Josie no customs, and they had no relatives who cooked national dishes or had customs. They had no clothes, no flags, no banners, no sayings, no ancestral lands or villages or folktales. When she was thirty-two, and wanted to visit some village, somewhere, where her people had come from, none of her relatives had any idea at all where to go. One uncle thought he could be helpful: Everyone in our family speaks English, he said. Maybe you go to England?

The Sam Cooke song ended, the radio news began, the word "lawsuit" was uttered, and Josie felt a white flash of pain, saw the face of Evelyn Sandalwood, the stabbing eyes of the old woman's litigious son-in-law, and felt sure no one cared one way or another that her business was taken from her, was certain the world held only cowards, that work meant nothing to anyone, service meant nothing, that pettiness and guile and treachery and greed won always—nothing could defeat the thieving weasels of the world. Eventually they would wear down the brave, the true, anyone who wanted to go about their lives with integrity. The weasels always won because love and goodness was an ice-cream cone and treachery was a tank.

When, eighteen months ago, she'd told Carl they should end their pretend romance and just move on as parents of Paul and Ana, he walked out of the house—the house he'd wanted and then, once bought and renovated, loathed; the Occupy movement had instilled in him the idea that home ownership was not just bourgeois but a tangible crime against the 99%—then took a walk around the neighborhood. Twenty minutes later he'd come to terms with it, and had a plan for visitations and everything else. She'd entered the discussion terrified and inspired, but afterward she was depleted. In his ready acquiescence he managed to take from her whatever triumph she hoped to feel, and he'd gone straight into logistics.

Now, at forty, Josie was tired. She was tired of her journey through a day, the limitless moods contained in any stretch of hours. There was the horror of morning, underslept, feeling she was on the precipice of something that felt like mono, the day already galloping away from her, her chasing on foot, carrying her boots. Then the brief upward respite after a second cup of coffee, when all seemed possible, when she wanted to call her father, her mother, reconcile, visit them with the kids, when, while driving the kids to school—jail the people who abandoned the manifest right to school buses—she instigated an all-car sing-along to the Muppets soundtrack, "Life's a Happy Song." Then, after the kids were gone, an eleven-minute mood freefall, then more coffee, and more euphoria until the moment, arriving at her practice, when the coffee had worn off and she grew, for an

24

hour or so, more or less numb, doing her work in a state of underwater detachment. There were the occasional happy or interesting patients, patients who were old friends, some talk of kids while picking at their wet mouths, the suction, the spitting. There were too many patients now, it was a runaway train. Her mind was continually occupied by the tasks before her, the cleanings and drillings, the work requiring precision, but over the years it had become far easier to do most of it without paying full attention. Her fingers knew their tasks and worked in close partnership with her eyes, leaving her mind to wander. Why had she bred with that man? Why was she working on a beautiful day? What if she left and never came back? They would figure it out. They would survive. She was not needed.

Sometimes she enjoyed people. Some of the children, some of the teenagers. The teenagers with promise, with a purity of face and voice and hope that could obliterate all doubt about humankind's dubious motives and failures. There had been Jeremy, the best of them all. But Jeremy was dead. Jeremy, a teenager, was dead. He liked to say "No sweat." The dead teenager had said "No sweat."

Noon was the nadir. The noonday sun demanded answers, the questions obvious and dull and unanswerable. Was she living her best life? The feeling she should quit this, that the office was doomed, uninspired, that they were all better off anywhere else. Wouldn't it be wonderful to throw it all away? Burn it all down?

Then lunch. Maybe outside, in some leafy courtyard, the

smell of fluted ivy, with an old friend who had just screwed her carpenter. Screams of laughter. Admonishing looks from the other diners. A few sips from her friend's chardonnay, then a handful of mints, and plans to go away for the week-end together, with kids, no, without kids, promises to send photos of the carpenter, to forward any suggestive texts he might send her.

The boost after the meal, the ascendant glow of one to three p.m., *The King and I* coming loudly through every tiny speaker, the sense that their work, that dentistry, was important, that the whole practice was an integral part of the community—they had eleven hundred patients and that was something, that was significant, these were families who counted on them for a crucial part of their well-being—and some fun when it was obvious to all that Tania, Josie's most recent hire, had gotten laid at lunch and was abloom and smelling of animal sweat. Then 3:30 and utter collapse. The feeling of desolation and hopelessness, all was lost, what was this shit? Who were these shitty people who surrounded her? What was all this? This didn't matter, and she still owed so much money on these machines, she was a slave to it all, who were these shitty employees who had no idea the vise-like grip all this debt had on her skull.

Then the relief of closing at 5 . . . or even leaving at 4:40. Finished at 4:40! The release while driving home, thinking of her bright little home, her filthy couch, the broom standing in the corner, guarding that which she'd swept last night but couldn't bring herself to pick up and throw away. Wait. Maybe there would be new flowers in bloom in the backyard. Sometimes they appeared between nine and five. They could grow in a day, sprout and bloom! This she loved. Sometimes it happened. Pull into the driveway. No flowers, no new colors. Then open the door, say hello and goodbye to Estaphania, maybe write her a check, wanting to tell her how lucky she was to be paid this way, no taxes, cold cash, are you saving enough, Estaphania? You should be, given what I pay you under the table.

Then holding her children close, smelling their sweat, their matted hair, Ana showing some new weapon she'd made or found. The rebound while drinking some cabernet while cooking. The music on. Maybe dancing with the kids. Maybe letting them dance on the counter. Love their tiny faces. Love how much they love your liberality, your abandon, your fun. You are fun! You are one of the fun ones. With you every day is different, isn't it? You are full of possibility. You are wild, you are wonderful, you are dancing, looking up, shaking your hair free, seeing Paul's delight and horror and tentative smile—you are untethered, singing, now with your head down, your eyes closed, and then you hear something break. Ana has broken something. A plate, a hundred shards on the floor, and she won't say sorry. Ana climbs down from the counter, runs, doesn't help.

The collapse again. The feeling that your daughter is a deviant already and will only get worse. In a flash, you can see her as a feral adolescent, as a dirty-bomb teenager, a burst of invisible and spreading fury. Where is she now? She's fled, not to her room but somewhere else, a closet, she always hides somewhere disturbing, a place befitting a German fairy tale. Believe strongly that the house is too small for all of you, that you should be living largely outdoors, in a yurt with a hundred acres around—wouldn't it be better if the kids were outside, where nothing could be broken, where they could be kept busy hunting vermin and gathering firewood? The only logical option would be to move to a farm. A thousand-mile prairie. All this energy and these shrieking voices kept inside these small walls? It wasn't sensible.

Then the headache, the blinding, the unspeakable. The stake being driven from the back of your head, coming out somewhere above the right ocular cavity. Ask Paul to find Tylenol. He comes back, there is no Tylenol in the house. And it's too late to go to the store, not at dinnertime. Lie down while the rice is cooking. Soon Ana will come into the room. Hiss at her about the plate. Make some generalization about her not caring for nice things, about her being reckless and never listening and never helping or cleaning. Watch Ana leave the room. Wonder if she's crying. With great effort, your head a sinkhole swallowing some happy home, get up and walk to her room. She's there. See her kneeling, hear her talking to herself, her hands on her Star Wars bedspread, unfazed, playing so sweetly, voicing Iron Man and Green Lantern, both of them sounding very kind, very patient in their lisping compassion. Know that she is indestructible, far stronger than you. Go to her, and see that she has already forgiven or forgotten, she is a battleship with no memory, so kiss her on the head, and the ear, and the eyes, and then it's enough kissing, Ana will say, and she will push her mother away but her mother will defy this pushing-away, and will lift Ana's shirt and kiss her stomach and hear Ana's guttural laugh, and she will love Ana so much she can't bear it. Bring Ana into the kitchen and put her on the counter again and let her check the rice while Paul is nearby. Hug Paul, too, finish your glass of wine and pour another and wonder if you are a better parent in all ways after a glass and a half of red wine. A tipsy parent is a loving parent, a parent unreserved in her joy, affection, gratitude. A tipsy parent is all love and no restraint.

A string of lights passed through the woods in front of her. Josie got out of the Chateau, the air faintly toxic from some unseen fire, and ran to the road, where she saw a convoy of fire trucks, red and chartreuse, racing by. The firefighters inside were only blurry silhouettes until the last truck, the seventh and smallest, where a face, in the second window, seemed to be looking into a tiny light, maybe some instrument panel, maybe his phone, but he was smiling, and he seemed so very happy, a young firefighter on his way somewhere, his helmet on. Josie waved to him like some European villager liberated in WWII, but he didn't look up.

Anyway, she was done. With the town. With her practice, with ceramic fillings, with the mouths of the impossible. She was done, gone. She had been comfortable, and comfort is the death of the soul, which is by nature searching, insistent, unsatisfied. This dissatisfaction drives the soul to leave, to get lost, to be lost, to struggle and adapt. And adaptation is growth, and growth is life. A human's choice is either to see new things, mountains, waterfalls, deadly storms and seas and volcanoes, or to see the same man-made things endlessly reconfigured. Metal in this shape, then that shape, concrete this way and that. People, too! The same emotions recycled, reconfigured, fuck it, she was free. Free of human entanglements! Stasis had been killing her, had in actuality turned her face numb. A year ago, during the start of the lawsuit spiral, her face had been numb for a month. She couldn't explain it to anyone and in the emergency room they'd been stumped. But it had been real. There had been a month where her face was numb and she couldn't get out of bed. When was that? A year ago, not a good year. A thousand reasons to leave the Lower 48, leave a country spinning its wheels, a country making occasional forays into progress and enlightenment but otherwise uninspired, otherwise prone to cannibalism, to eating the young and weak, to finger-pointing and complaint and distraction and the volcanic emergence of ancient hatreds. And leaving was made inevitable by the woman who had sued her for apparently causing her cancer or otherwise not holding back the tidal onslaught of carcinoma that would eventually kill her (but not yet). And there was Elias and Evelyn and Carl and his Goebbelsian plans. But most of all there was the young man, a patient since he was a child, who was now dead, because he'd said he was enlisting to build hospitals and schools in Afghanistan, and Josie had called him honorable and brave, and six months later he was dead and she could not wash the complicity from her. She did not want to think about Jeremy now, and there were no reminders of Jeremy here. No. But could she really be reborn in a land of mountains and light? It was a long shot.

II.

JOSIE WOKE TO A KNOCKING, a relentless hollow knocking somewhere beneath her. She opened her eyes to find that at some point she'd gotten back in the Chateau and had climbed up to the sleeper. It was dark outside and Paul and Ana were both out cold, though Ana had found a way to rotate herself such that her feet were now at Paul's head.

The knocking paused, then came again, louder. It was Carl. He'd found her. She'd done something illegal. Crossed state lines with her children? Was that unlawful? She hadn't bothered to check. In truth she didn't check because she knew it might be unlawful and she didn't want to know for sure.

Then a voice. It was a man. A different voice, not Carl's. She thought about where she could hide the kids. She thought about the velvet bag of cash she'd hidden under the Chateau sink.

"Wake up in there. State trooper."

Josie climbed down to find a man in uniform walking

outside the Chateau, his flashlight scanning with quick slashing strokes.

Josie had no reason to disbelieve this man was who he said he was, a state trooper, but the night was grey and the dark mythology of her dreams were still with her, so she did not open the door. Instead she sat in the driver's seat and waved to him.

"Hello," she said through the closed window.

The trooper did not ask her to open the window. He didn't ask her to provide identification or insurance or any explanation at all.

"Can't park overnight here," he said through the window, and pointed to a sign in front of her that said the same thing. "Okay?" he asked, now gentler.

She felt a rush of gratitude. Her recent life was full of gushing moments of gratitude to strangers, whenever they did not yell at her, curse her, almost kill or harm her in some way. Any time she escaped an encounter unscathed—and more so when someone was actually kind—she nearly swooned with appreciation. "Good. Okay," she said, and gave him a thumbs-up. "Thank you so much, Officer."

When he was gone, Josie started the engine and the dashboard clock read 2:14 a.m. She was a fool. Now the kids would be off their sleep schedule more or less permanently. And where would they all sleep if they couldn't park this thing, a recreational vehicle, in an enormous parking lot overlooking a postcard bay? Stan had said something about the RV parks all over the state, but Josie hadn't thought this would be their plan. What she had wanted was the freedom to just pull over anywhere, and eat, or sleep, or stay indefinitely.

She contemplated waking Paul and Ana and strapping them in before driving off, but she harbored an irrational hope that if she left them alone they might sleep through the night. It was improbable—it was a joke, really—but her style of parenting was predicated on hoping for things over which she had little or no control.

She turned on the radio and found nothing. She spun the dial left and right, then, thinking she'd found a faint signal, turned the volume up. It faded, and there was nothing for miles.

Then: "I've got big balls!" It was a man's voice. A song played by a man in a schoolboy's uniform. She turned it down, hoping it hadn't woken up the children. This had been the rule since they'd left Stan's driveway: the radio, which he'd called temperamental, would find no sound for hours, then would come alive with a sudden burst of song.

She drove south, looking for signs, but instead she saw the face of Evelyn, the dying woman who now owned her practice, and she saw Evelyn's malevolent son-in-law, and then she saw the face of the dead soldier. What fool goes to Alaska alone in a vehicle like this? She had guaranteed herself limitless stretches of driving like this, her children occupied or asleep, while all she could do would be to contemplate her many mistakes and the fundamental mistake of knowing other people, all of whom would ultimately die or try to kill her.

Finally she saw the words RV PARK on a hand-painted sign, and pulled into a gravel lot. She drove slowly past a tall wigwam, a totem pole next to it, leaning heavily to the right. The office was a pink aluminum trailer, and within there was one dim amber light. She knocked on the door, producing a weak tinny sound.

"Second," a woman's voice said from somewhere deep within.

"Thank you," Josie said to herself and said it again to the woman who answered the door. The woman was about her age, with black hair done up in a beehive. The sight of it, almost a foot high, brought Josie briefly to a cheerful 1950s place where the future was bulbous and sleek and reaching upward.

"That yours?" the woman said, her chin giving a quick acknowledgment of the Chateau. "One night?"

Josie confirmed one night and, in a rare burst of chattiness, asked the woman, "How you doin' tonight?" dropping her *g* for no reason she could account for.

"Hoping for rain," the woman said. "Need some rain."

Josie nodded, not immediately understanding why—she thought of farms, crops, droughts, not knowing Alaska to be a major agricultural state, but then remembered the fires. She'd heard a radio report that day that counted at least a hundred and fifty currently burning. "Hope you get some," Josie said, still using her new, fake accent.

The woman charged her forty-five dollars and told Josie she could stay parked where she was, or park anywhere in the lot that suited her fancy. The entire lot was empty.

"Breakfast at seven if you want it," the woman added, and closed her door. When Josie returned to the Chateau, the kids were awake.

"Did we move?" Paul asked.

Josie explained they had moved, but left out the part about the state trooper. She couldn't predict how the presence of any police officers would affect either child. Sometimes police made them feel safe; other times they implied the closeness of chaos and crime. More so than any other earthly threat, the kids were preoccupied with the idea of "robbers." Every third night in their Ohio home Josie had to explain that there were no robbers in their town (there were), that they had an elaborate alarm system (they did not), that there was no remote possibility of any robber ever getting within a mile of their house (the house next door had been burglarized in the early evening, three months earlier, by a pair of meth addicts who had beaten the owner senseless with his own tennis racket).

"Let's go back to sleep," she said, knowing it would not happen. Her children were hungry. Ana wanted to see the wigwam. Josie noted it was almost three a.m. and the world was asleep, but the children had no interest in that news. And so, after feeding them cold quesadillas and raw vegetables from a plastic bag, she let them watch *Tom and Jerry* en español above the cab.

She poured herself a splash of the second pinot she'd bought in Anchorage and stared into the woods before her. She found her *Old West* magazine, turned to "Trails Grown Dim," and found a doozy:

"My father, Addison Elmer Hoyt, lost his genealogy book of the Hoyt family in or near Polson, Montana, about 1916—at least before World War I—and was too ill to search for it. Our family Bible shows Hoyt ancestors in Worcester, New Braintree, Massachusetts, about 1723 or earlier. The first Hoyt listed is Benjamin, born 1723, killed in the Battle of Ticonderoga. Benjamin had a son, Robert, born May 6, 1753, married to Nancy Hall, daughter of Zakius Hall and Mary Jennison Hall. After all these years do you suppose that the Hoyt book is still in existence? Possibly there were ink sketches of horses, little birds and fine penmanship in the book as Father loved to sketch and draw. He was born in Greene County, Illinois, son of Albinus Perry and Surrinda Robinette New Hoyt. I would like to hear from descendants of our lineage who are willing to share information."

Josie, thinking of redirecting her life to help the Hoyts, thinking of renaming herself Surrinda, climbed up to the bed over the cab. It was wide enough for three of them, though the head clearance was coffin-tight. The mattress was flimsy and the sheets and pillows smelled of mildew and dog, but she knew she would fall asleep in minutes. Ana's face appeared, her eyes wild with disbelief, seeing this as some enormous traveling bunk-bed, and Paul followed. Josie grabbed them, tickled them, pulled them into her, wrapped her arms around them both, Ana sandwiched between her two guardians. What would that be like, Josie wondered—to know there were people around you always, committed to your well-being and safety? To the best of her knowledge, Josie had not had such a person in her life in twenty-five years. She closed her eyes.

"I'm not tired," Ana said.

"Then maybe Paul can read to you," Josie said, and felt herself drifting off very quickly, while also knowing that if her children rolled the wrong way they would fall five feet to the floor below. She rearranged them so she was facing out and they were contained, stuffed into the front of the compartment like luggage.

She heard the sounds of Paul and Ana having one of their conversations, often made within earshot of Josie, where Ana would ask existential questions about herself and her family, and Paul would answer as best as he could, having no inclination at all to ask for Josie's help.

"Are we going to school here?" Ana whispered.

"Where?" he whispered.

"In Aska," Ana said.

"Alaska? No, we're on vacation. I told you that," he said.

"Can robbers come into here?"

"No, there are no robbers who rob RVs. And there are huge locks and alarms all over this. And police who guard us and who see us from above."

"From hellcopters?"

38

"Yup. *So* many helicopters."

"What's above the hellcopters?" Ana asked.

"The sky," Paul said.

"What's above the sky?" she asked, and after a long pause he answered, "Space. Stars."

"Are they good?" Ana asked.

Ana had gotten this from Paul. Every day, Paul wanted to know if something, a movie or car or park or person, was good. *Is he good? Was that good?* He didn't trust his own taste, or hadn't developed it yet, so always with great seriousness, and with finality, he wanted to know, *Is it good?* The one question he didn't seem to ponder was *Am I good?* He seemed to know he was.

"You mean are they nice?" Paul asked.

"Yeah."

"The stars are *really* nice. And I forgot to tell you that between the sky and the stars there's a whole layer of birds. And the birds guard everyone below."

"Are they big?" Ana asked.

"The birds? Not so big. But there are millions of them. And they see everything."

"What color are they?"

The boy's patience was astounding. "Blue. Light blue," he said, and after a pause during which Paul must have had a realization that impressed even himself: "That's why you can't see them. They blend into the sky."

Josie loved her children, but had heard this kind of thing from Paul before, and so put a pillow over her head to drown

39

out their voices, and soon felt Paul climbing around her, and then down to the kitchenette, and then sensed him returning. He crawled over her and she heard him turning the pages of a book, whispering words to Ana, and Josie could picture their faces, their heads joined, and soon knew from her silence that Ana was asleep, so finally she found it, too.

III.

BUT THIS WAS NOT YET a land of mountains and light. What they'd seen so far was just a place. There were mountains, some, but the air was jaundiced and the light plain. The little oval window that faced forward presented the real Alaska to her: a parking lot, a wigwam, a sign telling passersby that the wifi was free. It was seven a.m. She looked down to find her children awake and exploring the cabinets.

"Let's have some breakfast," she said, and they dressed and walked across the gravel parking lot to the diner. Inside there were a pair of firefighters, a man and a woman, both seeming managerial in age and demeanor. Their shirts said they were from Oregon.

"Thank you for your help up here," the waitress said to them, refilling their coffee. Periodically Josie would catch other diners nodding to the firefighter table, closing their eyes in gratitude.

Paul and Ana ate eggs and bacon, Ana sitting on her foot, vibrating. Josie had told her that there was no plan for the day and this, to Ana, seemed to unleash all possibility of mayhem.

"How's the food?" Josie asked Paul.

"Fine," he said, and blinked his long-lashed eyes. His lashes were spectacular, and no matter what happened in his life he would have them, and these lashes would imply to all he was gentle and kind and, framed by his ice-blue eyes, that he was intelligent and wise and perhaps saw the future. Paul was an extraordinary-looking person, his face a long oval of polished stone, his eyes startling from forty feet.

It was hard to see Ana, though, because she existed as a blur. She did not stop moving, even while eating. She'd been born four months premature, had entered the world weighing just over three pounds, was beset by a series of gothic afflictions—sleep apnea (being the occasional twenty-second delay between breaths), necrotizing enterocolitis (intestinal problem causing swollen belly and diarrhea), a bout with sepsis, then a blood infection, a half-dozen other full attacks on a creature the size of a shoe. But she got stronger daily, was a beast now, still underweight, still having something in the eyes that said *Holy hell what happened? But aha! I'm here! You couldn't kill me!* but somehow her head had grown huge and heavy, and every day she seemed possessed by the need to prove she belonged here and would use her days fully, recklessly. She woke up ecstatic and went to bed reluctantly. In between she took five steps for everyone else's one, sang loudly songs she created and which made no sense, and also attempted at every opportunity to cause herself harm. From a distance she resembled a perpetually drunk adult—bumping into things, yelling randomly, making up words. She could not be trusted in parking lots, near electrical outlets, near stoves or glass or metal or stairs, cliffs, bodies of water, vehicles of any kind, or pets. At the moment she was swaying back and forth like a buoy, doing a sitting dance to music only she could hear. In her left hand was a piece of toast, and surrounding her mouth like a messy new galaxy was syrup, eggs, grains of sugar and a film of milk. Now she stopped moving, and took in her surroundings in a rare moment of what could be construed as contemplation.

"Do they speak English here?" she asked.

"Yes," Paul said to Ana, then gently said, "We're still in America." And then he patted her arm. The boy was freakish in his devotion to her. When Ana was one, two, three, Paul insisted on helping put her to bed, and every night created some new song for her to lull her to sleep. "Ana is sleepy now, Ana is sleepy, all the Anas in the world are so sleepy now, they hold hands and drop away . . ." He was a startling lyricist, really, at four, five, six, and Ana would lie there staring at him, her eyes unblinking, sucking on her bottle, listening to every word. And his artwork! It showed a different level of devotion: he signed everything he created *Paul and Ana*.

They ate their breakfast, Josie sitting across from her children, staring at the heartless landscape of blue sky and white mountains, and remembered Carl once saying, joking but not joking, that their children had their genders confused. Paul was exquisitely sensitive, thoughtful, maternal. He didn't wear girls' clothes but he did play with dolls. Ana liked motorcycles and Darth Vader and had hit her giant head on so many things, falling, ramming, that her skull was wildly misshapen and lucky to be covered with her riot of red curls. Paul listened, cared more for people than objects, and was wounded deeply by the thought of any suffering endured by any living soul. On the other hand, Ana really did not care.

Then there was the matter of honor. Though his father was an invertebrate, Paul was already a great man, a tiny Lincoln. A few months ago, for his after-dinner treat, he chose a tiny packet of peanut M&Ms from the candy left over from Halloween (Josie kept it in the cabinet over the fridge). There were six M&Ms inside the packet, and Josie said he could have four. Josie took Ana to bed, while Paul ate his treat in the kitchen so Ana wouldn't see or want some of her own. The next morning on the counter, Josie found the packet with the two extras in it. Paul was so honest that he wouldn't sneak the last two and eat them—something Ana, or Carl, or even Josie, would likely do without a second thought.

Finished with most of her food, Ana left the booth and ran to a gumball machine, which she yanked on hard enough to bring it down—it would have gone down if it weren't bolted to the floor. Josie could not remember Ana ever seeing a gumball machine before, so how was it that she knew

44

exactly how to harm one? And what had she imagined would be the results of her efforts—broken machine, a floor of glass and gum, punishment inevitable? What was the appeal? The only explanation was that she was receiving instructions from extraplanetary overlords. That, and Ana's tendency, once a week, to look at Josie with otherworldly eyes, old eyes, knowing eyes—it was unsettling. Paul was always Paul, self-contained, earth-bound, but Ana, sometimes, would stop being a child and look at Josie, her mother, as if to say, For a second let's stop pretending.

"Can you get her and bring her back?" Josie asked Paul.

Paul slid out of the booth and went after her. Seeing him coming, Ana grinned and ran toward the bathrooms. In seconds there was a loud crash, an odd delay, then Ana's wail overtook the diner.

Josie rushed to the bathroom and found Ana inside, on her knees, holding her chin, screaming.

"She was standing on the toilet and fell," Paul said.

Paul always knew. He knew everything—every event, every truth involving Ana. He was her personal coach, her historian, assistant, caretaker, governness, guardian and best friend.

"I'll get a first-aid kit," Paul said. Josie knew her son, only eight, could do this. He could find a waitress, ask for the first-aid kit, bring it back. He could answer the phone, could run into the grocery store to buy milk, could go to the end of the street to pick up the mail. He was so calm and reasonable and composed that Josie considered him, most of the time, her peer in parenting and also, possibly, some shrunken reincarnation of Josie's own pre-breakdown mother.

Josie lifted Ana to the bathroom sink, looked under her chin and found a tiny red line. "It's just a scratch. There isn't really any blood. I don't think we need a first-aid kit." She held Ana close, feeling her rabbit heart thrumming as she heaved and choked on tears.

Then Paul, who had returned with the kit, gave Josie an urgent look, a clenching of his teeth, meant to convey that he knew there was no blood, but that Ana would not stop crying until some remedy was placed on her chin.

"There's got to be a good band-aid here," Paul said, and at this, Ana's eyes opened and followed his quick long-fingered hands as he opened compartments. Finally he arrived at the right one. "Found some," he said, and held up a clump of simple, if oversized, bandages. While Ana watched, no longer crying—in fact rapt, holding her breath—he pored through the band-aids like a normal boy would do with Magic cards, baseball cards. "I think this one," he said, and took a small one from its wrapping. "Maybe we should put some cream on first. What do you think?"

Josie was about to answer but realized Paul was talking to Ana, not to her. Ana nodded gravely to him and insisted that he, not Josie, put on the cream. In seconds he had some kind of lotion in his hands, and was rubbing it between his palms.

"Let's make it warm first," he said. After it was whatever

temperature he deemed right, he applied it to her chin with the utmost delicacy, and Ana's eyes registered a pleasure so great they had to close. After the cream was spread evenly, he blew on it, "so it dries quicker," he told Ana, ignoring Josie utterly, and then carefully attached the band-aid to her chin, pressing it lightly on both adhesive ends. Then he stepped back and assessed his work. He was satisfied, and now Ana was calm enough to speak.

She asked for a meal.

"You want a meal?" Josie asked. "You haven't finished your breakfast."

"No!" Ana roared. "I want a *meal*."

"A meal?" Josie was lost.

"No, a meal!"

Paul tilted his head, as if he was on the verge of understanding.

"Are you hungry or not?" Josie asked.

"No!" Ana yelled, now about to cry again.

Paul looked to Ana, his eyes probing. "Is there another way you could say it?"

"I want to see it!" Ana wailed, and immediately Paul understood.

"She wants a *mirror,* not a *meal,*" he told his mother, a flash of delight in his ice-priest eyes. Ana nodded vigorously, and a smile overtook Paul's face. This was treasure to him, this was joy. All he wanted was to know his sister better than anyone else.

Josie lifted her so she could face the small mirror hung

high over the sink. She showed Ana the wound, fearing she'd wail again, shocked by the bandage overtaking her chin. But Ana only grinned, touching it lovingly, her eyes alight.

They got back on the road, heading south toward the Kenai Peninsula, with an eye toward Seward, about which Josie knew nothing. The kids sat at the banquette in back, Josie unsure exactly how that was safe, given the walls of the Chateau were dangerously thin and the benches of the banquette had seatbelts as old as herself. But the kids were loving it. Ana couldn't believe she didn't have to be in a car seat. She felt like she was getting away with some fantastic heist.

Ana yelled something from the back. It sounded like a question, but Josie couldn't hear anything. "What's that?" Josie yelled.

"She asked if you ever lived here," Paul yelled.

"In Alaska? No," Josie yelled over her shoulder.

Ana thought her mother had lived everywhere. It was Josie's fault; she'd made the mistake of mentioning her travels before their births, her many addresses. Her kids were too young for this, both of them were, but she found on too many occasions that she couldn't help it. When they'd heard mention of Panama in a documentary about the canal, she told them she'd lived there for two years, explaining the Peace Corps, the village on a hill where she and two others with no particular training in mountainside irrigation tried to help the residents with mountainside irrigation. She couldn't help herself, and assumed her kids would forget it all. Ana forgot most things, but Paul forgot nothing, and as if to thwart her efforts to write the past in disappearing ink, he made his own copy, like some tiny deranged monk. They knew that after the Peace Corps and before dentistry school she'd gone to school, briefly, to train seeing-eye dogs (she dropped out after a month but the prospect held great fascination for them). They knew about Walla Walla and Iron Mountain, two of the four places she'd lived as a child. She thought it too soon to tell them about how she'd emancipated herself at seventeen, about Sunny, the woman who supported that insurgency and took her in. They occasionally wondered about Josie's parents, where they were, why they didn't have biological grandparents, why they only had Luisa, Carl's mother, living in Key West. They knew something about London, the four months in Spain—that period of whiplash moves, driven by whim and calamity. Why was it important to her that they know she'd been somewhere, had done more than dentistry? Was it wonderful to have changed so many times? She suspected it was not wonderful.

Now Paul was talking, but he was quieter than Ana, and Josie heard little more than wisps of consonants and vowels.

"I can't hear you!" Josie yelled.

"What?" Paul yelled back to her.

The Chateau was rattling and heaving and drowned all voices. By its nature a recreational vehicle carried along all manner of kitchen items—in this case, secondhand castoffs of Stan and his white-carpet wife—and every dish rattled, every glass clinked against every other glass. There were plates, and tea sets, and coffee cups, and silverware. There was a coffeemaker. There was a stove. There were pots and pans. There was a wok. A blender. A mixer in case anyone wanted to make a bundt cake. All of these were contained in cabinets, cheap lightweight cabinets like they had at home, but at home these cabinets were not hurtling through space at forty-eight miles an hour, carried on ancient shocks and tires. And because the vehicle was a dying machine, even the cabinets were poorly assembled and only casually attached to the vehicle. The sound, then, was like one would hear during an earthquake. The silverware shook like the chains of some restless ghost. And the cacophony grew far louder when they slowed down or sped up, or drove over an incline or decline or bump or pothole.

IF NOT YOU, THEN WHO? a lighted sign on the side of the road asked, and Josie felt found and accused until the sign changed to read DON'T PARK ON DRY GRASS and she realized these were messages meant to prevent forest fires.

After an hour, Josie pulled over. Going from forty-eight to a stop was a task akin to holding back an avalanche. All the weight was carried in the rear, so the front of the car heaved and shuddered, the wheels shaking. They parked in a wide lot by the water, but Josie's nerves were shot.

She climbed up from the cab and sat on the couch opposite the banquette. She told Paul and Ana they had the unique opportunity to help with an extraordinary project. They were intrigued.

"We're putting the kitchen in the shower," she said.

Intuitively they understood.

Ana opened the cabinet under the sink and found a pot. "Like this?" she asked, heading for the bathroom.

"Wait," Josie said, "let's get towels first."

So they lined the shower floor with towels. Then they wrapped plates and glasses and put these on the shower floor. When they were out of towels, they opened their duffel bags and wrapped plates and silverware in clothes they could spare, and they placed each bundle on the shower floor. They emptied the kitchen of plates, pans, cups and glasses, put them all carefully in the shower, and closed the door. When Josie started the Chateau again, and pulled back onto the highway, the sound was wonderfully muffled and she appeared to her children some kind of mastermind.

"What if we need to cook?" Paul asked.

"I don't want to cook," Josie said.

She didn't want to drive, either, the road giving her no peace, only faces. She saw the smooth handsome face of the young soldier in whose death she was complicit. No, she thought, give me another face. She saw the yellow eyes of the cancer-ridden woman who stole her business. No. Another. Carl, grinning on the toilet. No. The face of the woman's lawyer, her son-in-law, cruel and mercenary. Josie finally arrived at the onion-skinned face of Sunny, a face she tried to conjure when she sought peace. For a moment her mind rested there, on Sunny's bright black eyes, imagined Sunny running her bony fingers through her hair—Josie had allowed it even though she was a teenager and furious at the world—and then and now, for a moment, she felt something like calm.

In the afternoon they made it to Seward, and Seward felt like a real place. It was muscular and clean. It sat at the end of a great fjord, freezing water stampeding in from the Gulf of Alaska. The town's main strip was lousy with souvenir shops, tinkly glass shelves full of cartoon abomination T-shirts, but on the outskirts, Seward was raw, an actual place of business. Fishing boats came and went, and tankers, and small container ships, and they all passed through the narrow inlet called Resurrection Bay, a name for grizzled explorers and saints.

They arrived at an RV park outside of town, and parked facing a wide seaweed-covered beach. Across the water, half a mile maybe, there was the Kenai range, a wall of immaculate mountains—sawtoothed, silver and white, monumental and defiant. Along the shore were occasional stumps of trees rising from the sand, petrified in white.

"Stay here," she told the kids, and walked to the park office.

The man at the desk asked for her name and address, and Josie wrote it down, scribbling her name illegibly, giving him a PO Box she'd memorized from a credit card company, and then paid in cash. She had the vague sense that when

Carl realized what she'd done he might come to find her and the children, or send someone to find them, but then again the man had never held a real job (this new one in Florida didn't count)—could he really assemble and carry out a reconnaissance mission? He'd gotten halfway through the triathlon he'd trained for. Maybe he'd get halfway through finding her.

When Josie walked back to the Chateau, she found an irate man.

"This is not your spot!" he roared. Idling behind the Chateau was another RV, this one new and far bigger and with a Norwegian flag flying from its antenna. The Norwegian's face was red, his hands held behind his back as if to restrain them from doing some Norway-specific harm to Josie. He had been rehearsing this, it was clear. He'd been building a good head of steam for the fifteen minutes she'd been gone. Now, she was sure, he would mention her children.

"And you leave your children driving!"

She looked up to find that Paul was in the Chateau's driver's seat, and Ana was on his lap. All four of their hands were on the wheel.

Josie had some thoughts. She thought how much she loved her children, how they looked like little delinquents, even though Paul was angelic and Ana had never hurt anyone but herself. She wondered why this Norwegian would come four thousand miles to look at Alaskan fjords. It was perverse. Norway was better, cleaner. And didn't they give you things for free in Norway? Health care and the like? Go home.

Without a word, she got into the Chateau, shooed her children into the back, and ceded the spot to the angry Norwegian. All the spots on the shore were taken, though, so they drove around the park until they found a berth in the woods. It was fine, still less than a few hundred feet from the water, but where the shore was bright and facing the illuminated mountains, the woods were dark, dank, hinting at Tolkien and trolls.

Josie had spent a week there, in Norway, with Paul when he was two. It was a conference on teeth whitening. How strange the Norwegians were with Paul! (Carl stayed home, thought he might be getting sick, didn't want to risk it. A paragon of a man.) So in Oslo, and especially on that ferry trip through some pristine fjord, the Norwegians acted like she'd brought a wolverine on board. Paul had been a well-behaved toddler, a little citizen, almost effete, almost too mature, but on that ship he'd been a pariah. He opened his mouth and it was as if he'd ruined the journey, the very sound of his voice some kind of American dirty bomb.

Josie had heard every musical and thought an addition to the canon should be called *Norway!* It would feature a chorus of women in the same all-white outfits—everyone she'd met in Norway wore all white, and they all had the same suspiciously tanned skin, the same narrow black glasses—all these

Norwegians pretended to be happy people, civilized people, singing benign songs about fjords and state-sponsored culture funded by oil, but meanwhile they were trying to eliminate all children so they wouldn't have to share their limited amounts of white cloth. As she performed teeth whitenings, Josie often mused about the musical, picturing the finale, all the white-clad Norwegians singing some song with electronic accompaniment. Why did she do this? She spent her idle time conceiving of musicals that would never be. It was the only medium that could properly express our true madness and hypocrisy—our collective ability to sit in a theater watching lunatics sing nonsense while the world outside burns.

The teeth-whitening conference had otherwise been a boon—the treatments were like printing money. A patient was in the office for about an hour, ten minutes of which involved Josie—the hygienists could handle most of it—but she billed seven hundred dollars and everyone was happy to pay it. Thank you, Norway!

They got out, and Josie removed the electrical hookup from the side compartment—basically a thick extension cord hidden in a rickety particleboard door near the rear wheel. She plugged the vehicle into the outdoor outlet and, not bad, they had electricity. She led Paul and Ana to the shore, avoiding the Norwegians, who were now taking pains to be friendly, standing over their weak grey fire, waving.

The bay was full of otters. Ana and Paul had already

spotted them, fifty yards from shore. What child doesn't love otters? Josie sat on one of the ancient white tree stumps and let the kids go out on the waterline to get a closer look. The otters were maniacal they were so cute, swimming on their backs, holding actual rocks on their stomachs, using them to break open actual clams. Such an animal could not be conceived by any self-respecting creator. Only a God made in our image could go for that level of animal kitsch.

Now Ana was on the ground. Now Paul was examining her hand. This was Josie's preferred method of parenting: go someplace like this, with grand scale and much to be discovered, and watch your children wander and injure themselves but not significantly. Sit and do nothing. When they come back to show you something, some rock or mop of seaweed, inspect it and ask questions about it. Socrates invented the ideal method for the parent who likes to sit and do very little. Through judicious questioning, her children could learn to read and write right here, on this beach in Seward. Of course they could. Read the name of that ship. Quick, read that warning on the side of the water taxi. Read the notes about voltage on that outdoor plug-in.

The air was clear. They were by the water, and the fire danger here was low, or at least lower, and somehow the winds that carried the burnt air were heading in some other direction. Josie breathed deeply and raised her closed eyes to the sun. She heard the complaints of some shorebird. The movement of gravel somewhere in the parking lot. The long shush of a breeze moving through the forest behind her. The crisp entry of a paddle into the bay. Now the squeal of a child. She opened her eyes, assuming it was Ana, hurt again, this time more seriously. But Ana and Paul were still where she last saw them, and now were stacking stones. She turned to the other side of the beach and saw another family, two parents, two children, all dressed in bright lycra and waterproof windbreakers. The children, about the same size as Josie's, were upset about a trio of dogs, strays, circling the family like some kind of 1950s greaser gang. The family had no idea what to do.

The adults of the group looked to Josie, outraged and imploring, assuming the dogs were hers. That these uncollared feral dogs were somehow hers. Because she looked feral? Because her children looked dirty, mangy, wild—the kind of people who would bring dogs to the beach to harass beautiful people in matching lycra. These were the people Josie had come to Alaska to escape.

These were the breed of people who had overtaken Josie's town, had overtaken the kids' school. No one seemed to work; everyone had matching lycra and found time to be at every one of the three or four hundred yearly events at school. How could someone like Josie have a job, and be a mother, and yet not be a failure, a pariah, at this average school in this average town? She had been led to believe that having a job in the U.S.A. meant working forty hours a week. Debate it if you will—we should work less, we don't work enough, so much time at work wasted with online pornography and break-room grinding—but still, forty hours a week is the expectation, the norm, the key to the national prosperity. But the schools, and these children, and their activities, and the parent-organizers of these schools and activities, and most crucially their judging eyes, were preventing the working of forty-hour weeks, and were thwarting this prosperity, and the answer to the question of decline in the U.S. might very well be these parents, their judging eyes, these schools, these activities. Was it not a generation ago when there were four one-hour school activities a year that a parent was expected to attend? There was the parent-teacher conference in the fall, its twin in the spring, there was the fall—no, *autumn*—music production, the spring music production. That was all. Maybe a winter program, but never two in one semester. Maybe a school play. Maybe a recital. But in any case there were four events considered mandatory, and most were at night, after work. Otherwise the family's breadwinners or breadwinner was at work forty hours a week, was a hero to make it to any of the four events, was a champion if she or he managed to attend the games on the weekend, was a verifiable saint to coach a team, but in any case the parent could be considered a paragon for attending just three of the four mandatories, period, full stop.

But now there is something else. Now there are, creeping like a well-intentioned but ultimately suffocating and murderous weed, these new and vague half responsibilities, which are choking the life from all growth in this garden, which could also be considered human productivity and the national GDP. These optional things, these middling things, they sneak and kill like rust on flora. Like communism. No, not like communism. The communists knew balance, and worked hard. Did they work hard? No one is sure. But these other parents and their judging eyes: When do they work? Their jobs are attending these events. That is their work, they imply, and they also imply that you, and *your* actual work, are fine but also neglectful and sad. They don't say that, though. They say, *Don't worry if you can't be there, at the mid-fall solstice sing-along, the late-winter sledding-song craft fair and potluck.* Not a big deal with the mid-spring parent-student doubles badminton under-the-lights evening funmaker. No problem with the mother-daughter pajama party on every third Wednesday movie day *Sound of Music* bring your own guitar or lyre. No need to bring treats on your child's birthday. No need to come in for career day. No need to swing by the opening of the new art studio which features real clay-throwing technology. Don't care about art? Not an issue. No need, no need, no need, it's fine, no problem, though you really are selfish and your children doomed. When they are first to try crack—they will try it and love it and sell it to our culture-loving children—we will know why.

And so Josie calculated, for her own amusement and for some likely future deposition, the hours it would take to actually attend all of these middle-mandatory events in a given November, and she arrived at just over thirty-two hours. That would sum up the time in the school, on campus, watching and cavorting, thanking and congratulating.

But wait. Consider the time to get from and back to work, through traffic, against traffic, everything, all the tragedy of driving at all, it added up to forty-six hours. Forty-six hours in one month to attend the daytime and nighttime events, all of them optional, for which you are not expected, no problem, no worries, everything is optional, your children are doing so wonderfully, don't worry, we know you need to work, Josie.

Josie did have to work, because there were the kids, and Carl did not know how to generate income, personally contributed no funds whatsoever—his mother Luisa supported him, though she was anguished about it, and she paid for Ana and Paul's things occasionally, too. It did not help that Josie had not taken on another dentist into her own operation, she was a fool not to, and it did not help that she offered her services on a sliding scale. None of it helped. All of it was ill-advised, and proved she should not have started a business, should not be living with her children in that town, with those gleaming people who balanced joy and obligation effortlessly. Every time she would attend some event, some cupcake soiree, some ceremony of the cupcakes of the oral presentation of the choral club, she saw them. All of them. The dads were there, the moms were there. They were all there, and when she saw them, inevitably and firstly, they would want to talk about the last event, the one the week before or the day before. The event she did not attend. *Oh, it was great,* they would say. *The class killed it. They killed it!* The parents would say this with wonder, with wonder at it all, the things these kids do, that these young children are capable of, and while saying this, they may or may not be aware of the shiv they were sliding between Josie's ribs. They may or may not have any idea. But then they would turn the knife: *And your* son, they would say, *wow, he was the* star. Another twist: *I think I have him on film, at least for a second. I'll send you a link.* Was this an Ohio thing? Was it happening everywhere? Was it helpful that Paul sang both "The Long and Winding Road" and "In My Life" in some daytime talent show that Josie hadn't gotten proper notice of? It was not helpful. One parent said, afterward, *Better you weren't there. It was too sad seeing Paul sing those words.* She really said this. Meaning this eight-year-old understood the words, connected them somehow to Josie's split with Carl. This happened.

The wonderful apex of it all was the email from a woman, another mother, a week later. "Dear Josie, As a service from the school community to our working parents, we've started an innovative program we call All in This Together, whereby each student whose parents can't be at schoolday events is 'adopted' by a parent who *can* be. This parent will take extra time with your child, will take pictures at events and post them, and in general give the child the support enjoyed by the students who . . ." The email went on for another page. Josie scanned to the bottom to see who had been assigned to her children, and found it to be this woman, Bridget, who she remembered being precisely the kind of mother she'd never leave her children with—loony-eyed and fond of scarves.

Josie had chosen this kind of environment. She had left her former tribe, the searching ranks of Peace Corps alums, to go to dental school, to move to Ohio, to come to live in this suburb, among stable people—so stable they were willing to "adopt" her children during the school day—but she remembered her other people, other friends from the other life, those still roaming the planet like the undead. None of the Peace Corps friends had had kids. One had spent a year in bed, her healthy limbs unable to take commands (she'd since recovered). One had moved back to Panama, another learned Arabic and found some mysterious consulting job in Abbottabad and claimed to have watched the bin Laden raid from his rooftop. One was dead of an apparent suicide. A now-married couple ran a llama farm in Idaho, and had asked Josie to come, to move in, to be part of their commune (*It's not a commune!* they insisted), and Josie had almost done it, or had almost thought about considering it, but yes, the rest of the ragged race of Peace Corps people were still wandering, unwilling to stop, unwilling to live in any traditional or linear way.

Only Deena, a mother of a boy in Paul's class and manager of a pet food store, understood, seemed to have any past at all. Josie had mentioned her emancipation to another couple and they had not been able to hide their horror. They'd never heard of such a thing.

"I didn't know that was possible," the man said.

"I ran away once," the woman said. She was wearing

capris. "I slept at a girlfriend's house and came back in the morning."

Another time, at Moms' Night Out—no three words more tragic—Josie had mentioned the Peace Corps and Panama, how she'd known someone, Rory, who had managed to become a heroin addict there. Josie thought she told the story in a funny way, an American smuggling drugs *into* Central America, but again there was the chasmic silence that implied Josie was bringing some hint of apocalypse to their fine town.

But Deena understood. She was a single mother, too, though her husband was not a deserter, but dead. He'd been a contractor in the Nigerian delta, was kidnapped, ransomed, freed, and, upon returning to the U.S., died two months later of an aneurysm. Deena's other child, also named Ana but spelled Anna, was adopted, and between that and the dead father, Deena, too, had been threatened with Anna being adopted by the scarf woman from All in This Together.

Josie and Deena talked about being the only people in the school that anything had ever happened to. Josie felt right telling Deena anything, but she hadn't gone far into her own childhood, her parents' broken world. Those were untouchable years. It was one step too strange, so with Deena they left it at the particular absurdities of being a single parent—the making of money to pay children to watch their children so they could make money to pay these people to watch their children. The confiding in their children, complaining to them, lying too long with them at bedtime, telling them too much.

"We should move to Alaska," Deena said one night. They were at Chuy's, a burrito place where the kids could run around and scavenge and Josie and Deena were free to have their mojitos and take off their shoes. Deena was watching her daughter spill a basket of chips on the floor, pick them up and eat them. She didn't move a muscle to help, she didn't utter a word in admonition.

"Why would Alaska be any better?" Josie asked, but the idea stuck in her mind, in part because Sam lived there.

On the beach, the family in colorful new windbreakers disappeared behind a boulder down the shore, and Josie's relief was great.

Ana approached carrying something carefully with two hands. Paul was right behind her, then by her side, his hands hovering around hers, ensuring that whatever it was they'd found would not fall. Josie stood, hoping to discourage them from dropping it in her lap. "Look," Ana said with the utmost solemnity.

"It's a head," Paul said.

And now the stray dogs were among them, sniffing the head. Josie's kids barely took notice of the dogs, and the dogs seemed to have no interest in eating or harming the skull.

"One of dem otters," Ana said, and waved toward the bay. She had a skull in her little pink hands, and Josie noticed with horror that it had not been picked clean. There was still cartilage on it, and whiskers, and fur, something viscous, too. Josie conjured Socrates and thought of a question. "Why in hell did you pick this up?" In solidarity, the dogs lifted their heads to Ana and Paul, then ran off.

At night they went to a real restaurant in town. Josie retrieved the velvet bag from under the sink, retrieved six twenties, feeling it illogical but inevitable that she would spend most of them that night.

When they hit the main strip, they saw that a cruise ship had docked and Seward was full of identical couples in their seventies, all wearing slight variations on the same windbreaker and white sneakers. The town had been breached, the restaurants had surrendered, and Ana was running through the streets again. Josie and Paul caught her and Josie tried to appease her with a piggyback. No. Her little body, all muscle, moved like a barracuda: bending, twisting, anything to be free, so she let Ana run on the sidewalk. No negatives motivated her. Josie threatened to take away her Batman sticker book. No effect at all; she knew there were others. Josie told her she'd never watch another DVD; she had no sense of the future so she didn't care. But if Josie said she'd *get* something, some dessert, some object, she would toe the line. She was the purest sort of materialist: she wanted things, but didn't care about things.

The restaurant they went to was the cheapest one they

could find, but the prices in Alaska were science-fictional. Josie looked at the menu as they were waiting to be seated. Every pickle was twenty dollars. This was what she had tried to avoid. Back home Josie was so tired, so bone-weary of spending money. It crushed the spirit. Every day she found herself at the drugstore or grocery store and always the bill was sixty-three dollars. She would go into Walgreen's for milk and Ana's nighttime diapers and somehow would end up spending sixty-three dollars. Always sixty-three dollars. Sixty-three dollars, three or four times a day. How could that be sustained?

But this menu, in the brightly lit hellhole they found themselves in, wanted more than that for dinner. Josie did a rough calculation and knew she would spend eighty dollars for dinner with her two children, neither of whom would care one way or another if they ate here, or ate mud and grubs dug from shallow holes. Ana, always happy to puncture the pretense of any situation, found her opportunity. After the busboy wiped down the table, Ana wiped it again, with her own napkin, saying, "Oooh yeah! Ooooh yeah!" She made it uncomfortably lewd. Josie laughed, so Ana did it three more times.

Paul, though, was in a contemplative mood. He looked at Josie with his ice-priest eyes.

"What?" she said.

He said he didn't want to talk about it.

"What?" Josie asked again.

Finally he beckoned her closer, promising a secret. Josie

leaned over the table and a plate tilted, knocking against the wood.

"Where do the stray dogs go at night?" he whispered, his breath hot in her ear. Josie didn't know where Paul was going with this so said, "I don't know." Immediately she knew this was the wrong answer. His face crumbled and his eyes, so pale and cold, told her he wouldn't sleep for weeks.

She'd forgotten Paul's thing with strays. Back at home, he'd heard about stray cats—there was some demented socialite in their town who had made the homeless cats' plight her calling, and the ads were all over the buses and in the local newspaper, offering shelter and the HIGHEST QUALITY MEDICAL CARE! for these strays—and Paul made Josie put milk out every night for any wandering felines who happened to be passing by their home. Josie had also made up a story about how they often dropped by their house on their way home—there was an Underground Railroad for the strays, she'd explained, and they were one of the partici-pating homes. The fiction lasted weeks, and it was Josie's fault. She'd made up the Railroad, so had to make up the milk-being-available, and had to empty the milk at night, watch Paul check it in the morning, discuss it with him over breakfast, and so how had she forgotten his concern for these wayward animals?

Later, after she'd paid for dinner—eighty-four dollars, everyone involved going to hell—and while Ana ate an ice-cream sandwich on a bench on the boardwalk, Josie clarified some things for Paul while entertaining herself a bit, too. The stray dogs, she said, all live together in a club-house. And this clubhouse was built by Alaskan park rangers because the stray dogs, being pack animals, prefer to live together. They're fed there, she said, three meals a day, by the rangers—omelets for breakfast, sausage for lunch, steak for dinner.

Paul smiled shyly. Someone who did not know Paul would assume he knew this was all made up, that his smile acknowledged the absurdity in all this—the silliness of his concern for the strays and the madness of his mother's explanation—but this was not the meaning of Paul's smile. No. Paul smiled because something that was wrong in the world had been righted. Paul's smile confirmed the true north of the moral world: How could he doubt the preeminence of order and justice? His smile confirmed rightness. His smile laughed at his temporary doubt in this rightness.

Ana was finished with her ice-cream sandwich, and handed the wrapper to Josie on her way to inspect, a few feet down the pier, what seemed to be a bloody fish head. They were near the cleaning station, where the fishermen weighed and gutted their day's catch. The boardwalk was pink with watery blood and a last fisherman was finishing his day. Ana stood below him and looked up, then down at the head of the fish, its silver skin stained with bright plasma. She picked it up. She picked the head up.

"This yours?" she asked him.

Before he could answer, she'd dropped the head, and, in an incredible feat of dexterity and fine-motor skills, kicked the head, on the fly, into the dark water below. She laughed, and the fisherman laughed, and Josie wondered just how this child was hers. "What's my name?" Ana asked the frothing water where the head had disappeared. Josie had not taught her this expression, and Paul certainly didn't know it. But Ana had said this before, and had also said "You want this? You want this?" And "What'd you expect?" These confrontational phrases she insisted on yelling to rocks, trees, birds. She often spoke disrespectfully to inanimate objects, and often walked around practicing gestures, facial expressions, like a clown preparing backstage.

The fact of Ana's existence, and her will to live and run and break things and conquer, was all attributable to her birth. After living for a month in a plastic box, and spending her first two years looking like a withered old man, she shed her preemie skin like Lady Lazarus and became a world-ender. Carl had long before abdicated any responsibility. When they first brought Ana home from the hospital, Carl thought it a good time to start training for his triathlon—there was suddenly such urgency to it—and Josie soon gleaned he was not likely to be instrumental in Ana's care. So she deputized Paul. Your sister is very small and not strong, she told him. When she comes home she'll need your help. They talked about Ana's homecoming every night and every night Paul seemed to take his impending responsibilities more and more seriously. One night she found him on the floor with a hand vacuum, cleaning the room waiting for Ana. He was three. Another time he'd found an old greeting card, a burst of balloons on the cover, and dropped it into her empty crib. Josie's intent was to be sure that Paul, a sensitive boy but nevertheless a boy, would be careful not to accidentally smother tiny Ana, or break tiny Ana's bird bones, but instead she created this boy who came to understand his role as something akin to caretaker of the world's most delicate orchid. He slept in her room, on a mattress next to, and then under, her crib. By the time Ana was three months old he knew how to feed her and swaddle her. When Josie or Carl did either he sat nearby, adding frequent notes and corrections.

Ana grew stronger, and by two she was running without fear or limit, though she was still Pinocchio-thin and her eyes were circled in pale blue shadow—temporary evidence, Josie hoped, of her traumatic journey thus far. As she grew in confidence and awareness of her power of ambulation and self-determination, as she became more aware of herself and the world, she became less aware of Paul. He sensed it and felt betrayed. There was a time when she was two and Paul five, when he came to Josie, anguished. "She won't let me hold her," he wailed. He was on the verge of tears, while Ana barely knew he lived in the same house. Reaching full strength, she had no interest in anyone, really, least of all him. She wanted to see things, to roam, to climb and plummet. She was attracted to the shiny, the moving, the blinking, the rustling, the fur-covered. Paul was none of those things so he held no interest.

But something happened when she turned three, and

after that Paul was known. Now when she did something, usually something dangerous, she wanted Paul—Paulie—to watch. Paulie, Paul-ee. Paul! Eee! Watch. Watch. Watch-watch-watch. Paul acted aggrieved by Ana's demands but satisfying them was his life's calling. He loved her. He brushed her hair. He clipped her toenails. She still wore a diaper at night and she preferred that he put it on. When Josie would wrap a towel around her after a bath, Paul would rewrap it, tighter, more carefully, patting it down just so, and Ana had come to expect this.

Now, as they stood on the deck stained in pink fish blood, an older man was suddenly too close and was talking to them.

"You kids like magic?" the man asked. He seemed to be leering. These lonely old men, Josie thought, with their wet lips and small eyes, their necks barely holding up their heavy heads full of their many mistakes and funerals of friends. Everything these men said sounded hideous and they didn't even know it.

Josie nudged Paul. "Answer the nice man."

"I guess," Paul said to the mountains beyond the man.

Now the old man was delighted. His face came alive, he dropped twenty years, forgot all the funerals. "Well, I happen to know that there's a magic show tonight on our ship."

The man owned a ship? Josie asked for clarity.

"I'm just a passenger. I'm Charlie," he said, and extended his hand, a pink and purple tangle of bones and veins. "Haven't you seen the *Princess* docked here? It's hard to miss."

Josie came to realize that this stranger was inviting them, herself and her two kids, the three of them unknown to this man, onto the cruise ship docked at Seward, where, that evening, there would be an elaborate magic show featuring a half-dozen acts including, the old man was thrilled to convey, a magician from Luxembourg. *"Luxembourg,"* he said, "can you *imagine?"*

"I want to go!" Ana said. Josie didn't think it mattered much that Ana wanted to go—she had no intention of following this man onto a magic-show ship—but when Ana said those words, "I want to go!" Charlie's face took on a glow so powerful Josie thought he might ignite. Josie didn't want to disappoint this man and her daughter, who continued to talk about the show, what tricks a man from so far away might be capable of, but was she really about to follow this old man onto a cruise ship in Seward, Alaska, to see a Luxembourgian magic show? She couldn't deprive them, she knew. They had only one grandparent, Luisa, who was spectacular but who was too far away, so Josie frequently succumbed to these grandparent manqués, who bought her children balloons and gave them candy at inappropriate times.

"We're allowed to have guests, I think," the man said as they walked the gangplank. The kids were astounded, stepping slowly, carefully, holding the ropes on either side. But now their host, this man in his seventies or eighties, was suddenly unsure he could have friends over. So Josie stopped and her kids peered down into the black water between the dock and the gleaming white ship. Josie watched as Charlie approached some man in a uniform. A few dozen elderly passengers went around them in their windbreakers, small bags of Seward souvenirs dangling from their arms.

"Let me talk to this man," Charlie said, and motioned them to hang a few yards back from the door. Charlie and the man turned around a few times to inspect and gesture at Josie and her children, and finally Charlie swung around, telling them to come aboard.

The ship was garish and loud, and crowded, full of glass and screens—the décor was casino crossed with Red Lobster crossed with the court of Louis XVI. The kids were loving it. Ana was running everywhere, touching delicate things, bumping into people, making elderly women and men gasp and reach for walls.

"I think it starts in twenty minutes," Charlie said, and then again looked lost. "Let me see if we need tickets." He wandered off, and Josie knew she was a fool. Parenting was chiefly about keeping one's children away from unnecessary dangers, avoidable traumas and disappointments, and here she had dragged them to Alaska, and had driven them around unchosen parts of the state, and then to Seward, where no one had recommended they go, and now she had them following a lonely man onto a ship designed, it seemed, by the insane. All to see magic. Luxembourgian magic. Josie paged through the years of her life, trying to remember a decision she had made and was proud of, and she found nothing.

Finally Charlie returned, holding the tickets in his hand like a bouquet. "Are we ready?"

There was an escalator, an escalator inside a ship. Charlie was ahead of them, and rode upward while looking back at them, smiling but nervous, as if worried they might flee.

The auditorium seated at least five hundred and all within was burgundy—like being inside someone's liver. They sat in a half-moon booth near the back, Paul next to Charlie. A waitress in bright red hurried by and Charlie made no move to order anything. Josie asked for a lemonade for the kids and a glass of pinot noir for herself. The drinks arrived and the lights went down. Her glass was the size of a crystal ball, and was nearly full, and Josie felt kissed by the anonymous and irrational generosity of humankind. She relaxed, anticipating a few hours of not having to do anything but sit and watch in silence, getting harmlessly plowed.

Charlie had a different plan. The show started, and Josie realized that Charlie intended to talk throughout. And the words he wanted most to say were "See that?" For Ana, the answer was always "See *what?*," so they made a beautiful pair. Charlie would notice something that every member of the audience had seen, and then would ask Josie and her kids if they'd seen it, too. Ana would say "See what?" and Charlie would then explain what he had seen, talking through the next five minutes of the show. It was wonderful.

The first magician, a pretty man in a tight silk shirt, had, it seemed, been told to make his act more of a personal story, so his monologue returned again and again to the theme of how he had always welcomed magic into his life. Opened the door to magic. Said hello to magic. Or how he had learned to appreciate magic in his life. Did he say he was married to magic? Maybe he did. It all made little sense and the audience seemed lost. "Life is full of magic if you look for it," he noted, breathlessly, because he was moving around the stage in a thousand tiny steps, as a woman in a sparkly one-piece bathing suit vamped behind him with long strides.

The pretty magician produced some kind of flower from behind a curtain, and Josie struggled to see this as magical. She and Charlie clapped, but few members of the audience joined her. Her children didn't clap; they never clapped unless she told them to. Were they not taught clapping in school? The magician was not impressing this audience, though who could be easier to impress than five hundred elderly people in windbreakers? No, they were waiting for something better than carnations produced from screens.

Josie began to feel for this man. He'd been a magician in grade school, no doubt. He'd been pretty then, with lashes so long she could see them now, fifty rows back, and as an adolescent, apart from his peers but not concerned about this, he and his mother had driven forty miles to the nearest city, to get the right equipment for his shows, the right boxes—with wheels!—the velvet bags, the collapsing canes. He'd loved his mother then and had known how to say it, maybe with a flourish, and his unguarded love for her had made his apartness unimportant to him and her, and now she was so proud that he had made it, was a professional magician, traveling the world making magic, welcoming magic into his life. All that, Josie thought, and these elderly assholes wouldn't clap for him.

Josie downed half her pinot and gave the pretty magician a whoop. If no one else appreciated him, she would. Every time he asked for applause, which was often, she yelled and whooped and clapped. Her children looked at her, unsure if she was being funny. Charlie turned to her and smiled nervously.

Now the long-legged woman was helping the pretty magician into a big red box. Now she was turning it around and around. It was on wheels! Everything in the act had to be on wheels, so it could be turned around. It was a rule of magic onstage that everything must be turned around and around, to prove there were no strings, no one hiding just behind. But in its absence did the audience ever wonder about the turning around? Did they ever ask: Um, why hasn't someone turned the box around? Turn the box around! My god, turn it!

Now the sparkly assistant opened the box. The pretty man was not in the box! Josie whooped again, clapping over her head. Where had he gone? The suspense was fantastic.

And now he was next to them! Suddenly a spotlight was on their table, or near it, because the pretty man was next to them. "Holy shit," Josie said, loud enough that the pretty man, whose hands were outstretched, again asking for applause, heard her. He smiled. Josie clapped louder, but again the rest of the audience didn't seem to care. *He was up there,* she wanted to yell to them. *Now he's here!*

You fuckers.

Up close she saw the magician was wearing a tremendous amount of makeup. Eyeliner, blush, maybe even lipstick, all seemingly applied by a child. Then the spotlight went dark, and he stood for a moment, next to their table, hands up, while a second magician appeared onstage. Josie wanted to say something to the pretty man, a heaving silken silhouette a few feet away, but by the time she arrived at what she would say—"We loved you"—he was gone.

She turned to the stage. The new magician was less pretty.

"This is the one from Luxembourg," Charlie whispered.

"Hello everyone!" the new magician roared, and explained he was from Michigan.

"Oh," Charlie sighed.

The Michigan magician, red-haired in a white shirt and stretchy black pants, was soon in a straitjacket and was hanging upside down twenty feet above the stage. He explained, his breath labored and his arms crossed like a chrysalis, that if he did not escape from the straitjacket in some certain amount of time, something unfortunate would happen to him. Josie, trying to get the attention of the waitress, had not caught exactly what that consequence was. She ordered a second pinot, and soon some part of the contraption holding the magician was on fire. Was that intentional? It seemed intentional. Then he was struggling in an inelegant way, ramming his shoulders against the canvas jacket, and then, aha, he was free, and was standing on the ground. An explosion flowered above him, but he was safe and not on fire.

Josie thought this trick pretty good, and clapped heartily, but again the crowd was not impressed. What were they waiting for? she wondered. Fuckers! Then she knew: they were waiting for the magician from Luxembourg. They did not want domestic magic, they wanted magic from *abroad*.

The man from Michigan stood at the edge of the stage, bowing again and again, and instead of the applause growing, it dissipated until he was bowing in silence. Josie thought of his poor mother, and hoped she was not on this cruise. But she knew there was a very good chance the Michigan magician's mother was on this cruise. How could she not be on this cruise?

Now a new magician appeared. He had a high head of gleaming yellow hair and his pants were somehow tighter than the pants of his predecessors. Josie had not thought this possible.

"I hope this guy's from Luxembourg," Charlie said, too loudly.

"Hallo," the magician said, and Josie was fairly sure he was from somewhere else. Perhaps Luxembourg? The magician explained that he spoke six languages and had been everywhere. He asked if anyone in the audience had been to Luxembourg, and a smattering of applause surprised him. Josie decided to clap, too, and did so loudly. "Yes!" she yelled. "I've been there!" Her children were horrified. "Yes!" she yelled again. "And it was *great!*"

"Lots of visitors to Luxembourg, I am pleased," the magician said, though he didn't seem to believe those who had applauded, least of all Josie. But by now, her spirit dancing in the glorious light of her second overpoured glass of pinot, Josie believed she *had* been to Luxembourg. In her youth she'd backpacked through Europe for three months, and wasn't Luxembourg right there in the middle of the continent? Surely she'd been there. Did that one train, the main train, go to Luxembourg? Of course it did. She pictured a beer garden. In a castle. On a hill. By the sea. What sea? Some sea. Puff the Magic Dragon.

The magician from Luxembourg did his tricks, which seemed more sophisticated than those of his predecessors. Maybe because they involved roses? Before him there had been only carnations. The roses, this was a step up. Women holding roses appeared in boxes, *boxes on wheels,* and the man from Luxembourg turned these boxes around and around. Then he opened the boxes, and the women would *not* be there; they were somewhere else. Behind screens! In the audience!

Josie clapped and hollered. He was wonderful. The wine was wonderful. What a good world this was, that there was magic like this on ships like this. What an impressive species they were, humans, who could build a ship like this, who could do magic like this, who could clap listlessly even for the magician from Luxembourg. These fucking assholes, Josie thought, trying to singlehandedly make up for their sickening lack of enthusiasm. Why come out to a magic

show if you don't want to be entertained? Clap, you crimi-
nals!! She hated these people. Even Charlie wasn't clapping
enough. She leaned over to him. "Not good enough for you?"
she asked, but he didn't hear.

Now Luxembourg was gone and a man was making his
way onto the stage. He was rumpled, his hair reaching
upward seven different ways, and he was easily twenty
years older than the others. Another man. Where were the
women? Were women not capable of magic? Josie tried to
conjure any female magician she'd ever seen or heard of and
couldn't. My god, she thought! How can that be? Scandal!
Injustice! What about Lady Magic? Lady Magic, yes! Why
do we allow all these men, all these silken heavy-breathing
men, and now this one, this rumpled one—he made no effort
at all to be pretty like the others. He had no lovely assistant,
and, it soon became clear, he didn't intend to do any magic.
Goddamn you, Josie thought, guessing all the magic was
over. And did she have money for another drink? She had
about twenty-five dollars, she guessed. Maybe the drinks
were cheaper onboard than on Alaskan soil. She had to count
on it. She looked for the waitress. Where was the waitress?

There was only the rumpled man standing at the edge of
the stage. Now he was telling the audience that he'd worked
for some time at a post office, and had memorized most zip
codes.

Holy crap, Josie thought. He'll get murdered. What
kind of world is this, she thought, when a man from the post

office follows Luxembourgian magic and why were they, she and her kids, on this ship in the first place? With incredible clarity she knew, then, that the answer to her life was that at every opportunity, she made precisely the wrong choice. She was a dentist but did not want to be a dentist. What could she do now? She was sure, at that moment, that she was meant to be a tugboat captain. My god, she thought, my god. At forty she finally knew! She would lead the ships to safety. That's why she'd come to Seward! There had to be a tugboat school in town. It all made sense. She could do that, and her days would be varied but always heroic. She looked at her children, and saw that Paul was now leaning against Charlie, asleep. Her son was asleep against this strange old man, and they were in Seward, Alaska. For the first time she realized how *Seward* sounded like *sewer,* and thought this an unfortunate thing, given Seward as a place was very dramatic, and very clean, and she thought it very beautiful, maybe the most beautiful place she'd ever been. It was here she would stay, and train to become a tugboat captain at the school that she would find tomorrow. All was aligned, all was right. And now, looking at her son sleeping against this man, this old man who was leaning forward, listening to the post office man talk about the post office, she felt her eyes welling up. She took a final sip from her second pinot and wondered if she'd ever been happier. No, never. Impossible. This old man had found them, and it could not be coincidence. This town was now their home, the site of this ordained and holy reunion, and all the people around them were congregants, all of them exalted and now part of her life, her new life, the life she was meant for. Tugboat captain. Oh yes, it had all been worth it. She sat back, knowing she'd arrived at her destiny.

Onstage, the post office man was telling the audience that for anyone who gave him a postal code, he could tell them what town they were from.

Josie thought this was some sort of a comedy bit, that he was kidding about the postal job, but immediately someone stood up and yelled "83303!"

"Twin Falls, Idaho," he said. "Unincorporated part of town."

The crowd erupted. The cheers were deafening. None of the magicians had elicited this kind of enthusiasm, nothing close. Now ten people were standing up, yelling their zip codes.

Josie, despairing for the waitress who had not returned, downed half a glass of water, and that act, the dilution of the holy wine within her, took her away from the golden light of grace she'd felt moments before, and now she was sober or something like it. Tugboat captain? Some voice was now speaking to her. What kind of imbecile are you? She didn't like this new voice. This was the voice that had told her to become a dentist, who told her to have children with that man, the loose-boweled man, the voice who every month told her to pay her water bill. She was being pulled back from the light, like an almost-angel now being led back to the mundanity of earthly existence. The light was shrinking to a pinhole and the world around her was darkening to an everywhere burgundy. She was back inside the liver-colored room and a man was talking about postal codes.

"Okay, you now," the postal man said, and pointed to a white-haired woman in a fleece vest.

"62914," she squealed.

"Cairo, Illinois," he said, explaining that though it was spelled like the city in Egypt, it was pronounced "kay-ro," the Illinois way. "Nice town," he said.

The audience screamed, hooted. It was a travesty. Now Paul was awake, groggy and wondering what all the noise was about. Josie couldn't bear it. The noise was not about magic and tugboats: it was about zip codes.

"33950!" someone yelled.

"Punta Gorda, Florida," the man said.

The crowd roared again. Ana looked around, unable to figure out what was happening. What was happening? Postal codes were making these people lose their minds. They all wanted to have their town named by the rumpled man with the microphone. They yelled their five digits and he guessed Shoshone, Idaho, New Paltz, New York, and Santa Ana, California. It was a melee. Josie feared people would storm the stage to rip his clothes off. Go back to sleep, Paul, Josie wanted to say. She wanted to flee, everything was wrong about all this. But she couldn't leave because now Charlie was standing up.

"63005!" he yelled.

The spotlight found him and he repeated the numbers. "63005!"

"Chesterfield, Missouri," the postal man said.

Charlie's mouth dropped open. The spotlight remained on him for a few seconds, and Charlie's mouth stayed open, a black cave in the white light. Finally the light moved on, he was in darkness again—as if a spirit had held him aloft and suddenly let go, he sat down.

"Hear that?" he said to Paul. He turned to Josie and Ana, his eyes wet and his hands trembling. "Hear that? That man knows where I come from."

Afterward, on the gangplank, Charlie offered to walk them back to the Chateau. Josie declined, and kissed his cheek.

"Give Charlie a hug and say thanks," she told her kids.

Ana rushed in and hugged Charlie's legs. He put his hand on her back, his fingers spread like the ancient roots of a tiny tree. Paul moved closer but stopped, hoping, it seemed, that Charlie would fill the distance between them. Now Charlie was on one knee and his hands were outstretched. Paul shuffled toward him and Charlie brought him in, and Paul's head dropped onto Charlie's shoulder with something like relief.

"Let's write letters," Charlie said into Paul's hair.

Paul nodded, and pulled back, as if to see if Charlie was serious. Josie knew Paul would obsess about these letters, and she was terrified by the possibility that she would have to offer their address to this man.

"How?" Paul asked. "Can we send a letter to a ship?"

Charlie didn't know. He fumbled in his pocket and brought out what turned out to be an itinerary. "Just take it," he said to Josie, and she saw that on it was the ship's every port of call.

IV.

IN THE WHITE LIGHT MORNING Josie had not slept well and her mood was apocalyptic. It was not a matter of falling asleep. After the magic show, they'd walked the mile home along the waterfront, the night brisk and the moon bright. They walked past the fishing boats, to the end of the docks, and then along the dirt road and through the woods until reaching the Chateau. Ana and Paul had been animated at first, recounting the show, asking questions about Charlie, where he was from and when he would die (Ana wondered this, throwing a stone into the cold water), but then, when they arrived at the Chateau, the kids were silent, somber, and didn't bother to take off their jeans or socks before dropping off to sleep.

After a nightcap of pinot—the last of the second bottle, she deserved it, given all she'd done and endured—Josie climbed up to join them, and fell asleep readily. But at first light she awoke, as she often did, her mind leaping with the realization that she had indeed killed that young man.

Some young prosecutor with Josie's own face—it was her, but younger and with hair in a high tight bun, a great suit. This legal version of herself was leaping around a courtroom, wood-paneled and filled with sensible citizens, insisting upon it. Convict this woman! Hold her accountable!

Josie opened the door to the quiet woods and walked to the waterfront. The sun was beginning to bring pale color to the mountains on the bay's far shore. She squinted at the water's blinding shimmer and beyond, the otherworldly glow of the low sun on the mountain snow. She walked across the beach, almost stepping on the otter skull her children had presented to her the day before. She sat down again on her petrified white tree stump and raked her hands through the gravelly sand, lifting a handful, letting it pass through her fingers.

Jeremy. He'd been a patient since he was twelve. One of those boys who said *Ma'am. Yes Ma'am. Thank you Ma'am.* He had beautiful teeth. Every time she saw him she hoped for cavities, loved seeing him that much, but it was only twice a year in the office, a cleaning, a checkup, some conversation, and the occasional sighting on the street. The kind of boy who, when they ran into him at the park, he would leave his group, a group of teenagers lying about, a pride of lazy lions doing nothing on the park bench by the creek, and he would jog over and crouch down and talk to Paul and Ana, would offer them whatever gum or mints he had in his pocket. His parents were not well-off but they were solid—both worked for the city and had good health plans. The father was from Venezuela, the mother from Cuba, and they began to come for check-ups, too, on his recommendation—Jeremy had vouched for Josie, was the light of the family, and though the parents weren't nearly as talkative or preternaturally aglow as their son, they all liked to talk about Jeremy. How could we make more Jeremys? He had four younger siblings, and he knew everything about each one of them. Josie could ask any detail, How's little Ashley? And he'd have a story. What's the baby doing now?

Then he was seventeen, eighteen, and had become a tall and strikingly handsome young man with a boomerang jawline. Tania, the hygienist, took notice of the way he filled a room, six two, his wide shoulders, and made sure to brush her breasts against him as she cleaned his teeth. His bright green eyes, his unblemished flesh, his impossibly smooth chin. He did not need to shave, he said. "No Ma'am. Once or twice a year is all I need right now." He smiled and ran his hands over his noble face. He played soccer, lacrosse, and then, at Josie's doing—she insisted when she signed up—he had been Paul's counselor at the rec center summer day-camp.

Paul was no athlete but had been treated with special consideration. Jeremy had given him a nickname, El Toro, because Paul had one day worn a T-shirt bearing the silhouette of a bull, and Paul grinned shyly when Jeremy yelled the name across the street, from his car window, whenever he saw Paul in town. "El Toro! Charge!" Josie had found it written on all the flyers Paul took home from camp. Under "Name of Camper," Jeremy had always written, in bold all-capitals, EL TORO! Even the exclamation point.

After summer camp she'd been one of the many mothers who asked Jeremy to babysit. So rare to have a male babysitter, she said, every other mother said. She'd been able to wrangle his services three times, and as far as she could tell he had spent each of those nights being attacked, with affection, by her children. Were they so starved of contact? When she got home she would find them asleep, their hair matted to the pillow, Jeremy on the couch, exhausted, smelling sweetly of sweat, and he would tell her about the night. They'd eaten their pizza, he'd say, and as they walked away from the table, Ana had leaped on him like a wolverine.

"I don't think she let go for the next three hours," he said. Paul was reticent at first, but soon the three of them were wrestling, were jousting with Jeremy's lacrosse sticks and shields made from couch cushions. "But mostly wrestling. Me on the ground and them jumping on me like little animals. They're pretty physical. Way more than Paul was at camp," Jeremy said.

Convinced that they were expelling some latent aggression toward their absent father, that this could only be healthy, she asked Jeremy to come back, and he did, two more times, and each time the battles grew more epic, the final one taking place in the backyard.

"They would have broken something in the house otherwise," Jeremy explained. "Ana called me *Dad* at one point. When I was brushing her teeth. It was pretty funny. Paul was embarrassed."

Josie was mortified. Did Jeremy know that Carl had moved out? Was he old enough to know that her children were starving for a male presence in the house, and that her daughter, being four, had virtually no memory, would be happy with Jeremy as a replacement man, that he could eclipse and erase Carl in a matter of weeks?

"So were you in Panama?" he asked, pointing to a photo of Josie with a dozen Peace Corps volunteers. She'd spent her two years in Boca del Lobo, and it was a mixed bag, a few successes, a few friends, the whole issue with her friend Rory, now in prison, but still. Good work could be done, she said.

Jeremy didn't know what he would do after high school. This was the fall of his senior year. She had assumed he would have had a sturdy plan by then, limitless college options.

"I don't want to be in more classrooms right away," he said, and turned at the sound of footsteps. It was Ana, awake, in her Buzz Lightyear pajamas. Josie stretched out her arms, and Ana rushed to her but then paused between them, as if wanting to fall into her mother's arms but afraid this would alienate Jeremy in some way, would hurt the chances he'd come back. Instead she did a sort of twist-dance on the carpet, and said "Champagne on my shoulders!" She'd been saying that recently.

"Step here," Jeremy said, crouched on the floor, putting

his palms out. Ana did not hesitate. She put one bare foot on each of his hands, balancing herself with her hands on his shiny black head. Her eyes betrayed that she didn't know what would happen, but was certain it would be incredible and worth any risk.

"Okay, now let go," he said. She obeyed.

Now he slowly rose to his full height, somehow balancing Ana on his palms with such sureness that she felt free to spread her arms wide, as if receiving the bounty of the sun.

"My dad used to do that with me," he said, barely exerting any effort, this forty-pound child still standing on his hands. Now he lifted her higher. "Can you get the ceiling?" he asked.

Ana reached, grunting, until she tapped it with her finger. "Down please," she said, and he lowered her slowly, then dropped her in a heap on the couch and pretended to sit on her, trying to get comfortable as she shrieked gleefully below.

"You're a great mom," Jeremy said to Josie, still sitting on Ana. "I mean, in general, but especially because you let me do stuff like this. Not all parents do. But kids are beasts. They need to sweat and scream and wrestle." Jeremy collected Ana in his arms and plunged his mouth into her stomach, making a loud wet raspberry. Ana's eyes were charged, her hands like claws in front of her, waiting for the next attack. But instead Jeremy smoothed her shirt, patted her tummy and stood her up on the carpet, as if restoring a fallen statue.

"Thank you," Josie said, overcome.

In return for Jeremy's kindness and strength, all Josie had ever wanted was to tell him how much she felt he was the hope of the world. Is that all she did? No. She said more, and this is why she should not speak, ever again, and why she cherished every day when she spoke to no one but her two children. She knew that the color of the sky affected her moods, the sun changed her outlook and words, and if she took a brisk walk during lunch and saw something beautiful she was liable to say something exuberant, or be too full of happiness for an hour or so, and this was when she made mistakes. In her exuberance she would reveal too much about herself. She would overpraise, she would urge people into tasks they could not complete.

It happened two weeks after that night. She had come back from lunch and was feeling some joy the fall air had given her, and could hardly concentrate. She had three patients that afternoon, and all were subjected to her inane bliss. First there was Joanna Pasquesi, a Rubenesque high-school sophomore who revealed she was considering going out for the school musical. It was *A Chorus Line* that year, and with altogether too much zeal Josie urged her to try out, to make their selection of her beyond debate, and went on a bit about the need for body diversity on the stage, though in reality she was trying to score a very belated victory against the gatekeepers who had kept her out of her own high-school musical, *Cabaret,* for which Josie was not called back. So Joanna Pasquesi, who had actually checked her watch twice while Josie rambled on, left feeling inspired—she said so, at least—though she might have been simply stunned into submission.

And then Jeremy came in, and they talked for a time about her kids, *Such cool kids,* he said, and they laughed about their hyperactivity, their madness, their need to wrestle with him, touch ceilings with him, and then conversation turned to her, and the Peace Corps, and though she rarely was so exuberant about it, this time she told him it was the greatest experience of her life, that they had made such a difference there, that it was just after the country had taken ownership of the canal, that there was such optimism then, so many changes, and that being part of that transition, representing the U.S. in Panama, this crucial partner, at a crucial moment—she went on and on, and it was wildly convincing. Even Tania was listening.

And then, with his smooth young face and sincerity, Jeremy told her he wanted to enlist. He wanted to be a marine. He wanted to make a difference in Afghanistan, help open schools for Afghan girls, work on clean water projects, bring stability to a country on the verge of great things. Josie's eyes filled and she squeezed his shoulder. She did not do what good people would have done, which would have been to say nothing. Enlisting during a war was such grave business that only an idiot would praise this notion. Josie should have been judicious enough to know that she could not, should not influence such a decision in any way—to recognize that this was between Jeremy and his parents. To know that she was nothing.

But she was a fool who knew no boundaries, and was not very sure about the state of the war—she was relatively certain it was winding down and would present little danger to Jeremy. So she told him that sounded wonderful. That he, as the hope of the world, a gentle soul, a formidable figure, could make such a difference. That the marines, that the region—that Afghanistan itself!—needed someone like him. Somehow she had confused her enthusiasm for Joanna Pasquesi's musical ambitions with Jeremy's nation-building hopes, and further had conflated her own time in Panama, the expression of American love through cisterns and the teaching of English by men and women in sandals and khakis (for the impulse did come from love, love of the world) with Jeremy's expression of the same love, though in uniform and carrying an AK-47. It was not the same thing, and now he was dead and his parents hadn't spoken to her since.

This has absolutely nothing to do with you, her friends said, bewildered that she would take any responsibility at all. But then why hadn't his parents been back? Josie had heard, later, that they'd been against his enlisting from the start. And what they didn't know, and she would never tell them, and had not told anyone, was that he had approached her, in the parking lot of her office one evening, at five—he knew when she'd be there, weeks after that visit where she squeezed his shoulder and said *Wonderful*—and told her that her support had been so important to him. That his parents had been unsure, they'd been worried, but they had respect for her, for Josie, his dentist, that her support had meant so much to them and him. He had enlisted and was killed six months later.

This is why she no longer offered advice, why she was happy to let go of her practice. Liberated. Thrilled. Away and free. This was why, outside her parenting duties, she had not left her bedroom most of January, her limbs unliftable and her face numb. No one had told her. Not the parents, none of their friends. The funeral had already happened. He'd been shot in some remote Afghani hillside and had bled for six hours before dying. He'd had time to write a note to his parents, which had been found on him, the contents of which Josie would never know. A boy of eighteen dying alone, bleeding alone, writing to his parents—how did all this happen? How was this allowed? Josie wanted no more of this. This idea of knowing people. Knowing people meant telling them what to do or not to do, providing advice, encouragement, guidance, wisdom, and all of these things brought misery and lonely death.

"Mom?" It was Paul.

Josie turned. Her son was in yesterday's clothes, and had somehow gotten out of the Chateau, walked through the woods, across the parking lot and found her there, on the shore.

"We're hungry," he said.

They ate in the camp cafeteria, the eggs and sausage excellent and costing only fifty-five dollars before gratuity. The Norwegians ate nearby, waving again.

There was a television hanging from the ceiling, showing a loop of the park's services—iceberg tours, glacier tours, whale watching, each excursion costing somewhere in the thousands per person—and every so often there was a public service announcement featuring Smokey the Bear. Josie had forgotten about his very existence, hadn't seen him since her Girl Scout days, and between then and now something had happened: he'd been working out. The cuddly and round-bellied old Smokey was now a burly bear with a flat stomach and arms like bent steel. In the animated message, his friends were trying to give him a birthday party, and they carried out a cake full of lighted candles. Smokey didn't like this. He gave them a disapproving posture, his huge arms on his waist, and Josie felt a stirring within her. Did she have a crush on this new Smokey?

Her table shook. Someone had bumped it. An older man turned to apologize but his wife spoke first.

"Nimble as a cat," the woman said, her voice a patrician purr. Josie looked up to her, laughed and took in the woman's face: it was beautiful, with an upturned nose, a delicate chin. She had to be seventy.

Hearing Josie's laugh, the woman turned again to her. "I'm sorry. He's just lost a step lately. He was a very debonair man—even last month." The woman smiled, turned away, evidently embarrassed. She'd said too much.

"Who are those people?" Ana asked.

Josie shrugged. Her daughter's face was streaked with dirt and dried snot. Josie had seen a sign for showers available at the campground, somewhere in a vast log cabin in the woods, so after breakfast they put on flip-flops, bought the necessary tokens and brought their shampoo and soap and towels.

They undressed, leaving their clothes high in a cubby, and stepped across the plywood floor to the women's shower area, where there were two young women, each of them facing out, unabashed and vigorously shampooing their hair. They were ravishing creatures, taut and tanned with tiny breasts alive and alert, and their teeth were white, their asses high and shiny and pubic hair artistically groomed. Josie stared at them as she would a pair of unicorns. What are you doing here? she wanted to ask, though she had no better idea of where they should be. Where does young beauty belong? Maybe stepping through fountains in Rome calling *Marcello! Marcello!* Or on a plane. Piloting a plane. Josie pictured the two of them flying a plane through pillowy clouds, each wearing white, their legs uncovered and so smooth.

One of the young women now was looking back at Josie, who in her reverie was caught staring, and now she was telling her friend they were being watched, and soon they were hustling out of the shower and into towels. Josie thought of her parents, both nurses at a veterans' hospital, how they taught her how to dry herself after a shower. Her mother and father mimed the brushing of all excess water from their arms and legs, left arm, right arm, left leg, right leg, saving the towel for whatever was left. Josie thought of their demonstration—they'd done it in the living room when she was eight—every time she showered; many days it was the only time she thought of them. What did that say about her? About the limits of memory, the threshold for the tolerance of pain?

Seeing they had the showers to themselves, Ana ran naked into the mist. Would she break into song? Josie got up and Paul followed, they hung their cheap rough towels on rough hooks and the three of them formed a tight circle, facing one another, the warm water falling between them. Ana looked between Paul's legs and said "Hello penis." It was not the first time she'd greeted Paul's machinery. He'd gotten used to it, and took some pride in being the only member of the household so equipped. Josie soaped their bodies and shampooed their hair, Ana making underwater sounds and stamping her feet. We gravitate toward comfort, Josie thought, but it must be rationed. Give us one-third comfort and two-thirds chaos—that is balance.

Their hair wet and bodies clean, they stepped out of the hygiene cabin and into the dappled sunlight and Josie felt they were in the right place. The last few days, their many trials, were only adjustments. Now she knew what she was doing. She had the hang of it and all was possible. They rested awhile in the Chateau, during which time Paul brought Josie a card, dictated by Ana and written by Paul, which said "I love you Mom. I am a robot."

That settled, they walked back into town.

"Mom?" Paul said. "Was that show good?"

"The magic show? Yeah," she said. "Did you think so?"

He nodded, utterly unsure.

Where the town met the onslaught of the rough black bay, there was a monument to Seward with a long accounting of why the town had been named after Lincoln's trusted advisor. Josie tried to explain it all to her children but they needed context.

"Okay, who freed the slaves?" she finally asked. Paul knew the answer, so Josie raised her finger to allow a moment for Ana to try.

Ana thought about it for some time, and then a light entered her eyes. "Was it Dad?"

Josie laughed, snorting, and Paul rolled his eyes.

Ana knew she had said something funny, so continued saying it.

"Dad freed the slaves! Dad freed the slaves!"

Near the monument there was a rocky beach decorated with wild debris and driftwood. They walked amid great rough-hewn beams, big as truck axles and thrown ashore like pencils. Paul picked up a steering wheel and Ana found the remains of a buoy, smashed into the shape of a child's torso. Josie sat on a round rock and felt the salt air rush at her. Happiness swelled inside her with equal force, and she wanted to stay there all day, all night, wanted to live in that moment for as long as was allowed. She was right when she thought, every hour, that children, or at least her children, needed to be outside, amid rough things, and all she needed, beyond feeding them, was to sit on rounded rocks watching them lift things and occasionally throw them back to the sea. The sand was damp, a deep brown dusted by lighter clouds of dry sand. Soon Paul and Ana sat on either side of her.

"What's that smell?" Paul asked, though Josie smelled nothing.

"It's really bad," he said, and then Josie saw something. There was a large stone in front of them, the size of a shoe, and it looked like it had recently been dislodged and replaced. Josie lifted it and the smell flew upward and filled the air. She replaced the stone but had seen, in a glance, a terrible thing. It was feces, and there might have been some sort of diaper there, too. She thought about it, examining the memory of what she'd seen. No, that wasn't it. The answer came to her: it was a maxi pad. It was a maxi pad covered in caramel-colored feces. "Let's move," she said, and hustled Paul and Ana up from the beach, past the monument to the great man, and through town.

There could be no doubt that humans were the planet's most loathsome creatures. No other animal could have done something so wretched. Someone, an outdoors someone, came to this shore, knowing it was beautiful and rough. Then they had shat here, even though there was a bathroom two hundred yards away. They had shat in such a way that most of the feces was attached to the maxi pad—the physics of it Josie couldn't conjure. And then, instead of bringing the shit-covered maxi pad to a garbage receptacle, one only fifty yards away, they had left it under a rock. Which showed some strange mixture of shame and aesthetics. They knew no one would want to see the shit-covered maxi pad, so they hid it, under a rock, where, they surely knew, it would never decompose.

So they walked into downtown Seward and Josie, feeling magnanimous to compensate for the depravity of the rest of humankind, allowed Ana and Paul to explore the souvenir shops, and bought them each horrifying talking-moose T-shirts and snow globes. They walked along the waterfront and after half a mile found a vast green park with an elaborate play structure full of blond and black-haired children.

"Can we go?" Paul asked, but Ana had already run ahead, crossing a parking lot where she narrowly missed being crushed by a truck backing out. For all her young life Josie had had to envision the tiny coffin, the words she would say, life without this girl. Ana was doing everything she could to bring herself to an early end and the force and focus she brought to the endeavor could not be overcome. Oblivious, she ran through the woodchips and would remain among the living for at least another hour.

Josie found a bench, set the bags of horrible souvenirs down, and watched Ana tear through the play structure.

Next to her, Paul was standing still, hands at his sides, carefully examining the playground, seeing its many features, judiciously deciding which would be best to experience first. Josie opened the free newspaper she'd been handed outside one of the stores, while keeping an eye on Ana, who she knew at some point would throw herself from the slide or find some new way to land on her head. Soon Ana stopped, had spotted a small skate park nearby, and was mesmerized by the teenagers in their gear. For no reason Josie remembered something Carl had written in a folded note, slipped under the pillow: *I will never tire of your sweet ass.* Was that sexy? His handwriting was a murderer's scrawl. Otherwise Carl didn't take sex seriously. He liked to make jokes during and after. "Well done," he'd say afterward, immediately afterward, obliterating any mood, extinguishing any afterglow. When Josie told him she'd rather do without the jokes, he was so sad. He loved his jokes. After that, whenever he'd finish, she could see him staring up at the ceiling, wanting to say "Good work," or "I think that worked out pretty well" but unable to. She'd squashed this crucial avenue of self-expression.

"Okay, locals against tourists," a kid yelled. He was in the playground, standing in an area between Ana and Paul, and seemed to be about twelve, black-haired and handsome, and was organizing all the kids on the playground. He was a leader—if there were ever a true thing it was that some people, some children, some infants, were leaders and some were not—and in seconds he had divided eighteen children into teams and Paul grabbed Ana and all the smaller children were dutifully listening to the boy's instructions. "This is how it works," the boy-leader announced, shaking his long raven-black hair out of his eyes. "It's like tag, but instead of being tagged it's like you're a zombie and you die if your neck's broken, like this." Then, as Josie watched, horrified and helpless, he took Paul, put his hands on either side of Paul's head, and twisted, quickly, mimicking the breaking of someone's neck as done in action films. "Now fall," the boy said, and Paul dutifully crumpled. "That's how it works. You're dead until the game ends then we start over. Everyone got it?"

Ana's eyes were huge, from fear or fascination Josie didn't know. But she did know she was leaving and her kids were leaving. Seeing a twelve-year-old pretend to break her son's neck had left her cold. She waved Paul over, as if she had some casual unrelated news or instruction, then grabbed his arm and didn't let go. "Ana!" she yelled, and they walked off. Ana soon followed.

Seward had been nice but it was time to go. They still had a day to kill before Homer so they packed up the Chateau, Josie filled the tank—$212, an abomination—bought a map and left town.

"Where we going, Mom?" Paul asked.

"Put a seatbelt on," Josie said.

V.

THIS WAS A DIFFERENT WAY OF MAKING PLANS. Sam
had said that she would meet Josie at five p.m. on Monday,
and because Josie had no phone and Sam never picked up
hers, that plan would have to suffice and be honored. By
Josie's calculations, if they drove straight from Seward to
Homer they'd make it by noon, five hours early. There was
supposed to be a barbecue on the beach to welcome them,
Josie and her kids.

She caught Paul looking at her in the rearview mirror.
He was assessing, gauging whether or not his mother knew
what she was doing. She looked back at him, projecting
competence. Her hands were on the wheel, she had her sun-
glasses on, she had a map on the passenger seat, and directions to Homer.

I'm dubious, his eyes said.

Screw off, her eyes responded.

Josie turned the radio knob left and right, occasionally securing a signal in the middle, and when it was clear,

it seemed to be broadcasting a Broadway marathon. Gwen Verdon in *Redhead*. These were obscure songs, songs known only to someone whose formative years were engulfed by the maniacal sounds of musicals known and obscure, failed and world-dominating—most of them sounding tinny now and desperate to please. Her relationship to the music was complicated at best, tied up as it was with her parents' work and devolution.

The musicals had happened when she was nine. She hadn't known her parents to be interested in any music at all. The family owned no stereo. There was a radio in the kitchen, but when it was on, rarely, it was tuned to the news. There were no records, no tapes, no CDs, but then one day there were boxes of records, vinyl black holes spread all over the floor. Her parents were nurses in the psych ward, though they brought little of the work home. As a child Josie heard them mention restraints and Thorazine burps, heard them discuss the man who thought he was a lizard, the man who made imaginary phone calls all day, using a spoon. But now there was homework. They'd been put in charge of bringing music to the ward. Their supervisor had encouraged them to keep the music upbeat and clean and distracting. Everyone had settled on Broadway musicals as the least likely to provoke murder and suicide.

With a borrowed record player and fifty LPs bought at an estate sale—a music teacher in the next town had died—their home was filled, for the next few years, with *Jesus Christ Superstar* (deemed too thought-provoking) and

Anne of Green Gables (wonderful, foreign, unrelatable) and *On the Town* (perfect, as it described a healthier approach to the home life of enlisted men). They would listen to a new one every night, were required to examine every song, every word, for its appropriateness, its ability to cut through misery and uplift. Patterns emerged: Irving Berlin was fine, Stephen Sondheim too complex, morally problematic. *West Side Story,* including as it did gangs and knives, was out. *My Fair Lady,* being about nothing the veterans recognized as their lives, was in. Older musicals about presumably simpler times prevailed. *Oklahoma!* and *Carousel* and *The King and I* quickly made their way into rotation, while *South Pacific* was shelved; they wanted nothing about soldiers still fighting any foreign war. So many well-known shows were tabled in favor of less troubling but forgotten shows that now only Josie could recall. Jackie Gleason in *Take Me Along*—a vehicle for Gleason to be Gleason. Richard Derr and Shirl (Shirl!) Conway in *Plain and Fancy,* about New Yorkers in Amish country. *Pippin* was out, the words circled by her father, then crossed out: "And then the men go marching out into the fray/Conquering the enemy and carrying the day/Hark! The blood is pounding in our ears/Jubilations! We can hear a grateful nation's cheers!" That wouldn't work.

The first musical Josie remembered well was *Redhead,* a show built around Gwen Verdon. The first seconds of the record were a revelation: everything was manic. The wall of delirious optimism appealed to her as a child, though her parents studied the words for controversy. They consulted her sometimes, danced with her occasionally—there was a time when their home had something in common with the bizarre happiness of dozens of people singing from a stage to darkened strangers who'd paid for joy and release. She remembered her mother, on her back with her legs in the air, doing some kind of yoga stretch, her father trying to put Josie on his shoulders to dance, finding the ceiling too low, her hitting her head, the two of them laughing, her mother admonishing, and the musical went on. Josie, in those years, pictured her parents' lives at work as a similar sort of non-stop party, the soldiers dancing, too, with their simple and solvable problems—broken arms and legs, a few days in and then out again, her parents serving them jello and fluffing their pillows.

"It smells," Ana said from the back.

Josie turned down the radio.

"What's that?" she asked.

Paul agreed, something was off. Ana suggested skunk, but it was not skunk. It smelled like something in the engine, but then again it wasn't the smell of oil or gears or gasoline.

Josie opened the windows in the cab and Paul opened the kitchen windows. The smell dissipated but was still present.

"I can really smell it here," Paul said. Ana said her head hurt, then Paul had a headache, too.

At a rest stop Josie pulled over and crawled back to the kitchenette. Now the smell was much stronger—it was a faintly industrial smell that spoke of great evil.

"Get out," she said.

Ana thought this was funny, and pretended to be asleep, her head resting on the kitchenette table.

"Now!" Josie yelled, and Paul unbuckled her and pushed her in front of him until the two of them were down the steps.

"Get on the grass," Josie said. Now she knew what it was. The gas was on. All four knobs had been turned full right. She had the momentary thought that she should jump out, that the whole vehicle might explode if she even touched the stove. But, inexplicably wanting to preserve the Chateau, their new home, she reached over, turned all four knobs hard left and then jumped down from the doorway, pushing Paul and Ana, who were standing on the grass, Paul behind Ana, hands on her shoulders, until they were all fifty yards away and panting. The Chateau stood still, unexploded.

A car passed, heading toward the RV, and Josie ran to the parking lot, directing them to make a wide berth around the Chateau. "What is it?" the man asked. He was a grandfather with three kids in the backseat.

"Gas was turned on. From the stove," Josie said.

"You should turn it off," Grandpa said.

"Thank you," Josie said. "You're very helpful."

He turned his station wagon around, and Josie crouched in front of Ana, who was holding her ThunderCats figure in front of her in self-defense. How had she grabbed that on her way out? She had found time to grab her ThunderCats figure while fleeing an imminent gas explosion. "Did you know you almost caused a very bad accident?" Josie asked her.

Ana shook her head, her eyes wide but defiant.

"She turned the gas on?" Paul asked Josie. He turned to Ana. "Did you turn all the knobs on the stove?"

Ana looked at her knees.

"Ana, that's really bad," he said. This was, Josie knew, the worst thing he'd ever said to her. Ana's chin shook, and she began to cry, and Josie stood, satisfied. She wanted Ana to cry for once, to feel remorse for once. Ana's nickname for most of last year was Sorry, given how often she had to say the word, but this had almost no effect on her tendency to put herself and her family in grave danger.

This is a kind of life, Josie thought. She stood, looking around, noticing now that they had parked next to a beautiful round lake, the surface so clean and placid that the sky was reflected in it, in perfect symmetry. Looking at it, Josie felt a certain calm as she cycled through some questions and observations. She wondered how close to death they'd actually been. Could they have all died at midmorning, on a sunny Alaskan day? She wondered, with some seriousness, if Ana was an emissary from another realm, disguised as a child but tasked with the murder of Josie and Paul. She wondered how long they needed before the Chateau was clear of deadly fumes. She wondered what a life was—if this was a life. Was this a life? And she wondered about the gene she possessed, some strangling DNA thread that told her, daily, that she was not where she should be. In college she changed her major every semester—first psychology, then international studies, then art history, then political science, and all the while she was on campus she wanted to be away, away from the pedestrian workaday nonsense of most of her classes and the directionless pathos of most of her peers. She went to Panama, and felt briefly vital, but then tired of shitting in a hole and sleeping under a net, and wanted to be in London. In London she wanted to be in Oregon. In Oregon she wanted to be in Ohio, and in Ohio she was sure she needed to be here, in Alaska, and now, she wanted to be where? Where, for fuck's sake? For starters, somewhere high above all this filth and calamity.

"Mom, take my picture." It was Ana. Her pants were around her ankles, her hands outstretched, as if ready to catch a falling man.

Josie took her picture.

They made it to Homer. It was only one o'clock. Josie pulled into the Cliffside RV park and paid sixty-five dollars for the night, and then they headed out again, down the road, toward the spit. Or the Spit. It was where most of the action in Homer was, Sam had said, so Josie descended from the hills and down the two-lane road onto the narrow promontory jutting into Kachemak Bay. Sure, it was pretty, Josie thought, without being Seward. For Josie nothing had compared to Seward. Maybe the closeness of those mountains. The hard mirror of that bay. The icebergs like lost ships. Charlie.

On the Spit's main drag there were some old buildings that had real or former fishing operations in them, and there was a stretch of stores and restaurants, so, realizing they hadn't eaten, Josie parked the Chateau next to another, far more luxurious recreational vehicle, knowing this would make its owners happy, to know they were better than her, than her children. Josie ducked under the sink, pulled a handful of twenties from the velvet bag, and they left.

She took Paul and Ana by their hands and crossed traffic, heading for a pizza restaurant that looked, from the outside, as though it had been made from broken ships—the exterior was a mess of bent walls and masts and crooked windows, everything blue-grey, like driftwood. The door was covered in stickers denying entry to those without shoes, with dogs, to unaccompanied children, to smokers and Republicans. Under that last admonition were the words "Just Kidding," and under that, "Not Really." Inside it was light-filled and warm and staffed exclusively by women. It seemed to be some kind of political pizza place, a pizza restaurant embodying its version of utopia. There was a giant stone oven in the middle of the first floor, and five or so young women buzzed about it, all in white aprons and blue shirts, all with short hair or ponytails. Josie ordered a pizza, afraid to look at the price, and the woman behind the counter, with a pixie cut and exhausted eyes, told her to sit upstairs anywhere.

The second floor was bright, glassed in and overlooking the sound. The sun was so hot there that they all took off their jackets and long-sleeve shirts and were still warm in their short sleeves. Ana asked if she could have a knife and Josie said no. Paul tried to explain to his sister why knives were dangerous but Ana had already gone to the bathroom and in seconds there was the sound of something falling. She returned to the table, saying nothing.

"Can you check the bathroom?" Josie asked Paul, and he leapt up, knowing he was on a mission that combined his dual loves: checking after his sister, and pointing out the wrongness of someone else's behavior.

He returned. "Looks pretty bad," he said, and turned to Ana. Ana wasn't listening; she had caught sight of a motorboat cutting across the bay.

Josie stepped into the bathroom and found a towel rack on the ground, knowing Ana had made it this way, and knowing that only Ana could have separated the towel rack from the wall this quickly. Hundreds, if not thousands, of customers had no doubt used this bathroom and this rack without breaking it, but Ana had done so in less than ninety seconds.

The political pizza place had had an intoxicating effect on her already, for Josie found herself not caring about the towel rack. In fact she was briefly stunned, undeniably impressed, that this girl had that acute a sense for the weakness of objects. That she could enter any room, any bathroom in Homer, and know the object most likely to be broken, and just how to go about it.

She went down and told one of the women that one of her kids had broken the towel rack.

"How'd he do it?" the woman said. A different woman—with feathered earrings—was pulling something from the oven.

"It was my daughter," Josie said, and now Josie knew she wouldn't have to pay for the damage. Her leverage was invisible but real.

"Just leave it up there," the woman said. "We'll get it."

Josie ordered a glass of chardonnay and two milks.

Upstairs, it was two p.m. but felt like sunrise. The light on the water was tap-dancing wildly, trying too hard, really, and there was some boat out there they were watching—some great yacht with a thousand white sails. Josie finished her chardonnay and when one of the political pizza women, a third, with a sheep's black curls all over her big head, brought the food up, a lumpy pizza served on what appeared to be a piece of bark, Josie ordered another glass.

This was why people linger. Sometimes a place asks you to stay, to not rush anywhere, that it's warm, and there's the tap-dancing water, and the powder-blue sky, and they had the second floor to themselves. Josie felt that if anyone else came up there she would drive them away, she would throw a knife. This was now their home.

Soon Ana was standing on the floor, using her chair as

her table, eating her slice with her elbows on the seat. She was a disgusting shark-child but Josie loved her monumentally at that moment. Her never-questioning confidence in herself, in how her limbs should work, made clear she would always do things her way and never wonder if it was the right way—this meant she could be president and certainly would always be happy. She wiped her mouth on her arm like a feasting barbarian, and Josie smiled at her and winked. The sun swished around in the gold in her glass and it sang a song of tomorrow. Josie drank it down.

The kids ate two slices each and Josie had two, and then wanted more wine. She asked the kids if they wanted anything. They didn't, but she convinced them they wanted some of the cookies she saw in a jar on the counter downstairs. Then she convinced Paul it would be great fun if they wrote an order down on paper, and if he brought it down to the political pizza women. Josie didn't want to see their eyes or puckered mouths when they heard her order a third chardonnay at three p.m. on a Monday. And besides, Paul was at a stage where he liked to be entrusted with making a phone call, with punching in ATM codes, with running into the 7-Eleven himself. He knew it would be a decade before Ana would be allowed to do this kind of thing. He knew he was responsible and he liked proving it.

She wrote out the order: *1 milk, 2 cookies, 1 chardonnay, and the check,* and Paul took it downstairs. He returned a few minutes later with another bark plate, all the items balanced on top. He was struggling a bit, and Josie thought, for a fleeting second, that she could get up and help him, but would he really want that? She stayed put.

He made it to the table, and looked at her with a terror that seemed to question whether or not his parent really knew what she was doing. To put him at ease Josie smiled benevolently, like a grandma-saint. She wanted to toast him, and briefly raised her glass, but thought the better of it. "Look at the new ship," she said, before turning toward the bay and realizing it was the same one she'd seen before.

The chardonnay ennobled her, made her stupid. Her tongue grew and could no longer form words. She didn't want her children hearing her slur in the afternoon so she said she was resting her eyes, to soak in the warmth of the sun, and she raised her face to the streaked glass ceiling. Josie saw Jeremy's face, then her father's, and heard her father, in his white nurse's uniform, joking about sticking his head in the oven. Josie opened her eyes and saw Paul and Ana standing, his face near the back window, watching a pair of dogs humping in the dunes.

After Carl she'd alternated between complete indifference to any carnal pursuits—she had no urges, no drive, made no plans, could muster nothing approaching an effort—and then, once every six weeks, there would be a calling within her, something like possession, and she would be in heat. She occasionally slept with Tyler, a high-school boyfriend. No, not a boyfriend. Someone she'd known glancingly in high school and with whom, through the miracle of internet nostalgia-sex, she had reunited. He'd written to her one day, attached a photo of her in her Halloween costume—she'd gone as Sally Bowles from *Cabaret* after her unsuccessful audition (I defy thy verdict, Ms. Finesta!). She recalled the feel of the tight satin on her legs in the cool night, the silver wig, and remembered her many admirers that evening and in the days after. A pair of satin tights, a black vest and the imaginations of hundreds of boys were alive for decades. So Tyler re-found some picture, called, said he was in town—passing through. Okay, fine. They ate pasta, drank numbing red wine and later, in his hotel, he did a fine job with his small cock until he became determined to stick his finger in her ass. He tried it once and Josie moved herself in a discouraging way. Five minutes later he tried again, and this time she gently pushed his hand away, assuming the matter settled. He tried once more, though, five minutes later, and this time she tried to make it funny, laughing a bit as she said, "Why are you so hellbent on sticking your finger in my ass?"—but despite her caution and obvious decorum he pulled away, pulled himself out of her, no great loss, and then—this part was delightful—he smelled his finger. Very slowly, very discreetly, as if he was just scratching his nose. He even looked away when he did it! Out the window! As if hoping he'd gotten at least a little bit of her feces on his forefinger before she'd thwarted him. That was why he'd been sticking his finger in there. To smell the finger afterward. He was memorable. And there was the other man, the one who died. The last man she'd slept with had died a few weeks later. How did she feel about this?

Vincent. He had been a kind man. A kind man who had said he would never leave her. For the children, he'd said, and she had appreciated this, his grave seriousness about not damaging her children in any way by entering and exiting their lives, for he knew about their father, Carl's powers of invisibility. *I won't leave you*, he said. *I won't do that to your kids*, he said. Never mind that he barely knew them and they couldn't pick him out of a lineup. It was too soon. She understood he meant well, but after two months of seeing each other, he had said that if they were ever to break up it would have to be her doing it. He could not abandon her. He would be in it for the long haul. She was flattered, maybe even impressed, but it was a bit constraining, no? She asked her friends: This was constraining, yes? To be told that this man would be attached to you, for the sake of the children he does not really know, for eternity.

He had a habit of watching her as she watched movies. He caught her tearing up during an Iraq War soldier-widow movie and after that, every time there was an emotional scene of any kind on the screen before them, he turned to her. She could always sense in the dark his face angling toward her, to see if she was crying, or about to cry, or welling up. To what end? What internal score sheet was he keeping? He didn't carry a handkerchief and never offered her a tissue. But he'd been indoctrinated. Stay with woman for sake of children. Watch woman and her displays of emotion.

"Come to Normandy with me," he said once. "The kids, too. I want you all to see something." He wouldn't tell her why he wanted to go to Normandy. He thought it would be some wonderful surprise. She explained the difficulty in leaving her practice, and trapping her small children for fourteen hours on two planes—all without knowing why they'd be going to that French beach. Finally he told her: He'd been learning more about an uncle—no, a great-uncle; he corrected himself the next day, apparently after some phone calls to his Salt Lake genealogists—who had fought and died on D-Day. He wanted to go, pay his respects, and apparently because he'd decided whatever was his was hers, he wanted to share it all, the field of graves, with Josie.

She'd suggested a few weeks away from each other and he'd nodded, agreeing, praising her wisdom, and then two weeks later he'd died. He'd collapsed on the beach. At Normandy. He'd gone to lay flowers at the grave of his great-uncle, then, apparently after that he'd gone jogging, and suffered a venous thromboembolism. The funeral, back in Ohio, was a mess of ex-girlfriends and sisters—the man had a life full of women, and they had all loved him, so why hadn't Josie tried harder?

The check from the political pizza makers arrived. They wanted eighty-two dollars. With a tip she would be paying a hundred dollars for a pizza, two cookies and three glasses of wine. This was Alaska. It looked like a cold Kentucky but its prices were Tokyo, 1988.

Josie paid and walked down the steps, out the door, and felt so free, out in the open, and happy that the women of pizza hadn't seen her, drunken afternoon mother. Then she felt the afternoon's new chill, and looked at her children, and realized they didn't have coats on. Where were their coats? Josie turned around to find one of the women of pizza, standing at the door, holding their coats and long-sleeved shirts, smiling like she could have Josie imprisoned.

Josie took the coats, hustled Paul and then Ana into them, and they wandered down the street. Three shops down was a kiosk full of hand-woven hats and sweaters and Josie was sure she'd never seen such beautiful things.

"Were these made here?" Josie asked the woman, grey-haired and with bright opal eyes. The woman was grinning with joy barely contained, as if to be in Homer, selling handicrafts, was more than she deserved.

"No," the woman said. "Bolivia, mostly." She purred the *liv* portion of the nation's name, implying this was the only place or way to do it, *to live,* and it seemed to Josie the only way to say the word.

Josie fondled the sweaters and hats, thinking she must purchase these Bolivian goods in Alaska, and if she didn't, she would have missed an opportunity to fully seize this moment.

"You let me know if you have any questions," the woman said, and sat on a nearby stool, raising her face to the sun with a beatific smile.

Josie found a scarf, wrapped it around Paul's neck and stood back to admire him. He looked five years older, so she took it off.

"Mom, how do you know Sam again?" Paul asked.

119

This was unusual for him. Normally she didn't have to tell him anything twice; his memory was airtight for unusual information about the adults in his life. Before she could explain, this time more memorably, he asked, "Have I met her?"

He had met her. Or Sam had met him, held him as a baby. Josie told Paul this, and made up something about how he had really bonded with her, that she was sort of a godmother to him.

"So she's my godmother?" he asked.

Josie looked quickly to the opal-eyed woman, expecting judgment, but her ecstatic expression hadn't changed.

The truth was that Josie hadn't given Paul godparents yet. When he was born, she held off, wanting to wait till his personality had formed, to better match him to the right people. It had seemed radically enlightened at the time, but since then she'd plainly neglected the task. Now, this notion of Sam seemed inevitable.

"Sure," Josie said.

Anyone would be better than Ana's godparents, friends of Carl's, who received the honor like a bad wedding gift quickly shelved. Ana hadn't seen anything from them—never a card, nothing.

Sam, well, it could go either way. She would not likely be a smothering sort of godmother, but perhaps she could be the distantly inspiring sort? She could ask Sam about it when they saw her. No one ever said no to being a godmother, so it was as good as done.

"Sam's the best," she added. "Did I tell you she had a crossbow?" Sam wasn't the best, and she was only guessing about the crossbow, but Josie was overcome with a sudden longing to see Sam, and to strengthen their ties over this godmother notion. She did love Sam in a complicated way, and hadn't seen her in five years, and they'd walked the same strange path, and above it all and most important for Josie this day, Sam was an adult. Besides Stan and magic-show Charlie, Josie hadn't said more than please and thank you to anyone over eight years old since they'd been in Alaska.

"She's your stepsister?" Paul asked.

This was true in a general sense. Telling the whole truth of their sisterhood wasn't possible, not to an eight-year-old. Though she'd tried, Josie hadn't arrived at a simple enough storyline to explain Sam to her children.

"Right," Josie said. "Pretty much."

Now the grey-haired woman opened her eyes. Josie caught her looking at Paul, as if assessing if he had the strength to live through all this—cloudy step-aunt and godmother, tipsy mother. Josie bought sweaters and hats for Paul and Ana, showing the woman her competence and love by spending $210 on bright Bolivian clothing that her children would wear only reluctantly.

Josie did some math and realized she had spent all of the money she'd brought, $310 in an hour, while in a state of being most would consider intoxicated. Across the street she could see the Chateau beckoning, warm and still.

"Who wants to watch *Tomás y Jerry?*" she asked.

They went back to the RV, the kids settled into the breakfast nook and she started the movie. Josie crawled upstairs, fully clothed, lay down on the sunny mattress. Before she fell asleep, she heard Paul say to Ana, "Are you going to get your coloring book? I don't know how long you can play with a carrot." Were they watching the movie or not? How did it matter? She drifted off, and woke up an hour later, sweating heavily. She looked down to find Paul and Ana asleep, with their headphones on, hair matted.

She closed her eyes again, feeling the heat of the afternoon, thinking that what she had done, taking the kids up here, notifying no one, especially not Carl, might be considered criminal. Was it illegal? Insane? Carl would use that word. For Carl, good things were insane. Bad things were insane. Josie was insane. "You grew up next to a nuthouse!" he would say, as if that meant something. As if the entire town where Josie had been raised would have been deranged by osmosis. As if Josie growing up near the Rosemont Veterans' Administration Hospital, formerly the Soldiers' Home, better known as Candyland, would explain whatever he hoped it would explain. He thought her childhood, her proximity to the scandal, her emancipation from her parents at seventeen, gave him some kind of leverage. He was from sturdier stock, went the implied logic, so he was entitled to drift—was allowed to do nothing. This was nonsense, of course. His father was part of a beef conglomerate that deforested some large swath of Costa Rica to make room for cows and grass, cows that would eventually be chopped into American steaks. That's why he grew up in some luxurious expat school in San Jose—Costa Rica's, not California's—and why he'd grown up with servants, and why he had no idea how to work, what work meant. And because he'd never seen any connection between work and the ability to pay mortgages and the like, he felt at will to judge Josie's every quirk. And because Josie had been born to two nurses—an occupation Carl associated with the servant class he'd exploited as a child—and because both of them were implicated in the Candyland scandal, any variance in her behavior, any flaw or weakness, could be exploited, tied to this VA tragedy.

When she and Carl were together, they'd decided not to tell the kids anything about Candyland, but now, as she lay in the Chateau, soaked in sweat, breathing the stale air inches from the ceiling, she knew she would have to be on guard around Sam. Sam, she knew, had told her twins about it all, Sunny and her own emancipation, and would be determined to bring it up in front of Paul and Ana.

Josie's parents had been nurses at a hospital. She could tell her kids that—she had told them this. This was enough for now. At Ana's age that was all Josie knew. Her parents wore white when they went to work at Rosemont, and came home together, changed out of their whites and said nothing about their day. Josie's knowledge of their work came in stages. When she was seven she realized their hospital was for veterans. When she was nine, there were the musicals at home, and she became aware of Vietnam, and that most of Rosemont's patients had fought there. But she didn't know what ailed them: she pictured rows of beds of happy soldiers with sprained ankles and black eyes. She didn't know, as a child, where it was exactly, if the war was still on or not.

Occasionally her parents talked about the patients. There was a man who spent the days knocking the side of his head, as if to free up some loose bolt. There was the man who, not wanting to disturb the perfection of the made bed, slept under it.

"I hope your parents aren't part of that Candyland mess." One of Josie's teachers said this one day. Josie had never heard of any Candyland mess. But the news that year became inescapable. The suicides. Rosemont had been overprescribing their psych patients and they were dying in alarming numbers. They slept eighteen to twenty hours a day and when they weren't drugged into a stupor they were killing themselves at the rate of one every few months. Most of the suicides happened in the psych ward itself, a few after discharge, and all were horrible in their strange detail. A man of thirty-two using a bedsheet to hang himself from a doorknob. Another drinking bleach, rupturing his lower intestine. A man of thirty-three throwing himself from the roof, landing on another patient's mother, breaking her neck, and then, realizing he was not dead, using a piece of broken glass to slice open his wrists and jugular, there on the sidewalk.

That was the one that opened Rosemont up to national scrutiny. The newspapers discovered the place had a nickname among the vets, Candyland, and that macabre touch stoked public fascination. Eighteen suicides in three years, five accidental overdoses, maybe more. The faces of each young man, most of them in uniform, stared out from the paper each day. *We sent them to Nam to be killed,* the editorials said. *When they came back alive, we killed them again.* The head of the ward, Dr. Michael Flores, was arrested, and most of the blame fell on him—"I only wanted them to live without pain," he said—but Josie's home became loud. Her parents had been questioned, had been blamed privately and publicly. Four of the suicides had happened on their watch, and the whispering grew. How could they have let it happen? Their colleagues at Rosemont stood by them, said they hadn't been negligent, but the doubts persisted and grew. The ward was closed, then the hospital itself was closed, her parents were out of work, and Josie learned the meaning of the word *complicity*.

Then, in what she saw, as a teenager, as a stunning display of irony, they both began abusing the very drugs, Dilaudid and Thorazine and Dilantin, that Flores had overprescribed. Just after her fourteenth birthday her father moved out and, a year later, moved to Cambodia, where he stayed and still lived. When Josie was sixteen, her mother was working as an in-home nurse for a family fifty miles away, caring for an elderly woman, Mrs. Harvey. "I'm in love, Joze," she said one day. She'd gotten involved with Mrs.

Harvey's middle-aged son, another vet, another addict, and wanted Josie to come live with them in this new home, with the dying woman and her son, making specious promises about their lives being good again.

Josie thought: No. She had two years of high school left. She broke down one day at the dentist's office, in the waiting room, and the receptionist had come to her, had brought her to the bathroom, had sat her down on the toilet and dabbed her face with a warm wet towel, and this had made Josie cry harder, louder, and soon she was lying in one of the examination chairs, face soaked with tears, and Dr. Kimura was next to her, initially thinking it was some body image breakdown. When the receptionist had caught Josie weeping, she had a *People* magazine on her lap, open to a story about heavy teenage girls being bullied. So she and Dr. Kimura thought Josie, who towered over both of them, was upset about her size, had been harassed at school. They brought her into a back room, where surgeries were done, and they huddled around her like saints. There was something in Dr. Kimura's wet eyes and chandelier voice that invited Josie to talk. And when Dr. Kimura asked the receptionist to leave, and told Josie she had the afternoon free, Josie told her everything. Her father was in Chiang Mai and, according to Josie's mother, lived with a paid harem of four women, one of them thirteen years old. Her mother had been sleeping on the couch for two years. Now she was in love, but was using again and was marrying an addict. There had been new people in the house. They were dealing, they weren't dealing, Josie didn't know. She remembered backpacks lined up in the foyer, always different backpacks, and the new men would arrive and leave with one of these backpacks. Josie began hiding in her room.

Through Josie's ramblings, Dr. Kimura said very little. But her eyes seemed to have settled on something. "Why don't you come here after school for a while? Tell your mom it's an apprenticeship," she said. "You need a calm place to be for a few hours every day."

The first week Josie sat in the waiting room, doing her homework, feeling the thrill of betraying her mother in this small way. But she grew accustomed to the calm, to the simplicity, the predictability of the office. People came, went, paid, talked. There was no chaos, no screaming, no mother on the couch, no mother interacting with skittish men with hollow eyes. Sometimes Dr. Kimura brought her back to show her something interesting—an unusual X-ray, how the molds were made. But usually she spent those hours in Sunny's office—Dr. Kimura had told her to use her first name—doing her homework, sometimes napping, occasionally wondering about the photo of a teenager, a dishwater-blond girl who looked so unlike Sunny that Josie assumed it was a patient. After the last patient, Josie would help close up the office, and Sunny would ask for updates about happenings at home. Sunny listened, her eyes angry, but never said a disparaging word about Josie's mother. They were about the same age, Sunny and her mother, somewhere in the late thirties, but Sunny seemed a generation or two removed, far more settled and wise.

One day she closed the office door. "I know this might be the last time I talk to you," she said. "Because what I'm about to suggest will trigger a series of events that might get me in a world of trouble and might cost me my practice. But I think you should pursue emancipation from your parents, and if you do it, I'd like you to come to live with me. I know a lawyer."

The lawyer, a quiet but persistent woman named Helen, was a friend of Sunny's. They met the next day. She had a tight mound of curly hair and unblinking eyes. The two of them, Sunny and Helen, sat across from Josie, shoulder to shoulder. "We won't do this if there's any possibility of it getting ugly," Helen said. "You already have enough drama in your life," Sunny added. "If your mother objects . . ." Helen began, but Sunny finished the thought: "then we can reassess. What do you think?"

Their eagerness was both unnerving and infectious. Josie wanted to do it. She wanted to be around these sober, functioning, efficient women who made grand plans quickly.

"Okay," Josie said, utterly unsure.

"Good," Sunny said, and took Josie's hand. "Come home and have some dinner with us tonight. I want to introduce you to someone."

So Josie called home, told her mother the truth—that

she was eating dinner with her dentist, and because her mother had lost all hold on propriety, she agreed, told her to be home by ten. Josie rode in the backseat, Sunny's car old but clean, Helen in the front seat, Josie feeling very much like they were in a getaway car, sure that the three of them would be thereafter best friends and an inseparable trio. She entered Sunny's house, walking between Sunny and Helen as if being protected, like a president or pope.

"Samantha!" Sunny yelled, and a girl tromped down the stairs and stopped midway. She was the girl from the picture.

So Josie was Helen and Sunny's second project. The realization knocked her back. Samantha had been taken in a year before, fleeing a mother who beat her and a trucker father who had photographed her in the shower. Samantha lived forty miles away, and Helen had been alerted to her case by a high school counselor there. Samantha's emancipation process was quick. Now Samantha was home-schooled in some self-guided arrangement that Josie didn't immediately understand. She didn't understand, either, why Sunny hadn't told her about Samantha before the emancipation discussions had begun.

"I couldn't tell you about Samantha before we were sure," Sunny said. After dinner that night, Sunny had suggested a walk, and so, under a dark canopy of trees, she explained Samantha's situation. "It's best if she keeps a low profile. We have the restraining order on her dad, but it's best not to risk it. You understand? Does the existence of Samantha change your mind about all this?"

It did. During the drive from Sunny's office to her home, Josie had believed Sunny was taking her in an act of bravery, of wild and even irresponsible courage. But it was more mechanical than that. She and Helen had a system.

"You coming to me after Sam was serendipity," Sunny said, trying to return the situation to something closer to a fairy tale. "You two are only a year apart, and could make each other stronger."

Or we could drag each other into a succession of feral teenage dramas, Josie thought.

"I know it's awkward," Sunny said that night and often thereafter. "But it's quiet here, and safe."

It was awkward. Josie and Samantha were put in the same room, meaning Samantha's room had been instantly halved and her personal space evaporated. "What have those two sluts done now?" she muttered to herself while loudly moving her belongings around the room to make way for Josie's. She cooperated, seething, competitive one month, then aloof, prone to occasional eruptions. Josie stayed in her school, and they had different friends, so their contact was incidental, and avoidable. Sam treated Josie like a freeloading drifter who had come in from the rain to share a room she'd paid for.

Eventually there was detente, and they revealed each other's weaknesses, only to have them exploited later. They were smart and angry girls who were not properly grateful to Sunny or Helen, who argued with their teachers, who flirted with each other's boyfriends, who stole or broke each other's things.

But their home was sane and calm, and Josie's own emancipation was accomplished without resistance. "I laid out the pros and cons for your mom," Helen said one day, and Sunny smiled—the implication was that they'd utterly overpowered Josie's mother; it gave Josie a twinge of guilt. Josie visited her mother every month for the next year, and their meetings, always at a highway Denny's situated between their two towns, were cordial and tense, and they talked mostly about how good it would be in a few years, when all was settled, when whatever resentment had burned off between them and they could return to each other as adults and equals. Ha.

There were some whispers about Sunny and Helen, just what they were up to—building some kind of cult, one lost teenager at a time? Were they lesbians? Were they lesbians starting a lesbian cult? But after Josie there were no more strays, not that year at least. Eventually Sunny's home became a known haven for young women fleeing calamity, and the power of Sunny's interest in Josie was diluted by all the girls who followed. Sunny knew it, and worried Josie and Sam would feel neglected. Don't worry, Josie told her. Never worry.

VI.

IN A FLURRY JOSIE WOKE THE KIDS, got them in their seatbelts and drove up the Spit and back to the Cliffside RV park, to meet Sam. They were late, stupidly late. In twenty minutes Josie was putting on their shoes in the parking lot, Ana's like little rubber bricks, and then they were all standing atop the bluff, looking down at Sam, who was with about twenty others, a barbecue in full swing on the beach below, all to welcome Josie and her children.

"Sorry!" Josie yelled down, as they made their way down the steep path, trying to smile, trying to laugh, as if they were all in this together, the Alaskan way, a life without schedules and set times for beach barbecues. "We fell asleep!" Josie said brightly, trying to make it sound adorable, as Paul and Ana dragged groggily behind her, so she kept a smile frozen on her face as they jumped the last feet from the path to the beach. Sam was quickly upon her, swallowing her in a wooly embrace, her hair and sweater smelling of woodsmoke. She was wearing shorts, boots with the laces open, and a handknit black sweater. Her hair was windblown and unwashed.

"Don't worry, you're only an hour late to your own party," she said, releasing Josie and grabbing Ana and lifting her high. "You've never met me but I plan to eat you," she said, and Ana's eyes went electric, as if alerted to another of her wild breed. Sam kissed Ana roughly on the ear while eyeing Paul more cautiously. "Is this Paulie?" she said, and put Ana down. Paul faced her, and seemed to be accepting the possibility that Sam would lift him, too. But she didn't. She squatted in front of him and held his face with two red hands. "I always remember those eyes of yours," she said, and then stood up.

The barbecue was being held close to the bluff, on a vast beach at low tide, the beach striped in orphaned strands of ocean water, silver in the low light. Across the water were the Kenai Mountains, but no one paid them any attention. The rest of the guests were accustomed to all this rugged beauty, all this driftwood and all these round grey stones, the vast tree trunks hollowed by the sea and bleached in the sun. There were introductions to everyone assembled—a mix of scruffy people who worked for Sam, scruffy people who had worked for her in the past, parents of her twins' friends, and neighbors, most of whom wore down vests or wool sweaters, all of them in old boots. All along, one man seemed to be standing very close to Sam, and Josie guessed this was some kind of boyfriend. Josie tried to remember Sam's approach to marriage. She'd been at Sam's wedding, to a commercial fisherman named JJ, but hadn't seen him since. Was it an open marriage? Something like that.

This man in front of her, leaning into Sam with obvious familiarity, could have been ten, fifteen years younger, but a thick rust-colored beard made it hard to tell. Sam introduced him last.

"This is Doug," she said, and held his hand up, high over her head, as if he'd just been declared the winner.

No. It wasn't an open marriage. Now she remembered. JJ was away for months at a time, and they'd made an arrangement: whatever happened while he was away on these trips didn't count. No questions could be asked, and he had only one request: No one she fooled around with could be anyone he knew. But here they were, among all of their mutual friends, and there was this man, Doug, who to all seeing humans was sleeping with her.

"Do you still have kids?" Josie asked. "Or do they already have jobs at a cannery or something?"

Sam raised her chin toward the shore. A few hundred yards toward the water two silhouettes were standing before a large boulder. On the boulder was a giant bird, and Josie laughed to herself, figuring that any second she would be told that it was a bald eagle.

"Bald eagle," said a man's voice, and she turned to find Doug, holding a brown bottle of local beer out to her.

"You guys want to go see Zoe and Becca?" Josie said, and gave Paul an imploring look. "Go say hi and come back to eat." Paul took Ana by the hand and walked toward the water.

Josie had a surging feeling that Sam had made a good life for herself here—she had many friends, friends willing to come out to the beach on a weeknight to greet Josie and her children.

"You get lost?" Sam asked. "We got here at four, set everything up and everyone showed up at five. We said five, right?"

Josie tried to flare her nostrils.

"We knocked on the doors of a bunch of the RVs up there," Sam continued, "but no one had seen you guys."

It was fascinating, Josie thought, how little she knew what to expect from Sam. Five years was a long time, and Sam, a shape-shifter to begin with, might have changed into some entirely new entity by now. But she was still a keeper of grudges.

Josie explained that they had been driving all day, and that they were off schedule, napping at odd times, that she didn't have a phone, and thus didn't have an alarm clock, and anyway so what, it's summer and Sam was among friends anyway, so who cares if she was late, does anyone really care anyway, ha ha.

At the end of her soliloquy, Josie saw that Sam was looking at her in a certain way, her eyes searching and her mouth amused, and she remembered that Sam had often done this, had presumed she had a direct line into Josie's elemental soul, could get messages no one else could receive or decipher.

"Don't do that," Josie said. "Don't act like you know me so well. I haven't seen you in five years."

This delighted Sam even more. Her eyes opened like cartoon headlights. "You left your practice and fled Carl. Or fled your practice and left Carl. That's what I heard."

The only person she could have heard any of this from would have been Sunny, who was anguished over the loss of Josie's practice and who would never have put it in such terms. But Sam had always been flippant about any loss, any tragedy. She felt it her right, as a survivor of a broken personal world.

"Well," Josie said, and couldn't conjure a way to finish the thought. She hoped the one word would suffice.

In the stretch of Josie's silence, Sam only grew more delighted. "Well indeed!" she said, as if they were engaged in some cute verbal dance they both knew and loved.

"My kids should eat," Josie said, hoping to focus herself and Sam on practical matters.

"Doug's on it," Sam said, nodding toward a bonfire, which Josie realized was also the barbecue. This was a barbarian arrangement—a vast open fire being fed with giant logs, and over it a grill held high by a complicated latticework of sticks.

"They like bratwurst?" Doug asked.

Josie said they did, knowing she would have to cut them into tiny pieces and tell her children they were hot dogs.

Paul and Ana returned with the twins, thirteen years old, identical, willowy and athletic, taller than their mother or Josie. Their hair was strawberry blond and thick, and with their light freckles and their eyes dark and bright and intense and laughing, they had the look of medieval warrior-women just back from joyous plundering and man-beating and whale-riding. They strode to Josie and hugged her as if they really knew and loved her. Josie, overcome, told them they were beautiful, that she couldn't believe it, and they each looked directly at her, actually listening. They were not quite of this world.

They took their leave, throwing sticks that the many large dogs could chase, and Josie gave her children plates piled with fragments of bratwurst and corn grilled in foil. Her kids sat on an enormous log, next to a line of boys, all of whom were nine or ten years old, and each of whom was holding his own carving knife. As Paul and Ana ate, the boys whittled, their fists white, their long hair covering their eyes. Paul was watching passively, but Ana was enthralled. Josie knew she would want a knife and would talk about nothing but knives for days.

"You look tired," Sam said.

"You're sunburned," Josie said. "That your boyfriend?" She indicated Doug, who was dodging the changing direction of the bonfire's smoke. Sam shrugged and went to Doug, rubbing his back and then ducking from the smoke as it enveloped her.

Josie glanced over to see that Ana had repositioned

herself. She was now sitting on the sand in front of the child-carvers, her eyes at blade level. The boys were laughing, thinking Ana was a trip, that this girl was the craziest thing they'd ever seen. Then Ana's eyes lit on an idea, and she lifted her sweater, the Bolivian one, all that heavy wool woven loosely, pulled it over her head with great effort to reveal a Green Lantern shirt underneath. She was showing the boys that she was no girl, no simple girl—that she was like them, that she liked Green Lantern, that she appreciated fighting evil with great supernatural force, appreciated the cutting of wood with big knives. The boys didn't care enough, though: they glanced, chuckled, but said nothing. Ana was not dissuaded. Shivering in her Green Lantern shirt—the temperature was dropping into the fifties—she squeezed in next to them on the log, every so often putting her hand on one boy's forearm, as if to participate somehow in the carving. As if, through this human transference, she could be carving, too. Josie served her a second brat on a paper plate and Ana devoured it, never taking her eyes off the boys and their knives.

Paul, meanwhile, took his plate and walked to the twins near the eagle and the boulder on the beach. Josie watched as he made his way directly to them, and then stopped short. The girls turned toward him and seemed to acknowledge his presence in some satisfactory way. He squatted on the beach and ate his food and the three of them looked at the eagle, and a pair of horseback riders trotted slowly across the horizon in the shallow water, until one of the girls threw a

rock close to the bird, and it lifted off, its shoulders seeming
tired, the movement of its wings far too slow and labored to
create flight, but then it was up, rising like it was nothing,
flight was nothing, the planet was nothing, nothing at all,
just another place to leave.

VII.

AFTER THE BARBECUE THE KIDS CLIMBED into the back of Sam's pickup, with Sam and Josie in front, and they drove back to Sam's house, passing young pines all the way, about a mile up a hill of tidy homes. The house, with a rolling lawn and orderly rows of shrubs surrounding it, had a clear view of the rest of Homer below. This was not some deep-country log cabin. This was a respectable and modern house, newly painted and sturdy and clean.

To be a bird-watching guide in Homer, wow. Sam had it right. She had gone up to Alaska and opened her bird-watching operation, no fuss, didn't ask anyone's permission. She had the run of the forest, some island off of Homer, and she had it figured out. Had she left society, as Josie wanted to? Yes and no. She ran a business, she had kids, the kids went to school, she paid taxes, she sent emails. She was as trapped as Josie was, but she had a boat, and wore boots, and her daughters were these holy outdoor creatures with long-flowing sweet-corn hair. She'd figured out a few things. She'd simplified.

Paul and Ana got changed and went upstairs, following the twins, and the twins said they would put them to bed. Ana was thrilled, Paul cautiously ecstatic. Josie had planned to tell Paul about Sam being his actual godmother, or announce this to Sam, but now she wasn't sure. She hoped Paul had forgotten.

"I have a surprise," Sam said.

She'd been making her own whiskey and wanted Josie to try it. Josie had never developed an appreciation for brown liquor, and was fairly sure Sam's would not be good.

Sam brought out a medieval bottle and poured anyway, and poured too much, and worse, she poured it into a coffee cup. Josie smelled it, and the stench was stronger than regular whiskey—it was wicked and fathomless, a predatory smell. Josie feigned sipping it, pretended to grimace, pretended to swallow and enjoy it in the brave rugged way Sam expected.

"Damn," Josie said.

Sam was pleased. The purpose of the whiskey maker, it seemed, was to make the drinker gag.

"So good," Josie said. She hadn't tasted it yet.

They took their cups out to the back deck. Sam grabbed a heavy blanket and turned on a propane heater and brought it close. The night was cooling and the sky was grey with low cloud cover. They sat with their feet touching, their bodies making a V facing the dark trees.

Josie assumed deep talking was about to happen, and so took a long pull on the whiskey, wanting its effects without experiencing its taste. But the taste was inescapable and wretched. It burned. She thought of tennis shoes on fire. "This is awful," she said.

Sam smiled and refilled her cup.

"So what the fuck are you doing up here?" Sam asked.

Josie laughed. Sam laughed. They laughed loudly, so loudly that an upstairs window opened and one of the twins, Josie couldn't tell which, leaned down and her dark face said, "Quiet out there, missies. It's bedtime for the little ones."

The window closed and Sam turned to Josie.

"So Carl didn't want to come?" She was kidding. "Seriously. Are you in touch with him? He in the picture?"

Josie gave Sam an accounting of his participation in his children's lives, which took eight or nine seconds.

"Too bad," Sam said. "Remember when he nicknamed Ana *Oh No* and then *My Bad*? He was funny. Actually pretty good with kids." Both of these things had been true to some people at some point, but somehow his disappearance made him seem, to Josie at least, both less funny and less child-friendly. Whenever she heard Carl praised, she conjured his comical crimes. He had, more than once, *asked* Josie to fake an orgasm. She was ready to present this to Sam but Sam was moving on.

"And did I hear right, that you sold your practice? You're not a dentist anymore? And wasn't your face numb for a year or something? You're not planning on driving that RV off a cliff, are you? Stop me if I'm prying."

"No," Josie said. She couldn't think of anything else to say. She thought, *You, who fled to Alaska and is somehow married but not married—you're judging me?* But chose not to. There was no point. Josie took another long sip of the sickening whiskey and felt she could just let the night pass over her, an hour until she could claim exhaustion and go to sleep. The night air was warm, and the crickets or frogs were making their noise, and there was a breeze and far off, some road hummed a forgettable tune.

Sam topped off Josie's cup. "So you quit? You sold the practice? What did Sunny say about that?" Sam asked, and Josie was glad that Sam had stopped calling Sunny *Mom*. The last time she'd seen Sam, she was using that word, Mom. Neither she nor Sam had called Sunny by that name when they lived with her, and hearing her use it, twenty years later or whenever it was, was jarring—as if Sam had assessed what Sunny had been to her and had given it a name. Hadn't she once called her Sunsy? She had! Sam liked names, nicknames. These names did what—they helped Sam define, or redefine, what she and Sunny were to each other. They gave her some control, as if to call her *Sunsy* put her in her place, as a small and aging woman, whereas Mom had been a holy honorific. But now she was Sunny again. Sunny was just her name. The name as they'd known her. Let's settle on something and leave it alone, Josie wanted to say.

She sipped her whiskey, looked into the obsidian sky. This could be the cause of all modern neurosis, she thought, the fact that we have no immovable identity, no hard facts. That everything we know as foundational truth is subject to change. The world is running out of water. No, actually, there is enough water underground to cover the surface of the earth six hundred feet deep. So there's no water problem? Well, only six percent of that underground water is drinkable. So we're doomed? Well . . . The hedging and backtracking never ended. The scientists, the astronomers being the worst offenders. We are matter. No, we are surrounded by matter. There are nine planets. No, eight. We are exceptional, our planet singular in its ability to sustain life. No, there are billions of Earth-like planets, most of them bigger than ours, most of them likely to be far better developed. Sunny. Sunsy. Mom.

Sam was saying something. Josie focused on the words. "She must have been devastated. *De*vastated."

Oh this. Josie had expected this. When she'd taken up dentistry in college, Sam was cruel. "You don't have to suck up like that, Joze." That Josie had gone through with it, and had opened her own practice. Sam had been livid. Paralyzed. Then she'd moved up to Anchorage, then Homer, and there was an unspoken theory among Sunny, Josie, and Helen, that Sam had chosen Alaska as her way of ceding victory and territory to Josie. Josie had won, she'd secured Sunny's greater love, and thus could have her and have the Lower 48.

There was a thumping of Sam's unlaced boots. She put her feet, huge in their heavy wool socks, on the grey picnic table.

"Sorry, shit," Sam said, and suddenly her face was directly in front of Josie's. Their noses touched. "I'm not mad at you. Or jealous," she said. "I'm nothing. Nothing like that. But I know you've always thought I was bitter." Josie remembered, suddenly, a time when Sam had accused her of positioning herself to inherit Sunny's practice. She'd been so nasty, so often, again using her excuse that it was all fucked up, so what. "I love you. We're sisters," Sam said, and now Josie's eyes were welling and Sam was crying. "I want to hear about what happened. It helps to talk."

Josie felt this a dubious claim. Usually it did not help to talk. It hurt like hell to talk. It was like saying *Standing still helps* to a person sinking in quicksand. In this case, Josie was sure the pain would be searing, that she would think about it more vividly that night, later, lying on Sam's basement pull-out. She knew, in fact, that she would lie down there, cold and with a head full of bad whiskey, and run all this through her mind again, while also thinking of her children sleeping two floors above, who very well might wake up in the middle of the night and would not know where their mother was—they wouldn't guess the basement, and would find that terrifying, their mother asleep in a basement. Josie was sure talking about all this was a terrible idea—talking about horrors had not been helpful to her, she was better off forgetting, structuring her life around forgetting, but Sam wanted to know, and in a moment of whiskey-driven weakness Josie thought it a wonderful idea to open this wound.

She had such a gentle face. Her hair was white, her cheeks pink, anyone who met her would have thought of Mrs. Claus. How could a woman like that, a woman named Evelyn—Evelyn Sandalwood! A name to soothe the tired and weary!—how could this widow with five grandchildren become such a demon? Josie thought of the strange monuments in the desert, the hunched and hollowed shapes that wind and rivers had made of respectable mountains.

Evelyn had been Josie's patient. Years without a problem. She had a dirty mouth, yes, she was a smoker with soft teeth, two dozen fillings, poor gums. But nothing far out of the ordinary. Usually one could sense the troubled patients—they had so many worries, they would jerk around in the chair, grip the armrests, would look at you with resentful eyes before spitting into the sink. Afterward they would ask so many questions, would stay far longer than they should, they would ask for second opinions from her hygienists. Josie had broken up with so many of these patients in the past, sending them to cheaper or more expensive dentists, anywhere.

But Evelyn was one of the good ones. They talked about the creek near Josie's practice, how Evelyn used to take a canoe through its sulfurous waters as a girl. She occasionally mentioned her dead husband in a lovely way, nothing morbid, knowing he was gone, feeling lucky to have had him so long. She was not angry about anything, had no confrontational bones. She seemed an honest woman. And so why did she come at Josie like she did? Josie sensed forces around her. A son-in-law who was a personal-injury attorney. A niece who had seen some documentary about malpractice. Josie heard things but wasn't sure. It was a small town, Josie couldn't know what was true, what happened in her home, in her mind.

She did know that one day Evelyn Sandalwood's records were subpoenaed from her office. Christy, the receptionist, opened the letter, from an attorney known to be a holy terror, asked Josie about it, and Josie said of course send them, send the records, anything. But she couldn't breathe. She stared at the letterhead. This attorney was an animal. It was three in the afternoon, she had only one more patient, just a cleaning and checkup. She glanced at the letter, afraid to read it, but saw the words "gross negligence" and "significant delay in diagnosis" and knew her practice would not survive. She let Christy close, and stopped by the grocery store on the way home, getting herself an oversized bottle of prosecco. She got to the parking lot and went back for gin.

Josie should have seen the tumor. That was the claim. In any checkup Josie would do a standard oral cancer screening, and for someone like Evelyn, a smoker, she took her time. She lifted and examined that filthy tongue, the color and texture of a car's floormat. She remembered vividly doing so,

147

remembered finding nothing, remembered marking *negative* on her chart.

But sixteen months later Evelyn had Stage 3 cancer and wanted two million dollars. Josie didn't know who to call. She called Raj. "Come see me after work," he said. Raj had his own practice in town, and she and Raj talked frequently, gave second opinions on root canals and, for fun, sent each other their most annoying patients. He was a round man in his late fifties with a booming voice, given to dubious philosophizing at high volume. He would stand with his legs firmly planted, as if ready to withstand a sudden gust of wind, and say things like "I love my work, I cannot deny it, because I love all people!" Or, on a less happy day, "The only problem with our profession, Josephine, is the people and their terrible mouths."

This time, Josie arrived at his office to find him standing in the empty foyer, arms outstretched. But instead of embracing Josie, he began one of his pronouncements. "I told my daughters, 'Don't go into medicine!'" It was just the two of them but he was talking loudly enough for an open-air political rally. "Can you imagine, an Indian man telling his daughters not to be doctors? It's these lawsuits! This constant blame. This culture of complaint! We are not the givers of immortality! We are fallible! We are human!" Josie asked him if he'd ever had a patient subpoena anything, and he said sure, back in Pennsylvania once, but he didn't know a good lawyer in Ohio. She spent the rest of an hour hearing him talk about his own problem patients, the dozen times he'd narrowly avoided lawsuits of his own.

When Josie finally found a lawyer, a young woman who had just left the district attorney's office in Cincinnati, she knew she was beaten. She'd hired a kid lawyer to defend her against a woman dying of cancer, a woman who happened to resemble Mrs. Claus. She did not stand a chance. It was a matter of settling and for how much.

The notion of giving the practice away came to Josie one day when she was arriving at the office. The moment her key turned the lock, the idea struck her with gorgeous simplicity. She would hand the business over to Evelyn Sandalwood. The woman had poisoned the business, and now it could be hers. Her lawyer was hinting at a settlement of two million dollars. Josie's insurance topped out at one million, and she thought the business could be worth about five hundred thousand, so she offered them a trade. She would hand over the entire thing, the equipment, the clients, everything, and walk away. They could get all that, a million and a half, now, or wait forever for less.

Evelyn's lawyer said it was ludicrous, no chance, until the former DA explained how long it would take for Evelyn to extricate the same amount from Josie in cash. Her house, even if they sold it, was only half hers, and after the sale and split and taxes and fees it might bring Evelyn one-fifty.

The rest would come in wage garnishments for the remainder of Josie's life—and Josie had made it known she didn't plan to practice dentistry again, so that level of income was never to return. The business was Evelyn's to own. That was Josie's offer. And it was Josie's idea to give Evelyn's people seventy-two hours to decide. In those three days Evelyn's people sent experts through the building, assessing the value of the machines, the lights, the tools. In the middle of it all, Raj called. "I'll buy it for a million," he said. Josie told him it wasn't worth that. "I think it is!" he said—he roared. He was somehow louder over the phone. Josie told him he was a saintly man. "I want happiness for you, Josie!" he yelled. "I want you to forget this ugliness and find serenity! You are now free!"

Even before Evelyn, the work wasn't fun anymore, wasn't even tolerable. One day Josie arrived at the office to find a note taped to the door. "How *could* you?" it asked in a sturdy all-caps hand. The note terrorized her for weeks. Who'd written that? What did it mean? Was it about Jeremy or someone complaining about overbilling? Josie grew skittish. She started to mumble. So afraid to give advice, to impart wisdom that might get someone killed in some lonely Afghani valley, she had begun saying next to nothing. The anxiety of influence! In her country, at this particular deranged moment, a dentist had the power to send a man to his death. A dentist! She had said wildly encouraging things to Jeremy about his ability to change the world, and he was shot dead. Then, she had gone the other direction, marked a box "negative" and that had, Evelyn or her carnivorous family claimed, led to that sick woman's cancer. Well, enough. It was better to say nothing, to avoid all people. She was done with all mouths, beginning with her own.

"Don't worry," Raj said. They were walking through her empty office. Everyone was gone. Raj would soon take over, rehire most of the people. She loved him for it. "Josie," he said, holding both her hands like they were about to square dance, "the lost will always prey on the competent. Just as someone drowning will pull down someone merely treading water."

The last meeting with Evelyn and her people—it was an ugly thing. Months had gone by since the first subpoena, and the old woman had lost thirty pounds. She couldn't talk, and her once kind eyes had grown hard. Josie wanted to feel for her, but felt nothing. She wanted to be gone. Evelyn accepted the terms, took the money, her son-in-law watching her sign the papers with those withered, yellowed fingers.

And Josie was free.

"That's why your face was numb?" Sam slurred. They'd refilled their cups twice during the tale.

"I don't know," Josie said. "Sure."

Josie looked into the black night.

"Is this the way you're supposed to live?" Josie asked.

"What does that mean?" Sam asked, and stood, and looked into the night, trying to see what Josie was seeing.

151

"Do you feel like you're doing what you're supposed to be doing? That you're using your time here properly?"

Josie laughed, to undercut what she'd just said, but she knew, even in her stupor, that this was the central thought that had occupied her mind for the better part of twenty years. Wherever she was, she could be content, and could do her work, or feed her children, or temporarily love a man like Carl, and live in the town she lived in, in the country she'd been born in, but a thousand other lives presented themselves to her daily and seemed equally or more worthwhile.

Sam didn't answer. Then Josie realized she hadn't said the words out loud. Josie had wanted to say them, but now the moment had passed and she couldn't.

Instead she said, "It's okay," and by that she meant that they, Josie and Sam, should be better to each other. We all should be better to each other, she meant to say. Evelyn shouldn't have gotten cancer, and shouldn't have taken Josie's livelihood in recompense, and why was it again that she hadn't heard from her father in eleven years and that Jeremy was dead? How was that acceptable?

"What were you looking at?" Sam asked.

"It's okay," Josie said again, and then said, "I think it's time to sleep."

But she didn't sleep. She went down to the basement and lay on the foldout couch there. Her business was gone, and there were no plaques, no thanks. Her employees blamed her, not Evelyn Sandalwood, not the cannibalistic legal climate, not the abyss that was moral order, but Josie, for the demise of the practice and the loss of their jobs. Tania had scolded her for not having the proper insurance. Tania! *Who she'd insured!* All these young women—they came to Josie looking for work, yes, but more important, they wanted insurance. A dentist's office surely had the best coverage. They had unknown lists of pre-existing conditions and they could not help themselves—they asked about insurance in the first ten minutes of any interview. Josie took care of Tania and Wilhelmina and Christy, took care of all these people and none of them lost money. All the money to be lost was hers, and they took their pay and considered themselves cheated. There was no reason to run a small business and employ people. These people had been brought up to feel aggrieved at any employer, to feel cheated by every paycheck. Josie had repeatedly brought up the idea of a co-op, a system whereby everyone at the practice shared the profits and shared the risks. No one wanted any part of that. They preferred to be aggrieved.

She closed her eyes.

And was met by the face of that certain zealous woman at the school, the one with the scarf, always some scarf, who thought Josie was some kind of shirker. "How can we get you more involved around here?" she'd asked, her crazed beady eyes and wild black hair like a broom of brambles. No, no. New thought. Jeremy. Not Jeremy. Someone else. Not Carl. *I read a book about html!* Carl once roared, the only time

Josie had ever heard him yell. *I read it cover to cover!* This, for him, was a kind of work. This justified his sloth. This might have been the greatest thing he'd ever done outside the bathroom. Remember the time he bought two twelve-packs of toilet paper? He had to; he went through a roll a day. No. No more Carl. Josie swept him away. Patti? Whatever happened to Patti, that friend of hers from nursery school? Patti was good. Patti was funny, ribald, knew the bullshit when it was bullshit. With a shock of recognition, Josie realized it was her fault—Patti had reached out repeatedly last spring and Josie had what? Forgotten to write back? To call. No, Patti had moved. Divorced and moved. Why couldn't she remember these things? Running a business murders your ability to be the kind of friend people expect or deserve. Days and weeks go by and there can be no keeping up. Her best friends were her oldest friends, who did not expect constant contact. Everyone else was disappointed.

That was the primary response she provoked in others: disappointment. Her employees were disappointed in their hours and pay, her patients were disappointed in their care, in their cavities, in the fact of their dirty mouths, their soft teeth, in their slippery insurance plans. The suggestion box, the staff's idea, had been a disaster. *Kinda disappointed. Very disappointed. Super disappointed.* She put away the box, had a few happy years, then the customer-review websites appeared, jesus, so many aggrieved, all these anonymous patients avenging her every slip, every imperfect moment. Disappointed in her bedside manner. Disappointed in the diagnosis. Disappointed in the magazines in the waiting room. Every disappointment a crime.

We live in a vengeful time. You didn't get the orange chicken you ordered *or* the sticky rice? And now you're already home? Meaning you'd have to drive all the way back to get the orange chicken and sticky rice you ordered? Injustice! And thus avenge. Avenge the proprietor's crimes! This was our contemporary version of balance, of speaking truth to power. Avenge the proprietor on thy customer-review site! Right the imbalance! Josie had done it herself. Three times she'd done it, and each time it felt so good for two or three minutes, and then felt base and wasted. It meant nothing to the world. Forget it. How had she stayed in business that long? I'm disappointed, too, she wanted to say. Disappointed in your halitosis, by your hard-on when Tania leans over you, pressing her breasts into your pubescent shoulder. Disappointed in the way you hold the armrests as if I'm hurting you, fuck you, I'm barely touching you. You crybabies. You big babies. Bramble-haired mom was disappointed. Evelyn most disappointed of all. Oh shit: It was a show: *Disappointed: The Musical*.

Think of it: the audience leaves *Disappointed*. What'd you see? How'd you like it? *Disappointed*. That would be the ad! *After This Show, You'll Leave Disappointed*. It couldn't lose. Lying in the basement, apart from her sleeping and drooling children, her eyes now open, Josie thought about getting a notepad. No, she'd remember. It was better than *Norway!* Every song in *Disappointed: The Musical* a litany of

155

complaint set to a jaunty score. The set a kaleidoscopic orgy of colors and products, the unimaginable array of things and conveniences available to us, all somehow falling short, all letting us down. Products to be disappointed in. Our friends: disappointing. Our parents: disappointments. Airlines: disappointing. Our nations and leaders, all disappointments. The show would make the disappointment four-dimensional. The actors would sing and dance in phenomenal outfits that would somehow fall short. The seats in the theater would be comfortable, sure, but could be better. At intermission there would be refreshments, but they would be not up to par, and the time before Act II not quite long enough to enjoy these beverages. Ticket prices: not quite outrageous, but definitely a disappointment. Availability, also disappointing. The show would be too long.

But Evelyn would be the star. Whoever played her would be in her seventies, but her opening number would be about all that she had to live for, the thousand possibilities ahead of her. We'd see an aging woman, and a woman who was not quite able to bound around the stage—and she'd be smoking, too, and possibly not even moving so much at all, perhaps just sitting on a stool—and she would sing a song as if a vivacious new arrival to the big city: all the things she wanted to do. But then. But then, she sees the dentist, who is somehow oblivious, somehow causes her cancer—that would be the end of Act I—this dentist causes cancer by not catching it. Her second solo number would be a tragic song about lost horizons, about finite time, about disappointment. The show-stopper would be that song "Every Disappointment Is a Crime," and for it Evelyn would be joined by her children and grandchildren, all lamenting her fate, but expecting some measure of satisfaction when justice is served, when the negligent dentist is punished and cast away—perhaps some trapdoor in the stage? The show would end that way, with the dentist descending at the same moment Evelyn ascended—she would rise to heaven, amid a sweep of cornets and French horns, and then of course she would be disappointed there, too.

VIII.

JOSIE WOKE TO THUMPING from the rooms above, and knew these were the sounds of Sam and the twins eating and dressing and, Josie prayed, leaving soon. She had no clock nearby and didn't want to know the time. She wanted only for these people to vacate the house before they woke up Paul and Ana. Sam had to work in the morning, she had said, lead a group from New Jersey, and the twins would be at school, so Josie and her kids would be left alone till the afternoon.

The front door closed with civility, then the screen door with a cannon bang, and Josie put a pillow over her head. Then the door opened again, the screen banging three, four more times. It was some kind of joke, Josie thought. But finally it was quiet, and Josie was very warm, and briefly thought she would fall asleep again, only to find, when she closed her eyes, the face of Jeremy, and his mother, and her accusatory eyes. Presented with the choice between waking up far too soon, or closing her eyes again to fight off these faces and their accusations, she threw aside the blankets and pillows and got up.

The first floor was silent and clean. Sam and her children left no mess, no sign they had eaten or in any way inhabited these rooms just moments before. In Josie's home, dishes were not cleaned after dinner; it seemed better to leave them until the morning, as if to clear and clean them too quickly would be to prematurely erase the memory of a fine meal. Josie walked around, and, her mind awakening slowly, thought with some small pleasure that for twenty minutes or so she might be able to explore the house without being observed or interrupted. Sam had no coffee, so Josie brewed tea and walked through the kitchen, opening cabinets and drawers.

The organization was astounding. There was a cabinet for glasses, another for plates and bowls, and no interloping had occurred in any of them—no rogue tumblers or platters. There was a drawer for plastic bags. A cabinet for pots. The silverware drawer had silverware in it and nothing else—no carrot grater, no corn holders. Those outliers had their own drawer. In vain Josie looked for the drawer or bin or closet where all the uncategorizable things were held, or hidden during desperate cleanings, but found nothing. The refrigerator, though an older model, was clean and bright, and inside were plastic tubs of leftover pasta and garden burgers. The milk had been somehow conjured from hemp, and the orange juice had been squeezed and bottled in Homer. A half-eaten banana had been carefully entombed in plastic.

Josie stood in the doorway to the living room, sipped her tea, and contemplated the strangeness of being in a house at all. Josie and her children had been away from home for only a few days and already this, this large house with its sturdy walls, walls so strong pictures and mirrors could be hung from them, was some foreign and unfathomable temple to solidity. Josie found herself touching the walls, leaning against them, lavishing in their strength. There was a fireplace that appeared to get use, a tidy wall of quartered logs on one side, a smaller pyramid of kindling on the other. On the mantel were some old family photos that Josie recognized, one of Sunny and Helen and Josie and Sam, an unsurprising array of the twins' school photos and lacrosse trophies, and a large plaque that Josie passed over quickly the first time, only to realize, when she returned to it, that it had been created to commemorate Sunny's retirement. How did *Sam* have *that*?

From above, she heard two small feet drop to the floor, and guessed from their nimbleness that it was Ana. In the mornings Paul was slower to re-enter the world. It would be better, Josie thought, if her children had a father like Zoe and Becca's: heroic and faraway, rather than nearby and cowardly. It was far better and Josie tried to stifle the envy that was washing through her. How did Sam afford a place like this by giving birding tours for three months a year? It was ludicrous and not fair. Why should her fatherless children be so beautiful and strong? Why should she have arrived at effortless solutions to everything while Josie's head was in a vise?

"Mom?" Ana called from above, having no concern for her sleeping brother.

"Down here," she said, and Ana tromped down the stairs.

Ana was hungry, so Josie found yogurt and they ate a cup together. They found grapes and crackers and ate them. They found eggs and Josie made omelets. While eating her second helping, Ana noticed the play structure in the backyard and ran to it. Paul was still asleep, so Josie went back to the fridge, found chocolate kisses and ate six of eight. She opened the front door, hoping to find some answer to the question of her unhappiness that day, but found only the morning newspaper.

She brought it back to the kitchen and paged through it while keeping an eye on Ana, who was busy finding weak spots in the play structure. Josie knew she would break some part of it, and knew also that Sam's kids were far too old to play on it. With Ana, Josie did calculations daily: How likely will it be that she breaks this? What will it cost in time or money to repair it? She scanned the structure, looking for the worst Ana could do, and arrived at the conclusion that it would involve the thin chains that held the swings to the thick posts above. The chains were the structure's weakest point and Ana knew this, and was already pulling wildly on them.

Josie refilled her cup with tea and turned her attention to the local weekly newspaper. The cover stories concerned a city employee who had made away with twenty-five thousand dollars in quarters he'd pilfered, over three years, from parking meters. The paper was astonished, wounded, but Josie thought: that is some extraordinary planning and follow-through. That man had some talent. A few pages later, the Announcements page graphic featured two words in large letters: *Births,* accompanied by a rattle and bottle, and *Police,* with a picture of handcuffs. These two words and pictures were next to each other, tilted jauntily, and were above what was mostly a police blotter of extraordinary clarity.

8/16

An anonymous caller reported a semi-truck traveling down the road with a tire on fire on East End Road and Kachemak Bay Drive.

A caller reported an aggressive dog on Beluga Court.

A caller reported an injured otter on the beach. The Alaska SeaLife Center, consulted, said to let the otter have time to see if it would go back into the water.

A caller reported neighbors being loud outside her window on Ben Walters Lane.

8/17

A caller reported he found a black lab on Baycrest Hill.

A man on Svedlund Street reported being yelled at by his woman all the time. He stated he did not want officers there.

A woman turned in a found purse.

8/18

Someone reported an overturned trailer on Ocean Drive Loop.

A caller reported that her husband was assaulted while walking along the roadway.

A caller reported theft of an outboard motor on Kachemak Bay Drive.

A caller reported a man walking down the road wearing shackles.

8/19

A man came to the police counter and advised he thinks someone stole his golden retriever.

A caller reported an injured sea otter.

A woman reported a bright light filling her home.

It was all very lucid and yet Josie had many questions. Was the man in shackles somehow involved in the assault of the husband on the roadway? Was it the same otter on 8/16 and 8/19?

Paul came downstairs and something in his eyes echoed Josie's own thoughts about this house: it was warm and solid and made Josie's family's existence in the Chateau seem utterly irresponsible and cheapened their humanity. Josie made him an omelet and poured the last of the hemp milk, while his eyes asked just what they were doing—in the RV, in Homer. Why couldn't they live here, or like the people here? A loud whine cut through the day's quiet and Josie looked out the window to find a man wearing some kind of jetpack attached to a vacuum cleaner. Oh no. A leaf blower. The easiest way to witness the stupidity and misplaced hopes of all humanity is to watch, for twenty minutes, a human using a leaf blower. With this machine, the man was saying, I will murder all quiet. I will destroy the aural plane. And I will do so with a machine that performs a task far less efficiently than I could with a rake.

Sam had said she'd be back by three, so at two, realizing they had done nothing but eat all day, Josie knew they'd have to go grocery shopping. She dressed the kids and they made their way down the road, enjoying the new experience of being able to walk to the store. Josie was sure she'd seen a food market down that way the day before, but the store they found was half hardware store, half discount grocery, and wasn't the one Josie had in mind. The ceilings were high and the shelves piled precariously with wholesale goods, enormous bags of rice and flour, and a remarkable variety of food for dogs. All the brands were different from any Josie had seen before, none of them recognizable. The kids were confused. The cereal aisle was indistinguishable from the aisle, next door, that sold garden supplies.

They found what they could and paid some irrational sum for it all. Walking home, Josie carried four bags, and the kids each carried one, and in a steady drizzle they made their way up the hill. All was routine until Ana began splashing in the puddles, Josie unwisely allowing it. The water eventually weakened Ana's paper bag and her groceries fell through and onto the street. The kids began retrieving them, but there were cars speeding by, and there was no sidewalk, so Josie positioned Paul and Ana on the narrow strip of grass between the road and the ditch, and arranged the stray groceries in their remaining bags, gave one soggy sack to Paul and carried the others herself, and they resumed their journey. Dignity was at an ebb.

With the house in view, three blocks up the hill, Paul turned to Josie. "Why are you sighing?"

"I was yawning."

"No, you were sighing," he said.

She told him she didn't know what she'd done or why, and it was raining so they should hurry. When they turned the corner Josie saw Sam's truck, and her heart split. She was home early, and Josie had the unmistakable feeling that she was about to be scolded.

"Boy, you sure did some house-exploring, ha ha," Sam said after a moment, without anything like mirth. "And eating! You guys must have been hungry!" Josie tried to recall. Had they opened drawers, left them open? Closet doors? They must have.

"We bought food," Josie said, holding the bags high in the air. She brought them to the kitchen, and as she began to unpack them, she realized they hadn't done any kind of organized replenishing. She'd bought some basics, eggs and milk—regular milk; they hadn't had the hemp variety Sam favored—some stuff she and her kids wanted, some stuff the kids put in the cart and then a fair number of items even

Josie wasn't sure they'd eat. She looked back upon herself from just an hour ago, at the store, and couldn't fathom anything at all about that person who had done that.

"Looks like I'm going grocery shopping, ha ha," Sam said.

"Just make a list," Josie told her. "I'll go out again."

"It's fine."

"Let me go, Sam."

"No, it's okay. You're the guest. You relax."

To make her point as clear as possible, and to be the biggest ass she could be, Sam got her keys and went out then and there.

An hour later Sam returned, her hands full of newer, better groceries, and a wide smile on her face. It was as if, having proven her point—Josie could not be trusted with any task—a grand benevolence had overtaken her. She seemed under the impression that she and Josie were close again, that the dressing-down she'd given Josie an hour ago was right and just and had been dutifully absorbed. Grinning like they were in pajamas and still sharing a bedroom, Sam suggested a plan for that night whereby the twins would babysit Paul and Ana, and she and Josie would go out on the town. When the kids got wind of the possibility of staying alone with Zoe and Becca, ordering pizza and watching TV, it was over.

Soon Josie was in Sam's truck, and they were driving to a

bar Sam insisted was for locals only, as if what Josie wanted and needed more than anything in the world was to drink with locals—that drinking with or near tourists was not right.

"This is my place," Sam said, and Josie nodded appreciatively. It looked like a VA bar. This was Sam's place. Sam had a place. The walls were decorated with pictures of fish and battleships. It seemed a pivotal and regrettable moment, when you had a place at all, and it was a place like this. Sam ordered margaritas not from the bartender, but from Tom. He was a large man with a pink face that seemed to be prematurely falling, like a wax figure in the midst of melting.

"We hooked up once," she said to Josie, loud enough to be heard by Tom and anyone else. He smiled to himself while turning a glass upside down and setting it in a mound of salt.

"Cheers," she said, and clinked Josie's glass. As a teenager, Sam didn't drink. Not through college, either—she was a puritanical young woman fueled by her sense of control, her ability to avoid all substances and temptations. Sunny couldn't get her to take aspirin. Now Sam was this. She'd downed half her margarita and had hooked up with the bartender. When?

Above the bar, a football game was in the middle of some celebratory moment. "Look at that," Tom said.

It wasn't a touchdown, though. The players now rejoiced after every play. Whether they were winning or losing, every time they did anything, they found something to celebrate.

"I have to pull my girls from school," Sam said, her eyes on the TV, where an adult male in silver spandex was doing some dance involving a football and a towel. "You ever hear of girls giving boys a rainbow blowjob?"

Josie had not. Tom had stopped moving, was visibly listening, thinking so hard his forehead had sprouted twin diagonals from his temples to the bridge of his nose. He couldn't wait to hear about the rainbow blowjobs.

"Apparently this is done," Sam explained. "A girl puts on red lipstick, and gives a guy a red ring on his dick. Then her friend puts on orange, another ring. Then another girl with yellow, another with green, blue. Would it be blue next?"

Tom was nodding vigorously. Yes, blue.

"Now I have this to think about," Sam said, finishing her first drink and ordering another. "Will one of my girls be doing this? I mean, there's no right way. Either I let them do whatever they want and they go and give rainbow blow-jobs, or I try to control them, and to spite me, they go give rainbow blowjobs."

None of this seemed possible in Alaska, not with these girls. All the girls she'd seen, especially Sam's twins, seemed of an entirely other world, another time, apart from any contemporary teenage nonsense, more likely to harness and ride a whale than want to be indoors with tiny boy-penises.

"They're how old?" Josie asked.

"Thirteen. I have a friend, an older woman, who offered to take them to live with her, in the woods. Like Sunny did with us, in a way."

Sam spotted someone across the bar and waved. "Old friend," she said by way of explanation. Soon he was walking over, and he was as advertised: old. Sixty. As he got closer, he seemed to be getting older. Sixty-five, seventy.

"*Old* friend," Josie said, and Sam took a second, as if deciding whether to pretend the comment was funny or pretend it was offensive. She chose to blink a few times.

Then he was upon them, and looked seventy-five. He was a sort of Alaskan Leonard Cohen, tall and handsome but with no fedora.

"Robert," he declared, and shook Josie's hand. His touch was both wrinkled and oily, like some dying fish. He looked between Sam and Josie a few times, nodding. "This is my lucky night!" he said loudly, his voice high and limp. Tom heard but did not smile. Josie felt she was in the middle of a slanted love square—love parallelogram?—but Robert was either oblivious or didn't consider Tom a worthy part of it.

Josie glanced back to the TV. Again the players seemed to be celebrating some minor achievement. It offended the eye at first, then Josie grew to understand it. That's what's missing in my life, she thought. The celebration of every single moment, like those fucking idiots on TV.

"Jager shots for the ladies," Robert said to Tom. Tom's wax face tightened, as if struggling with this, the fact that he had no choice but to serve. He had chosen a life where he had to serve any kind of human, had to hope for a good tip from a bad man.

Robert seemed surely a bad man. There was something

about him, everything about him, that was disagreeable, untrustworthy, lecherous and leering. His shirt was open to the crease where his sunken chest met his sudden belly.

"To sisters," he said, saying the word *sisters* in a strangely lewd way. Sam winked at Josie under his raised glass. She must have kept it plain with him, telling him they were simple sisters.

He ordered another round, but Josie hid her share of the second batch behind her elbow. He didn't see or care.

"Josie's up from Ohio," Sam said.

"Oh yeah?" he said, now taking this geographic information as license to scan Josie, neck to knees. Arriving back at her eyes, he let loose what he would surely consider the night's great bon mot. "I'd like to go down there sometime."

Sam didn't seem to catch his meaning.

"Okay," Josie said, trying to yawn. "Think I'll head home."

"Don't go," Robert said, trying to touch Josie's hand. Josie pulled it away so quickly she hit the man behind her.

"Sorry," she said to him.

"Don't be sorry," Robert said. "Just stay."

Sam wasn't following any of this. She was two margaritas and two shots in, was now holding Robert's hand, and seemed intent on making a night of this, of Alaskan Leonard Cohen. Tom was on the other side of the bar, looking up at the TV at what seemed an uncomfortable angle.

"C'mon," Sam said, "there's so many people here you could meet." Robert wanted a threesome, and Sam wanted to be alone with him. She scanned the bar for people she could pass Josie on to, and came up empty.

"I'll see you back at the house," Josie said.

Josie turned, not expecting Sam to allow her to leave. When she made it to the door, she turned to catch Robert plunging his seventy-year-old tongue down Sam's young throat.

In the sky there were low white clouds, and clouds of steamship grey, but there were visible stars, too, and a crisp white moon. Josie walked back up the hill, thinking of Sam's face, Leonard Cohen's face. She was sober, and she was furious, and she was thrilled to have escaped that bar, and so thankful to have been spared the sight of the inevitable dancing that Robert would want to do with Sam, the delicate swaying drunk old leches want to do in public, their gyrations, their gropings—they no longer cared about hiding any of it. Josie was intermittently confident she could get home without getting lost, and soon was reasonably sure she saw the church at the end of Sam's street, but then looked at her watch and saw it was only ten thirty. The kids would still be awake, and would think their mother was unwilling to give them any space, time alone with the twins.

Josie stood on the side of the road and thought some thoughts, including the certainty that despite her tidiness and Popeye boat and beautiful children Sam was a monster, an immoral animal, and that she was finished with her. And she also thought: This is me living my life. And she thought: Was Sam a Leonard Cohen fan? Was that the attraction? Josie decided they shouldn't have come to Homer.

Consistency. *I need to be consistent,* she thought. The sun was consistent, the moon. Life on Earth thrives because it can depend on the sun rising and setting, the tides coming in and out. Her kids needed only predictability. But so why had she brought them to Alaska, a new place every night? She must be consistent. Bedtimes must be the same. Her tone must be the same. Atticus! Atticus! She must be Atticus. It was simple to be the same. How simple! But what about *not* being simple? What about being interesting? Parents could not be interesting, could they? The best parents rise and fall like suns and moons. They circle with the predictability of planets. With great clarity Josie realized the undeniable truth: interesting people cannot bear children. The propagation of the species is up to the drones. Once you find you are different, that you have moods, that you have whims, that you get bored, that you want to see Antarctica, you should not have children. What happens to the children of interesting people? They are invariably bent. They are crushed. They have not had the predictable suns and so they are deprived, desperate and unsure—where will the sun be tomorrow? Fuck, she thought. Should I give these children away, to some dependable sun? They don't need me. They need good meals, and someone to bathe them dutifully, and to clean the house not because they should but because they want to. Not someone to keep them in this particle-board RV, carrying their dishes in the shower, their feces in a tank.

But wait, Josie thought. Maybe they could could live here. Maybe there was destiny and symmetry in her coming here to live near Sam, her fellow feral. But who could live here? It's beautiful now, yes, but the winters were surely a holy fucking horror. The clouds continued to move above her like troops in formation.

She would leave Homer tomorrow, she decided, but she didn't know where to go. This town, because it had people like Robert in it, was an unlivable place, no better than the town she'd left, and that town had been overtaken. What had happened in her little town? "I really have to get out," Deena said one day. "I can't hack this place anymore." She'd grown up there. Once it had been an actual place, a small-ish town with an actual cobblestone square where children rode their scooters and were chased by tiny lamentable dogs, perversions of selective breeding, off leash and barking. Now the place was crowded, there was no parking, women in ponytails drove at dangerous speeds on their way to yoga and pilates, tailgating other drivers, honking, cheating at four-way stop signs. It had become an unhappy place.

The crime of the ponytail ladies was that they were always in a hurry, in a hurry to exercise, in a hurry to pick up their children from capoeira, in a hurry to examine the scores from the school's Mandarin-immersion program, in a hurry to buy micro-greens at the new ivy-covered organic

grocery, one of a newly dominant national chain begun
by a libertarian megalomaniac, a store where the food had
been curated, in which the women in their ponytails rushed
quickly through, smiling viciously when their carts' paths
were momentarily waylaid. In its radical evolution toward
better food and health and education, the town had become
a miserable place, and the organic grocery was the unhappi-
est place in that miserable town. The checkout people were
not happy being there, and the people bagging groceries
were apoplectic. The butchers seemed content, the cheese
people seemed content, but everyone else was murderous.
The same terrible women (and men) who drove aggressively
to yoga now drove aggressively to the organic grocery store
and parked angrily—they stole the last parking spot from
some elderly citizens hoping to use the nearby pharmacy,
got out and rushed from their cars, half-livid, to buy havarti
and prosecco and veggie burgers. These people were now all
over Josie's small town, endangering her children with their
predatory driving and barely contained fury.

The town, green and hilly and with streams running
through it, though not far from an abandoned steelmill,
had been discovered by these hordes and their anger, and
all their new money and new anger had culminated in the
incident, the Bike Pump Maiming—only Josie called it this,
but still—in the middle of town. The incident involved a
man in a pickup truck and a man on a bicycle, and the result
had been a fight that left one man half-dead. But it had not
been the pickup man who had beaten the bicycle man, not at

this moment, in this town—no, this was the contemporary inversion, the version where the bike-riding man, wearing spandex and riding a five-thousand-dollar machine, triumphs over the kindly lawn-cutter in his rusted truck. The bicycle man had apparently taken umbrage at the pickup driver, who scraped out a living trimming grass and doing one-man landscaping gigs, who apparently had not given the bicyclist wide enough berth while passing. They were both on the road, traveling along the tiny pond that an environmental group had preserved for migrating ducks and stationary herons. So at the stop sign, the bicyclist pulled up, yelled his choice words, at which point the pickup driver stepped out and was promptly struck in the head with a bicycle pump. The driver went down and was struck again and again until the bicyclist, in his spandex and tiny special shoes, had fractured the lawn-cutter's skull and blood covered his face and spattered on the rhododendron that had recently been planted on the median by the Retired Gardeners' Club (RGC), which had supplanted the Association of Green Retirees. It was inside out, utterly backwards but perfectly emblematic of these new angry people rushing to and fro, always rushing to angrily go jogging, to angrily explain, to angrily expound, to explode when interrupted or slowed down, ready to be disappointed. These were the people! Josie made a mental note. The bicycle man, the maimer, would be in her *Disappointed* musical. Could there be some nod to *Mame*? Would that be too much?

Josie had known the man, the bicycle man. He'd been

a patient. When he'd first come in, a few years earlier, he'd had an agenda, saying, *Can we skip the cleaning? I know what I want.* He wanted to replace his six silver fillings with ceramics. The silver was near-black now and he'd married a young woman who found his mouth in need of improvement, so he scheduled two appointments on successive Friday afternoons, biked to the office in full florid regalia, clicking his way across the stone floor in his special orange shoes and spandex leggings, his racing shirt sweet with sweat. He was a diminutive and tightly wound man who checked his phone as his new ceramic fillings dried, who asked that the music in the office—it was *Oklahoma!* that day—be turned down a notch, thanks. He was an abomination and did no time in jail after the maiming. He was facing some civil charges but no one expected him to suffer much.

Josie had biked to work for a while, hoping her commute would be transformed in some way. For a week or so it was. But then it wasn't. She tried taking a bus, which left her half a mile away, and she had to walk along the highway like some quixotic hitchhiker. But no matter how she traveled she was still passing the same buildings, the same parking lots. How does anyone stand it? After her parents and their atomization, she had always identified with the stayers, the homesteaders. But she knew no one who stayed anywhere. Even in Panama, most of the locals she met would just as soon live somewhere else, and most of them asked her casually or directly about getting visas to come to the U.S. So who stayed? Were you crazy to stay anywhere? The stayers were either of the salt of the earth, the reason there are families and communities and continuity of culture and country, or they were plain idiots. We change! We change! And virtue is not only for the changeless. You can change your mind, or your setting, and still possess integrity. You can move away without becoming a quitter, a ghost.

That Ohio town, then, was in Josie's past. The past could be a delicious thing, to be done with something, with some place. To be finished and able to package it, beginning, middle, end, box it and shelve it. The town had once held hippies, Ohio hippies, all of whom seemed to Josie preternaturally grateful people, who were happy for the trees, happy for the rivers and the streams and birds, and the fact of their lives, and the existence of their weed and ready sex. They built their homes from mud and twigs, here and there a dome, here and there a hot tub. But now they were older, and were moving or dying, being replaced by these bicyclists, these fast-driving women in ponytails who desired everything, who so wanted the world that they would not accept limitations, interruptions, babies at restaurants or scooters on the sidewalks. Ohio, birthplace of most of the country's presidents, was now home to most of its assholes.

IF NOT YOU, THEN WHO? Another one of those signs. This one was hand-painted, stuck on the embankment. Was there danger of forest fires here, too? Josie could see Sam's house up ahead. It looked like a happy home, and her heart expanded as it grew closer. IF NOT YOU, THEN WHO? Josie smiled at the beautiful stupidity of the question. How about you *and* me? Me *and* you? Why the negativity? Why divide us? She was suddenly overcome by the cool wind, the granite sky, the fast-moving clouds, and she felt firmly placed in the world. Sam's world was solid, was new to her but was solid, deeply rooted, logical. Josie's children were inside that solid house, ecstatic with their cousins. They would stay a few days. She could park the Chateau on Sam's block. Her kids and Sam's would eat breakfast together. They could have many contented weeks, months. It was too soon to think of school here, but still. Sam could be her anchor. Tonight was a fluke, was just some thing. More important to remember was their long history together, their common narrative. How many young women are emancipated as they were? She was petty and crazed to give up so easily on Sam, wasn't she? She needed to attach herself to this world, this hardy and rational world Sam had created. She could and would. But what was that rushing sound, that unholy white light?

IX.

LEONARD COHEN WAS WATCHING her children. This
seemed to be what Sam was telling her, holding her hand
like she was dying. Evidently they were in a hospital.

"Is it cancer?" Josie asked.

"You were in a ditch," Sam said.

Now Josie remembered. She was run off the road by a
truck, and she skidded down the road embankment and
then . . . Then she didn't know what. Something else must
have happened. Her arm was wrapped in gauze and Sam was
saying that Robert was at home with the kids. With Josie's
children. Who was Robert? Then Leonard Cohen's face
appeared before her.

"They've been asleep for hours," Sam said. "It's four a.m.
They don't know you're here. You were asleep or passed out."

"Is Leonard Cohen molesting my children?" Josie asked,
and Sam assured her no, he wouldn't, he couldn't, that he
was a grandfather of six. Josie laughed. It hurt. Sam, who
was married, was dating a grandfather.

"Did I break anything?" Josie asked, thinking it must be her ribs. Breathing was painful.

"I don't think so," Sam said, and now it was obvious she was still drunk. While Josie was being struck by a delivery truck and sent into a ditch, Sam had been at the bar, getting plowed.

Josie looked at Sam's sweet face and wanted to punch it. Sam squeezed her arm, thinking they were having a moment. She hadn't said anything about sorry yet. In her life Josie had heard only one or two people apologize. Wasn't that something? Wouldn't that be significant to future anthropologists? This was a time in history when no one was sorry. Even Ana, whose nickname for a year was Sorry, was still never sorry. Sorry took too much courage, too much strength and faith and rightness to have a place in this cowardly century.

"Am I on any drugs?" Josie asked.

"I don't think so," Sam said.

Josie figured it out. She was next to that IF NOT YOU, THEN WHO? sign when the truck swerved too close. She'd turned too quickly, and had slammed her head into the corner of the sign. Thus the laceration on the side of her head.

"Can I leave?"

"I don't know. Let me ask."

Soon there was a doctor by Josie's side, a bald and bearded man with a worry-free face. He looked like everyone's ideal high-school counselor. He introduced himself, but

Josie couldn't decipher the name. Dr. Blahblah. She asked him to repeat it, and he did, and now there seemed to be a hocking sound in the middle. Dr. Blachblah?

He asked her how she felt.

She told him she felt wonderful.

He told her they'd checked her neuros, they were fine, no sign of concussion, no dilated pupils.

"Did your sister tell you about the stitches?"

"No." Josie looked at Sam, but Sam was looking out the window.

"Eight in your head. Over here," Dr. Blachblah said, and touched an area above her ear. Now Sam's eyes were back to Josie and were welling. "We were initially worried about a concussion," he said, "because the EMTs said you were singing when they found you."

Now Sam's face hardened, as if Josie had dropped from pitiful to something lesser, something untouchable. Singing in a ditch—that had been the turning point.

"I understand you're a dentist?" Dr. Blachblah asked. "I think your teeth are okay, but that's your field." He smiled, thinking he'd made a joke.

They got back to Sam's house at five a.m. Leonard Cohen was sitting up on the couch, asleep, like one of those statues they put on public benches to scare children. Hearing the front door close, Sam's grandfather–sex partner opened his eyes and looked around as if the world, and his limbs, had been replaced with new, unfamiliar versions during his slumber. When he got his bearings he stood up, a scarecrow given the gift of life, and kissed Sam on the cheek.

"They never woke up," he said, and then realized how morbid that sounded. "They're sleeping like angels," he said, making it worse.

Josie wanted to know only this: Are my kids dead or what?

She went upstairs to check on them and they were asleep, the four of them, in the twins' room. Her two were on a mattress set on the floor. They would sleep on cut glass if they could sleep next to those two young warrior-women.

Downstairs, in the bathroom mirror, Josie looked at her wound. They'd shaved a tasteful three-inch square from the side of her head. It almost looked intentional, like she'd gone to some 1980s throwback stylist and asked for something that told the world she couldn't be trusted near the office supplies and shouldn't ever have children.

She returned to the basement bed, and, prompted by the hospital, the rubber gloves, she had some unproductive thoughts, starting with Jeremy and Evelyn. Jeremy bleeding out on a dusty hillside. Evelyn's black tongue. No, she thought. Not that, not now. She could write a letter to Jeremy's parents. No. She'd already done that, and had gotten no answer. She thought of the many letters she'd written in the last year, none of them returned. Why wouldn't they answer her letters? An unanswered letter made the sender feel like a fool. Why send letters? Why feel like a fool? Why leave the house? Why pick up a pen? Am I rotting? Josie wondered. She smelled something sour, and realized it was her.

The pain woke her up. It was dawn and her brain was swollen. She was on the couch, and Sam was upstairs with Leonard Cohen, so Josie couldn't ask her for Advil and Sam hadn't thought to leave any out for her—though she'd assured Dr. Blachblah she had plenty at home.

Josie lay on the couch, watching the sky turn gunmetal blue then grey then white. Moving her head was impossible without inducing a hot blade of pain, slicing her head lengthwise, so she closed her eyes and planned exactly how she would leave Sam and Homer. Something had changed—was it being run off the road? Had that altered the chemistry of her visit?—and now a quick exit, while Sam was at work, held a certain appeal.

Josie tried to conjure the name of the day. Was it Friday? Wednesday? Was it? She could leave. Sam would be going to work soon and they could leave then. Josie could write a note, telling Sam they were heading north and would come back soon. Maybe they really would return. Josie went to the kitchen, and of course found a tidy pad of paper with a pen attached to it. She picked up the pen and began writing, and then, for the first time, Josie had the familiar sense that she was making a choice that was contrary to what would be best for the kids. Her children, she knew, would prefer to stay here, with Zoe and Becca, learn from them, worship their older twinly ways, and to use regular plumbing, to be for a time free of the unknown dangers of the Chateau. Josie's pen hovered over the pad, saying nothing.

Leonard Cohen came downstairs, looking somehow older now, his face not unlike the mummified banana in the fridge, and Josie hid in the pantry. He put on his shoes and exited quietly. Josie went back to the couch, suddenly unsure of her plan, and fell asleep.

Sam thumped loudly down the stairs at seven, making no attempt to be quiet. She made breakfast for all the kids, and Josie allowed herself to be served while still sitting on the couch. All the while, Sam said nothing about Josie having been in the hospital, near-dead, hours before. This seemed uniquely Alaskan, and Josie grudgingly admired it—being hit by trucks and found in ditches, it was a valid way to spend a weeknight, nothing to get too excited about.

"How do you feel?" Sam finally asked.

"Like a champ. I feel like a champ," Josie said.

"You want any of the Vicodin?"

Josie declined. "You keep it," she said, feeling stoic and superior. She wanted badly for Sam to keep the Vicodin, which would imply that Sam would use it sometime in the future, and when she did, Josie would archive some small and meaningless victory.

Now Sam sat down on the coffee table in front her.

"Listen, I forgot to tell you last night. They called Carl."

Josie stopped breathing. She held a finger up, and

sharpened her eyes, wordlessly telling Sam to shut the fuck up. She grabbed Sam's elbow and led her outside, to the back porch, and there, Sam explained that when Josie was unconscious, she'd told the nurses that she, Sam, had to get back to Paul and Ana, the patient's kids, and then the nurse asked about the father, and Sam had maybe fucked up—her words, *maybe fucked up*—a little bit by explaining some rough outline of the situation, that the father was back in Florida, and that the nurse very nicely suggested they could call the father, and maybe, Sam said, she got flustered, said No!, and the nurses got suspicious and then it turned into a real thing, with everyone, including Dr. Blachblah, insisting on calling Carl, and then it got a bit weird for about an hour.

"You couldn't just tell the nurses *you* had called Carl?"

"My job isn't to lie for you, Joze."

"You're right," Josie said, already knowing she and her children would be on the road within an hour of Sam leaving for work. "You're right. Thanks for all you've done."

Sam was taken aback, and grew gentle and idiotic. "Maybe this is good. Relieves the pressure." Again she put her hand on Josie's arm.

Having the father know not just that Josie had kidnapped the children, but exactly where she'd kidnapped them to, was not likely to relieve any pressure. "You're right again," Josie said, holding back a laugh. "You better get ready. Don't want you being late for work."

* * *

When Sam had gone to her boat and the twins to school, Josie packed her kids' things, choosing not to tell Paul and Ana they were leaving for good.

Josie found Sam's perfect reminder pad.

We're heading out, she wrote.

"What're you writing?" Paul asked.

"A note for Aunt Sam."

"What's it say?"

Ana came to look.

"That's a short note," she said.

X.

THE SHAVED SQUARE ON THE side of Josie's head was
fascinating to Paul. This is why he wanted to sit in the passenger seat. They'd left Homer and were approaching the
confluence of many highways, going east and west and north.

"Does it hurt?" he asked.

"No," she said. "Does it look good?"

Paul shook his head slowly. His eyes conveyed how scared
he was by this square cut into his mother's scalp. It was not
motherly. It would shake him, just as Josie had been shaken
by seeing her own mother return from the hospital with
her head wrapped in gauze. She'd fallen on the back deck,
clumsy on mixed meds. This was when she started taking
the drugs they were giving the soldiers, before the scandal,
before Sunny. Josie turned her head to look at the shaved
square, the lines so clean. She did not want to scar her son
this way, with the knowledge of her frailty, her aptitude to
be abandoned by her pseudo-sister and to get hit by Homeric
delivery trucks, sent into a ditch. But the introduction of

frailty in a parent—is this so terrible? It should, perhaps, be introduced right away, so the shock is not so great later. We are better when we expect tragedy, calamity, chaos.

"Budget!" Raj had said to her in one of his wild revelatory rants. "You just need to budget!" he said, or exclaimed. He was the only human she'd ever known who actually spoke in a way that could warrant that verb, *to exclaim*. The word was a strange one, so common in the picture books she read to her children. There, in the fifties and sixties, everyone was exclaiming, but in real life she'd never known the verb to be true. But then there was Raj, with his wide eyes and loud voice, exclaiming all the time. "You need to make a life budget!" he exclaimed. "You ever make a household budget?"

Josie said she had not. Not really, no. She had chosen instead to guess her savings, more or less know her checking balance, to over-report her earnings and underestimate her expenses.

"Never?" Raj exclaimed. "Well, it can give you great peace when things are tight, or when things feel chaotic. A dozen bills can feel like an assault, but within the framework of a budget, of expectations, they're reasonable, powerless even. You expect them, and have means to dispose of them."

Josie had looked around, hoping for escape.

"So think about it the same way with your life, with the country or world. Any given year you should expect certain things. You can expect to see some horrifying act of terror, for example. A new beheading of a man in orange is a shock and will make you want to never leave the house, but not if you have budgeted for it. A new mass shooting in a mall or school can cripple you for a day but not if you've budgeted for it. That's this month's shooting, you can say. And if there isn't a shooting that month, all the better. You've come out ahead on the ledger. You have a surplus. A refund."

Raj was one of the reasons she thought all her colleagues in the medical or semi-medical world were one synapse away from real madness. "Budget for your children incurring some injury before they're ten," he continued. "Half of your friends will get divorced. One of your parents will die younger than they should. Two of your straight friends are actually gay. And at some point someone, some stranger, some patient, will wake up one day and decide to try to destroy you and take your business!" he said. He exclaimed.

Josie had dismissed this conversation and Raj's theory until every aspect of it came to pass—the beheadings, the shootings and then Evelyn—all within weeks. The man was a prophet.

"Where are we going?" Paul asked.

"I'm thinking north," Josie said. She harbored the hope that she could make her children think that this was the plan all along, that they had planned to stay at Sam's for only two nights, and then leave, without saying goodbye and with no destination in mind. She made a mental note to buy a hat.

"We'll come back," she said.

Now Ana became aware that something was happening. "Where we going?" she asked.

"We left Aunt Sam's house and we're not coming back," Paul told her, and Ana began to cry.

"I think we should go back," Paul said. He meant it as a threat. He'd demonstrated his power to make Ana weep, and seemed to imply he could and would do it again.

"There's no point," Josie said. "Sam's working and the kids are in school. And after school, the girls play lacrosse. We'd just be sitting around all day."

A long silence gave Josie the mistaken impression she'd scored a knockout blow. Why indeed stay at someone's house when they were gone all day and tired at night? She'd just convinced herself that it made no sense. The trip to Homer, which she'd left open-ended, was more rightfully brief. Josie looked in the rearview mirror and caught Paul squinting.

"Why aren't *we* in school?" he asked.

Josie looked at the road.

Ana stopped crying. "Is it time for school?" she asked the two of them.

"No, sweetie," Josie said.

"Yes it is," Paul said to her, but loudly, legally, announcing it to the Chateau's speeding hall of justice. "It's September. We should have started school Monday. Everyone's in school without us."

Now Ana was crying again, though she had no idea why. She didn't care at all about school, but Paul was creating the impression that all order had fallen away, that there was no past, no future.

"Why'd we come here right when school started?" Paul asked.

"I want to be in school!" Ana wailed.

Josie wanted to explain it all to them. She yearned to. At least to Paul. He'd actually understand her point of view; he harbored no great loyalty to Carl. Not since Carl had signed up to lead his adventurer's club. He and Paul had conceived it together, but then he'd simply not done it. Paul had gotten four other boys to sign up to hike into the woods every Saturday evening, Carl at the lead, but when it came time to do it, Carl had not shown up, had pretended that no such plans had been made, and if they had been made, they weren't firm, c'mon. The four boys stayed all night at Josie's house, indoors, reading inappropriate comics.

But Paul was too young to hear all this.

"No more discussion. Five minutes of quiet," Josie said, and then thought of a nice coda. "And this trip is educational. I checked it all out with your school. This is independent study."

"That's not true," Paul said.

"Get in back," Josie hissed. She'd had enough insolence. He was eight. "And it *is* true." It was true. She'd actually told the assistant principal, a mischievous older woman who dressed like a sexy mortician, all about Carl, and the assistant principal had given Josie permission to enter the school year sometime later in the fall. "No one should have to put up with that," she'd said, and every time doubt crept into her, Josie thought of Ms. Gonzalez and the delicious way she rolled her eyes at every one of Carl's misdeeds.

The misdeeds were many, and he was known by all who knew him to be a ridiculous man, but this new plan was too much, was Caligulian, Roveian, and she had no obligation to cooperate. Like so much about Carl, his request—his near-demand—defied all propriety, was so unprecedented in its depravity that it took one's breath away. How to explain it? He was getting married, to someone else, to a woman named Teresa, of course it was Teresa, she had no choice but to be named Teresa. She was from some kind of established family, and there were those in the family who had their doubts about Carl. Doubts about Carl! When Josie had heard this, through an intermediary, she cackled, loving those words. Doubts about Carl. Doubts about Carl. His name could not be uttered without doubts. His name necessitated punctuation: Carl? It wasn't right without the question mark.

"Mama?" Ana called from behind her. "Been five minutes."

Josie looked in the rearview mirror, saw Ana, then looked in the side-view, seven or eight cars backed up behind them. She pulled over to let them pass, cursing the devil Stan. After the caravan moved on, glaring at Josie, she pulled back onto the road.

"Five minutes more," Josie said.

Carl had called one day, had explained it in his way. "I'd love to have the kids out here for a week or so," he'd said, as if they did this regularly, split time like this, as if every month they catapulted the kids across the country for visits with their wonderful quick-shitting father. "Teresa's family wants to spend time with 'em," he'd said, adopting some kind of folksy Floridian diphthong he'd invented completely (he was from Ohio), "and a'course I'd like to show 'em off."

Speechless. She was often speechless. How could a few sentences contain so many crimes of language and ethics? But since their cleaving, any time she interacted with him, she was agog, stunned, breathless, aghast. It was worth answering the phone when Carl called because always there was something so toweringly craven, so doubtless important to anthropologists and students of deviant psychiatry. There was the time he'd watched some news segment about soy and called at ten thirty at night to talk about it. "I hope you're monitoring the soy intake with the kids. Especially Ana. They say it accelerates a girl's entry into puberty." He really said this. He really said and did so many things, so precious few of them within the boundaries of predictable human behavior. Now this visit to Punta del Rey. "They'll love it," he'd said. "They can swim, get to know their new grandparents. Play golf. Maybe Jarts." Jarts, he said. Jarts, which had been banned in the eighties. It was wonderful, it was perverse, it was Carl. Carl?

Finally, through some intermediaries—well, the same intermediary, Carl's mom, who liked Josie more than Carl—finally Josie got the full picture: The wedding was in the fall, but there were those among Teresa's family opposed to the union, thinking or knowing Carl for what he was—a deadbeat father, an abdicator, a man born without a spine—so Carl (and Teresa? It was unclear how much she knew) had concocted this plan to show them he was close to his progeny, that he was part of their lives. And Josie thought, you know what, goddamn you to hell. You're in Florida? I'll be in Alaska.

But she did not tell him this.

"Are we going back to the red house?" Ana asked from the depths of the Chateau. She'd unbuckled her seatbelt and was standing near the bathroom.

"Sit down and put your seatbelt on," Josie said.

"Paulie said I didn't have to," Ana said.

"Paul, you're on probation," Josie said.

"Thank you," he said.

What the hell was happening? Paul now knew sarcasm. Ana sat down again and buckled herself in.

"Of course we are," she said, answering Ana's question. Their house was not red, it was grey, but the trim was maroon, so Ana had taken to calling it the red house, and Paul and Josie had never corrected her.

Had she told Ana that they wouldn't be going back? Or if they did go back, it would only be to move out? Josie's feelings about the house were a barbed, snarling thing. She and Carl had thought buying a house a sensible thing, an objective not often debated in the civilized world. They had seen houses, and debated their merits, and finally bought one, a home needing work. Carl said he would do the work, would at least oversee the work, and do some of it himself (he had no idea how to do any such work) and she thought it would keep him busy and focused, even if he were just watching others labor. So they got themselves a loan, and bought the house at its asking price, and it was all very simple, and while they remained in their rental, Carl undertook (oversaw) (occasionally dropped in on) the first basic renovations, three months' worth, until they could move in. Which they did, they moved in, the kids gleeful, really, they couldn't get enough of the new bedroom they'd share, their unusually big closet, a strangely small and terrifying basement, and then, after a week of sleeping in this house, which was a fine solid house priced at the average price for the homes in their town, Carl began to lose his mind.

"This is wrong," he said. "This is decadent." He was standing in their bedroom, looking around like they'd entered the Vanderbilts' Newport spread. "Look at this!"

Josie looked around the room, and saw only a mattress, an unassembled bed and a small window with a view of a lopsided apple tree. Josie was stunned, but not quite as stunned as she would have been had Carl been someone sane or stable. "What? Why? We just moved in."

It turned out Carl was conflicted, torn, shredded, by the juxtaposition—was it a paradox? What was it? he wondered, What is it? he wailed aloud—of having just bought a house, and being in the middle of renovations. He said the word *renovations* like it was some filthy thing, as if they'd been burning money at the feet of orphans—all while the Occupy movement was trying valiantly to alter the foundations of our financial system. How could they, Carl and Josie, be debating what kind of wood floors to use? History was being made elsewhere, everywhere, and they were choosing paint colors and whether their lamps should have nickel or copper finishes. At the hardware store one day, when they were supposed to choose a cabinet for under their bathroom sink, he couldn't get out of the car.

"I can't do this," he said.

"The door handle is just there, below the window. Pull on it," Josie said. She already knew his state of mind. Carl was mercurial and surprising but he never surprised in his shape-shifting. He was inconsistent in all things but his cowardice. His unreliability could be counted on. Should she point out his impossible hypocrisy? The fact that he was the son of a cattle rancher who'd decimated some untold miles of Central America to feed cows that would feed Americans and Japanese? And that he'd never had a job? And that to have him judge her, their life, the life she paid for—

It was impossible. There was nowhere to start, nothing to say.

"No! No. You go," he said. "I'll stay here."

Were they really about to spend six hundred dollars on a cabinet? he wanted to know. Did they really spend five hundred and fifty dollars on beds for the kids?

"Otherwise the kids sleep on what?" she asked. She thought he might really have an alternative.

"I don't know," he said. "But I think we need to start asking these questions."

She laughed out loud. It was not planned.

He couldn't participate in the spending of money like this, he said. Money he had no hand in making anyway. When they'd met, Carl had been fired from a vague position at an ad agency; he'd never held a job more than a year. Had she really allowed him to drift? Was it her fault? Had she actually told him to—had she said the words *pursue your passion*? Lord. Carl had no conception of how to earn money for his children or himself, had no sense of the steps involved between waking up one day and sometime later being paid for work done. He knew how to wake up, and knew how to cash a check, but everything in between was a muddle. All his bosses had been ogres and psychopaths—chiefly, it seemed, because they'd tried to tell him what to do. That itself was some high crime.

All those months of Occupy were disastrous. He was paralyzed. She found him in bed, lying on his back, on their capitalist mattress, a towel on his face. She found him on the floor of the children's room, splayed like he'd fallen in a ditch. He said he had migraines. He said he couldn't go through with it. He called off the renovations, sent the workers away, leaving the house full of plastic sheeting, billowing loudly from the open windows.

"Now these guys don't get paid," Josie said. "Don't *they* need work, too?"

"That's not the point," he said, but his eyes showed some recognition that it might be part of the point. Carl had never been one to see the connection between any of his own actions and the running of the finances of their household or town or world.

All he really wanted was to be in Zuccotti Park, not in Ohio. That was the point. The average age of the Occupy campers was about twenty-four, Josie said. There are no parents of small children there. There are no children there. And if there are children, they're living in squalor. He agreed, but he was catatonic. He couldn't live day to day. He went on fifteen-mile runs, then got drunk. He slept half the day then looked at graduate school applications. He searched for places to live in Bali. Looked up international schools for the kids in Brazil. Then he went on a twenty-mile run and got drunker.

"Why are we here?" he asked.

"On Earth?" Josie asked. She was joking but he was not.

"How did we get so far away from everything?" he asked, and Josie realized he really meant this. He had somehow come to confuse himself with some Weather Underground revolutionary who had lately gone soft. Josie couldn't conjure anything vaguely revolutionary that Carl had ever done. She knew he'd once voted for the Green Party. Maybe that was it. Now he pined for his Occupy brethren as if Josie had personally come to steal him from his place at the barricades. But aha, the day the protesters left Zuccotti Park, Carl's mood brightened. The activists went back to their homes, and Carl, it seemed, was ready to live in a house himself.

Then the triathlons began. Carl joined—he paid to be part of, spent Josie's money to be part of—a group of men and women coached by a former marine. They ran, biked, climbed on fake walls indoors. Josie came to know all their names: Tim, Lindsay, Mercury, Warren, Jennifer. Wonderful to know so much about them. This training took him all over Ohio, and away most of every Saturday and most Sundays. Josie had arranged for the care of the kids during the workdays, but thought it helpful to have their father around on the weekends.

"I feel so good about this," Carl said.

About the triathlons, not his children. Carl never ran in one. But he was gone every weekend, and Josie found herself shattered by the sameness. Alone with Ana and Paul, after breakfast she was determined to get the morning's errands done by eleven. At eleven, the errands done, she would fight off the desire to nap. Paul went next door, to unhappily play with the hyperverbal only child who said cruel things to him. So it was Josie and Ana, and Ana didn't really care what they did. Maybe they could watch a video on her phone. Then yes, a nap for twenty minutes, next to Ana—an attempt, anyway, for during those twenty minutes Josie would think of the sixty or seventy worst things she'd ever done, the stupidest things she'd ever said. She would open her eyes, scalded. She would put on her running shoes, then take them off. She would consider pouring herself a drink. Who would know? She'd pour a drink and immediately pour it back into its bottle. How would the hours pass?

Carl would come home in the afternoon, and after any workout or pretend-workout, he would be randy, and he would be unfussy about how the spilling of his seed happened—he was just as happy using his hand or hers, but somehow the manual labor always took longer and was twice as boring. Afterward, lying on their backs, the ceiling so white, they would share a moment, having accomplished something, but then again nothing. Then he'd click his tongue and get up. "Gotta go to the can," he'd say.

Her memories of Carl involved either him shitting or lying, paralyzed by the heroes of Zuccotti. Oh wait. That was better than *Disappointed: The Musical.* Think of it: *The Hero of Zuccotti.* This would be about Carl, a man in Ohio, the son of a land baron who raped a thousand miles of Costa Rican forest to feed his cows. Now Carl was the Hero of Zuccotti. A child of wealth, dedicated to the cause of the poor, even though he did not technically ever go to Zuccotti, or do anything overtly to support the Occupiers. Maybe he was part of the 99% because technically he had no income? Was that the connection? The show would center around him running—running at night with a headlamp! On a treadmill. Just running. His thoughts, his dreams, represented by video of various protests and marches, projected behind him as he ran, as he stretched out after running, as he rubbed his legs with Ben Gay after running, as he drank a cold beer after running, as he watched some women's soccer on his phone after running, jerked off in the downstairs bathroom after running—here we could show Josie, upstairs and alone in bed—all the while, the rest of the world was happening on-screen behind him, the tents and placards and marches and altercations with cops, and every so often he would look up and nod meaningfully, as if one with the protesters, even while he was alone, his dick in his hand.

A few months after their split he'd gotten a job in Florida and was gone. His employment out of state, it seemed, gave him license to become a ghost. He found this logic unimpeachable. I can't be in two places at once, he said. A college friend had given him a sales job, commission only, in a start-up. Could you call it a start-up if they sold roof racks for compact cars? Child support was never discussed or contemplated. For six months he wasn't seen at all. But when he reappeared, he acted like he'd been there all the while. "Are you sure about this school they're in?" he'd asked last fall, the last time he'd visited. "Are they being fully challenged?" When he said this, he was wearing shorts and sandals and a visor. These were beach clothes, Florida clothes, but he was in Ohio. He'd flown in for the weekend, rented a car, shown up at their house. Who was this man? Where had he found this visor? Josie actually asked him, she had to know.

"Where'd you get the visor?"

He told her that he'd bought it online. And thus! And thus in this world existed a man who ordered visors online and said things like *Are they being fully challenged?*

Josie had since met others in her position, single parents who had these ghost-appendage partners, people like Carl who did nothing, who were simply not there, not in any way part of their children's lives—but who walked around perfectly confident that they were pulling their weight. Josie was sailing the ship of her children's lives, hoisting the sails, turning the winches and bailing water, and Carl was not on that ship, Carl was sunning himself on some faraway unnamed island—wearing his visor!—but he believed he was on the ship. He believed he was on the ship! How can someone be on the ship when they are not in fact on the ship? When they are in fact on some faraway island? Carl had seen his children once in the last fourteen months, but in his mind he was tucking them into bed every night. What evolutionary mutation permitted this kind of self-deception?

All this could figure into the musical. All throughout, as Carl jogged, and stretched out, and jerked off, his family and Occupy would be going on around him, projected on the screen behind him, though he would confuse this with actually being there. And at the end of the show, during which the actor playing Carl had done nothing at all for anyone, he would arrive on stage and bow, and take curtain calls, and say *Thank you, thank you, I thank you so very much.*

Now all Josie wanted was to be left alone. She wanted to say to him: Do not reappear. Do not offer advice. Do not enter my home and comment on my housekeeping. Do not comment on the role of soy in my daughter's entry into puberty. No, she would not send her children to Punta del Rey. She would not be party to his ploy. Was this small of her? Embittered? Ungenerous? Ridiculous to flee her home for Alaska, where she and her children could not be found for his photo-op? Yes, he, and Teresa, and her parents, and whoever the fuck else, wanted photos of him with his children—to show he was a real father. Look at him frolicking with his daughter and son! They wanted to frame this photo, these photos, and have them there on the bridal table, central to whatever display they would assemble for their godforsaken guests. Some descendant of Goebbels was now a wedding planner and had been hired by these jackals to produce this fiction.

"Mom, there's a smell."

It was Paul.

"What's that? Did we have five minutes of quiet?"

Josie had lost track.

"It's a really bad smell," he said.

Josie inhaled deeply. It was both familiar and foreign—pungent, a mixture of organic and chemical.

"Spray some of that sunblock," she said and Paul did, and the Chateau took on a creamy pineapple air. It didn't last long. The previous smell was too strong. Josie opened her windows and looked around for fires, or firefighters, but saw nothing. Finally, up ahead she saw a stream of smoke leaving the chimney of an industrial building. "It's probably that," she said, pointing to it. She closed her window. They drove in silence for ten minutes, until they were far out of range of the building and its chimney.

The only legitimate man in her life since Carl, besides the man who wanted to smell his shit-covered finger, was Elias. She'd read about him in the local paper. He was a lawyer, and was assembling a class of plaintiffs to sue a nearby coal-burning plant over various environmental violations. The story made him out to be an everyday attorney who decided, on his own accord, to take on a billion-dollar company. There were thousands of homes within range of the plant, all subject to unknown dangers of particulates in the air, fly ash and unburned coal combustion byproducts settling onto lawns and roofs. He was asking anyone within a three-mile radius to come forward and hold GenPower accountable.

Josie was surprised to find she was within range of the plant—it was only two miles away—so she sent him a letter, and he called her, and she found herself driving into the city to see him. She expected him to work in some warren of legal offices, papers stacked neatly on the floors, boxes of documents being carried by aides. But he worked alone, and his office was tidy, spare, no papers anywhere.

There was relief in this. Since she'd written to him she'd felt strange, watched, treasonous. If Elias had operated out of some shadowy basement office, Josie would have ascended from worried to paranoid. But he was young and open-faced and smiled easily as he shook her hand. He had great teeth.

They walked to a café nearby and he asked if she would join the class action. In an irrational burst driven by his unblemished skin and bright eyes, she said yes. She asked about the possibility that his lawsuit might provoke retribution from the company, that they might countersue or do something less legal and more nefarious. She'd read about these things. "Could be," he said, but didn't seem the least bit concerned. He filed the lawsuit, now with her name among the lead plaintiffs. She took pride in this—her standing in the community, he said, made her a prize.

A few weeks later Elias came over to update Josie on the case, and she showed him the white van that had been parked on her block for a month, and they walked around the van together, laughing at themselves, but still wondering why a nondescript van like that would be parked in front of her house, exactly the same spot each time, never down the street—never even across the street—and with the back window covered.

"I dare you to knock on the side," she said. She was fourteen again, her heart leaping, bursting. "See if anyone's in there with headphones." Elias did knock. She gasped.

"You're the one who lives here," he said, and they laughed as they rushed from the van and back inside her house.

Josie had fallen a little bit in love with Elias, though his eyes told her he felt he was too young (or more meaningfully, she was too old). He was no more than thirty, and looked younger. When they rushed inside, and closed the door, gasping and laughing, she thought it at least possible that they would fall into each other, kissing and groping. But he said he had to use the bathroom. All the men in her life preferred to be alone in the bathroom rather than be alone with her.

After the bathroom, Elias brought out from his bag the actual lawsuit, the two hundred pages of it, with its standard and utilitarian but strangely beautiful cover page. She thrilled at seeing her name on it. What did it mean? Having her name above theirs, GenPower, as if her place above them codified her moral superiority. Then the word versus, a display of defiance and aggression. I sue you. I am versus you. I challenge you. I hold you accountable. I name you, I name me.

As she and Elias were looking at the lawsuit, and their shoulders were touching, innocent but not entirely innocent—Josie could feel the heat of him through his bright white shirt and she felt her own high heat as a result—there was a knock on the door and then Carl's face re-entered her life.

Josie could not prove that this was when Carl decided to marry his then-girlfriend Teresa with an alacrity new to him, but it would not be improbable. He entered before she invited him, and then he registered the two of them, Josie next to this handsome lawyer with his clean white shirt. Josie and Elias were bent over the papers, and Elias's full size and height was obscured, and so Carl rushed forward, thinking he would confront, in his way, in some way, this new man standing in the house he used to own—or at least lived in—but as he got closer, Elias straightened himself and revealed his full size, six two or so, and Josie's heart almost burst. She loved to remember it now, watching Carl take in tall and handsome Elias. She recalled watching Carl as he slowed, reassessed, and as he stretched out his hand to shake Elias's, no longer confrontational, now deferent, feigning friendliness—it was delicious.

"Sorry to interrupt," Carl said.

"I should go," Elias said.

"No, don't," Josie said. But soon Elias was gone and Carl was in a state of ecstatic agony and confusion and rage suppressed. Who was this other man, this tall man in his clean shirt, his shiny shoes? In the same kitchen, a moment of intellectual intimacy she'd shared with Elias devolved into an idiotic spat with an idiot.

"What are you looking for?" Josie asked.

Carl was pacing around the kitchen, looking on every surface, opening drawers like a monkey new to the complex interior of a human home. He was wearing a hoodie and huge colorful sneakers, which in contrast to the younger Elias in his minimal palette made Carl look even more childish and lost.

"A key to the storage unit," Carl said, lying.

"You took it with you. I know you did," Josie said, though she had no idea what the key looked like or if he'd taken it.

"Dishes stacked in the sink . . ." Carl now said—he

seemed to have given up the pretense of the key—and he made a tsk sound, like some grandmother from the fifties. And why are the dishes in the sink the universal emblem of domestic squalor and parental failure? Is it the stacking? Dishes shouldn't be stacked—was that the conclusion? Or is it that they're in the sink? It's okay that they're stacked, but not in the sink? Should they be stacked elsewhere? In a closet, on the bed?

"Your key isn't here. You should leave," Josie told him.

"The kids are home from school soon," Carl said, looking at his watch, seeing it was only one o'clock, when he knew (or did he? He didn't know! He didn't know!) that they didn't finish until two. "I was hoping to see them."

"You can't wait for an hour," Josie said. "Not here."

"Wait. Ana's in preschool till two? That's a long day."

Josie saw a knife on the counter, and thought how easily she could end all this. Now he was looking at the window over the sink, from an angle, examining it for cleanliness. It was not clean. Was he taking mental notes for some later lawsuit? He was.

"Did I interrupt some tryst you were about to have?" he asked, bringing his tiny green eyes to her. Who is this man? Josie thought. Was he always this ludicrous? And afterward came—it had come so many times after their split—the crashing realization that she had been with this ferret-man for eight years, that she had two children by this low scavenging mammal, that she would never escape him. After he left—he did leave, and perhaps had saved his life, the knife

in her hand felt so right—she had to go for a brisk walk
to try to clear her mind of the cycle of self-recrimination.
She would not say the words, or think the words, *I wasted
my youth on,* but of course she had. Or not her youth—she'd
wasted her middle thirties, a time of blooming for her,
when she had grown professionally comfortable, had taken
full control of her body, had brought Paul and Ana into the
world and was ready to look out and build. She'd wasted so
much time with Carl. Eight years. Eight years with invertebrate Carl, jobless Carl, confused Carl, and now she was forty,
and she was too late for Elias, anyone like Elias. Anyone with
courage. Now she was in a state surrounded by firefighters.
Would that yield options?

"The smell's worse now," Paul said, and Josie knew this was
true. It was an acrid smell, something like the burning of
garbage.

This time, before Josie knew that he'd unbuckled himself, Paul had gotten up to check the stove and reported that
all the knobs were as they should be.

"Open the windows," Josie said, and she reached over to
roll down the passenger side. The smell dissipated but not
by much.

They drove on, and though there was no evidence to
believe it, Josie continued to believe that the smell—it had
earthy tones with a certain toxic topspin—was coming from
outside. She was happy, though, that Paul was in a spirit of

cooperation—or at least had abandoned his posture of open hostility. The smell had united them.

They drove that way five miles, maybe ten. Looking back on it later, Josie could admit that she drove much farther than a more responsible person would.

Finally Paul said he felt sick, felt he might throw up, so Josie pulled over, this time without an adequate shoulder, such that when they stopped, the Chateau was at an angle so oblique that a strong wind would have tipped it over like some buckshot elephant.

The kids got out and Josie directed them to run down the embankment until they were standing next to a lone spruce tree, squat and bent heavily by some past storm. Josie hustled into the living area, and though she knew Paul incapable of error, she checked the stove, and confirmed it was not turned on, but the smell closer to the stove was far stronger than it had been in the front seat. She opened cabinets, thinking she might find rotting fruit or a dead animal. She found neither, but was sure, then, that dead animal was the answer to the question of this smell. She opened every drawer, looked under the cushions. She looked in the bathroom, finally, expecting the answer to be there, but though she found only the pile of dishes and towels in the shower, she discovered the smell stronger. She lifted the toilet seat, thinking that one of the kids had dropped a secret there, and found the toilet empty but the smell emerging with great assertiveness.

She left the Chateau to gag, and joined her children

on the side of the road for a few moments, taking in the trash-laden highway. Someone had thrown a tampon out a car window, and in seconds, given its proximity to Ana and the way she was eyeing it, Josie knew that while she was in the Chateau, Ana had picked it up and been told, by Paul, to drop it. Ana was eyeing Josie warily, wondering if she was about to see her mother vomit for the first time, but she was also keeping the tampon in her peripheral vision—waiting for the opportunity to examine it more closely, or possibly put her mouth on it in some way.

"I found the smell," Josie said.

But she had not quite found the smell.

She went back into the Chateau, wondering about a way to tape the bathroom shut, or wrap the toilet in plastic or some material impenetrable to fecal smells. And while making her way back to the bathroom, she saw something she had not seen before. On the wall just next to the stove was a switch, which Stan had not told her about, because Stan was a motherfucker. This switch looked like the kind of small metal switch in abundance in old airplanes, the kind of switch that provides a satisfying click to the user. Above the switch were the words Tank Heater.

Josie noted that the switch was turned on, meaning that some tank was being heated. She thought first of the gas tank, but knew better than to guess that there was a switch, between the kitchen and bathroom, that heated a tank full of highly flammable gasoline. The only tank, then, she could guess at was the tank of feces and urine that was below the toilet.

A gasp escaped from her mouth. It began to come together. The Chateau featured a tank-heating mechanism. Why? Josie deduced that in the winter owners would not want their feces being frozen, because frozen, the feces could not be drained through the sky-blue ribbed tube, and so there would be no room for new feces. The feces had to be kept warm and in liquid form, so it could be drained, and new feces could be put in the tank.

Ana had turned on the feces-heating mechanism. She had done this in August, when the feces didn't need to be heated. So Josie and her family were driving through lower-central Alaska while not only carrying their feces but heating them. Cooking them. What would that be? Josie searched for the verb. Broiling? When the heat is coming from the interior surfaces of the oven, as opposed to gas or flame? She was sure the word was broiling.

She turned the switch off, returned to Paul and Ana by the lone spruce, and told them they should not turn any switches on, anywhere in the Chateau. She told them what had happened, about the feces and the broiling of it, and they nodded, very serious now. They believed this story without hesitation, and she marveled at this pure stage of life, when a child is first told about such things, about how to broil feces, why they shouldn't do so in the summer.

They got in the Chateau and drove on. It was a great day to be alive.

XI.

"'I AM TRYING TO CONTACT Mr. and Mrs. Wright. I have lost their first names,'" Paul read aloud. "'There were three boys, L.J., George, and Bud Wright. There were two girls that I knew of, Anna and another whose name I have forgotten. My brother Wheeler and I worked for them in 1928 or 1929 in the wheat harvest. We also threshed some flax, the first and only flax we ever worked in or had ever seen. The Wrights lived in a sod shanty at Chaseley, North Dakota near Bowdon, North Dakota. The last I ever heard of them, George was married and lived near Scottsbluff, Nebraska. We loved those dear ones. Would like to hear from anyone who can give me any information as to their whereabouts.'"

The idea to have Paul read "Trails Grown Dim" to her as they drove was a brilliant one, Josie thought. They had gone about a hundred miles north of the scene of the feces-heating, with the windows open, and the air in the Chateau was reasonably better now, though they wouldn't be the best judges—they'd been breathing human-waste fumes for so long they wouldn't know the difference.

They passed a large parking lot, attached to an abandoned shopping center, where a firefighters' staging ground had been set up. FUEL TRANSPORT said one sign. FIRE SHIRTS SOLD HERE said another. A half-dozen red and yellow and white fire trucks of various sizes waited for orders.

"Do another," she said.

"Okay," Paul said, a serious but delighted look on his face. He was sitting up front with her, and Josie was reasonably sure this was against the law, even in this renegade state, having an eight-year-old in the front seat, sitting on a stack of towels. But Josie was enjoying his company too much to let him disappear into the back.

"Here's the last one on the page," he said. " 'I am interested in finding the whereabouts of my great-uncle, Melvin H. Lahar (pronounced Liar). He was born in Washington State between 1889 and 1893, son of Charles A. Lahar and Ida Mae Gleason Sharp. He had one full sister, Nancy L. (nicknames Emma and Dottie) Lahar Farris. He was last seen in Washington just prior to World War I. No one in the family has seen or heard of him since. He was raised in Colfax, Washington in the household of his aunt, Mrs. Minnie Longstreet. There is some talk, too, about him having been a bank robber, involved in a shootout in Bend, Oregon. Any clarity or information would be appreciated.' "

"That's a good one to end on," Josie said, hoping Ana hadn't heard the word "robber." It would provoke a string of questions, if not keep her up all night. "Is she asleep?" she asked Paul.

He didn't have to turn around. "No. She's just looking out the window." He nodded toward the ATVs. This was a new phenomenon. The main roads were paralleled by narrow dirt paths where men and women and families traveled to and from town, with groceries or anything else, on four-wheeled ATVs. These alternate paths were everywhere now, in this part of Alaska, wherever they were.

"Why can't we go like that?" Ana asked from the back. Josie turned to find Ana's face was pressed against the glass.

They watched mothers with small children sitting in front of their ATVs, helping steer, as they went up and down the gentle hills of their dirt roads, and Josie, too, thought it seemed a logical way to travel. Finally they caught an eight-year-old piloting his own vehicle, a scale-model ATV, and Josie knew Ana's imagination would ignite. She mouthed the words just before Ana said them: "I want one."

"You can't have one," Paul said. "You're five." Now he turned to Josie. "Okay, you want me to go through my school day?" He said this as if she'd been bothering him about this for weeks and he'd finally relented in telling her. This was a new Paul: able to dismiss Ana quickly, feeling worthy of dominating the conversation. Had sitting in the front seat emboldened him that much? Josie told him she'd be delighted to hear about his school day.

Recounting it all took him fully thirty-five minutes. There was a good deal of explanation of the rows. There were four rows in his classroom, he explained, and one of them, the blues, was stacked with the rambunctious kids, and Paul.

"Were you put in the blue row as a balance against the bad kids?" she asked.

"I guess so," he said.

He told her about the time when a police officer came to class to talk to the kids about crosswalk safety and stranger danger, and almost immediately four different kids volunteered the information that their fathers were in jail. The officer didn't know how to handle this, and had to tell the kids to stop raising their hands.

The Ohio town where they'd lived—it was exhilarating to think of it in the past tense—had a private school, too, where the other half of the children went, and hearing Paul tell this story, thinking it interesting, Josie had the thought that for the parents in her town, a paramount purpose of private school, and its ludicrous cost, was that these private-school children would not be sharing their scissors and glue with children whose fathers were in prison. This was the march of civilization. First there is barbarism, no schools at all, all learning done at home, chaotically if at all. Then there is civil society, democracy, the right to free schooling for every child. Close on the heels of the right to free education is the right to pull these children out of the free schools and put them in private-schools—*we have a right to pay for what is provided for free!* And this is followed, inevitably and petulantly, by the right to pull them from school altogether, to do it yourself at home, everything coming full circle.

"Archery," Paul said. There was a sign up ahead. ARCHERY. LESSONS. TARGETS.

They had nowhere in particular to be, though Josie hoped to get to Denali the next day.

"Can we?" Paul asked, and because he so seldom asked for anything, Josie pulled over, descending the highway and onto the long gravel driveway, the Chateau like a tired mule groaning in protest to be led this way.

They followed the signs half a mile and then saw it, the wide green field, the red and white targets. But they saw no people. Still they got out, and without waking Ana, who was sleeping, soaking in her sweat, they looked around. There was a wooden booth of some kind, painted pine green, where one would usually pay and be given a bow and told where to go. The door to the booth was closed, but a window was open. Josie peered in but saw no one. There were no other cars, so they should have presumed it closed. And it probably was closed.

"Look," Paul said, pointing to a tree near the rightmost target. There was a bow leaning against it, an old thing, some ancient model. Josie saw no harm in Paul looking at it, so he ran off across the field, and returned with both the bow and three arrows he'd found in the thicket nearby. One arrow was bent into a parenthesis.

"Can I try?" he asked.

Paul never hurt himself, had never risked any injury to himself or anyone around him, so Josie told him he could. He took the bow in one hand and the arrow in another, and it took him some time to figure out how to do it well, but soon Paul was at least sending the arrows forward, though the bent one squirmed like some airborne snake.

Josie's eyes wandered, and soon found their way back to the archery booth, and its open window. She leaned in and saw the booth was mostly bare but for a sleeve of styrofoam cups, a bin of broken bows and, hanging from a nail, a green visor with the words STRAIGHT ARROW printed across its horizontal swath. Josie immediately knew she would take the visor, but knew, too, that she would debate taking it for a few minutes as she watched Paul shoot. Finally she reached in, grabbed the visor, tried it on, found it fit, and then arrived at an excuse—it was in the garbage—to use when Paul would see it on her and ask about its provenance.

"Where'd you get that?" he asked, returning from the target with his bow and arrows, looking strangely adept and professional.

"I saw it on the ground next to the booth," Josie said, adapting her story slightly, on the fly, feeling this lie becoming whiter and more inconsequential. "It hides the bald spot."

Paul peered around the side of her head, and then pulled the visor gently upward, better covering the gap, and then returned to his archery. Eventually, by practicing and by getting ever closer to the target, Paul struck near the middle a few times and then did not want to leave. So they stayed. They had food in the Chateau, and they had nowhere to be, so Josie brought out the lawn chair, sat and watched Paul shoot until Ana woke up. The sun was dropping behind the tree line on the high ridge behind them when Ana came down from the Chateau, briefly stuporous, until she saw the visor on her mother's head.

"Like Dad," she said.

Josie told her the story about finding it next to the booth, Ana finding it believable and very much what she would do in the same position—Paul, if he could, would have brought it to the police station to be claimed—but having Ana remind her of Carl, and Carl's tendency toward visors, sapped Josie's STRAIGHT ARROW headwear of much of its appeal. She thought about tossing it, and decided she would, as soon as an alternative arrived.

Josie watched her children shoot their arrows, running and giggling, and realized that a child's forgetting of joy is the principal crime committed upon a parent. Raj, in one of his rants, had said as much. His daughter was seventeen. Oh god, he said. The seventeen-year-olds, they will rip your heart out. A whole joyous childhood, and they will tell you it was all shit. Every year was a fraud. They will throw it all away. Josie had felt for Raj, and had feared the wrath from her own children, but then remembered: Hadn't she emancipated herself from her own mother and father?

But for her own children, Josie was determined to thwart this crime of forgetting. She would remind them of joy. Document joy, tell tales of joy at bedtime, take photos and write diaries. Journals of joy that could never be denied or conveniently forgotten. She began to conceive a new theory of parenting, where the goal was not the achieving of a desired result. The object is not to raise a child for some future outcome, no! Times like these, together in the pines amid the fading light, as the kids run through long grass, her son gravely teaching himself archery while her daughter tries to induce some self-injury, these moments alone were the object. Josie felt, fleetingly, that she could die having achieved such a day. Get to a place like this, get to a moment like this, and that alone is the object. Or it could be the object. A new way of thinking. Stretch some of these days together and that's all one could want or expect. Raising children was not about perfecting them or preparing them for job placement. What a hollow goal! Twenty-two years of struggle for what—your child sits inside at an Ikea table staring into a screen while outside the sky changes, the sun rises and falls, hawks float like zeppelins. This was the common criminal pursuit of all contemporary humankind. *Give my child an Ikea desk and twelve hours a day of sedentary typing. This will mean success for me, them, our family, our lineage.* She would not pursue this. She would not subject her children to this. They would not seek these specious things, no. It was only about making them loved in a moment in the sun.

Ana walked over to her chair and leaned against it. Her bow was around her shoulder in a startlingly professional way.

"Mom?" Ana said. "Are there robbers here?"

"No," Josie said. On cue, a distant siren knifed through the air. "That's a fire engine," she said, pre-empting. Paul was nearby, still shooting his arrows.

"But are there bad guys?"

"No."

"Where are they then?"

"They're really far away," Josie said, and caught Paul's eye. Why tell her there are bad guys at all? he seemed to be saying.

"You'll never see them in your whole life," Josie said. "And we have army guys fighting them." Again she caught herself saying unhelpful things.

"What about the Joker?" Ana asked.

"What about him?"

"Is he real?"

"No. He's pretend. Someone just drew him, the same as I could draw him. Someone like me made up the Joker."

"Someone like you?"

"Yeah. Or someone like your dad. More like your dad."

"What about skunks?" Ana asked.

Josie tried not to laugh. "Skunks?"

"Are they real?"

"Sure, but they're not dangerous. They can't hurt you."

"But are monsters real?"

"No, there are no real monsters."

"How do we know about monsters then?"

"Well, people made them up. Someone came up with an idea and drew it and made up a name."

"So someone can make up a name like Iron Man?"

"Sure."

"How about Randall?"

"Randall?"

"Yeah, is that a name?"

"It is. Did you hear that name somewhere?"

"I think so. I heard that word." Ana's brow furrowed. "I didn't know if it was a name."

"It's a name," Josie said.

Another pair of sirens threaded through the sky. Ana listened, her eyes concentrating on Josie's arm. She was tapping it with her tiny fingers, as if sending a coded subterranean message.

"Are the army guys big?" she asked.

"They are. Much bigger than the bad guys."

"Are they monsters?"

"Who?"

"The army guys."

"No. They're regular people. They have kids, too. But then they put on a uniform and they fight the bad guys." And to try to end the discussion, Josie added, "And they always win."

"But they killed Jeremy."

"What?"

"Someone killed him, right?"

Ana had been building up to this, Josie realized. She had heard the entry from "Trails Grown Dim," the words *robber* and *shot* and had been sorting it through ever since.

"Who told you Jeremy was killed?"

Now Ana turned to Paul, who had stopped his archery, having heard it all. When Ana turned back to Josie, her eyes had welled. Josie had not told Ana about Jeremy's death, and had not told Paul, either. She looked to him now, disappointed.

"Mario told me," Paul said, petulantly. Mario was another camper, another boy Jeremy had babysat. And then, as if to answer Josie's next question, he said, "Ana should know. Otherwise she thinks someone's alive when he's dead. That's stupid."

A mechanical wheeze sounded behind Josie, and she turned to find an enormous vehicle, slowing to park behind the Chateau. There was dust all around, but when it settled she saw that it was a silver pickup truck with a wooden home, pitch-roofed and painted black, sitting in the bed. The little house had windows, and a tiny tin stovepipe, looking altogether quaint but for the words "Last Chance" painted on the front-facing wall. Below those words, in smaller print, were the words "Beholden to None."

"What's that, Mom?" Ana asked.

Josie said nothing. She expected that one of the truck's doors would open momentarily, and didn't want to be caught describing the inhabitants. There was good reason to pack her children up quickly and leave, given the friendliness of the people steering a vehicle like this, which could not possibly be street-legal and hinted at the end of the world, was not guaranteed.

"Paul, come here," she whispered, and he brought his bow and arrow to her, and she subtly arranged both him and Ana such that she stood between them and this harbinger of doom.

The door opened. "Are we open?" a cheerful voice said.

It was a young woman with a brilliant mane of raven-black hair. She emerged from the truck in a two-footed jump, her heavy boots making an assertive sound of arrival in the white gravel. Wearing a loose black T-shirt and denim shorts, she began to stretch, one arm raised high, revealing a lithe and busty torso, while her other hand pushed the passenger seat forward, allowing the release of three children, all athletic and tanned, from the depths of the truck. They each jumped from the truck as she had—that is, as if landing on the moon. All seeming to be within the age range of Josie's kids, they ran directly to the empty booth, having assumed Paul and Ana had gotten their bows there. The driver's door opened and a short man emerged, no taller than the woman, and said, "Is it open?" He leaned back, stretching with a loud groan. Broad-shouldered and muscular, he wore a V-neck undershirt and canvas workpants tucked into hiking boots. He made his way around the truck and down the slope toward the archery field.

"I asked her but she didn't answer," the woman said, nodding her chin toward Josie. Her tone was familiar.

"Sorry," Josie said. "I didn't know you were asking *me*. I don't work here. We just got here and have been messing around."

"So it's free," the man said. He had an impish, closed-mouth smile but his eyes were tight and bright and lit with a kind of mischief that could go either way—practical jokes around the house, or handmade bombs in the shed.

"There's no more bows, Dad," one of the new children said. This was a girl of about nine. She and her younger brothers had investigated the booth and found it empty.

"You bring those?" the woman asked Josie, indicating the bows and arrows Ana and Paul were holding.

"No, they were just in the field," Josie said. "Your kids are welcome to use them. We've been here for a while." By this Josie meant that she and her children would be ceding this field to this family, and would be fleeing quickly.

"No, no. We came because we saw you guys out here. We can wait," the man said, and extended his hand. "I'm Kyle. This is Angie." Josie shook their hands and introduced Ana and Paul. Kyle and Angie's kids were soon upon them, and were introducing themselves—Suze, Frank and Ritter—with the utmost civility, making Paul and Ana look skittish and impolite by comparison.

"Do you live there?" Ana asked. She was pointing to the black home sitting in the truckbed.

"Ana," Josie said, then turned to Kyle and Angie. "Sorry."

"Don't be sorry. We sleep there at night, yup," Kyle said to Ana, squatting down in front of her. "You like it?" Ana was noncommittal at first, then gave a slow nod. "Sure you do," he said, smiling his closed-mouth smile, his bright eyes shining in their devilish or saintly way. His grin grew, and now Josie saw his teeth, oversized incisors, lending his face a wolfish cast. "We built it ourselves," he said. "You want to look inside?"

"No, no. That's okay," Josie said, but found herself and her children being led to the truck by the eager Kyle. Angie stayed with her children, who were now using the bows and arrows dropped in the high grass by Paul and Ana. Kyle jumped onto the truck's back bumper and opened the back door of the structure, which resembled a chicken coop from the outside and inside, an army barracks, with a series of bunks on either side, the floor covered in a carpet remnant. There were also stacks of towels, and magazines, and baseballs and bats, blankets. At the end of each bed, a flashlight hung from a hook.

"Cool, right?" Kyle said.

Ana readily agreed, then said, "We live in a car, too."

Kyle laughed. "Well, then it's good we all met up, right? Fellow travelers. Mom, let me get you a chair." For a second Josie thought Kyle's mother was somewhere in the truck, too, perhaps in a compartment underneath, then realized he was referring to her.

He pulled a short stack of folding chairs from the chicken coop—the structure was yacht-like, a paragon of space and economy—and set them out, three in a row, with a commanding view of the field. In moments Josie had been given a bottle of hard cider, was sitting beside Angie and Kyle, the three of them watching the five kids taking turns, complimenting each other, acting with stunning civility.

Kyle tapped Josie's bottle, then Angie's, in a kind of toast without a toast. "So where you headed?"

Josie told them she had no fixed itinerary.

Angie's eyebrows leaped, and she gave a conspiratorial look to Kyle. "I told you," she said. "Single mom with two kids, using an abandoned archery field. Our kind of people, I said."

Josie and Kyle and Angie compared notes about Homer and Seward and Anchorage and the rest stops and attractions in between. Kyle and Angie had been to the tragic zoo outside Anchorage, too, and had noticed the unmistakable pathos of that one certain antelope. He'd been looking to the mountains for salvation when they'd seen him, too. Angie was a beautiful woman, Josie realized, and she and Kyle were younger than she had first thought. There wasn't a wrinkle on either one of them, though it was clear they didn't stay out of the sun. They looked like coeds from the seventies, the silken-haired and well-tanned types once featured in cigarette ads.

"You gone for good?" Angie asked.

"How do you mean?" Josie asked, though she understood implicitly. She meant: Are you ever rejoining mainstream society? Josie had not, until then, thought much beyond August and September.

"I don't know," she said.

Kyle and Angie smiled. They were gone for good, they said. She'd been an accountant for an oil company, and he'd been a teacher, high-school earth science. In a flurry they outlined their plan to get to the northernmost point of Alaska then make their way around the western coast, and back down, then on to Canada. Their complaints about their previous life included living in a neighborhood of fenced and barking dogs, commuter traffic, but seemed most centered on taxes—income tax, property tax, sales tax, capital gains. They were finished paying any of that. "He's the *evader*," Angie explained. "I'm the *crusader*." They both let that sink in. It was apparently wordplay they were acutely proud of.

"No income, no property, no taxes," Kyle said, and Angie, the accountant, added, "We've considered renouncing our citizenship, but I think we'd have to become Canadian to do that. We're looking into staying stateless."

Josie's mind, which normally would have registered their near-madness and would be planning escape, was instead occupied with Angie's perfect face. Her cheekbones were high, her eyes smiling—she seemed to have some Native American blood, but could Josie ask? She couldn't ask. She realized she was staring at Angie—her teeth were magnificent, too, fantastically white—so she looked away, and to the field, where she saw Ritter, their younger boy, about to release an arrow. Ana was standing next to him, her hand gently holding the tail of his shirt, as always finding a way to touch the bearer of violence. But where was Paul? Now she caught sight of him. He was bent down, retrieving arrows that had landed beyond the targets.

"Ritter!" Angie yelled.

He was about to let go while Paul, at the sound of Angie's voice, stood up. Ritter, startled, released the arrow, but it fell feebly a few feet from his bow.

"Sorry," Angie said, and rushed to her son. She leaned

over him, her arm around his shoulder, her raven-black hair all over him, scolding, pointing to Paul, who was loping back to the group, his hand full of arrows. The danger had not been great, given Ritter was only six and Paul was fifty yards away, but still.

"Keep your head up," Josie yelled to him, trying to sound calm. In the days ahead she would wonder why it was so important to her to seem calm, or to stay at that archery field, to stay in that folding chair drinking her hard cider, trying somehow to impress those two beautiful young people.

"My kids are usually more responsible," Kyle said.

"Stay aware," Josie said to Paul. And by this, she meant that it was normal enough to be retrieving arrows in an active archery field. That it was normal enough to be doing so with three children you had just met, who lived in a wooden shed atop a pickup truck. That it was her son's responsibility to look out, in case a child-stranger might be shooting a life-ending arrow in his direction.

"You hunt?" Kyle asked.

Josie admitted she did not.

"Angie!" Kyle shouted. "You think I can shoot just one?"

Angie looked up from Ritter and shrugged. Then she seemed to change her mind, and shook her head no.

"You see anyone around here?" Kyle asked Josie. She hadn't. "She'll let me do one," Kyle said. "You saw her shrug. She always lets me do one. And the targets—hard to resist, right?"

With a conspiratorial smile in Josie's direction, he leaped from his chair and jogged over to his truck. He returned with a handgun and a rifle, setting the handgun on the chair and leaning the rifle against it.

"No, please," Josie said.

"Almost forgot," Kyle said, and flew back to the truck again. He returned with a plastic bin that rattled loudly. Bullets.

"Paul! Ana!" Josie yelled, and they ran to her, recognizing something new in her voice, something unhinged. "It was my turn," Ana said, as Josie grabbed her hand and pulled her close.

"Your children are gorgeous," Angie said. She was sitting next to Josie again, her hand now on Josie's knee, squeezing it twice, once for each syllable of *gorgeous*.

Josie thanked her, again getting momentarily lost in Angie's youth and beauty, thinking, she still looks twenty-four. She must have been fifteen when she had her oldest.

A crack split open the air. Josie wheeled to find Kyle kneeling, his arms outstretched, his handgun pointed toward the target.

"Kyle!" Angie roared. "Give us a heads-up at least." She turned to Josie. "Sorry. He's such an idiot."

"Was that real?" Ana asked, hoping it was.

Kyle jogged to retrieve his target, and Angie confirmed it was real. "You ever see a real gun go off?" she asked Ana, who was paralyzed, frozen somewhere between joy and terror.

Josie wanted to leave, but Angie's hot hand was still on her knee.

"Damn," Kyle said, standing at the target.

Why am I here? Josie continued to ask herself, as the afternoon grew pale and darkened, but Kyle set up a barbecue, and Josie and her kids were still there, and soon he was grilling hamburgers, which Josie's children ate greedily, standing up, and Josie was drinking her second hard cider, still wondering just how she could remain there, amid all this insanity. But Angie continued to touch her, on the arm, on the shoulder, and each time she did Josie felt a stirring, and though she worried about these two, and though every fifth sentence they spoke had something to do with evading or crusading, she wanted to stay near them, and was getting too tipsy to leave.

"One more?" Kyle asked Angie. "Before it's dark?"

The children were far off in the darkening field, each of them with a flashlight, meandering like giant fireflies, and Josie had convinced herself that these were her people. Beholden to none indeed. Their children were happy and strong and polite. The family did as they pleased. Everyone had perfect teeth.

But then another shot rang out. Josie screamed.

"You didn't ask!" Angie yelled.

"I did!" Kyle yelled back, laughing, holding his rifle at the end of the field. "Josie heard me," he said, walking toward the target. Josie remembered that he had said "One more" but she hadn't registered it.

"That's the end!" Angie said to him, and he lifted his hand over his head, in a halfhearted wave of acquiescence.

"Well, I think we should take off," Josie said, vividly conjuring the speedy collection of her kids and swift escape. She had in mind being on the road, and away from these people, in under a minute.

Angie squeezed her arm. "You can't drive. No way." Then she yelled to Kyle, "Josie was planning on driving tonight."

Kyle's head dropped, and he said nothing until he returned to Josie's chair, laying his rifle on the grass before her. He looked at Josie like he was still a teacher and she a disappointing pupil. "You can't drive, Josie. That would be irresponsible." He looked to Angie, and a moment passed between them, during which they seemed to be weighing whether or not to bring up some unspeakable thing.

"My mom was murdered by a drunk driver," he said.

"I'm sorry," Josie said.

"You shouldn't drive," Kyle said gravely. "Please. Your keys."

She didn't drive. She gave this man her keys. All went sideways. She sat with Kyle and Angie as the night went black and the bugs became ravenous. The sirens continued their sporadic wailings, and she sat with Kyle and Angie, who laughed full-throated laughs, who seemed to be enjoying Josie, and this night, immeasurably. Periodically one of the kids would rush back to them, and ask if they could do some new thing, chicken fights or climbing a nearby dirt heap, and each time Kyle and Angie considered it with

Solomonic seriousness. The children squealed and cackled in the gloaming, but finally Ana came back, resting her head on Josie's lap, and it was time to retire. Josie and Kyle and Angie said good night with swaying hugs, and they gathered their children, and Josie felt sure that it was over, that whatever had happened was over, but then Paul asked if one of the boys, the older boy, Frank, could sleep over. Angie and Kyle thought it was the most wonderful idea, not really worth debating, and soon he had his sleeping bag and a pillow and was installed in the bed over the cab, squeezed in with Paul and Ana, all of them giddy.

Josie made the lower bed for herself, doing the math, realizing these strangers had her keys and she had their son, and just as she was settled under the covers, there was a loud tap on the window. She jumped. "Just one more!" Angie said.

Josie said nothing, being somehow still unclear on what was about to happen. A hollow pop split the night, meaning Kyle had fired another gun, or maybe it was the rifle this time.

"That's the end!" Angie yelled, now farther away. "Night!"

Josie returned the sentiment, and the kids did, too, but no one slept. Her children were vibrating with the newness of the night, with the gunfire, with the presence of the strange tanned boy next to them, and Josie was thinking seriously that she had lost her mind. How could she stay here? Her keys were in the hands of the crusader. Or was he the evader? Up in the overhead bed, she heard Ana asking

Frank about the guns. There was some affirming discussion about how Kyle would shoot any robbers, and Ana giggled to hear it.

And there were the sirens. Something had happened nearby, some kind of accident. Or the fires were getting closer. The sirens were louder now. Sleep was impossible. Her mind raced through dark woods. Had she really stayed the afternoon with these people, with the father shooting guns fifty yards away? What did she know about them? Nothing. Somehow she had to trust that they would use their bullets on targets, not on her family, that nonsensical trust seeming to be the core of life in America. She thought of her own stupidity. She laughed at her own surprise at finding people like this here, in rural Alaska. What was she expecting? She had fled the polite, muted violence of her life in Ohio, only to drive her family into the country's barbarian heart. We are not civilized people, she realized. All questions about national character and motivations and aggression could be answered when we acknowledged this elemental truth. And why was this other child in her RV? And what about that bastard Mario, who told Paul about Jeremy? He had no right. And Paul had no right to know. Another siren, this one wild and lonely, followed by the howl of a coyote, eerily similar, as if the animal had mistaken the siren for kin.

XII.

JOSIE STARTLED AWAKE. It was still dark. The kids were asleep, and the night was quiet, but she knew everything was wrong. She sat up on one elbow, listening, and for minutes heard nothing. Then a thunderous rapping of knuckles on the Chateau door. The kids leaped up, Paul hitting his head on the ceiling. Josie dropped to the floor to answer the door. She heard movement outside. A car started. A voice in the distance yelled "Frank!"

Josie opened the door and saw Kyle, in a robe. "Gotta move," he said. "Evacuation. We're moving out in the next five minutes."

"Wait. What?" she said, and looked down the road, and saw, far beyond, through the trees, the red, blue and white flashes of a pair of police cars. Kyle ran back to their truck, and Angie appeared, poking her head in the Chateau door.

"Frank," she said. "Wake up." As Frank climbed down, she explained a change in the winds had sent a wildfire south and it had accelerated far quicker than anyone had anticipated, that it could arrive within the hour. "We're going north," Angie said, leaving with Frank wrapped around her. "Follow us."

Josie closed the door and inside found Paul and Ana standing just behind her, eyes wide. "Get buckled," she said.

She didn't have her keys. She leapt from the Chateau and ran after them. "Wait!" she yelled. Kyle and Angie's taillights cast Josie in red.

"You have my keys!" she screamed.

"Sorry," Kyle said. "We would have noticed eventually, though. We wouldn't have left you here to burn."

He handed the keys to her. "Better hurry."

She ran back to the Chateau.

"Did they have our keys?" Paul asked.

"Yes," Josie said.

"Why?" Ana asked.

"No idea," Josie said. She followed them down the hill and toward the highway. Ahead of her she saw nothing strange—just a dozen or so red taillights blinking, beginning the process of leaving the area. The archery field was apparently not far from a small town, which was being cleared out by police. The silhouettes of a few people raced past but otherwise the scene was orderly. Josie followed the column of vehicles fleeing, but in the melee she lost Kyle and Angie.

Where the dirt road met the highway, most of the cars were going left, but she saw a man waving madly. She wanted to follow the other cars but this man—now she saw he was in a yellow uniform—was waving her the other way so passionately that she obeyed, going alone. After a few hundred yards she stopped and looked in her rearview mirror, trying to decide if she'd done the right thing. But the mass of lights was vague. One car seemed to be turning around to follow her. She decided that the other vehicles had been misdirected before, and were now all being sent her way, the right way. She would be the leader, and, she assumed, the farthest from the fire.

She drove on. For a mile or so there were no signs, but then she saw one, in the sudden headlights a startled green and silver, telling her the highway was three miles ahead. This seemed a good omen.

"Is there a fire, Mom?" Ana asked.

"Not near here," Josie said.

"Angie said it was close," Paul said, and then seemed to realize he'd erred. He was usually so careful about keeping news of danger from his sister.

"No," Josie said. "Angie said it would take an hour to get here. That's a long way off. And we're driving away from it, so every mile we drive we double the distance. In an hour we'll be two hours from it. In two hours we'll be four hours from it. You understand? We're heading the opposite way."

The road was empty, and Josie took this to mean she had been the first to leave the park, and would soon be the first on the highway. She felt like a lone spacecraft escaping an exploding planet—all was dark, all was quiet, and with her two children she had all she needed. In her jumbled mind, spinning with adrenaline, she briefly conflated the fire and this place with her own town, and pictured their house in the path of the fire, being taken by the flames, and she wondered if there was anything inside she would miss. She thought of a dozen things and then reversed herself, believing she would feel cleansed and free if everything inside was burned, gone, turned to ash.

"Where do we go?" Paul asked.

"We'll drive a few hours to be sure we're far enough, and then we'll find a different place to sleep. Or we'll park somewhere." Josie pictured a parking spot near water, like the one they'd used their first night, when the trooper had sent them on their way. She wanted to be near water in case they—in case what? Fire overtook them and they needed to jump in the lake? And they would swim in this lake? Or fashion a watercraft and sail away? She decided the specifics didn't matter. "Strange," she heard herself say aloud.

"What's strange?" Ana asked.

She thought it strange that she wasn't seeing any cars, but then corrected herself, remembering that she was the first to leave the park, and that it was midnight and this was Alaska, and there wouldn't be dense traffic on any night here, let alone with a wildfire at their heels.

"Nothing," she said.

"*What's* strange?" Paul asked.

"How much I love you," she tried.

"No really. Tell us. Tell me." And now Paul was in the passenger seat. He thought it was something only he should know.

"No. Nothing's strange."

"I don't want to be alone back here!" Ana roared.

"Mom," Paul whispered. "Tell me."

"Everything's strange," Josie said.

Now he was quiet. It was a plain and truthful statement that went nowhere. It was not the forbidden secret he'd hoped for.

Josie turned on the radio and found Dolly Parton, "Here You Come Again," and settled in.

"Can you go sit with your sister?" she asked.

He retreated to the back. "Is this Dolly?" Paul asked.

Josie affirmed it was and turned it up. Ahead of her, she found the highway and took the exit. Though she wasn't expecting traffic, she was surprised to see no cars at all, nothing in either direction. She felt even more like they were alone in space, in an ancient spacecraft, a loud spacecraft, but alone and with no directives to obey.

And now, sneaking around a high hill a quarter mile ahead, there was a light. It was an orange glow peeking around the curve of land, like a sunrise, and Josie found herself checking the time to make sure it couldn't be the sun. No. It was twenty after twelve. She slowed down. She assumed it was some safety thing, warning lights of some kind. She got ready to stop.

The road wound around the blind turn and when she emerged, a bright orange stripe filled her view. The hillside was on fire.

"Is that a fire, Mom?" Ana asked.

It was a fire, a mile wide and depth without end, but it couldn't be a fire. There was no one around. No police, no fire engines, no barriers. The road she was taking would more or less take her directly into the flames. Her spaceship was heading into the sun.

"Mom, what are we doing?" Paul asked.

Josie stopped the Chateau. Her heart was leaping but her eyes were mesmerized by the strangely passive sight of the wall of flames. A gust of white wind overtook her view, a burst of dust.

The loud clapping of a helicopter emerged from somewhere above her, and a spotlight appeared on the hillside, and then focused on the road before her, and finally it flooded the Chateau. White light cut through the blinds, striping the faces of her children.

"My arm's glowing!" Ana said brightly.

A voice barked something from above. She couldn't make out the words. She opened the window and immediately choked. The air was acrid, poisoned. She coughed, gagged, and closed the window.

"Mom, you have to turn around," Paul said. "That's what they're saying."

Now Josie heard it, too. "Turn around immediately," a woman's voice said from above, sounding like a god both mechanical and annoyed. "Turn around and go. Move, now."

Josie did a three-point turn as the helicopter hovered above her and then she was on the road, going in the opposite direction. Over the next few miles the helicopter periodically swooped into view as if to confirm Josie was not some suicidal driver bent on self-destruction.

"Remain on this road," the voice said. "Do not turn around. Continue north." The helicopter soon lost interest in her and they were alone and in the quiet black again.

"Was that a real fire, Mom?" Ana asked.

"Of course it was," Paul said. "A forest fire. It was a million acres."

"Will it burn us now?" Ana asked.

Josie told her no, it wasn't a million acres, wouldn't burn them. Nothing could, and anyway they were far away already, that they were safe, would outrun any fire.

She drove north for an hour, two hours, and the kids finally fell asleep. There were no signs in this part of the state, no rest stops or signs of human settlements. It was madness to keep driving, having no idea if they were heading into the dark heart of the state—wasn't it mostly national park, ruled by bears?

Josie looked for any kind of accommodation or RV park, but found nothing. She drove on, and finally saw a sign that said BED AND BREAKFAST, and stopped. She checked the time. It was four thirty. They pulled into the dirt driveway, the kids waking to the change in speed. The property was a spread of about three acres set against the high bluff. The main house was a two-story family home with bicycles and tricycles out front, and even a child-sized motorized car, upon which Ana's eyes had already seized. In the darkness Josie and the kids got out and looked around the house, trying to figure out which was the front, then rang the bell. No one answered.

A small amber light was visible through the thicket behind the house and Josie guessed it to be the guest cottage. She led Paul and Ana to it. "Are we staying here?" Ana asked, and Josie thought of the strangeness of what they were doing, tramping through a path in the woods, to a cottage high on a bluff, long past midnight, alone.

The cottage came into view and looked new. The amber light came from a sconce on the porch, happy with new chairs and heavy cushions. There was a light on inside, too, and Josie, while feeling half-sure that the cottage was occupied, and that there was some outside chance someone would appear, angry or armed, also had a distinct confidence that the cottage was empty. She peered in and waited for movement. There was none. It was an A-frame, and all within was visible and built of new pine: a tidy kitchen, a pair of couches and matching chairs, a loft above where a large bed, empty, was visible, covered in a thick yellow comforter.

"We can't go in there," Paul said.

"Why not?" Josie asked.

"We didn't ask anyone," he said.

Josie had already decided they would either sleep in this cottage or sleep in the Chateau while parked in the driveway. She would not drive again tonight, and this property seemed accustomed to guests.

She turned the doorknob to the cottage. It opened. Inside it was clearly new, all of it well built, still reeking of cut wood and lacquer. It was solid, clean, seemingly never used. She walked in.

"Come," she said to her children. They were standing on the porch, Paul holding Ana back with one hand.

"We tried to ask. They're not home," Josie said, then had an inspiration. Paul needed order, and needed to stay on the path of the moral right, and also, happily, he liked tasks and was proud of his handwriting. Josie wrapped it all together.

"The way bed and breakfasts work," she said, changing her tone to one of almost blasé authority, "is that often you arrive after the proprietors"—she knew Paul would not know the meaning, but the word would heighten her authority—"go to sleep. And sometimes they live nearby but not on the premises. So the standard thing to do"—now she was really blasé, she considered yawning—"is that you write a note and tape it to the front door."

"This front door?"

"No, the main house. Can you be the one to do it, Paul?"

Of course he would do it. He would write it, and fold it, and tape it to the front door, and would take on the work with seriousness and joy. The only trick would be to get him to do it soon. Given his exactitude and caution, tasks like this usually took him an hour. This had been mentioned at school—good and tidy work, but time management an issue.

So they went to the Chateau, and while Paul sat at the banquette to work on the note—he needed no instruction;

he knew the gist and intended to breathe new life into the form—Josie gathered their toiletries and packed a quick bag of clothes and toys. By the time she was ready Paul had finished the note.

"Greetings! We saw your Sign. We are sleeping in your wunderfull Cabin. Thank you!"

It seemed enough, actually, and Josie said so. Paul's face fell.

"Or you could keep going," she said, "but we have to get moving." She suggested that she and Ana set up in the cottage while Paul stayed in the Chateau to finish, and he didn't even look up.

"I'll stay with him," Ana said. She had moved next to Paul and was watching his work intently.

Josie went back to the cottage and opened the door, smelling cleanliness and good taste. The house had been built with great attention to detail and to the overwhelming comfort of its visitors. There was a new refrigerator, new oven, new coffeemaker—in fact, there were a half-dozen appliances throughout the kitchen and not one looked as if it had ever been used. She opened the fridge and found that it was on, and cold, but empty, untouched.

They were undoubtedly the first to stay there.

She returned to the Chateau and found Paul and Ana unmoved, Paul's tongue protruding meaningfully and his hand working, pressing too hard with his pencil—always too hard. She asked if he was almost done.

Ana shook her head, as if she was his assistant and had been tasked with fending off distractions.

"Almost," Paul said, without looking up.

"Can I see?" Josie asked.

He said no, but in a few seconds he was finished.

"Greetings!" the note said. "We saw your Sign. We are sleeping in your wunderfull Cabin. Thank you! We knocked and rang your bell but no one answered. Maybe you are sleeping? We will won't wake you. Please don't wake us in the morning. We saw a forest fire and we are tired. Thank you,

"Josie, Paul and Ana

"P.S. We will pay you for useing the Cabin."

After Josie pointed out the will/won't problem, Paul corrected the note and taped it to the front door of the main house. Josie led the kids back to the cottage, and inside they sat in every chair, and Ana quickly made her way up the ladder to the loft, and from above, pretended to fall. "Oh no!" she yelled. "I almost died."

The bed upstairs was big enough for them all. Ana kicked and squirmed in some expression of her comfort and joy, and Paul folded his pillow. Josie lay with her children, in this house they had more or less broken into. If someone showed up now, it would not look good. If someone arrived in a few hours, after she was asleep herself, it could be very bad. Would they read the letter Paul wrote? Josie had a thought they should have also left a note on the door to the Chateau, referring the reader to the cottage. Paul would have loved that, the sense of treasure-map control and continuity.

But they were doing something acceptable, she told herself. It was within the bounds of appropriate and even legal behavior for the wayward. There was a time, was there not, when it was right and good to go on a journey, and find an unoccupied cabin in the woods, and spend the night there, and then clean it, leaving it as they found it, ready for the next tired traveler? All this should be allowed. She and her children, so comfortable and warm and tired in their loft bed smelling of cedar and pine, should be allowed.

After reading from the cabin's only magazine, *Yachts and Yachting*, Josie climbed down, locked the door, turned off the light, climbed back up the ladder, and the three of them huddled under the heavy comforter. Only then did they notice there was a skylight, and through the skylight they could see a sliver of the moon, the slightest of smiles.

Ana was asleep in seconds, but Josie knew without looking in his direction that Paul was awake and taking in the moon.

"I heard you with Ana the other day," she said. "When you invented that story about the ring of birds around the world."

She could see the vague shape of Paul's face as he turned to her. She thought he was smiling but couldn't be sure.

"You're beautiful with her," she said, and now she was crying.

She was sure Paul was staring at her. He said nothing, but in the dark she sensed him telling her that he knew her. That he knew everything about her. How weak she was. How flawed. How small and human. He conveyed to her that he loved her this way. That she belonged in the world, was no heaven-sent and infallible being—such a thing would be harder for him and even more so for Ana.

I know you were scared tonight, his eyes said to her.

You were scared, too, she conveyed.

You handled it well. And you brought us here. I understand why.

Then, as if this exchange was finished or was too intense to continue, he turned to fall asleep.

Josie closed her eyes and drifted off, and soon settled into a deep sleep, the comfort a kind she hadn't felt yet in this burning state.

XIII.

THE HAZEL MORNING DROPPED through the skylight, featherlight and warm, and they were still alone, still in bed. It was almost ten. Josie sat up and looked through the window to the main house, seeing Paul's note still there. No one had come. She stretched, feeling like she'd slept in a cloud. It was the most decadent bed she'd ever known. She looked at Paul, who was still far gone and dreaming, under the covers, only his eyes and hair visible. Now Ana was awake, rubbing her eyes. Josie brought her finger to her mouth to ask Ana not to wake Paul, and Ana nodded—an unusual display of restraint. The three of them had gotten away with something here, something innocent, stealing a night of sleep.

Paul's head turned. "Are we getting up now?"

"No," Josie said, and closed her eyes, hoping he would, too.

But the sound of Paul's voice had activated Ana, and Ana was a comet—she could not turn back. She was up, and soon was standing on the bed, then under the covers again, kicking furiously, exultantly. Then she was up again, and sitting on Josie's stomach, and dropping her heavy head toward Josie's face, a wrecking ball covered in red fur.

"I'll get us some food," Josie said.

She went to the Chateau, passing the main house, still no sign of any occupants, no new vehicles. Inside the Chateau, the rear living area brought on a terrible sadness. Now more than before the vehicle was a filthy thing. They were filthy people who belonged in this filthy machine. But then again, they were beautiful creatures who were at home in an immaculate cabin on a hundred-foot bluff. She retrieved milk and cereal and apples and returned to the A-frame.

Outside the cottage, birds were gossiping, the sun was rising. The wall of mountains beyond the bay took in the streaming sun with magnanimity. Josie and Paul and Ana ate, and washed the dishes with the faucet's wonderful water pressure, and dried the dishes with the kitchen's soft and absorbent paper towels. Josie decided they could stay another day. That they could make the beds and straighten the cottage such that it wouldn't be obvious they had slept the night. They would linger on the grounds, see what came, and then, if by the afternoon no one had arrived, they could sleep there again. It was ideal here, considering anyone might be looking for them now: police, child services, Carl, someone sent by any one of them. Here their vehicle was hidden, they were hidden, there was no registry, no record of their presence. In fact, Josie thought that their reversals, their driving through the fire, might have served, unintentionally but brilliantly, to throw off whoever might have been on their trail.

After breakfast they explored the property, Josie ready at any moment for the arrival of the owners or caretakers. They removed the note from the door, deciding that if anyone came, she would pretend she and the kids had just arrived.

They found a path through the woods, leading to the bluff. But before the edge it bent and took them to a small white gazebo standing a few yards from the edge of the cliff, and she took this to be some sort of wedding location. Maybe the whole place was rented out for ceremonies, where five or ten families could gather and watch the vows and stay the night. Ana began running in circles in the gazebo and after the third lap was dizzy and holding on to the railing, panting. They could think of nothing else to do.

They returned to the main lawn and soon Ana had a soccer ball she'd found, and was kicking it, then running after it, attacking it as a cat would a giant ball of string. Paul thought this was very funny, and the lawn was wide and flat, and the sun bright and sky clear, so Josie saw no harm in sitting in one of the plastic lawn chairs and letting the kids run around while she did nothing. Could I live here? Josie wondered. Miles from anything. The road inaudible from your yard. The occasional moose. The possibility of bears and wolves. This spectacular view. The inability of your neighbors to complain about your leaving broken machinery in your yard. She thought of staying here indefinitely, but staying would mean waiting to get caught, and then there would be a negotiation, and she would have to contend with the look of distrust from whoever found them. If only, from now on, she could avoid judging eyes, she could survive. But all eyes were judging eyes, so better to move, and see without being seen.

But then again, this home, this property, was evidence of the glory of the land, this country. There was so much. There was so much space, so much land, so much to spare. It invited the weary and homeless like herself, her worthy children. She had the blurry thought that all the world's searching and persecuted could find a home up here. Alaska's climate was warming, was it not? It would soon be a forgiving place, with milder winters and uncountable millions of unpopulated acres, and so many empty homes like this, waiting to take in the desperate travelers of the world. It was a wonderful thought, a numbing notion. Josie closed her eyes, not expecting sleep.

When she opened her eyes, the air had chilled and her children were nowhere to be found. She startled to her feet, called for them, her mind popping with images of the two of them jumping over the cliff—of Ana jumping first, Paul trying to save her, the two of them tumbling downward, wondering where their mother was in all this. She'd been asleep in a plastic chair.

She found them in the barn, sitting on an antique tractor. It was not entirely safe, but not dangerous, either. Paul was up on the old metal driver's seat, and Ana was on his lap, her little hands on the steering wheel. She turned to Josie, grinning.

"Look Mom!" she said.

The garage was full of mounted animal heads. Which seemed odd, to go through the trouble of killing and stuffing them all only to hang them in this dark unvisited place. Think of that! To kill animals, and care so much for them, or be so interested in celebrating the kills, that you would pay hundreds of dollars to mount them, only to warehouse them in this unseen room. It spoke of the endless bounty of the animal world, legions of replaceable mammals, more than enough to stuff and hide away some great percentage of them.

Josie thought of her own basement, the things she kept there even while knowing she would feel freer without them. She knew she felt liberated outside that house, and felt freer without her job, freer away from those hot dirty mouths. She felt freer here than at home, freer here alone than surrounded by her purported friends, and she felt sure she would be far freer without her bones weighing her down and her flesh draping over her bones, all this ugly aging skin needing food and water and moisturizer. To be a ghost! To see all, to see anything, but never to be seen—this might be bliss.

"We should go," she said to them.

Paul was outraged. "You mean leave?"

She had just been struck by a strange feeling. The heads on the wall had done it. The sinister nature of their deaths had gotten to her. She'd been lucky the night before, and that luck could, would, fade or, more likely, change abruptly.

"No Mom," Paul said. He then laid out an entirely rational argument. That they had been there one night already. That no one had come. That they had left the note on the door. That he could leave more notes—on the windows, on the door to the Chateau, to the cottage. That the worst that could happen would be that they would pay for two nights. The towering tragedy of a single parent is that your eldest child becomes not just confidant but valued counsel.

They decided to stay, with Josie reserving the right to change her mind at any time that day. The sky stayed blue all through the morning and they had an extravagant lunch of hot dogs and rice and pastrami, using the cottage stove and microwave and eating on real plates and with glasses made of glass, sitting on stools by the kitchen counter, and afterward Paul and Ana returned to the lawn, where they set up and played their own version of croquet. They found a tiny frog and Ana somehow caught it without fuss and carried it around in her little fat hands for an hour. And Josie watched from her chair, and finished her "Trails Grown Dim."

A good one: "My great-grandfather James A. Layman, a Confederate veteran, Pvt., Co. D, Cavalry, Co. A, received an honorable discharge May 10, 1865, and entered Confederate Soldiers' Home at Higginsville, Missouri, October 19, 1900, from Pulaski County, Missouri. He was listed as a resident there as late as 1902. He left to enter the home at Pewee Valley, Kentucky, and was there January 31, 1905, in Room 31 in the south wing. Here my record stops—no death date or place and no burial place. Will appreciate any help."

The day was overtaken by dusk, Josie was exhausted, and there was very little food left. But she managed to make omelets and a bizarre salad containing lettuce and watermelon and bacon bits and pieces of sausage. The kids devoured it and by eight they were all ready for sleep.

"Can we?" Paul asked.

"By all means," Josie said, and Ana climbed the ladder to the loft, and Paul followed. He reached down for *Yachts and Yachting,* which he planned to read to Ana, and Josie handed it up to him, looking around the cottage for anything left to do. There was nothing. The simplicity was complete. Maybe, she thought, they all needed one long rest—a twelve-hour binge to feel right again. She turned out the main light, leaving the cottage with only the porch light and the bedside lamp next to the kids, who she could hear under the covers, Paul reading in low murmurs to Ana.

The door opened so quietly that Josie assumed it was one of her children. But her children were in the bunk above her. Then it must be the wind, she thought. She hadn't closed it tightly enough, and the wind had pushed it open.

"What's happening here?" a man's voice said. Josie jumped at the first word. She turned to find a young man in camouflage pants, a sleeveless shirt and baseball hat. His eyes were small, blue, his goatee black. In the single second that lingered between them, Josie had time to hope that he was a gentle man, a proprietor who found the note and understood, had found Paul's child handwriting endearing. There was the possibility, in that second, that this man only wanted to know what was happening, and that Josie could easily explain it, that he'd accept their money and welcome them to stay.

"Who the fuck are you?" he said instead.

Josie didn't breathe. His small blue eyes, his hunter's outfit—anything could happen.

"We left a note," she managed to say.

"Is that your RV? Are you a squatter? Who are you with?" he asked. He hadn't seen the children yet. He stood in the open doorway, Josie standing five feet away, his feet ready to move, as if unsure he wanted to be with her in the closed room, as if he'd encountered a bat in the cottage and wanted to allow passage for it to fly away.

Josie looked up, to see where Paul and Ana were, and saw nothing. They were hiding in the loft. She couldn't imagine how they knew to hide, how Paul was keeping Ana quiet, but she had a split-second moment of admiration for them. She thought of Anne Frank.

"You just let yourself in?" he asked.

Josie had already decided she wouldn't mention the night before. She would tell him they'd just arrived, had written the note, had money, would settle all this. "We saw the sign," she said, hearing her voice so thin and scared. "No one answered the door. There was nowhere else to stay."

"So you broke in?" Now his volume spiked. Something had turned. He could be on drugs. His hands were fists. Josie looked for a weapon. Then looked up to the loft again. No sign of the kids.

"Who's up there?" he asked, still yelling. "Who the *fuck* is up there?"

"Please. Take it easy. We'll leave."

"No, we'll call the police. That's what we're doing. You stay here."

And he left. She didn't know where he'd gone. Maybe he didn't have a cellphone, or had left it in the main house? But he'd left them alone, so she had a few minutes. She rushed up the ladder and found Paul and Ana under the covers and awake. Their heads were pressed together, Paul's arms around her, in some kind of death embrace, a Pompeii pact.

"Let's go. Now," she said.

Josie grabbed Ana and flew down the ladder in two steps. She reached up and took Paul from the first step, pushing them both out the front door. She returned, found their duffel bag, stuffed it with the clothes she'd removed, and met the kids on the porch. She paused, looking and listening for the man. There was no sign of him.

They needed to get to the Chateau but couldn't use the path. "Follow me," she said. She picked up Ana and led Paul by the hand through the woods, toward the bluff, intending to follow the cliff side to the driveway. The man wouldn't see them until they'd gotten inside the RV.

"Mom, careful," Paul said, pointing to the sheer drop, only a few feet to their left.

"Shh," she said, moving swiftly toward the driveway.

Now she saw a man emerge from the main house. He had a phone on his ear, the cordless receiver of a landline, and was looking in the direction of the cottage. She assumed he was calling the police.

Fine, she thought. Now all she had to do was get to the Chateau and go. The police might chase her, but they couldn't be anywhere near here. She'd have a twenty-minute head start. Her heart was in her mouth, her ears. She watched the man, standing outside, facing the cottage. He was looking for movement from her, assuming she was still inside. All she needed was for him to return to the main house, or go to the cottage to find them. That would give her time to get to the RV and leave.

She turned to Paul. "We're running to the Chateau. Any second. Ready?"

Paul nodded.

The man took the phone from his ear, pressed a button, and the orange lights of the receiver went dark. He tucked the receiver into his pocket and strode to the cottage, his white form crosshatched by the thicket.

"Now?" Paul asked.

"Wait," Josie said. When he was just before the cottage, she hissed "Now," and they sprinted out of the woods and across the lawn and toward the Chateau. They were at the gravel driveway when their footsteps gave them away.

"Hey! Get the fuck back here!" the man yelled.

Josie opened the cab door and threw Ana inside. Ana hit something with a thump; Josie knew she would cry but that she was unhurt. Paul stepped in and Josie shoved him over. Before she got in she saw the man hurtling toward her, across the lawn and down the driveway. He was astonishingly fast. She closed the door, threw the key in the ignition and started the engine. She threw it into gear and the Chateau lurched forward just as a loud bang hit the rear bumper. She'd hit him. No. He was banging his hand on the back of the Chateau. Now the side. The back of the Chateau dipped. He'd grabbed the ladder. He was riding on the back. Impossible. No, possible. He was the kind of man who would jump on.

"Go, go, Mom!" Paul said.

"I'm going!" she hissed.

She slammed the pedal down. The engine groaned and the gravel spit. They lurched forward and turned heavily to the right as the driveway wound toward the highway. There's a man on this car, Josie thought. She imagined him hanging on the back, crawling forward to her. By the time he reached her he would be ready for murder.

Ahead the driveway rose suddenly to meet the highway and she sped up, thinking the sudden incline might toss him from the ladder. The front bumper slammed into the pavement, and the hood leaped up with a crunch. The Chateau bounced and squealed as she turned and sped onto the highway.

"Get in the back," she told her children. Ana was bawling but Josie hadn't heard her until now. What if the man was on the back and got in? Through the roof. Some other way. "No, stay here," she told Paul. "Stay here, both of you. Hide down there," she said, and pointed to the floor of the passenger seat. She wanted them near her, within view. Paul obeyed and huddled with Ana in the dark.

They were on the highway now, and reached twenty, thirty, forty. She could only assume the man was still on the ladder, but there was a chance he'd jumped off, had fallen off. But she couldn't stop to be sure. If he was still hanging on, the man was now crazed and desperate, and would harm her. But she couldn't just drive on, speeding on the highway with a man hanging from the ladder, could she? She had to. So she did, while waiting for the sound of the man climbing, or pounding, or the dip of the back end as the man jumped off.

In a flash of inspiration she realized she could stop at a gas station and there, under the lights, she could stop and be safe—he wouldn't try anything. So she drove north another fifteen miles until she saw the blue-white lights of a gas station looming. She slowed, listening closely for any movement—the sounds of a man crawling on the tin box she was driving. When she pulled in, she saw a figure inside the green glass, a woman standing at the counter, watching a tiny television. Josie looked to see if the woman saw anything strange on the Chateau. The woman glanced her way then returned her attention to the screen.

Josie stopped the Chateau as close to the door to the station as she could and waited. He might choose this moment to attack, to avenge his harrowing ride. But again there was no movement. An idea occurred to her. She honked the horn. The volume was tripled under the canopy and echoed against the glass of the food mart. The woman at the counter startled and looked to Josie, eyes wild.

Josie waved, said she was sorry through three layers of glass, and frantically beckoned the woman out. The woman shook her head, no. She couldn't leave her post. What reason could anyone want her to leave? The only possibilities were all dangerous.

But eventually Josie cajoled her into leaving the counter. The woman opened the front door of the food mart and poked her head through. "I can't come outside," she said.

Josie rolled down the passenger-side window.

"You see anything on the outside of this RV?" she asked.

"What's that again?"

"Is there anyone on the RV? A man hanging there?"

"A man on your RV?" The woman had been scanning the Chateau all along, but her eyes had not alighted on anything. "No."

"So there's no one up there? On the back either?"

Now the woman's eyes looked scared, confused about

Josie and the task she had been assigned. Still, she craned her neck around to look over the back of the vehicle, and shook her head.

"No."

Only then did Josie feel comfortable opening the door. In another ludicrous calculation, she tried to think of the man's possible point of attack, just outside the door, so she decided to leap from the doorframe, into the open blue-light area of the gas station, creating as much distance as possible between herself and the Chateau. Maybe he would jump, miss, and land on the pavement?

She opened the door, leaped, and nothing happened. She lunged back to the door to close it—for hadn't she just left her cowering children in danger?—and then quickly paced around the station, looking from every vantage point for a man in camouflage pants who might have been clinging for the last hour. She saw no one.

The woman inside, though, was on the phone. Most likely reporting Josie to the authorities. Josie thought briefly about staying, because she hadn't done anything that the food-mart woman could claim or any police officer could prove.

She got back into the Chateau and drove off, picturing a bottle breaking against her face. This hadn't happened recently, but this vision, a bottle breaking against her face, had been an intermittent part of her life since she was twelve. She could not explain this phenomenon to anyone without provoking grave concern, so she never mentioned it, because it was not problematic or a symptom of some flowering psychosis. It was not related to the numb face. It had predated the numb face by twenty years. She had been in sixth grade, just after Candyland, when it started and it occurred regularly since then, and it was not a big deal. It was just a recurring vision of a bottle breaking against her face. Of the tens of thousands of thoughts she, like anyone else, had in a given day, a couple times a day there was the vivid picture of a bottle, a seventies-era soda bottle with its curves and striations, breaking against her face, and it was not a big deal. Exactly who was holding the bottle was never clear, and their motives were not known, but in any case the bottle would swing into her vision and shatter against her nose and cheek, the shards spreading like rain. It was never painful. It was not troubling. It was just a bottle breaking against her face. It had something to do with punishment, but it was also a little slapstick, too. It was a bit of pie-in-the-face, a bit of corporal punishment at the hands of an angry clown-god.

It was nothing, really.

Her children were still hiding on the floor.

"You can get up now," she said.

"She's asleep," Paul said. They were so entangled that Paul couldn't move, either, without waking Ana, so Josie left them there on the dark dirty floor and kept driving.

XIV.

JOSIE AWOKE TO A SHRIEKING. She was sleeping on the kitchenette couch, her children sleeping above, and they were in an RV park she'd found somewhere around midnight. She had no idea where in the state they were. Through the kitchenette blinds the day seemed balmy and clear.

Six hours earlier she'd been driving through the night, had found the sign, the gravel road, and she'd paid forty-five dollars to park with full power. She'd gone to the office and woken up the manager, a handsome man in his fifties or sixties named Jim, and he'd been kind and understanding and had given her keys to the shower and a code for the clean-out (she didn't tell him she wouldn't be using it). He'd given her a shot of bourbon, too, guessing she needed it, and afterward she'd walked numbly to the Chateau and fallen asleep on the couch.

Now it was morning, and Josie was awake, and someone was still shrieking. It was somehow obvious that it was

happy shrieking, though, cheerful shrieks of "Hello!" and
"Here we are!"

"Mom?" Paul called.

"Down here," she said.

Paul climbed down from above and while she lay on the
couch he spread himself on top of her like a cheetah on a
heavy bough. Ana followed, climbing down from the loft
and then on top of Paul, stacking herself carefully. Josie
absorbed all their weight, and briefly thought it was wonderful, then knew it would soon kill her.

"Off," Josie said.

They stretched and ate cereal and when the sun rose past
the tree line they left the Chateau and Josie remembered
where they were. In her mind she replayed the drive there,
the grey light of her headlights scraping across the parking lot gravel, then into the office, meeting Jim, the bourbon, him showing her the layout of the park and the most
secluded spot. There was the main house, the office—a large
and solidly built structure of red logs and white putty, a
wide porch. There was the gravel parking lot facing the
river, and then a loose grid of RVs and mobile homes tucked
against the woods. The two-lane interstate was nearby,
above, but quiet and passed over the river on a simple stone
bridge. When she stepped out to feel the day, she noticed she
was parked next to another vehicle, this one seeming more
or less permanent. There was a white picket fence around it,
and in its windows there were flower planters and flags.

Josie thought about what day it was and realized it was

Saturday. There would be a wedding that day, at this RV park, involving the shrieking women. If they shrieked at eight a.m. while bringing plastic forks into an events hall, what noises would they make when the ceremony was underway?

The events building was between the Chateau and the river, and so it seemed natural enough for Josie to set up her folding chair facing the wedding party. She went inside, made herself tea and returned to watch the proceedings as she would the morning news on television.

The door behind her opened with a whine and Josie turned to find Paul and Ana, dressed in yesterday's clothes.

"Who's getting married?" Paul asked.

They were very young. The men were dressed in their groomsmen suits, their jackets off, while the bridesmaids wore shorts and tanktops and would change later, and together they began decorating the building with streamers and white carnations, while uncles and fathers brought tables and chairs inside. A great time was had by all, with the bridesmaids occasionally lifted off the ground by the groomsmen, who threatened to throw them in the river, provoking more shrieking. They were so young and Paul was walking slowly toward them, as if drawn by some unseen force.

Josie said nothing, wanting to see how far her son would go. Three steps and he stopped, watched. Four more steps. Ana was uninterested, was playing in the Chateau's shadow, talking urgently to herself while holding a muscular green man, but Paul was in a trance, his hands in front of him, his fingers twisting fingers.

"There's someone in my class I could marry someday," Paul said without any emotion, as if noting a passing cloud.

"Helena?" Josie asked.

"Yeah," he said, his eyes fixed on the guests still arriving.

And now, from under the bridge, riding on a path along the river, came a group of six. First there was a man of about fifty, wearing a black vest, and black pants, and a button-down of sky blue. He was riding a mountain bike, and seemed to have won a race, because he said "Ha!" as he passed under the bridge and entered the gravel parking lot. Behind him was a woman in her thirties, in a pilgrim's dress, a conservative cotton garment grey and trimmed in white, its hem tickling her ankles. She was wearing a bonnet and was grinning, her face red and alive, so happy that she'd come in second.

So they were Mennonites, Josie thought. Or Amish. But they drove here, that was certain, so that would rule out the Amish. So Mennonites. She'd once seen a Mennonite family praying before a meal at Burger King, and that Burger King had been in the middle of nowhere. Thus that was allowed—driving to the Burger King, eating at the Burger King, driving to RV parks in Alaska with a trailer of bicycles. She settled on them being Mennonites, and sat in the grass, with one eye on her children and the other on this Mennonite tableau still developing.

More bicyclists followed, three children—boys of eight

and twelve, a girl of ten—and then, most intriguingly, another woman, who seemed to be about twenty, too old to be the daughter of the first woman. They all got off their bikes, laughing and whooping and wiping their brows. They'd just had the greatest time. The boys were in black pants and all wore the same sort of blue workshirt as their father. The girl and woman wore something similar to the second-place woman. They parked their bikes, each carefully positioning their kickstands in the gravel.

"Whoo boy!" said the father.

A smile overtook Josie's face. She spun around to see if she was the only one witnessing this. She looked to her children, who were now stomping in the shallow water, oblivious.

Josie turned back to the Mennonites. The man was husband to one of the two women, but who? The kids were by the older woman, she was sure. So the younger woman was along for fun. A niece, a fellow member of their church, their village. Her parents had died? She'd been orphaned, taken into this other happy family? Josie contemplated who she would have been had she been born or married into this family. What would she want? Would her desires have been simplified? All she would want, perhaps, was this, a good vigorous bicycle ride along the river, coming in second, just behind the handsome husband, how marvelous it all was, Whoo boy.

"Look," Ana said, and pointed downriver, where it bent. A tribe of kids were playing in the shallow water, amid a

267

tiny forest of high reeds. Before Josie could stop her, Ana had run down the bank. Paul followed, warning her to be careful.

There were about twelve kids, from four to ten years old, and their interest seemed to center on a huge downed tree, which lay dead in the shallows, its branches rising tragically, diagonally to the sky. Half of the kids straddled or hung from its branches, and periodically dropped into the ankle-deep water below. It was only after watching the group for a few minutes that Josie realized she was the only parent present.

Josie looked down the riverside, not believing this could be true, and finally found what appeared to be the parent charged with looking after the twelve children. She was a woman of about sixty, a grandmother perhaps, standing in the shallow water, talking on the phone, smoking, gesticulating, laughing a hoarse happy laugh. She looked up to find Josie, and she managed to both wink and wave simultaneously. Her smile was very warm, her wink seeming to acknowledge the beauty of the river, of the day, the gorgeous madness of all the kids playing together, of the two of them allowed to simply stand in or sit near the river, doing nothing.

Josie waved back. Feeling the other woman could handle it for a minute or two, Josie retrieved her folding chair and brought it to the flat grassy riverside and sat and watched. Now there were fifteen children, then twenty. The children of the river were trying to move the large tree. The alpha boy, shirtless and wearing pajama pants, had taken control of the platoon and was insisting that the tree be moved, and he was directing the other children to grab here, and there, and there, and you over there at the end. At one point he even said, "Lift with your legs!" His voice was husky and impatient.

Josie's own children happily submitted to his directives. He was the foreman of all the work being done, and he knew how to lead. Josie puzzled for an explanation of why the log had to be moved, but the children under his command labored, unquestioning.

Now he seemed burdened. He stood, watching his workers, hands on his hips, dissatisfied. Something was wrong. He lowered his head, came to some conclusion, and raised it.

"From now on," he said, "we'll have to use fart power."

He said it in a tone of seriousness, of resignation. They had apparently run out of electricity, fossil fuels, and now they would use what was left. Josie had long wondered how pioneers, how bands of cavemen, knew where to stop and settle. Along this trip so far, Josie had seen a few places where she thought, There's a lake, and there's a mountain, and there's a rolling meadow where she could watch her children play. But there had been easy reasons why none of those places seemed suitable places to stay. Most were near highways. But this park, sitting at the bend of a river, spoke of welcome and permanence.

Then again, Josie thought, looking at the road where it crossed the river, there was at least some possibility that the quiet of the morning could be broken by sirens looking for her. She had a quick vision of this woman with her by the water, and the invisible parents of the river children, rising up to protect her. She hadn't spoken a word to them, but believed that they had formed some kind of community, watching the children moving logs under the power of young flatulence.

"Hypnotic, right?" It was a man's voice. Josie jumped. She turned to find Jim, the man who had checked her in last night. Now he was standing behind her, holding a blue cup out to her. It seemed to be pink lemonade. He had a cup of his own.

"No thanks," she said, but he made no effort to remove the cup from her view, so she took it.

He clinked his plastic cup against hers. "I checked you in last night. Is that your name or your way of life?" he said, and nodded toward her visor.

"I found this," she said, and saw that he was disappointed: he thought he'd delivered a zinger. But, she wanted to say, nothing good can ever come from noticing anyone else's clothes.

She sipped the lemonade, discovering that he'd spiked it with what tasted like rum. She decided that because it was noon, and because she had escaped an innkeeping madman the night before, she deserved this. "Thank you," she said, trying to see him. The sun haloed his head, putting his face in purple silhouette. She remembered him as handsome.

"You on vacation? On the run?" he asked.

"Will you sit down?" she asked. "I can't talk to you standing above me like that."

He had no chair, so sat on the grass next to her.

"You don't have to sit on the ground," she said.

"I want to," he said, and ran his fingers through the weedy grass like it was plush carpeting. "Mmmmm," he said. "Your stay good so far?"

"The best," she said, with a useless sarcasm she did not endorse. He explained that the establishment was his, that he'd bought it five years ago, after moving up from Arizona. Josie assumed he knew she was single, and wanted to convey that he was not a clerk at the inn but its owner. Jim was younger than she'd remembered from the night before. About fifty-five? Sturdily built, strong shoulders, a round belly. There was a tattoo on his bicep, only partially visible, something military; she could see the claws of an eagle. He was a vet. The right age, build.

"There's a swimming hole around the bend of the river," he said, pointing downstream, where the river made a hard right into the woods. "Just an eddy about three feet deep, but it's got a rope swing. You like to swim?"

"Are you like one of those chefs who won't leave the customers alone?" she asked, meaning it lightly, but her voice sounded barbed.

"Guess I am," he said, and stood. "See you around campus."

As he walked away, the bottle broke against Josie's face, but it was not a big deal. It was just a bottle across the face.

* * *

All day Josie allowed her children to wander near the wedding party, eating outside within sight of the preparations, and then playing in the river with the other kids, all of them with one eye on the men and women in black and white rushing back and forth between trucks and vans and the building.

"Go see what state they're from," Josie said to Paul.

Paul smiled and ran. "Alaska," he said when he returned. "Are they really getting married today?" he asked, and when Josie said it seemed so, he asked where the groom and bride were, and Josie was not quite sure. All the men were dressed the same, but there was one young man who seemed slightly less joyful than the rest, moving slower, weighted with the trouble of his responsibilities, and she assumed this was the groom.

"Let's take a bet who the groom is," she said to Paul, and he asked if he could get a piece of paper to catalog the possibilities. He flew up to the Chateau and returned with the Yahtzee pad, which he turned over and began writing down differentiating details for each of the men. *Tall skinny red hair,* he wrote. *Shorter brown hair beard,* he wrote. *Glasses and limping,* he wrote.

At about two, a new car arrived and parked behind Jim's office, close to the Chateau. The bride, Josie assumed. She watched as three women rushed from the car into the office, an older woman holding the white dress over her head. Soon a stream of new cars appeared in a cloud of dust. A bald and portly man emerged from one of them, wearing a tuxedo, the first man yet to seem comfortable in it.

"The father of the bride," Josie said, and sent Paul to listen in on any conversations nearby, to confirm her suspicions.

He returned ten minutes later with no hard facts.

"Must be happening soon," Josie noted aloud, thinking at least one of her children could hear her. But neither was within earshot.

Young people in sportcoats, and blue suits, and black suits, one white suit, all the women in very short dresses and very high heels, emerged from their vehicles and stepped through the gravel to the staging house. For an hour there was no movement, no sound. They were getting married, and Josie couldn't hear a thing.

At dinnertime, she retrieved a few plates from the shower, and they ate inside the Chateau, a frozen pizza and greying vegetables, and as the sky bled orange the kids heard the laughter of other kids.

"Can we go see?" Ana asked.

Josie saw no reason why not, outside of her wanting them to stay with her, inside, watching a movie while their heads rested on her chest. She wanted them near her, and wanted to drink white wine while half-watching an animated movie. She was ready to let this day peacefully burn to embers, but they wanted to extend it.

"Sure," she said. She could not keep her children from whatever happiness was outside.

Paul helped Ana get her shoes on, and while she watched

Paul tie her laces, she looked back at Josie, and said, "I have diseases!" Paul finished one shoe and began the second. Ana was casual about it, as if getting her nails done, talking to a friend in the next chair. "Do you know how to spell diseases?" she asked, then answered her own question. "D-Z-Z-Z. Diseases."

"I don't think so," Josie said.

Ana took Josie's face in her hands and said, "Josie, I have *diseases*."

Paul finished with her shoes, stood, and the two of them opened the door, Josie following them. Paul and Ana looked around, not immediately seeing the other children, but finally seeing the tribe not far off. The kids had made an impromptu seesaw using a wide plank sitting atop a balance beam. The alpha boy was standing in the center of it all, his arms crossed in triumph.

Josie sat in the doorway of the Chateau, watching as Paul walked toward the tribe, Ana following. Suddenly Ana turned back to Josie.

"You forget something?" Josie said.

"Yes," Ana said, and took Josie's face in her hands. Josie laughed, and kissed Ana on the nose.

"No," Ana said, and repositioned her hands to get a better grip on Josie's face. This time Ana came in for a more romantic kiss. It was all there: the closed eyes, the puckered lips, and Josie let her daughter go for it. She kept her eyes open, wanting to see what Ana would do, but after a moment of lips-to-lips, Ana seemed satisfied, and withdrew with great solemnity. Then she wiped her mouth with the back of her arm, said, "See ya."

Night came on, and Paul and Ana returned, sweaty and complaining about falling off the teeter-totter. They were settling in for the night when a thumping reshaped the air. Josie assumed it was from a car passing over the road, but the pounding only grew louder.

"The wedding," Paul said.

Josie went outside to see if this really could be music, and not some kind of military assault. She walked to the meeting house, where the lights were bright inside, and saw the silhouettes of a hundred people crammed tight and moving in sudden diagonals. Paul and Ana followed her, unbidden.

"The reception," Josie said, and explained the idea to them, that the ceremony and dinner had happened quietly and now there was this, so loud, and it would go late. She thought about leaving the park. She thought about what she could stuff in her ears to muffle the sound. But there would be the thumping—in the ground, in the air. They would not sleep.

"We should stay here," Paul said, and stood, squinting at the meeting house, as if they'd bought tickets to some outdoor concert and had found just the right spot. Josie sat down and brought Ana into her lap. From their vantage they could see the festivities through the large window, the guests passing across its bright picture-screen like actors in a party scene. The bride had bright blond hair and arms covered in tattoos. The groom was very tall and bearded, and seemed to be crying, laughing, lifting one guest after another off the ground and spinning them around. The music bled one song into the next, and the heads kept bobbing, and Josie pushed her chin into the furry mass of Ana's hair as Ana drew ovals on Josie's arm.

It was not novel for Josie to be apart and stare. As a teen, during the worst years of Candyland, she'd been through a very long few years of aloneness, a brutal and wonderful and terrible time of luxuriating in her tortured mind, her suddenly heavy thighs, her growing nose, the rumors about her parents, the word Rosemont on everyone's tongues, always implicating her parents, her feeling of being horrified at being alone on weekend nights but not wanting to be among people, either. She railed against the injustice of her always being alone, but she loved being alone. As some sort of compromise, she'd taken to long walks at night, and that led her into the woods behind homes all over town, and when she walked behind these homes, keeping herself deep in the trees, often there were bright lights, and the people inside were illuminated as well as aquarium fish.

So on these long walks she would often sit and watch the families sit, or cook, or undress, and she found it reassuring and necessary. At a time when she doubted her place, doubted she was doing anything right, doubted her skin was really hers, doubted that she walked correctly or dressed correctly and at a time when she covered her mouth any time it was open, watching the quiet tedium of everyone else's lives gave her renewed confidence. Her family was considered strange and unholy, a twisted family awash in VA drugs, but these other families were no better. All were deeply boring and sedentary. They barely moved. She would sit in the patchy woods, watching a house for an hour and scarcely see anyone move from room to room. She watched classmates and they were dull. She watched a classmate's mother walk around in a bra, watched another classmate, a burly athlete, shockingly kind to all at school, come home and imme- diately get thrown across the room by his father. She saw certain things, scenes of violence loud and simmering. Being deep in the surrounding woods, she was never close enough to hear a word. And so in those dark woods, in the blue light of these sad homes, she realized she was no less normal than any of these sorry souls.

"I'm tired," Josie said, and by that she meant she was tired of being apart from the world. They had been alone and on the road for many days, and those days had seemed like weeks, weeks where she had only her children to talk to, and there was nowhere they knew to be home, and now they were watching again, or Josie was watching again, people who belonged in the world, who were rooted and reveling in their place, who were dancing triumphantly inside. It was never good to think about Carl, his then-disdain for weddings. She didn't want to be with Carl. What if they'd been married? Good god.

But a wedding would have been nice. She'd never had everyone in one place, the people she loved. Could you have a wedding like this at forty, forty-one? A raucous thing like this, the women barefoot in their tight dresses, dancing naughtily? You could, she could. Or perhaps she had made too many mistakes. Two children from one eel-like man, a fractured past, no family. Was she a drifter? Josie had a heavy warm child in her lap, Ana's red hair smelling like lemons, and she had another child standing next to her, above her, leaning against her, and he was a noble human and always would be. And yet her life was that of a drifter. Where are you from? *Here and there.* Where are your parents? *Doesn't matter.* Why aren't your kids in school? *We're doing an independent study.* Where are you going?

And then a door opened in the meeting house, a bright white sliver that enlarged into a yellow rectangle. Light poured out from the building, and down the lawn all the way to Josie and Paul and Ana, caught in the light. A man was in the door, and seemed to be relieving himself. It couldn't be. There had to be bathrooms in the building. But no. He stood, one hand on the wall of the building, the other holding his fly open, a man pissing dramatically, and even from their distance, Josie could hear the spatter of urine against the clapboard wall. When he was finished, he turned, as if to take in the night air and bask in good work well done, but he seemed to freeze, as if he'd seen Josie and her children and was appalled by them.

And now he was walking toward her. Shame came over

her at once. She knew he would scold her for sitting there and watching their sacred event. It had been a vulgar thing to do, to just sit there like it was all some show for their amusement. She would tell him she was nearsighted and couldn't possibly see that far. That she was blind and was just listening to the music.

Now the father of the groom was upon her.

"You and your beautiful children have to join us," he said.

He was standing over her, his face round and kindly and bright with drink and sweat. His hand was outstretched as if asking her to dance.

"No, no," she said, and suddenly she couldn't breathe.

"Oh no," he said, "I didn't mean to make you cry."

Josie apologized. "No, no. It's very nice of you." Why was she crying? Her face was soaked and she was choking. "No. I didn't mean to," she managed to say, but couldn't complete the thought.

But he understood. He understood that she'd spent the day wondering why she hadn't had happiness like this, Jesus Christ why had she made all the wrong decisions, these stupid teenagers getting married knew how to have a beautiful and humble wedding by this Alaskan river, goddamnit, why did she make it all so difficult when it could be so simple? And now the father of the groom was taking her hand and leading her to the lights of the party. She choked desperately on her tears but the father only held her hand tighter. She turned around and took Paul's hand and he took Ana's hand

and like a string of construction paper people they walked to the white tables and the lights and music and when they arrived Josie was still crying, and expected to be deposited at some far table and given cake.

But the father pulled her and her children deep into the dance floor, and they were suddenly in the wild heart of it all, with the groom and bride making their fluid thrashing movements, everyone jumping and no one questioning for a second why Josie was there. And now Ana was on the groom's shoulders. But how? And now a bridesmaid had lifted Paul to her level and was dancing with him, cheek to cheek. Everyone was turning, turning, and somehow Josie managed to dance, too, finding the rhythm and drying her face and smiling as much as she could, to tell everyone she was okay and knew how to dance, too.

The band played until two, and when the band left, the guests retrieved instruments from car trunks and drunken music was made until four. Josie couldn't recall when she'd gone to bed. The kids were asleep on their feet at midnight, and she carried Ana to bed at one, the red-haired groomsman carrying Paul, and for some time Josie lay, trying to sleep in the Chateau, so close to the campfire laughter, and finally she returned to the party, was welcomed to the fire, and one by one the guests passed out as the best man, knowing his duty, kept the fire fed.

XV.

WHEN SHE WOKE AGAIN and ventured outside, the park
was bright and empty. The guest cars parked near the over-
pass were gone. The vans and trucks were gone. The flowers
were gone, the tent was gone. It was just before noon. The
right thing would be to leave. Josie knew this. The park
was desolate without the wedding guests, and Josie had
already stayed too long. More than a few days in any place
was unwise. She knew they should go. But instead of leaving
she went to the office and told Jim she was staying another
night, and asked if he'd like to eat lunch with them.

"I just had lunch," he said.

"Dinner," she said.

"How about I make you some salmon?" he said. "My
brother sent me a bunch from Nome and I need to eat it. It
won't keep much longer in the fridge."

The kids played in the river with a new group of kids
who had arrived that afternoon, and at six they walked
to Jim's cabin, a hundred yards or so through a birch for-

est, and found him at the grill, wearing ironed jeans and a peach-colored polo shirt.

"Made you a mojito," he said, and handed her a glass of cut-crystal. She took a sip. It was cold and far too strong.

"Got a head start," he said, indicating his own empty glass, and poured himself a second.

Josie stared at him, imagining what he would have looked like as a young man. He looked like he'd gotten everything he wanted.

"Grenada," he said.

"Okay," Josie said. Nothing surprised her anymore— certainly not a man suddenly saying "Grenada" while holding a spatula.

"I saw you inspecting the ink," he said, and pointed to his arm, the military tattoo. He raised his sleeve, to reveal the words obscured before: Operation Urgent Fury. Josie had never heard this moniker. These words, Urgent and Fury, applied to Grenada seemed a wonderful joke.

"It's just a joke now," he said, and Josie relaxed. She was relieved, first of all, that he was not a Vietnam vet, and that they wouldn't have to talk about that, or about her parents, or Candyland, and she was so grateful that though he'd been part of the invasion of a country the size of the Mall of America, and though he felt, or had felt, some pride in this (the tattoo), he didn't take it too seriously. In an instant Josie pictured a show, *Grenada!* No. It would be called *Grenada?* A dozen soldiers would parachute onto the stage, and ask themselves where they were. "Grenada," one would say.

Another would ask, "Grenada?" This would go on throughout the show. People would die, helicopters would crash, medical students would ostensibly be rescued, a petty dictator would be overthrown, and all the while the U.S. soldiers would keep forgetting where they were. One would knock down the door of a local home, pointing his gun at a family of five. "Where are we?" he would demand. "Grenada," they would say, their hands in the air, a baby wailing. "*Grenada?*" the soldier would say, mugging for the audience. You could call it a comedy.

"Don't judge," Jim said. "Grenada made Kuwait possible."

Now Josie was confused. What in the hell was he talking about?

"You don't remember the national mood in the seventies and early eighties, do you?" he asked. Josie was a child during much of that time, and had not been paying attention to the national mood, no.

She needed to change the subject. If they went down this road, soon enough they would arrive at her mother and father, Candyland, Jeremy—Jeremy had already stepped into her consciousness and darkened the gauzy happiness of the day.

"You have a wonderful awkwardness," Jim said, and for a moment Josie thought the evening was being ground to dust, first by his nonsense about Kuwait and now this, an oblique insult. "You're beautiful, but you wear it so lightly. This," and here he touched the small of her back with an open hand, heavy and warm, "this is where the self-satisfied women, the uppity ones, lose their appeal." Somehow he had known to change the subject, and had effortlessly chosen a very chaste and very erotic place to put his hand. He was so confident, her sense of time shifted, broke down. Hadn't they just started talking? Now his hand was firmly on her back; they were ready to dance. "The other women, they're stiff here," he continued, his voice lower now, a rumble, "they carry all their tension and outrage and impatience right here. It's a catastrophe. But you, the way you bend, the way you shift hip to hip, it's fluid, it's just a breeze through long grass."

Shit, Josie thought. Shit shit. To be described is to be seduced. Shit. One turn of phrase. One thing noticed that she'd never noticed. It worked always. Hilariously, though, Carl had no idea. The one original thing, the one time he'd noticed something about her that she could remember—would not forget—he'd said while watching TV one night, a crime show. The detectives had shown up at the coroner's office, and he'd pulled open a cold steel drawer to reveal the corpse of a young woman. "That looks just like you!" Carl had said, leaning forward on the couch, and Josie had thought, *Will this harmless man kill me?* "He seems harmless," his mother, Luisa, once said to Josie, "but he has a terrible resolve." What did that mean? Josie thought of that often: *He has a terrible resolve.* That and the comparison to the corpse: It made their last year together somewhat less carefree.

Now, though, there was this man, with his Grenada tattoo, his POW/MIA flag, and he was so gentle. She knew a mistake with this man was inevitable. The only hope was to contain the damage somehow, release the lust, complete the seduction without too much mess.

After dinner, Jim brought a set of markers and a stack of printer paper from his cabin, and Josie assumed he planned to suggest the kids occupy themselves this way while he made a move on her. But instead he sat down and asked Ana what her favorite animal was.

Josie knew Ana's answer changed depending on the day and what show she'd last seen, so was curious to hear the answer.

"Winnie the Pooh," Ana said, and Jim repeated the word as Ana had said it, "Windy da Pooh," imitating her but somehow in a respectful way that seemed to confirm to Ana that her pronunciation was correct.

He cracked his knuckles theatrically and began to draw. Quickly the kids realized he knew what he was doing, he could draw, and they floated closer to him, one on either side, rapt. Ana soon had her hand on his arm, again demonstrating her belief in the transference of magic. It was a heartwarming scene until Josie came around to see the progress of Jim's drawing and found an anatomically correct elephant, standing upright like a human, and holding a beer, a flaccid penis pointing to the earth between its legs.

"You guys run to the vending machines for a second," Josie said, giving them a dollar each—only the second time in their lives they had held a dollar of their own. The kids ran through the birch woods and Jim sighed and sat back in his chair.

"Elephants have penises," he said in his defense. "Paul has one. Have you seen a whale's?"

"Your elephant even has pubic hair, you jackass," Josie said.

"It was *flaccid*." Jim grinned at her, thinking she was kidding.

She took the picture and crumpled it. "No more penises," she said.

The children returned from the store, Jim drew for them again, everyone having a blast. For half an hour he drew whatever they asked, and they colored his pictures—but why did Ana grunt while coloring?—and then laid them out on the grass around his house, holding them down with stones. The evening had arrived at a place of perfect serenity, and Josie and her children, and this stranger named Jim, were a perfectly functioning little family. Jim couldn't have been happier. He was not the least bit bored.

Ana put a blank piece of paper before him. "Can you do a giant, but a nice giant?" she asked.

Jim threw himself into that one, moving his mouth as he drew. Josie watched him, and a truth revealed itself to her: Older men are not confused. They aren't going in seven directions. A retired man knows what he doesn't want—and to those of us who have been ground into dust once or twice or more, and have somehow found a way to carry on, knowing what you don't want was far more important than knowing what you did want. Maybe a retired man is the real prize. An older man like this (or Sam's Leonard Cohen!) no longer worried about money; his ambitions had been satisfied or ignored, and he could now afford to draw pictures for children for hours at a time, had nowhere else to be, could take his time.

"Who wants to play air hockey?" he asked. Josie didn't want to play air hockey, or watch anyone play air hockey, but her children had jumped and danced at the idea, so off they went. They walked back through the birch forest and to the office. Jim plugged in the air-hockey table and turned to Josie.

"Why don't you go somewhere?" he said. "They're fine here."

"Go where?"

"Didn't you ask about the bikes the other day? Take a bike. Any one you see in the shed."

Josie dismissed the idea, because she had expected this air-hockey idea to be a ruse to get her alone in the back office—she'd glimpsed a couch there, and pictured herself sloppily on it—but Jim was soon playing with her children, and barely giving her a thought. So Josie found herself considering the bike ride, then wanting it, then calculated the probability that riding the bike in her drunken state would end in her crashing and drowning in the river. But then she thought of the Mennonites, and their bicycle joy, and wondered what lay on the other side of the underpass that had made them so happy.

"You kids keep going and I'll come back to keep score," Jim said, and led Josie to the shed, where a motley array of bicycles stood entangled. He was behind her, and she could smell his fermented male smell, and for the third time that afternoon she assumed he would take her, press himself into her.

"Try this one," he said, and pulled from the chrome thicket a blue women's bicycle with a wide white seat. He checked the tires and found them functional.

"Whose is it?" she asked.

"Someone's. I don't know. They might have left it. Or else it's someone's who works here. I don't know. It's yours."

By drawing vaguely in the dirt, Jim mapped the bike path as it ran along the river, across a wooden bridge, through what used to be a lumber forest and then back, along the river's far shore and across another crossing, this one a pedestrian footbridge made of steel.

She held the bicycle, and threw her leg around it, feeling the sensation that it was crooked. The handlebars were pointed decidedly leftward. She did not think it was a good idea to ride this bicycle. Her children were with a stranger and it was getting dark, and she was tipsy, and she had two or three miles to ride on a bicycle with handlebars that pointed due left.

"See you in an hour or so," Jim said, and turned himself

toward her children, whose silhouettes she could make out, through the window, hunched over the air-hockey table, pushing some hovering disc at each other with great urgency. They were fine. And so she pushed off, and immediately ran into the side of the bicycle shed.

"You got it?" Jim yelled from some invisible place in the woods.

"I'm good," she said, and decided she needed to prove she was good, so rode across the parking lot, adjusting her sense of direction and equilibrium to the handlebars, which were tilted down, too.

She looked up at the path, wanting to move forward, believing she could move forward, but the machine under her was mangled and had other plans. It defied logic that she could make this work after a potent mojito, but after a hundred yards she was riding more or less straight. Then again, she passed an older woman who stared at her, aghast, as she passed. To see oneself in another's eyes is no gift. It's always a shock, always a disappointment to see their own shock and disappointment. You look so old. You look so tired. What are you doing to your children? Why are you riding a crooked bike drunkenly on this lovely path? How is this the right use of your time, your humanity? Have we wasted precious space dust on you?

But soon the riding was comfortable enough and the landscape was drifting by, and because the sun was setting, setting so late, it occurred to her all at once that she'd never been more connected to the land, and nothing around her had ever seemed more alive and glowing and beautiful. The purple wildflowers, the grey dirt, the smell of the pine needles cooling. The tall tree halved by lightning. The waning sun on the hills in the distance, bright blue and white. Whose bike was she riding, anyway? A log-hewn fence. The wail of a faraway truck slowing. The monotony of an unburned forest on the sun-drenched hillside. Why did she have to be tipsy before she could notice anything? A rabbit! A rabbit was just down the slope from the path, small, tawny, and staying longer than expected, looking at her with absolute recognition of her humanity, of her equal right to this land so long as she remained humble. After it evaporated loudly into the thicket, there was the metallic hum of crickets. The butterlight of some cabin in the nearby woods. The heat of the pavement below her, the faint smell of tar where someone had sutured its tendril cracks. The click of her gears, the awed hush of the highway beyond the trees, the pointless drama of all of its rushing travelers. "You know what time it is?" asked a voice.

Josie looked around, the landscape spinning in green and ocher, and saw a man on a parallel road. He was on a bike, too, standing, straddling his, outfitted in an explosion of colorful gear. After he asked the question, he took a sip of water from a tidy black water bottle. All of this, he believed, made him both virile and monumental: the bike, the gear, the straddling of the bike, the sipping of water right after asking a stupid question.

"Eight thirty," Josie said, because she knew it was probably true.

"Thanks," the man said, but in a way that implied he was a paying guest and she was some kind of bike-path clock keeper—that she worked on the path and was in charge of time. She thought of the bicycle man in her town, the one responsible for the maiming, the furious and florid sense of themselves these men felt. *I am wearing these clothes and have gone fast. Move from my path. Fix my teeth. Tell me the time.*

"Fuck you, you motherfucking asshole," she said, not loud enough for him to hear, loathing all of humanity, and then continued on, in seconds happy again, again connected to the land, feeling everything gorgeous around her, hoping the lightning tree would fall on that man and improve the world by the subtraction of one.

She turned around a bend in the path and saw a stream, and then a pond, an empty bench facing the water, and she thought of old people, and dead people, and dirty pigeons, and then dirty landscapers, dirty housepainters. A fox! Was it a fox there, ahead of her, near the pond, staring at her? It could be a coyote. Christ, she thought, it was beautiful, with its rich coat, its luxurious grey coat, its eyes like Paul's, Paul's eyes always looking old, as if seeing her from a different wiser, sadder epoch.

Like the rabbit, the fox lingered far longer than she thought plausible before jogging away, into the high grass. This was dusk, when all the animals appeared. Dusk was all that mattered. Midday was nothing, nothing. Midday was for humans, for the drones of mankind, who bustle about in the heat of day like imbeciles, while the animals always waited till the cooling of the earth, waited till the light was low and the air cooling, till they appeared to do their business.

The sun wouldn't set for another half-hour and now, as she passed between two hills, one in violet shadow and the other dirty blond with sunset light, she realized this was the time when she and everyone should be out, should see these things, share the world with the foxes and voles and moles and rabbits. The light as it passed through the cotton of the willows! The light as it haloed the trees and grass and weeds! But she was usually not out at this time. Usually she was feeding her children, putting them to bed, all of these prosaic activities that kept her from the beauty of the world. Our children keep us from beauty, she thought, then corrected herself. Our children are beautiful, too, but we must find a way to combine these things, so we're not missing one for the other. Could it be so hard?

Ahead she saw a gentle decline from the path to the riverside and decided she would sit there and put her feet in the water. She found a large stone that resembled a pillow and she set her head on it, extending her feet to the river and found that her toes touched the cold water. She closed her eyes to the sun and yawned a happy yawn and woke up when? The light was the same. She'd only dozed. She looked around her, expecting cobwebs to tell her she'd slept a hundred years, her children were now grandparents, all was different, but instead she saw a small snake appear from between the rocks at the water's edge, a water snake of some kind, and without taking any notice of her, come out and inspect a snail making its wet way across the slick rock. With a snap of its head the snake swallowed it, and then retreated back into the dark water.

Josie stood and felt the uncertain earth beneath her feet. She steadied the land and thought again about staying, at least until she sobered. No, she thought, it will be good this way, to bike home this way—she had the powerful thought that this was the way it was meant to be, that it was all so beautiful she could hardly bear it. She took a long last look at the river, moving like a thousand silver knives. The rocks on the far shore, cooling in the shadows. She turned and climbed up to the bridge.

Getting on the bike was a kind of seven-dimensional chess. Was she drunker now than before? The river and the sun had inebriated her. The bike seemed a foot taller now than when she'd ridden it hours ago. She hoisted herself onto the seat, pushed off, and immediately careened into the shrubbery to her left. Okay, she thought. Okay. She squinted into the sun and mounted the bike again and this time shoved herself forward with enough velocity that she was propelled more or less straight.

The air was cooler now, and she hoped it would sober her. Her eyes watered as she rode, sideways, her mouth open. But she regained her balance, and said these words to herself:

Great night. Good evening. The greatest night. The beauty of this
nowhere world. I love this. Where are my children? Can I love this
without them? I can and I do. This is my best life. Among this
beauty, on my way to them.

Soon she saw the rooftops of the RV park. Now she saw
the first trailers and trucks, and passed a child on a scooter.
Now the path connected with the dirt road that connected
to the gravel road that connected to the paved road and now
she saw the underpass, and it felt so good to follow in the
Mennonites' footsteps, grinning while careening under it,
knowing she would see her children now, would reclaim
them from Jim, and she would kiss Jim in some way. Innocent, simple, maybe a long and tight embrace and later
she could pleasure herself in the passenger seat. But what
about Jim? Here she was, able to be at liberty at dusk, on
this wayward bike, to enjoy the beauty of the world, alone,
because of Jim. This was the boon of a second parent—he
could provide these moments alone, the temporary clarity of vision to see this golden light and see these gorgeous
mammals, to see the play of shadows on the hills. She
had the thought that she could stay. Her children loved it
here, and Jim was so calm, and they could live in his log
cabin, and she could become an innkeeper's wife. She had
never had a partner, never a real partner, in her parenting,
Carl being a child himself. What if she had an actual man
nearby, who could catch and gut and grill fish, and could
draw well-endowed elephants but could be dissuaded from
that in the future? But that would mean living here, and

with Jim, who she did not think she could love, who had an Urgent Fury tattoo on his arm and who knew what else on his chest and shoulders—he could have some kind of battleship, a squadron of bombers. What to do with a life? One second she believed fervently that it was enough to be with her children, the next moment they bored her to tears and were an impediment to all her dreams. Goddamn them, her terrible robber children, robbing her of so much, giving her everything and robbing her of everything else, her gorgeous perfect thieving children damn them, bless them, she couldn't wait to lie down with them, holding her old cold hands against their hot smooth faces.

She dropped the bike messily in the shed and walked to the office, where she found a unnamed clerk but not Jim, and no sign of her children. "He took them back to your RV," the clerk said. At the Chateau she expected them to be outside, watching him draw or whatever other outdoor activity he might conjure, but no one was outside, and the door was closed, and rushing to the Chateau Josie paused. Had this man put her children to bed or was he doing something terrible in there? She listened and heard a man's booming voice talking about giant poos.

She stepped up and found Paul and Ana up in their bed over the cab, and Jim sitting in the dinette, reading from a paperback Captain Underpants book. He had brought it himself.

"Again," Ana said to Jim, and then to Josie: "Jim's gonna do it again."

Jim then read a passage about a villain accidentally turning himself into a forty-foot-tall walking and talking feces log. After this passage Jim turned the book to show Josie the picture, revealing that the giant feces-man was wearing a cowboy hat. The kids were giggling wildly, delighted that this older man had validated and honored this story with his theatrical reading. Finally he closed the book with slow gravitas, as if he'd just wrapped up some long and distinguished volume, and placed it on the kitchen counter.

"Night, guys," Jim said to the children, and stepped down from the RV.

Josie climbed up and kissed her children's foreheads as they dangled over the ledge, and then stepped down from the Chateau and returned to Jim.

XVI.

IN THE RELENTLESS MORNING SUN Josie drove,
exhausted and angry and tired of watching the bottle break
across her face, but knowing she deserved it. What kind
of person takes it from behind in a trailer park, with her
children sleeping mere feet away? From a retired man named
Jim, veteran of Operation Urgent Fury? In her visions, the
bottle sometimes broke against her head, but today, first,
it just bounced off with a loud low ring, like a gong. Four,
five times it would strike her head, making the sound of
the gong before finally breaking and spraying her face with
glass.

What had she done?

After kissing her children good night she had stepped
outside and all was right, all was appropriate. This older man
who had babysat her children masterfully, who had allowed
her the glorious ride through the forest at dusk, was sitting
in one of Stan's chairs, and she took the other, and she told
him what she'd seen. She told him about the fox, and the

rabbit, and the light on the hills, and Jim took pleasure in this, and feeling her mojito glow fading, Josie told Jim she'd fix them up, and stepped up into the Chateau, happy to find her children already asleep. She could only see Ana's face but could hear Paul's steady breathing.

She found a bottle of chardonnay, three-quarters full, and went to the bathroom to retrieve two glasses from the shower floor. The wine was warm, so she found ice in the freezer and was pouring generously for herself and Jim when she felt his presence behind her. The sound of the ice rattling in the glasses had allowed him to sneak up behind her unnoticed and now his breath was hot on her neck, his hands on her hips, and then, very much like an animal would do, he began to rub his hardness against Josie's waist.

"Let's take this off," he said, and removed Josie's STRAIGHT ARROW visor and began kissing her neck. Had he seen the bald square on her head yet? Whatever was happening here, whatever wholly wrong physical nonsense, would end when he saw the stitches' crooked smile on her skull.

"Hm," he murmured, touching it briefly, then sweeping his hand back through her hair and down to her chest. That was all the interest he had in the wound. He didn't care. He returned to his grinding and the systematic kissing of every exposed part of her neck.

There are appropriate people, she thought, as she drove away from Jim. So many appropriate people, who know how to act with dignity. Think of the wedding party! she thought. Think of the father of the groom, with his generous, forgiving eyes and outstretched hands. Think of the groom carrying Ana around. The red-haired groomsman who brought Paul to bed. These were decent people who knew how to behave. There were no people at that wedding allowing an older man to rub his hard penis against their waists inside the Chateau. They knew the limits of propriety. They knew what separated humans from beasts.

But not Josie. Josie, at that moment, thought it was wonderful. Wonderful that this strange man, in his late fifties, was rubbing his hard penis against her, in the Chateau, in Bumblefuck, Alaska. She found it wonderfully spontaneous and alluring, and even had a momentary conflation, imagining it was burly Smokey the Bear, not Jim, behind her. His stove-pipe arms, his barrel chest. She thought of an elephant, too, an elephant with a man-sized penis. No, this is Jim, she noted. Grenada Jim, who you don't know. Meanwhile her children were sleeping sweatily above. Ana's sleeping face was visible! Paul's was not. Then Jim, the retired man who ran the RV park, was kissing Josie's neck, and Josie was wet, and he did some masterful things, maneuvers that showed he had learned things in his many years, had retained some knowledge and could act on it. His arm had come around her, and was resting against her chest, like a bolt laid across a door. Her pants dropped silently to the floor, far quicker than she might have been able to get them off herself. His hand was on her stomach, then two long fingers plunged in and up. She had certain thoughts: that she wanted him inside her, and also—this was important—that she believed, given his roaring arousal and heavy breathing, that whatever was about to happen would not take long.

This was Carl's fault. If that were Carl roaring in from behind, so aroused and breathing heavily, it would be over in seconds, while they were there standing up. Josie had come to expect this kind of blitzkrieg from Carl, and it was frankly perfectly fine, to stand up at the kitchen sink, Carl in heat, Josie knowing he would be finished before she turned around.

But Jim was more practiced, more controlled. Ninety seconds passed, then a few minutes, everything slow, steady, thickly filling, and she knew they needed a plan. She pulled up her pants and led him outside, and came up with an idea—at the time thought it a fantastic idea—to sit him down on the picnic bench, an arm's length from the Chateau and her sleeping children, and then to sit on him. With the last minutes of sun pouring through the woods, her mind was lost utterly, she was a being of pure light and radiating warmth, and somewhere in the sun Paul asked what they were doing.

"What are you doing?" he said in his even wolf-boy voice. He was outside. He was standing at the door of the Chateau, with a clear view of his mother, who was naked from the waist down, sitting on Jim.

Paul knew what they were doing. From a young age, he had sought out anatomical and reproductive knowledge, asking about Josie's parts, and his parts, and asking Carl about his parts, about the purpose of each, why Carl's were bigger than his, why all the hair. So he knew the mechanics just as much as he knew the basics of flight and the internal combustion engine, and when Paul asked what they were doing, he meant not "Mommy, were you exercising on top of that man?" but "Why is my mother screwing this man six feet away from her sleeping children?" He knew what he was seeing.

But she couldn't get up, not like that—Paul would have really gotten an eyeful. So she said, "Go inside for a second," and he obeyed, and when she could see his back turned inside the Chateau she jumped off Jim, hustled to the woods and dressed herself. When she returned to Jim, he was clothed, too, and was smiling, holding out another mojito. Again he was so unlike a younger man, a man like Carl. What had happened with Paul didn't seem to matter much; he conveyed that it would pass, that the best thing to do would be to continue outside, more or less in their same positions, sit and talk, close but not on top of each other now. Perhaps Paul's memory of what he saw could be muddled, replaced.

Josie's nerves were shot, so she drank her mojito, Jim repoured, and soon she was sloppy again, far less coherent than she'd been when swerving the crooked bicycle through the forest, and she found herself telling Jim about Jeremy, because in the heat of her loins and mess of her mind she thought Jim would be the very best person to share Jeremy with—there'd never been a better person, her addled brain told her. "I thought it was the right thing," she said, "I

wanted him to honor our country," she said, sounding
unlike herself but thinking it would endear her to Jim and
his tattoo.

"He died last year?" he asked.

She nodded, sipping her drink, feeling very dramatic.

"In Afghanistan?" he asked.

Again she pumped her head up and down, yes.

"We ended combat operations in Afghanistan on January 9, 2013," Jim said, and followed up with a litany of
numbers and dates, using words like "draw down" and
"post-occupation" but mostly using the word "exit" until
Josie doubted herself. It was likely the mojito, but could it
be that Jeremy hadn't died in combat? Her image was of
him shot, bleeding on a hillside, but now Jim, a veteran,
was saying this was impossible. Had Jeremy actually been in
Iraq, not Afghanistan? (Jim was insisting this was probably
the case, that Josie was mistaken, and couldn't it have been
more like 2009, he wanted to know.) But then she remembered where Jeremy had been killed, Herat province, and the
date, February 20, 2013. Jesus fucking Christ of course he'd
died in Afghanistan. "I'm right," she said, she slurred.

Jim rolled his eyes and poured himself another drink.
They argued this way for the better part of an hour, as
the night darkened around them, neither of them ceding
ground, neither of them sure whether or not their country
was still at war in Afghanistan. There were moments when
Jim seemed almost wavering, almost believing that Josie

could be right, that perhaps there were some combat troops still in the country . . . But then he dug in, disbelieving.

And so in the morning she'd left Jim's RV park and watched the bottle break against her face, and mile after mile as she drove away, she thought how interesting, humorous even, someone from that part of the world might find it, that an American man who had fought in a conflict no one remembered didn't know that his country was still fighting a different, larger war, still, had been since 2001. How funny! Coast to coast, most Americans would not be sure that war was still on, that we were still there, that men and women like Jeremy were still fighting and dying, that Afghans were still fighting and dying, too. Wouldn't an Afghan, and countless future generations, find that very funny in some way?

XVII.

WHAT CAN WE DO to erase a terrible sight from the minds of our children? We can show them other things, brighter things. It so happened that ten miles from the site of Josie-on-Jim, they came across what appeared, from a distance, to be the Batmobile.

"Look," Josie said, wanting to point it out to Ana especially, but knowing if she wasn't right there would be trouble. So she waited until they got closer, careening along the highway toward it, and when they arrived, and she was sure that some lunatic had placed an actual full-size Batmobile approximation on the side of the road, in a parking lot attached to a fireworks outlet, with the sole purpose of luring in people like herself and her children, she finally told them.

"Do you see what I see?" In the wake of what she'd allowed Paul to witness the day before, this sounded more lewd than intended. She amended quickly: "Ana, you see a certain vehicle outside?"

When she did see it, there was pandemonium, and they

stopped, and Ana jumped out of the Chateau and ran to it, running her hands across it. Its rough surface appeared to have been painted with black housepaint.

"Dis isn't da real one," Ana said, but she seemed to want to be disproved.

"It's *one of* the real ones," Paul said. "It's a backup car. The main one is still in Batman's cave."

This satisfied Ana's sense of balance, because surely Batman would have backup cars, and it was logical that he would keep at least one in an Alaskan parking lot, so she took to the car anew, her eyes allowing all the vehicle's glaring discrepancies and anomalies, including the fact that it had no interior gauges, lights or even a stick shift. It did have a steering wheel, and Ana was reaching for it, looking back at Josie, waiting to be told *no*.

But while Ana had been inspecting the car, and Paul had been explaining away all its flaws, Josie had noticed that the fireworks outlet, the one using the Batman car as bait, was closed, boarded up hastily. Of course it would be closed, during a summer of wildfires, a few of them no doubt blamed on bottle rockets and M-80s.

"You can get in," Josie said to Paul and Ana, feeling hopeful that this would eclipse forever the image of her grinding atop the RV park proprietor who drew elephant penises.

Paul climbed over the door (welded shut), and Josie lifted Ana in. They sat side by side, Paul in the driver's seat. Ana looked to her brother as if fervently believing that because he was sitting in Batman's seat, he was Batman. Josie watched the two of them, forgetting for a moment how badly she needed this to erase yesterday's indiscretion. *I know what you're doing*, his eyes told her.

There will be other mistakes, she said in return.

Josie took their picture, Ana looking straight through the windshield, as if scanning for evildoers, and Paul looking at Ana. And for the first time Josie felt the crushing tragedy of their aloneness, that they were only three, and had no one else, and were more or less on the lam, and that she had slept with Jim, and had no destination in mind—that they would leave the Batmobile and have nowhere else to go, that this would be the closest thing to purpose they would know today. "Ready?" she asked them. "We should go," she said. But where? Why? They stayed.

When, an hour later, they finished with the Batmobile and were back in the Chateau, slowly pulling away, Ana unbuckled herself and came to Josie and kissed her on the cheek.

"I love you, Mom," she said.

It was the first time Ana had ever said these words unprovoked, and though Josie knew what Ana meant was *I love Batman. I love Batman's car. And I love you for showing me Batman's car*, she was nonetheless moved.

They drove on, their path random, the sights bizarre. There was the strange geodesic dome, once part of a gas station, three stories tall and abandoned. They parked the Chateau behind it and stayed for a few hours, exploring within—they found a half-dead old kickball and played soccer briefly inside, and Ana collected an array of tool fragments and what seemed to be gears. They stopped at a garage sale, where the only other customers were firefighters from Wyoming. Josie bought Paul a book about heraldry and Ana a silver miner's helmet. For herself she bought a guitar with a bullet hole in it. *I couldn't learn, so I got mad*, the seller said.

They saw a moose, and pulled over to watch it lope without destination along the side of the road. But every car that passed their parked vehicle honked angrily, as if stopping for moose was not acceptable, or in bad taste, or endangered the moose in some way—Josie never knew. But she knew that seeing that moose was wildly anticlimactic, in the same way seeing a coyote, so small and weak and like the spawn of a hyena (the hunched back, the servile demeanor) and a housecat (its size, its dull eyes), was anticlimactic. This moose before them, which they were photographing with actuarial thoroughness, was a sorry specimen, thin and clumsy and not much taller than a pony.

It was important to stay off the main roads, but not to draw too much attention on the minor roads. The more they ventured away from the highways the more they saw evidence of the fires, their proximity coming with ample clues. The red and chartreuse trucks would pass her, going the other way, or would flash their lights from behind, in hopes they could go more than forty-eight miles an hour. Then the handmade or digital signs thanking the firefighters. Then the gusts of acrid smoke, the occasional stripe of haze overtaking the sky. ENTERING BURNED AREA. EXPECT FLOODS, said one sign, and Josie looked quickly to Paul, to see if he'd read it. The natural piling-on the sign promised—first fire, then flood—seemed unnecessarily harsh, and she worried about the nightmares a sign like that could provoke in a sensitive eight-year-old. But he was asleep, his mouth agape, Ana trying to balance her ThunderCats doll in his shirt pocket.

They were driving through a land of low hills, some of them charred black, when Josie saw a scrum of fire trucks ahead, creating a roadblock, their lights popping like flashbulbs. She slowed down and stopped before the group, ready to turn around, but when she rolled down her window, a police officer, looking not much older than Paul, approached. He had full, delicate lips.

"You passing through?" he asked.

"I don't have to," Josie said. She didn't know what to say. She had no destination in mind, but telling him that would seem suspicious. "I mean I can take another road—" She almost said "north" but she wasn't entirely sure she was heading north. She might have been going east.

"It's okay," the officer said, his lips pillow-soft, his eyes sleepy and amused. "The road just reopened. You're the first on it, outside of emergency vehicles. It's safe. Just be careful."

Josie thanked him, missing his lips already, his eyes,

thinking his parents must be proud of him, hoping they were. She drove slowly around the six or seven vehicles, and then found herself entirely alone on a wide four-lane road that passed through what had been a great battlefield. The hills on the left side of the road were largely green, untouched, covered with small pines and shrubs and stripes of wildflowers. On the right, though, the land had been rendered bald, leaving the occasional black stripe of a tree trunk, a few wisps of branches extended, the ground everywhere a plush grey.

Along the side of the road, fire vehicles were parked in bunches or alone. Here, a pair of red trucks, four firefighters sitting under a tree eating lunch on the rear bumpers. There, a single chartreuse truck, with a lone firefighter in matching gear walking up the hill, through the plush grey, carrying a shovel.

The road wound through the valley for miles, the scene serene and beautiful and empty. The valley was quiet, the sky was blue, the fire defeated.

Fire vehicles and firefighters appeared occasionally, some driving the opposite way, leaving the valley, but most of them parked on one side of the road or another, all of them acting independently, it seemed. It was, that day at that hour, more like a loose assemblage of firefighting freelancers, each allowed to do whatever they saw fit, than some coordinated, military-style attack. Or maybe it was the looser, cleanup fighting done after victory is assured.

Just then, she came upon a group of six firefighters surrounding a single large pine on fire, three hoses between them, two men on each.

"Look," she told her kids, and she slowed the Chateau.

It looked like some kind of execution. The tree seemed to be alive, defiant, gloriously on fire, wanting to be on fire, while the firefighters were dousing it, killing it.

Then a sound like a quick loud exhalation. The Chateau veered left, then right, then lurched forward.

"What is that?" Paul asked.

Josie pulled over and stopped, but she knew it was a flat. Stan had breezed through the procedure for changing a flat, and she'd seen the spare on the rear of the Chateau a dozen times a day, but now, knowing she would have to actually change it, change a tire on a decomposing vehicle weighing four tons, she briefly lost hope.

"Let's get out," she told her kids, and then the three of them were standing on the roadside, between the hills of green and the hills of grey, under the bright sun, the Chateau tilting rightward.

Ana found a rock and threw it in the direction of the firefighters at war with the burning tree.

"Some other guys," Paul said, and Josie turned to see that coming up behind them was a line of men in orange, ten of them, each of them carrying a shovel over a shoulder.

"Looks like you've got a flat," the lead man said. "Need help?"

He was short and stocky, his face striped in soot. The

group of them crowded around the flat, a few of them kicking the tire, as if that was in some way useful.

"You want us to help?" the stocky man asked.

"Could you?" Josie said, and the group of them began to fan out all over, like some kind of dance team—Josie was suddenly in the middle, and felt as if she should do some freestyle maneuvers while they clapped.

"You got the jack?" another man in orange asked.

Josie tried to remember where Stan had said it was, and could only think of the side compartment, where the lawn chairs were stored. She opened it, and three of the men rifled through the space—there were three of them doing any one thing—but found nothing.

"You want us to look inside?" another man, the tallest of them all, said. "My uncle used to have something like this." He nodded at the vehicle the way he might have pointed out a tick infestation.

Josie's bones told her not to allow ten men to tramp through the Chateau, opening every cabinet, especially given the velvet bag of money hidden under the sink. But a few of them had already seemed to be losing interest in the operation, and were standing a few yards down the road, as if moving on already, so to keep them interested she said sure, they could look through the Chateau, that maybe the tall man in orange had some insight, via his uncle, that she couldn't access. As the stocky one opened the side door and stepped in, she met Paul's eyes.

This is an example of making a bad situation worse, his eyes said.

But it was too late. Six of them were inside the Chateau, and Josie stood on the roadside, her children next to her, thinking that there was something unusual about this group of men, but unable to put her finger on it. Aside from the stocky one, they were smaller and thinner than the average firefighters, younger as a whole, all of them in their twenties, their arms grey with tattoos. She stepped closer to the Chateau to peek in, but the interior was a blur of orange. She turned around to find one of the men on his knees, obscuring Ana. He seemed to be talking to her.

"Ana, come over here," Josie said, her unease growing. Ana reluctantly shuffled to her, hands behind her back.

Josie scanned the hands of every one of the firefighters, looking for the velvet bag. The tallest man jumped from the Chateau door, a twisted piece of iron over his head, his other hand holding a mechanical device, this one rusted. "Got it," he said to everyone, and quickly there were orange men under the Chateau, and one was on the back ladder, removing the spare, and soon the vehicle was tilting high and they had removed and replaced the flat.

Just as they were lowering the jack, a new man, in chartreuse, was among them. "What's happening here?" he asked. He was an older man wearing goggles over deep-set eyes, canopied with heavy brows. He had a presence at once authoritative and gentle, a small-town judge wanting and expecting civility from all.

"Just helping this motorist change her tire, sir," the tall orange man said.

The men in orange had backed away from Josie and the Chateau, suddenly shy. A few of them had hustled to the roadside to pick up their shovels.

"Ma'am," the bearded man said to Josie. His eyes were alarmed. "Have these men harmed or bothered you in any way?"

"No," Josie said, confused, but adopting the tone of giving a traffic-accident deposition. "They've been very helpful."

The gentle-eyed man relaxed, and looked around at the orange men, his eyes registering that he was both disappointed and impressed. "You guys get your gear and keep walking, okay?" he said, and those of the orange men who hadn't done so already re-formed their single-file line and were tromping down the road. They passed the Chateau, none of them looking at Josie or Paul or Ana. The man in chartreuse watched their progress, his hands on his hips. When they were out of earshot, he turned to Josie.

"Did those men identify themselves as inmates?" he asked.

Josie's stomach seemed to evaporate. She shook her head.

"You know how we use prisoners in some fires, to cut line and such?" the man said.

Josie had no idea what that meant.

"They're low-level offenders. And happy for the work, it being outside and all," the man said, chuckling. "Anyway, we're short-handed, as you can see. Otherwise there's usually an escort with these guys. And I didn't know we were letting civilians through here. So a perfect storm, right?"

Josie was trying to follow. Prisoners are sent to fight fires, and the ten men who had flowed around and through the Chateau were all prisoners, and they had happily fixed her flat, and couldn't have been more polite, and now they were gone.

"Wait," she whispered, and climbed into the Chateau, rushed to the sink, opened the cabinet and found the velvet bag untouched.

"What was it? Anything gone?" the man asked.

"No, nothing," she said. She looked up the road. The line of men had taken an upward path into the charred hills.

"One of them give you that?" the man asked Ana.

Josie looked down to find that her daughter was holding a tiny yellow flower.

She could drive all night, she decided. She could pull over anywhere. It didn't matter. She was free and her children were safe. She felt powerful, capable, again heroic as she had when they'd left the bed and breakfast. She wanted a drink.

And here, up ahead, was what she'd been looking for in Alaska, an all-night diner with a neon beer sign in the window. She pulled into the parking lot, and saw that the place was oddly bustling for 9:23 p.m. She pulled over. The kids were asleep, but she needed to be around people, under strips of fluorescent light. She saw a pair of empty booths by the side window, and parked the Chateau so she could see it from one of the booths. She intended to sit and drink whatever they had, keep an eye on the RV that held her sleeping children, get some food for them to eat whenever they woke up. She had the feeling she would be talking to some stranger inside, the waitress at the very least. She was in one of those moods, she knew—once a month an ebullience came over her and she found herself small-talking someone at the checkout counter, people walking their dogs, nurses pushing the elderly down the sidewalk. *What a day, right?*

Seat yourself, the sign inside said, and Josie thought her heart might burst. She took one of the empty booths and opened the menu, to find not just the beer advertised in neon but two different wines, red and white. The waitress approached, and as she loomed close enough to appraise, Josie saw that she was a stunning woman in her forties, possibly the most beautiful woman she'd seen in Alaska. Her blond hair was streaked with white, which might have been age or might have been a style choice, it didn't matter. Her eyes were dark, and she had dimples, which announced themselves just after she'd asked Josie how she was and what would she have.

"White wine," Josie said.

Dimples. "Just a glass?" the woman asked, her eyes shining like those of a beloved childhood dog. "We have carafes."

"Yes," Josie said. "The carafe. Thank you. That's mine," she added, indicating the Chateau just outside. There was no reason to announce this just after ordering a carafe of white wine—as if she wanted the waitress to know what she'd be driving when she was finished drinking.

"You parking overnight?" the waitress asked. Dimples.

"Can I?" Josie asked.

Now the waitress was confused. Finally Josie put it together: the waitress had assumed that was why she'd pointed to the Chateau.

"Yes," Josie said, more assuredly now. "Do I pay here or . . ."

Dimples. "I can add it to the bill. I'll bring the registry over."

And now Josie was in a new kind of bliss, and felt sure she would get a little drunk.

The carafe arrived, and she finished her first glass greedily. She was thirsty, and followed the wine with water, and was still thirsty. She couldn't remember if she'd eaten since breakfast. She settled on the fact that she'd eaten half of a sandwich sometime in the afternoon, so she should eat now, should have a feast soaked in wine, and ran her eyes down the menu, ordered a chicken salad and started on the bread.

The diner was in full swing. Josie was in her flannel shirt, so she was invisible and enjoying a second glass of chardonnay. She looked around. There were two women who had come there, Josie was sure, to get laid; they were dressed like rock groupies. There were pairs of tired truckers, and a group of college-age kids who seemed to have spent the day rafting. One was still wearing a life vest. And then there was a man in front of her. Sitting in the next booth, facing her, as if the two of them had come with invisible companions and were stuck looking at each other.

He had one of those fat, round ageless faces that could be thirty or fifty. Lucky, Josie thought, to have all that fat in his face. He'll be set forever. He'll always look happy. And because he seemed so harmless and alone, she invited him to join her.

"You can come over here if you want," she said. She noticed he had ordered nothing but a cookie and a glass of water. "Bring your water and cookie."

The man reacted strangely. Josie thought it was not unreasonable to assume he would be glad to be asked by a woman to join her. Men did not often receive such invitations. But a long moment passed, during which his face took on looks of surprise, and suspicion, and assessment. Finally he tilted his head and said, "Okay."

He carried his plate and cookie over, and placed them on Josie's table, and she saw that he was a softly built man in loose jeans and a plaid button-down, even more harmless now that she saw him up close. He sat and looked at his cookie, as if gathering the courage to look up at Josie. She found him vulnerable, shy, unassuming, safe.

"I'm surprised you would invite me over," he said, still looking at his cookie.

"Well," Josie said, "we were both eating alone, and that seemed unnecessary. How's your water?"

"It's fine," he said, and as if to prove it, he lifted the glass and took a sip, finally peering over the ridge to look at Josie. There was something in his eyes, she thought. Something suspecting, as if he was still questioning her motives for inviting him over. She flattered herself, guessing he thought she was out of his league.

"I don't want you to be uncomfortable," she said.

He shook his head, looking down at his cookie, and as if knowing how long he'd been staring at it, he broke it in half.

Josie took a sip of her wine, knowing this wasn't going well. The longer he sat there, the more his strangeness was amplified. Every second of his tense posture, his inability to meet her eyes, seemed to increase the likelihood that he was not quite normal. "What's your name?"

He smiled to himself. "I don't know if that matters," he said, and looked up at Josie. Now there was something conspiratorial in his eyes, as if the two of them were engaged in some wonderful game.

"This yours?" a voice said. Josie looked up to see that the waitress was standing at their table, holding out a short stack of papers to the man. There were a few pages of printed maps, some pages with handwritten notes, and under those pages, an open-sided manila file folder and below that, a large closed envelope. The label featured a series of names separated by ampersands, all of it in a font both elegant and combative.

"Oh, thanks," he said to the waitress, and laughed a little laugh, looking quickly at the waitress and then to Josie.

"Would have defeated the whole purpose, right? Coming all the way up here and forgetting the envelope." He said this to Josie, and finally it came together. He was serving her legal papers. She was being sued by someone, thousands of miles away, and this shy man was an envoy delivering this aggression.

Josie stood up. "This man just propositioned me," she said loudly. "He said he wanted to do to me what he's done to other women around the state." She backed away from the table, moving toward the front door, and was satisfied to see that most of the customers in the room were hearing her. "I don't know what that means, but I'm scared." She said this louder, pointing at him, moving toward the front counter. She pulled two twenties from her pocket and placed them on the cashier's counter.

Josie was almost at the front door. The process server was frozen in his seat. "He said horrible things to me!" she said, allowing her voice to peak. "I'm scared!" she wailed, and burst toward the front door.

Not bad, she thought.

Outside, she ran to the Chateau and climbed in, finding Paul and Ana still asleep in their seats. She started the engine and looked into the restaurant's window. Two of the truckers, older men solidly built and awake to the possibility that they would create a justice event, had approached the table, and were hovering over the man, whose hands lay on top of his stack of papers. When Josie hit the gas and the Chateau lurched ahead, the man glanced at her, his face impassive, his eyes registering not defeat or surprise, but something like betrayal.

She pulled around the parking lot and passed the building again as she left the driveway and met the highway. Now there were three men and the waitress at the booth, the man obscured by the bodies surrounding him. The process server thought I knew who he was, Josie realized. He'd followed her there, and to the diner, and had been biding his time, sitting there, staring at her from the opposite booth. No wonder he was surprised she'd invited him over. He thought she knew.

The adrenaline sobered her instantly and made the driving easy. Her mind was alive, florid and supercomputing. She took every minor road she could while cycling through her thoughts and plans and questions. She had defeated him, all that he represented. The look on his face—Who sent him? Carl? What would the lawsuit say? Or Evelyn? She hadn't checked in with her child DA. Maybe there was something new on that front. Maybe Evelyn's people had found less value than promised. Maybe she was claiming fraud, false dealing—

Jeremy's parents. Could they sue? Try to sue?

No. It was Carl. It had to be Carl. This was the boldest thing he'd ever done. He'd filed some suit, and they'd hired someone to serve her. In Alaska. Holy shit. How much would a man like that be paid? A process server in central Alaska? Was he local? He didn't seem to be local. Likely from Anchorage. Anywhere you go there are people doing these terrible jobs.

Inviting him over had actually prevented him from serving her. After an hour of driving she was sure this was true. When she'd called him over, he'd left his papers. He'd been confused, put off balance. If she hadn't invited him to her booth he would have simply served her when she was sitting there. But she put him off his game, took control of the situation. She congratulated herself. Some extrasensory force had compelled her to suss out his nefarious purpose at the diner.

Was she invincible? She wondered if she was guided by some higher power. Was her mission, avoiding Carl, leaving civilization, a holy one? There was no other answer.

Somewhere near dawn, at another gas station lit in white, Josie got out, filled the tank, and felt compelled to check the Chateau for tracking devices. How else could the man have known where she was? He'd had a map, though. Would he have a map if he had some kind of tracking device? She got out of the Chateau and crawled under it.

"Everything okay?" a voice said.

She looked for the source, and saw a pair of boots. She stood and saw that the voice came from a teenager, no more than seventeen, wearing a pristine yellow shirt and skinny jeans. The boots were some incongruous style mistake.

"You work here?" she asked.

"Uh huh," he said. "You need help under there?"

She thought briefly about telling him she thought she was being followed, that she had been looking for some kind of black box affixed to the undercarriage, but then knew this would only stir interest, and make her more memorable, such that if or when someone asked if he'd seen anyone or anything unusual, he would have a story. Yes, a woman under an RV, looking for a tracking device, very nervous—

Instead, she had an idea. "You have a clean-out?"

He directed her to it, a tank buried behind the station. There was a tidy round hole in the cement ready to receive. "I'm supposed to charge you fifteen dollars," he said. "I mean, if you're unloading a full tank." Josie said the load was full, it was all the shit they'd been carrying around from the beginning, and paid the man.

"I don't know how to do it, though," she said.

Now the teenager's face hardened. "You don't know how to do it?" he asked, as if Josie, in her ignorance, had no right to pilot a magnificent craft like the Chateau, had no right to carry feces within. The teenager then drew a horrible and pornographic picture of a long thick tube extending from the side of the RV and snaking into a hole in the ground. "The waste should just shoot down into the tank from here to there," he said, drawing arrows moving up and down.

The teenager's drawing was benign, even beautiful, compared to the reality, which first required Josie to remove a twelve-foot white tube, inexplicably ribbed, from the bumper of the Chateau. It was stored there, tastefully hidden, a long cylinder tucked inside a long rectangle. She held it gingerly, knowing that unknown volumes of the waste of strangers—of Stan and his white-carpet wife!—had passed through. How could she know if there were leaks? Who could vouch for the end-to-end integrity of the shit-cylinder? She pulled it all out from the bumper, as it came and came, like a giant earthworm.

She attached one end to the right-sized opening on the bottom of the Chateau, just below the feces tank, and then dropped the other end into the hole in the ground, the clean-out. All she had to do now was turn the small and fragile lever that opened the tank and hope, when the human waste went hurtling down the tube, that the tube would stay attached and not fall off, spraying feces everywhere. But that seemed far more likely than it staying somehow fastened amid all that activity, the volume of waste shooting through its thin white membrane.

She reached under the Chateau, under the tank, turned the lever, and leaped to the side. The tube, though, stayed attached through the horrible business of it—the pumping, jerking, the terrifying rush. The jerking was the most unsettling, as the tube, which she realized was far outweighed by the volume of that which it conveyed, jerked and convulsed as the waste passed through in clumps and squirts. The sound was the haunting song of the feces rushing from its halfway house to its final home, not despairing its fate, but joyful and eager.

And then it was over, and all that was necessary was to detach both sides without getting the waste, which no doubt still coated the inside of the tube and the ends especially, on her fingers and shoes, and then replace the twelve feet of tubing, containing so much remembrance of things passed, into the bumper again.

The teenager reappeared. "All gone?"

"All gone," Josie said.

She followed the teenager into the office, washed her hands in the bathroom and, seeing that the store was stocked with food, bought enough for a week or so. Even stopping at RV parks from then on seemed too risky. They would stay in the Chateau, hidden in woods or valleys. She bought all the store's peanut butter, all its milk and orange juice and fruit and bread.

She bought a thermos and filled it with coffee, loaded the groceries into the passenger seat, climbed back into the Chateau and started the engine. Standing under the green-white light of the station, the teenager said something to her, but she couldn't hear it. She cupped her hand to her ear, smiling, hoping that would be the end of it, but instead he jogged around to her window.

"Enjoy the dawn," he said. The way he said it sounded like a statement of common inclination—that the two of them were united in preferring these small hours, to be alone and apart.

"Right," she said.

XVIII.

AT SUNRISE there was a sign. PETERSSEN SILVER MINE, 2 MI. They'd been driving for five and a half hours, going north and northwest, and staying off the main roads. A dozen times she'd hit dead ends and closed roads and had turned around, the state seeming determined not to allow her to travel in any direct path. The night finally eased, giving way to grey light. Josie was determined to find an obscure place to park, to hide the Chateau and herself. What she was looking for, really, was a cave, but knew this was too much to ask. A mine seemed a close approximation.

"You guys interested in an old silver mine?" she yelled back to the kids. They'd been asleep all night, and only now were making noises implying they were waking up.

Neither said anything.

"You still asleep?" she asked.

"No," Ana said.

"Let's go to a silver mine," Josie said. She was slap-happy, jittery from the coffee she'd bought from the last gas station and had drunk hot, then warm, then cool, then cold. A vague memory came to her, of her parents taking her to a mine in Oregon. All day she'd caught them kissing in the dark tunnels.

She missed the mine exit the first time, turned around and missed it from the other side. The turnoff was impossibly narrow and the sign was small and painted on wood.

The Chateau rumbled over the dirt road as it turned and climbed into a deep valley. "No one else here," Josie noted as they made their way two, three, four miles down the dirt road, seeing no sign of human habitation. She'd spent the night thinking to herself, and muttering to herself, and now, with the children ostensibly awake, she could talk out loud and consider it sane.

"Look at this," she said, "a river. Pretty."

If the man followed her again, intending to serve her anything, she felt capable of fleeing or doing him harm. If they were alone she was afraid of what she would do to him. She thought of rocks upside his fleshy head, leaving him alone and bleeding in some remote pullout.

She mused over the word *mine*. What a funny word for the extraction of precious metals from the earth: *mine*. She thought she would tell her kids her thoughts on this, the very funny confluence of the meanings of *mine* and *mine,* and then found herself whispering the words, *mine mine mine,* and noticed she was smiling. She was far gone.

"I need to sleep," she said aloud.

The Chateau crossed a narrow steel bridge over a clear

shallow river and soon there was another sign, telling them that the mine was three miles ahead. Time and space were bending. They were farther away now than when they left the highway. The landscape was lush with pine and wild-flowers and Josie was about to note this by yelling "Pretty" into the back, when she turned to find Paul's face between the two front seats, alarmingly close to hers.

"Pretty," she said to him, whispered to him.

Finally they saw a series of slapdash buildings of grey wood and rusted roofs climbing the steep hillside. There was a gate ahead, but it was closed and locked. She parked the Chateau and stepped down, heading to the gate, on which there was a handwritten sign.

CLOSED DUE TO GOVT SHUTDOWN.

NOT OUR FAULT.

Josie got back into the Chateau, told the kids the park was closed, and then informed them that they would go in and walk around anyway. An idea was forming in her mind.

"Can we?" Paul asked.

"Sure," Josie said.

Ana was delighted.

Josie parked directly in front of the gate, so as to announce to any ranger that might appear that she was not trying to hide from authorities. To them, she wanted to appear to be a mother who had stopped momentarily to show her kids around the old silver mine. They walked around the gate and through the parking lot and saw that there was a bathroom, a tidy one with a newly shingled roof. Paul ran to it and found the doors locked. In seconds he was peeing behind the building.

The mine had been well preserved, in that the park rangers and historians who had been caring for it were allowing it to decompose without much interference. Rusted machinery lay everywhere, as if dropped from a passing plane. There were informative signs along a path that led visitors up to the smelting building, and past the rooming houses and the old offices where the mining company kept their accountants and bookkeepers.

The kids were not intrigued. Josie often had no clue what would interest them; there had been a seafaring museum somewhere last year that Ana had gone mad for. And Paul was at least politely engaged in anything. But this mining operation held no appeal. One of the signs indicated there was a river somewhere nearby, but Josie couldn't see it or hear it. They followed the path to its end, to a pair of buildings where the silver had been processed, then just beyond it, off the path and amid a small pocket of dense foliage, she saw a newer, tidier structure.

"Wait here," she told the kids, and they sighed elaborately. They were standing in the low sun, and Josie winced while looking at their red and sweating faces. "Just need to look at this house here," she said.

She climbed over the low, period-appropriate fence, rough-hewn and grey, and walked along a winding red-dirt path until she reached the cottage. It was a pretty little thing, a log cabin, newly lacquered and with a cherry tint to it. She peered in the windows. It was finished nicely inside, with a fireplace, two rocking chairs, a futon, a small and plain but tidy kitchen. And it was empty. There was no indication anyone had been there for weeks, and whoever lived there last had cleaned it well before leaving. It was probably the caretaker's house. The ranger's residence. And the shutdown had apparently sent the ranger home, to some other home. Josie returned to her children. Her idea was now complete.

"Why don't you guys go back to the Chateau for a second?" she said. "Get something to drink. I want to look around some more."

Paul and Ana did not seem enthusiastic about moving anywhere, but when Josie presented them the key to the Chateau, they couldn't pass up the opportunity to unlock the door themselves. They would not get drinks or rest, she knew. They would play at locking and unlocking the door until she returned.

When they had run down the path and were out of sight, Josie went back to the cabin. She tried the front door and found it locked. She went to the back and it was shut, too. She had figured this, so then did what she'd planned to do, which was to walk back and forth along the back and side, looking for the smallest window.

The smallest window was in the kitchen, a grid of six panes. Josie took an elephant leaf from a nearby plant, wrapped it around her fist, and punched the glass.

It did not break. Her hand ached with the heat of a hundred suns. She dropped to one knee, cradling her fingers, cursing herself. In a few minutes she had recovered, and searched for a rock. She found a sharp one of about five pounds, and rapped it forcefully against the glass. Again the window did not break. She backed up, threw the rock underhand at the glass and missed, striking the side of the house. Finally she picked the rock up, held it overhead, and rammed it into the window. Now the glass gave way.

She waited, listening for any reaction from her children or anyone who might secretly be dwelling inside the cottage. Hearing nothing, she threw the rock away and went back to find her children.

They were playing with the key and the Chateau lock. Ana had cajoled Paul into being inside the RV while she was outside, trying to make the key fit.

"Knock knock," Ana said.

"You have the key," Paul said from within. "Why are you knocking?"

When Ana noticed Josie behind her, she looked momentarily crazy with alarm and guilt.

"Come with me," Josie said, and Ana relaxed. "I have something interesting to show you."

A very good thing about her children at this age: Whenever she said she would show them something interesting, they invariably believed her. They always thought she would actually show them something interesting. They dutifully followed her back up the sunlit trail to its end. This time she let them climb the fence, too, and she led them to the back of the cabin.

"What do you see?" she asked.

"Broken window," Paul said.

"What do you think we should do?" she asked.

The two children stared at her.

"What would happen if this was left open, this window, in a forest like this?" she asked.

"Animals," Ana said.

"They'd get inside," Paul added.

Josie had a plan but wanted her children to believe it was theirs.

"Right," Josie said. "So what should we do?"

"We should tape it shut or something," Paul said.

"But how?" Josie said. In that moment she observed herself critically, using the Socratic method on her kids in the hopes that they would suggest that Ana crawl through the broken window.

"One of us could crawl through and find a key," Paul said.

They were wonderful people, her children. Then she thought: Exactly how many misdemeanors would her family commit in this unassuming state?

"Or just open the door from the inside," Josie suggested with a noncommittal shrug.

Paul and Ana took the bait and set out on the path, seeming very serious about the task before them. After arriving at the broken window and allowing Paul and Ana to inspect it with the authority of glass-repair contractors, Josie relocated the cottage's welcome mat to the window sill and draped it over the broken window's lower ledge. Then she suggested, with all the moral seriousness of the naming of a saint, that Ana was the only human alive that could successfully make it through such a small gap, crawl down to the table below, then to the floor, then to the front door, to open it for her mother and brother.

Ana blinked hard. She couldn't believe it. The old restless soul in her seemed to know exactly what Josie was up to, but the actual five-year-old sharing Ana's corporeal form was alive to the adventure of it all and chose to ignore the voice within her that knew better.

Josie lifted her, Paul's hands ready below, and Ana's stomach shifted back and forth, like a beached shark, across the welcome mat, then, in an electrifying bit of improvisation, Ana did a front somersault—slow motion, never airborne—to get to the kitchen table below the window. Ana stood on the table for a moment, pretending to be assessing but actually just preening, knowing she was being watched and admired. Then, without fanfare, she jumped to the floor and ran to the front door as if she'd lived in that cottage all her life. By the time Josie and Paul arrived at the door, Ana had opened it and was tapping an imaginary watch on her tiny wrist.

Then she relaxed and smiled, like a host who had chosen to forgive tardy guests in the interest of preserving the mood. "Welcome!" she said.

Josie explained to them that they would need to tape the window shut from the inside—only from the inside would it work or hold through the rains and winds. So they went into the cottage, smelling its raw woods, the faint scents of mildew and detergent—of attempted order—and they looked for duct tape and cardboard. Soon they had found both and had repaired the window, or at least made it impenetrable to insects and small mammals.

But Josie's intention was not only to fix the window, but to stay here, at least until she'd decided on a next step. The location could scarcely be better. She rifled through the drawers in the kitchen until she found a key, tried it in the front door. It worked. She had a key to the cabin. "I think we should stay here tonight," she said casually, "just to make sure the place is safe and our window repair holds."

Paul and Ana agreed. Or just shrugged. They didn't care. There was no longer any logical pattern to their lives.

"Hold on a sec," she said. Leaving the kids in the cabin, Josie jogged down to the Chateau and pondered exactly what to do with the vehicle. She couldn't leave it at the gate.

She looked around and saw, inside the gate and across the parking lot, a prefab garage made of corrugated steel, its door open. She expected it to be filled with vehicles or whatever else the park rangers might make use of, but it was largely empty. The shutdown: this was where the ranger had parked his truck, and now he was gone. It looked tall enough to hold the Chateau.

Josie examined the lock at the end of the chain. It was a standard padlock that held together the heavy chain threaded through the gate and post. Her first thought was to attack the lock itself with one of the wrenches she'd seen in the Chateau toolbag. She had a jack there, too, but assumed that the padlock was designed to withstand the blows of simple steel and iron implements.

She stood in the lace-white light of the morning, staring at the gate, and when she thought of the solution, she laughed. It was ridiculous, and it would work, and once she had done it she would laugh about it always, in the years to come, the ease of the gambit, the fact that they had really done it. It was a criminal act, something between breaking and entering and simple vandalism, but it would work beautifully.

In minutes she was back at the cottage and had found the saw hanging over the mantel. And then she was running down the path again, the saw held over her head with two hands. She returned to the gate and began sawing the post. She started very low, so that when she returned the post to its position, the grass growing around its base might hide the fact that she'd cut through it. Working without rest, for she worried that at any moment her kids would be upon her, witnessing this, her most bizarre and criminal act yet, she sawed through. The lock was still attached of course, but it was now attached to a post that was unattached, that swung with the open gate.

She drove the Chateau through the gate and slowly guided it into the prefab garage, expecting the top to scrape any moment. It fit, though, was meant to fit, so she drove it in, and closed the doors to the garage when she was finished. The Chateau was invisible. She took a few hundred dollars from the velvet bag, shoved it deep into the corner of the cabinet, afraid to count what was left, and locked the Chateau door. She returned to the gate for the best part of it all. She replaced the post atop its foundation, balancing it such that it still looked like a functioning, unaltered pillar. If anyone touched it, or if a strong wind came, it would come apart, but for the time being it looked legitimate, unaltered.

They were likely free from any possibility of being found, at least for a day or two. Whatever park rangers were left in Alaska were occupied with the fires, or were far away, out of state even, enjoying fine weather on a shutdown holiday.

Josie and the children inspected the cabin, the children immediately finding the stairs and running up to the pitched-roof attic.

"Not much up there," Paul said upon returning. "Two small beds, but it smells."

Most of the cabin's life was on the main floor, with the fireplace determining the location of all other objects in the room. The futon and chairs were pointed toward the hearth, and most of the decorations surrounded it. On the mantel, a variety of fishing memorabilia, a horse carved from wood, a beaver rendered in a slab of bark. Crossed over the mantel like swords were a pair of wooden snowshoes, and over them, an ancient spear. To the left of the fireplace, the wall was covered with firewood.

In the kitchen, there were two old stoves, neither of them functional, and a formica table, three chrome chairs around it, each with a yellow plastic seat somewhere ripped and duct-taped. There was a sink, but no running water; instead, there was a water bubbler, almost full. A functioning refrigerator sat low in a corner, and next to it, drawers with aluminum foil, Tupperware containers, duct tape, scissors and string. A platoon of knives was magnetically attached to the wall, all facing right with soldierly anticipation. A small cabinet over the stove was stocked with canned soup and vegetables. Between the food they had in the Chateau and this, Josie thought, they could get by for a while.

"Look," Ana said. In the main room, the kids had found a stash of games, all of them forty years old, maybe more. Scrabble, Parcheesi, two decks of cards, Sorry! Josie half-expected to see Candyland, and have a brief spiral of stabbing thoughts, but when she scanned the stack, she didn't see it. Then Paul did. It was under the shelf holding the rest of the games.

"I've heard of this," he said, brushing the dust from the box. "How come we never had this game, Mom?"

"Who wants to make a fire?" Josie asked.

Paul and Ana delighted in choosing the right newspapers, kindling and logs, and in minutes there was a thundering fire. At the earliest opportunity, she planned to throw the game into it. But for now, she had distracted her children enough to hide it above the fridge.

In the kitchen, she found a transistor radio, turned it on and looked for news. Could there be some search going on for her? Some news of the death or maiming of a process server at the hands of diner vigilantes? She could muster only a faint signal, an evangelical message, telling listeners that God wanted them to prosper not just spiritually but materially. "Prosper is a word rooted in the three-dimensional world," the man said.

On the counter there was a photo of the man she assumed was the ranger who usually occupied the cabin. He was about forty, cheerful-seeming, with a red beard and wearing green and khaki. He had his arm around another man, also bearded, with the same cheerful eyes. A brother maybe, a lover, a husband? In any case she was contented to know the ranger who lived there, a man in love or capable of love, seemed less likely to chase them than the owner of the last cottage where they'd squatted.

"I have to sleep," Josie said. She hadn't rested in more than a day. Josie demonstrated the futon to the kids, and she could see their minds assessing whether or not they could all fit on it; she was sure they wouldn't want to sleep in the dark and drafty attic. She descended onto the padding, provoking a small cloud of dust. She did not care. Sleep pulled her down.

"Are we living here now?" Ana asked.

Josie fell asleep, thinking it a very real possibility.

XIX.

IN THE AFTERNOON, having slept through the day, Josie felt reborn. She raised herself from the futon, feeling unaccountably strong, and noticed that her children were nowhere in sight.

She called to them. No answer. She leapt up, her heart in her mouth. She pictured a pair of wolves carrying them off. She yelled their names.

"Out here," Paul said.

She threw open the door to find Paul and Ana outside, on the gravel walkway, huddled around a black mass of fur.

"What is that?" Josie roared.

The fur shook and whimpered.

"It's a dog," Ana said, and took its face in her hands and turned it toward Josie, as if to demonstrate the nature of the species to her unknowing mother.

"It was scratching at the door," Paul said.

They'd opened the door, and the dog had quickly slipped inside.

"We didn't want to wake you up, so we brought her out here," Paul said. He was telling the truth. He was frighteningly considerate. But whose animal was this?

"Does he have a collar?" she asked.

"Just this," Ana said, and pulled a plastic flea collar from its neck. Ana had moved to the side, revealing the full shape of the dog. It was tiny and black and looked like a malnourished pig, with short hair and triangular ears.

"It's shivering," Josie noted.

"She's hungry," Paul said.

"Keep your hands away from its mouth," Josie said.

"Her mouth," Paul said. "It's a girl."

"If you get bitten you'll be in the hospital for days," Josie said. "And we're not near any hospitals."

"Can we feed her?" Paul asked.

"Did you name her yet?" Josie asked.

"Ana did," Paul said.

"Follow," she said.

"That's her name: Follow," Paul clarified.

"Because she followed us," Ana said. Last year she named a fish Waterlover.

"I thought you said she scratched at the door," Josie said.

Paul had a way, when caught even in the whitest of lies, of staring at Josie, unblinking, for a few long seconds before he spoke. It was not done out of any sense of strategy. It was more that he was seized by, inhabited by, a kind of truth spirit that insisted upon full revelation. He took a deep breath and began.

"We went outside. Just to get some sticks," he said, indicating a small pile of sticks that, with orange duct tape, they'd made into swords. "When we were walking back, she started following us. We closed the door, and she started scratching on it."

Paul exhaled in a quick burst, as if in punctuation and relief. He was happy to have gotten through it, the unadulterated truth. His posture relaxed and he allowed himself to blink.

"Can we feed it?" he asked again.

So they had a dog. They brought Follow inside, and fed her old fried chicken and salad, and she devoured it. Josie knew what a bad idea it was to feed a stray like this, but the animal seemed traumatized, unable to stop shivering. She conjured a narrative whereby she was the ranger's dog, but had run away, and the ranger, unable to find her, had left without her. Then she'd returned to find him gone, the door locked, and her tiny self surrounded by a murderers' row of higher carnivores only too happy to lunch on her vibrating flesh. Somehow she'd survived the days since, but was a wreck of nerves and was starving to boot.

Josie examined the dog, looking for cuts or fleas or some sign of disease, and found her to be startlingly clean for a dog that had been out in the wild for days or weeks. "You can pet her," she told her children, and she sat on the futon, watching them fawn over Follow, as the dog shook and ate, and shortly after eating, fell fast asleep. They continued to pet her black fur as she slept, as she breathed unevenly, her hind legs periodically jabbing at the floor.

Josie had the feeling that with Follow, they had become some kind of frontier family. They broke windows and altered gates. They took in strays. And they hadn't even been in the cabin one night. The kids would not leave Follow, so they stayed inside as the night came on, and Josie built a fire, and the winds outside whistled an eerie tune. The cardboard they'd taped over the kitchen window inhaled and exhaled but held. She brought her children with her under the covers, and they slept through the night, Paul's arm hanging to the floor, where he could be sure of Follow's well-being.

A ringing woke her. It was still dark, the fire weak. Who could be calling? She hadn't even seen a phone. She slipped out of bed and to the kitchen, hoping the kids would sleep through it. In the dark she swept her hands over the counter, and finally, under a pile of maps, found a landline. It was still ringing. Three rings, four, each one rattling the cabin. She couldn't pick it up. Finally after six rings, it ended.

Paul and Ana were still asleep, but Josie knew she would be awake for hours. She brought a chair out to the deck and sat, jittery, listening to the night, running through possibilities. She wanted to believe the phone call was random, or simply intended for the ranger who lived there. But then there was the possibility that it was Follow's owners. Or the process server. Or the police.

No one is looking for us, she told herself. She even manufactured a scoff, meant to put herself at ease.

"Mom?"

It was Ana, alone, on the porch. Josie couldn't remember Ana ever getting out of bed alone. Usually, when she was out of bed after hours, it was part of a scheme Paul had conceived, a dual attack meant to prove that sleep was impossible for all in the house. Really, though, it meant that Paul hadn't been able to sleep, had woken up Ana and brought her with him. Only Paul was burdened with the near-death implications of sleep and the night's invitation to consider mortality and insignificance. Ana was too young to have come to these places.

She was standing in the doorway, her mass of red hair matted on one side, misshapen and a faded shade of orange, like the last pumpkin chosen from the patch. Her hands were stuck to either side of the doorframe, as if she were holding the two sides at bay.

"Are we staying here tomorrow?" she asked.

"I think so. Maybe for a few days," Josie said.

"Really?" Ana said, and her face and shoulders dropped in one beautifully coordinated collapse.

Ana had similar sentiments last winter, when they were headed back to school after holiday break.

"Do I go to school this week?" she had asked.

"Yes," Josie had said.

"And the week after that?"

"Of course."

Ana had been astonished. Winter break had brought something different each day, and now, going back to school, where things did not vary so much day to day, offended her. The repetitive nature of the system assaulted her sense of the heroic possibilities of a day.

"Go to bed," Josie said, but instead Ana came and crawled on her lap and pretended to suck her thumb.

"Don't worry, Josie," Ana said. "I won't tell Paul." Now she gave Josie one of her looks, a conspiratorial look that said they could drop all the formalities and role-playing, the silly game of parent and child.

"I don't like you calling me Josie," Josie said.

"Okay, *Mom,*" Ana said, making the word sound absurd.

"Go to bed," Josie said, pushing Ana off her lap. Ana fell to the rough porch in a heavy theatrical heap. She crawled back into the house, and though Josie expected to hear from her again, after ten minutes there was no sign that Ana was awake, which meant, for Ana—who usually fell asleep in seconds and stayed that way till morning—that she was actually asleep.

As if in protest at losing Ana for the dark hours, the howl of a coyote spiraled through the night.

The ringing again. Josie opened her eyes, saw that her children were already awake, huddled around Follow as she ate beef jerky, her tiny jaws snapping.

"Who's calling, Mom?" Paul asked.

"Wrong number," she said.

Josie realized that the presence of a dog did not help their situation. They wanted to be invisible, but wasn't there a chance Follow's owners would return for her? She had the thought that perhaps Follow belonged to someone else nearby, and that like many a puppy, she had simply been exploring when she encountered Paul and Ana and followed them to the cabin door. There was a chance the owners knew the ranger, that the dog had come here before, and they were calling to check if he'd seen her. Or there was the possibility that it was simply a telephone, that people made calls, that it rang, and none of it had anything to do with Josie and her children. She could unplug the phone, but what if the ranger called, found out it had been disconnected? She had to leave it be.

"Let's go for a walk," she said, not telling Paul and Ana that she thought there was at least some chance that Follow would lead them to her actual owner and real home. And so Josie packed a backpack with crackers and water from the bubbler, they tied a rope to Follow's flea collar and made their way up through the mine and into the woods beyond. The animal was tentative still, walking ahead, then circling back to the children, then running ahead for a spell before coming back again. She was either a deeply troubled dog or not very bright.

When they reached a stand of birch trees, though, some sense of purpose seized the dog, and she led them down a steady slope until they heard the sound of rushing water.

Follow brought them to a narrow stream cut through a tight valley, and drank deeply from the rushing water.

"Mom?" Paul said. "Where do languages come from?"

He wanted to know why there was Italian and Hindi and Swahili, and not just English, and why they spoke English, and was English the best language? Josie made a brief stab at the origin of languages, the vicissitudes of distance and isolation in the formation of foreign tongues. People living far from anyone else, she explained, as they were, might be the sorts of people who created their own tongue. They could, she said, create their own words for anything, and to demonstrate, she held up a rock in the shape of a man's head. "I could call this kind of rock *tapatok,* for example," she said. "And from then on all the people who came after us would call it *tapatok.*"

Ana picked up a rounder rock. "I call this *Dad.*"

"Dad is already a word," Paul said. "And why would you call that Dad?" His mood darkened, and Ana took note. Paul went down to the water to pet Follow, taking her into his tiny lap. Ana followed, then was distracted by something else, her head tilted. She took a few steps forward, stepping into a grassy bouquet of wildflowers, dropped the rock and pointed up.

"Waterfall."

There, cut through the cliffside above them, was a narrow white plume falling from fifty feet above. They all wordlessly agreed to walk to the waterfall. When they got close, the volume was far greater than it had seemed from the path. For a moment the falling water seemed utterly sentient, falling with joyous aggression to the earth, spitefully suicidal. The spray reached them first, and they stopped, sat, and watched the waterfall's ghostly white fingers. In the wall of mist, rainbows shot off like birds taking flight. Follow kept her distance.

Josie strode to the waterfall, stepping on the wet stones, trying to find a way not to soak herself, and when she was close enough, she put her hand under the flow, feeling its strength and its numbing cold.

"Can we drink it?" Paul asked.

Josie's instinct was to say no, of course not, but already the woods had calmed her, opened her, so she did something that she wanted to do but normally would not have done. She took their thermos out of the backpack, emptied it, and then held it under the rush. Immediately her hand was soaked, her arm was wet to the shoulder, and the bottle was full.

She turned to Paul and Ana, seeing their astounded faces, and raised the bottle to the sun and sky to see if it was clear. Josie and her children saw the same thing, that the water was perfectly transparent. There were no particles, no sand, no dirt, nothing. Josie brought it to her lips and Paul took a quick intake of breath.

"Is it good?" Paul asked.

"It's good," she said, and gave it to him.

He took a sip and smacked his lips. He nodded and handed it to Ana, who drank without caution. After she took her fill, Paul asked, "Are we the first to drink from this?" He meant the waterfall, but Josie took some liberty with her interpretation. This water, flowing at this moment? Yes, they were the first.

The days were like this, each was miles long and had no aim or no possibility of regret. They ate when they were hungry and slept when they were tired, and they had nowhere to be. Every few days Ana would ask, "Are we living here?" or "Are we going to school here?" but otherwise both children seemed to sense their time in the cabin was a kind of respite, apart from any calendar, that there was no inevitable end. In the mornings, Paul and Ana drew and played board games and cards, and near noon they walked to the waterfall, to splash in the shallow water. They were in the woods now, and the woods were unbreakable. Ana acted nobly, and her face shone with an otherworldly glow. Children, Josie realized, are truly like animals. Give them clean foods and water and fresh air, and their coats will be shiny, their teeth white, their muscles supple and skin bright. But indoors, contained, they will become mangy, yellow-eyed, riddled with self-inflicted wounds.

In those long days at the Peterssen Mine, Paul and Ana made bows from bent sticks and rubber bands. They created and destroyed dams in the river, they piled rocks to make walls and rock castles. They read by candlelight. Josie taught Paul how to start a fire in the hearth. They napped some afternoons, and other afternoons they explored the buildings of the old mine, the midday sun coming through the porous roofs in white bolts, dozens of tiny spotlights illuminating dust and rust and tools not held for a hundred years.

There were a hundred uncomplicated hours in every day and they didn't see a soul for weeks. Was it weeks? They no longer had a grasp of the calendar. During the day all was quiet but for the occasional scream of a bird, like a lunatic neighbor; at night, the air was alive with frogs and crickets and coyotes. Paul and Ana slept deeply and Josie hovered over them, like a cold night cloud over rows of hills warmed all day in the sun.

They were growing in beautiful ways, becoming independent, and forgetting all material concerns, were awake to the light and the land, caring more about the movement of the river than any buyable object or piece of school gossip. She was proud of them, of their purifying souls, the way they asked nothing of her now, they slept through the night, and relished the performing of chores, liked to wash their clothes—and they were immeasurably better now than they were in Ohio. They were stronger, smarter, more moral, ethical, logical, considerate, and brave. And this was, Josie realized, what she wanted most of all from her children: she wanted them to be brave. She knew they would be kind. Paul was born that way and he would make sure Ana was kind, but to be brave! Ana was inherently courageous, but Paul was learning this. He was no longer afraid of the dark, would plunge into any woods with or without a light. One day, on her way back from the woods, she caught the two of them on the hillside near the cabin, both barefoot, gently shushing through the shallow leaves with their bows, watching something invisible to her. She turned, scanned the forest, and finally saw it, a ten-point buck, walking through the birches, his back straight and proud. Her children were mirroring it on the other side of the hill, unheard by the deer. They had turned into something else entirely.

All along she had been looking for courage and purity in the people of Alaska. She had not thought that she could simply—not simply, no, but still—create such people.

But the food ran out one staple at a time. First they were out of milk, then juice, and were drinking only water, first from the bubbler then from the waterfall. They went through the vegetables, then the apples, and finally the potatoes. They lived on nuts, crackers and water for two days before a trip into town was unavoidable.

"We'll go tomorrow," Josie said.

"I don't want to go anywhere," Ana said.

The thought of driving the Chateau again, and exposing herself to the road, to the prospect of meeting anyone who might still be pursuing her family, filled her with a crippling dread. To reduce the risk she went out to the garage with a screwdriver, planning to remove the license plates. She was halfway there when she heard Paul calling.

"A map!" he yelled as he flew down the path to her, Follow running behind.

"Is this where we are?" Paul asked. He had it spread out on the ground between them. It was a dense thing, showing every foot of elevation, a maze of green lines, numbers and jagged paths, but they found the mine on it, and finally they arrived at the exact location of the cabin. "We're here," he said.

"Okay," Josie said.

"There's a town over here," Paul noted, pointing to a small grid that looked to be just over a ridge, only a few miles away as the crow flies. There seemed to be a trail that went over the ridge, bringing them to the town via a frontage road. They would appear from the trail like hikers, and then disappear again like hikers, and even if anyone took note of the three of them, remembering Ana's orange tumbleweed hair, they would be able to say only that they came out of the woods, or returned to the woods.

"And look," Paul said, pointing to a wide thread of blue. "A river, I think."

"The Yukon," Josie said. They were at the Yukon River, or within walking distance, and all this time they'd had no idea.

"Will we bring Follow?" Paul asked.

They discussed leaving her alone in the cabin, which seemed unwise—she'd tear the place up. They could lock her in the bathroom, but that would be cruel.

"I think we have to," Josie said, putting their fiery faces to bed.

Josie sat outside, listening to the lunatic night, her bullet-hole guitar on her lap. She didn't want to go to town. She had begun to think they could stay in the woods indefinitely. For the time being, she missed no one and nothing. She tried to conjure a decent chord and failed. She tried to pick a string, any string, to make a pleasing sound, and got nowhere. She put the guitar down, went inside, and found Follow, standing on the futon, as if waiting for her company. She lifted the dog, who weighed no more than a carrot, brought her outside and petted her until her black fur calmed and she returned to sleep. This was about the time the ringing had come before, so Josie's back was tense. The cabin door squeaked.

"Mom?" It was Ana.

"You can't be awake," Josie said.

"But I am," Ana said.

Ana came to Josie's chair and leaned against it. She was wearing her conspiratorial face, the one she wore when she called Josie by her first name. She traced circles on Josie's arm, her mouth moving, as if practicing something she needed to say.

"What is it?" Josie asked.

"Mom, I know Dad's dead." She produced an apologetic smile.

"What?" Josie said.

A flicker of doubt entered Ana's eyes. "He is, right?"

"No." Josie threw her arm around Ana and pulled her close. "No, sweetie," she said into Ana's thicket of hair, smelling of woodsmoke and sun and sweat.

Ana pulled away. "But then where is he?"

Josie put Follow gently down, lifted Ana into her lap and gathered her little legs in so she could wrap her arms around her daughter, hold every part of her. She considered how to answer Ana's question, how to hedge or say that her father was away, or they were away, or on vacation, or people grow apart, or make some half-promise to see him soon. But Josie knew it was time to call him. She felt a sudden tenderness toward Carl, because he had helped to create this child sitting in her lap, who had begun to think that if Jeremy was gone and dead, her father, who was gone, was dead, too. In the morning, in town, she would call Carl, and call Sunny, would tell everyone where she was and why, to let them know they would return.

XX.

IT WAS ABSURD TO lock a house where they were squatting, but Josie did lock it, knowing that if they returned and saw any sign of new arrivals—for example the rightful occupants—they could probably make it to the Chateau without being detected. She debated whether or not to take the velvet sack with them, but because the cabin was their home now, she felt it was safer inside than with them. She hid it behind the household cleaners under the sink.

They took the trail up past the last of the mine's buildings, a shack now with but one wall standing, stepped over the low fence and continued. The path rose up the hill for a quarter-mile before it turned and wound around another low peak, one they hadn't been able to see from the cottage.

"This must be Franklin Hill," Paul said, and Josie had the thrill of believing that this was possible: that they could set out in unknown territory, with a handmade map, and they would see actual landmarks that bore some topographical resemblance to the map in the cabin. They rounded the hill and passed through a huddle of pines and just like that, they could see the town below, very small, no more than a few hundred residents, most of the buildings standing by the bend in the river. The water was blue and brown, and traveled slowly but shimmered boldly in the midmorning sun. The rest of the walk, about a mile downhill, was giddy, the children galloping down the dusty path, with Follow ahead of them, then behind them, circling, everyone thinking they were doing something extraordinary.

Separating the trail from the town was a small RV park, a circle of vehicles surrounding a picnic area, white tables arranged in a half-moon. Josie stopped, looked at her kids, hoping they had the appearance of a family returning from a short hike in the hills. Ana was wearing simple sneakers and Paul was wearing his leather boots. Paul was carrying a school backpack and Ana was carrying a stick in the shape of a machine gun—she had assured Josie she would not fire it. They put Follow's rope leash on her collar, and emerged from the trail. The RV park was empty but for an older couple sitting on folding chairs, staring into the sun from the opposite side of the lot. When they arrived at the town's main street, they saw that it was not a regular day in town.

"Mom, is this a holiday?" Paul asked.

Josie had to think about it for a second. Was it Labor Day? No. Too late for that. But the streets had been blocked off for a parade. It was just ending, but Josie and Paul and Ana found a spot on the curbside and sat down just as a high-school band, small but loud, passed by, playing some seventies soul song Josie couldn't place and which was suffering greatly. The band was followed by a group of elderly women steering riding lawn mowers. Then a convertible carrying JULIE ZLOZA, TREE FARMER, TEACHER, who was running for state representative. Then a dozen or so kids on bikes, dressed like Revolutionary soldiers. A group from the local ASPCA, hoping to entice onlookers into adopting six or seven parading dogs, two of them missing legs. The local middle school had a float, where all the school's extracurricular activities seemed to be represented—twin girls in karate outfits, a tall boy in a basketball uniform, a small boy wearing a gold medal, likely some kind of academic decathlete? Walking behind the float was a lone boy in football gear. The final parade float carried a band, ten or twelve adults in close quarters, playing guitars and banjos and fiddles, all acoustic, sending an Americana sound into the air, to the general indifference of the dissipating crowd.

They followed the few hundred people in town to a park, where a sign gave notice that there would be a birthday party, starting in minutes, for Smokey the Bear.

"Who's invited?" Ana wanted to know.

"It's not that kind of party," Paul said.

"Can I see the invitation?" Ana asked.

When they got to the park, at the foot of a small wooded hill, they found most of the residents of the town, some gathered around picnic tables, others lining up for the bouncy house, in the shape of a cresting wave, complete with a trio of inflated surfers.

Already there was a table set up with a large sad sheet cake saying only SMOKEY, and around the cake were various brochures about fire safety, urging celebrants to support local rangers. Ana and Paul were drawn to a fire truck, where a goateed firefighter was demonstrating the use of his ax. Next to him, a woman in khaki, with a high bouffant, was showing the assembled kids the workings of a high-pressure fire hose. Josie thought of the strange math of the firefighting business at the moment. These two were here celebrating Smokey's birthday, all patient and nonchalant, while elsewhere in the state a platoon of inmates were trudging off into the unknown.

There was a gasp, and all heads turned. Coming down the hill behind them were a pair of women in overalls, each of them holding the hand of a giant bear in blue jeans. It was Smokey. But this Smokey had aged, had lived a sedentary life. This Smokey was walking very slowly, and he wore his pants high around his stomach. He emerged from the woods resembling an elderly man who had been in the hospital for many months, and was for the first time walking in the light of day, more or less under his own power.

Smokey stepped carefully in front of the audience and waved a small, tentative wave. He was not the same bear they'd been seeing on the ubiquitous television spots about fire safety. That Smokey was an insurmountable brown monument. That Smokey had intermingled with Josie's thoughts while Jim was pressing himself into her, in the Chateau, a lifetime ago. This Smokey, standing in front of a birthday cake (no candles) and still being held steady by the two assistants, had no idea where he was.

Ana and Paul grew distracted by the inflated wave. Ana asked, and Josie consented, and Paul followed his sister, relinquishing the dog's rope leash. Josie and the dog meandered across the park, then, not wanting to be in the circle of parents watching their children climb up and slide down—Josie was not ready for conversation yet—she stopped under a small pine, and heard the faint sounds of live music, starting and stopping, sounding like the band from the parade.

She looked around her, and finally saw, in a wooded corner of the park, a circle of adults playing guitars and harmonicas and was that an oboe? It was the same band, but now expanded to nine or ten. Their arms were strumming furiously, their shoulders turning, and one man, the one facing her most directly, was sitting bow-legged, flapping his legs up and down like a frog to the rhythm. When he lifted his head, though, Josie ducked behind a tree, and for a while she stayed there, feeling ridiculous, given Follow was clearly visible, her leash giving her away if anyone cared to look.

"I see you," a voice said.

Josie said nothing, did nothing.

"Behind the tree. We all see you and your pig-dog. Come over."

Josie wanted to run. They didn't know her face yet. If she

ran back, maybe she could return, later, not as the woman behind the tree, but as a regular person. She could bring the kids.

"Come on," the voice said, and Josie emerged, bashful, walking over to the circle, seeing that most of the faces were looking up at her, all of them smiling with perfect openness.

"Come sit," the first face said. This was the voice who found her, had spoken to her. He was bearded and thin, in the realm of forty, lithe and bright-eyed, wearing a plaid shirt and a baseball cap. He indicated a place near him but across from him.

"My kids are on the bouncy wave," Josie said, nodding to the giant wave-balloon across the park. She sat between a blond woman holding some kind of harpsichord and the man with the oboe. The bearded man began to play again, and the sound was bigger than before. She was in the middle of the sound, the crashing chaos of it, the diagonal violence of the strumming, the jagged strokes of the violinist, and yet the music was joyous, rollicking. What was the song? It was folksy, but had some bossa nova in there, and when she thought she knew it, a man near her, easily seventy and with a wild tangle of grey hair and grey beard, the swirl of it like an aerial view of a hurricane, began singing.

In che mondo . . .

Viviamo, im-pre-ve-dibile . . .

Was that Italian? She did not expect Italian language to come from this man's mouth in this remote town, in this park near the Yukon. His eyes were closed. He could sing.

What did it mean? Josie assumed it was something like "In this world/that we live in/incredible." Then he sang the same verse, or some version of it, in English, and it was not quite what she expected.

In this world.

That we live in. Unpredictable. Unpredictable.

In this world of sorrow, there is justice, there is beauty . . .

A beautiful song, far too beautiful for this park on this afternoon, far too beautiful for her. The sun was directly above, performing its intoxication, and Josie was immediately caught up, and nodding her head, bouncing her feet.

In che mondo . . .

Viviamo, im-pre-ve-dibile . . .

Josie glanced to her right, to see the man playing the oboe, and when he saw her watching him, his long fingers on that long black tube, he winked. Was there ever anything more phallic and less alluring than an oboe? Across the circle, a woman was playing the violin, though in this context it was probably a fiddle. Josie watched them all, their hands shooting up and down again. These were unnatural movements. Without sound the motions they made would look mad. These drastic gestures up and down, their chins and cheeks stuck to these wooden instruments, fingers touching strings in certain places at certain times.

And suddenly the song was over, and Josie felt spent. These people didn't know what they'd just done. What they were capable of. These goddamned musicians. They never knew their power. To those with no musical talent, to Josie, what they could do sitting in a park near an inflatable wave was both miraculous and unfair. They were sitting there, adjusting strings, smiling at her, murmuring about keys and about the weather, when Josie felt like she'd just heard something absolute in its power to justify her life. Her children justified her daily breaths, her use of planetary resources, and then this—her ability to hear a song like that, in a group like this. Those were the three primary justifications for her living. Surely she was forgetting other things. But what?

"We're just jamming," the bearded man said.

Goddamn you, she wanted to say. It's more than that. It's so easy for you, so hard for the rest of us.

"You have any requests?" he asked. "I'm Cooper."

Josie shook her head, now trying to shrink. She wanted just to listen, not to be part of this. She wanted to go back behind the tree to listen unseen.

"Anything," she said. She grabbed at a patch of grass underneath her and pulled. Was this a crowd that would know *Carousel*? she wondered. *Kiss Me, Kate*?

"Name something. I bet we know it," Cooper said. Now most of the faces were looking at her, actually wanting a request. Maybe they were bored with one another, these spoiled magicians.

"Okay," Josie said, her voice sounding hoarse. There were songs Josie knew, and there were songs she knew they would know, and there were songs she knew they would want to play, so she went for the third category.

" 'This Land Is Your Land'?" she said, shrugging, though

knowing they would love this. There was some nodding and grinning. She had made a good choice, and they began to get themselves into position. The harpsichord began, and the rest of the players followed. They went through the whole song, all six verses, eight choruses, and they insisted Josie sing, too. The song seemed to last twenty minutes, an hour. She glanced at the bouncy house periodically, catching sight of Ana and Paul climbing the inflated steps, sliding down, starting over.

"You play anything?" the oboe man asked her.

She told him no, she had no aptitude at all.

"Ever try to learn?" he asked.

"So many times, Jesus Christ," Josie said, and this was true. All the way through her teens and twenties she'd tried the piano, the guitar, the saxophone. She was equally inept at all of them.

And now she saw Paul standing at the bottom of the inflatable wave, looking around him, hand shielding his eyes, a scout watching for reinforcements.

"I have to go," Josie said, and stood. There were a few murmurs of regret, and someone, maybe Cooper, told her to come back again, that they played every Saturday and Sunday at noon, that anyone was welcome, and while he was talking, Josie realized it must be Saturday that day, thus the parade, thus everyone off work, and that tomorrow they would be playing again, that she wanted to be there.

She walked back to the bouncy wave, and for a while watched her children sliding down, jumping off, climbing back on. This was not civilized, though. There were too many kids, and they were all bigger than Paul and Ana, and bodies were everywhere, tumbling over one another on the way down, feet and elbows narrowly missing faces and necks. "Careful," she said, but her children were not listening. They were not afraid, they were capable of fending for themselves. Here Josie was watching resilience at the genetic level. She watched them climb the inflated steps, kids above them, feet stepping on their hands, and then watched them tumble down, their heads landing on the knees and stomachs of other children, and though Paul's and Ana's eyes were first round with shock and awareness that they could be aggrieved by their slight injury, they chose to roll off the wave, and climb back, again and again.

"Wait here," she said to Paul. "I'll be right back."

She turned around, walking back to the circle of musicians, but they were gone. She scanned the park, and finally found one of them, Cooper, walking toward the parking lot. She ran to him, making sure she could still see the wave that contained her children. He saw her approach, and a curious smile overtook his face.

"Woody Guthrie," he said, standing still, holding his guitar case.

"This will sound strange," she said to him, "given I don't know anything about music, but for a while I've had some music in my head, and ever since I heard you guys playing, I've wondered if you could help me."

"You have music in your head?"

She gave him an imploring look that said *Please don't mock*.

"No, no," he said. "I get it. You need a composer?"

Josie didn't know if it was composing or something else she had in mind. "I don't know," she said. "I think if you play some chords, I would know which ones were the sounds in my head, and we could go about it that way."

"Hm," he said, staring at the grass, a private smile overtaking his face. Josie knew he was thinking this was some excuse to get him in bed. She needed to keep this linear, and this required a lie.

"We're up here for a few weeks while my husband is in Japan on business," she said, happy her children were not near, hearing this canard. "But when I saw you guys playing, I had this thought. I could compensate you guys. I couldn't help noticing that dental care might be welcomed among some of your band. I'm a dentist."

Cooper rubbed the stubble on his cheek. "So, lessons in exchange for dental care?" he said. He seemed to find this a perfectly rational transaction.

"Not exactly lessons," Josie said, and explained that she wanted him to play, and she could listen, and when she heard something she liked, she might tell him to play it more, and faster or slower. She would know what she wanted to hear once she heard it. That she had no musical aptitude, but she knew music, or had heard it, and had composed countless tunes in her mind, or had thought of them at least, flashes here and there, but couldn't articulate the music in her head, or write music on paper, or even know which instruments made which sounds.

Cooper nodded slowly, taking it all in.

"Makes sense," he said.

"Where were you?" Paul wanted to know.

"Over there," she said. "Just near the trees."

For some reason she didn't want to explain the hootenanny circle to him just yet, though she couldn't figure out why. Paul, being all-knowing, knew she was withholding, made this clear with his searching and disappointed eyes, but he didn't press it.

"We're hungry," he said.

They walked through town, looking for a grocery store, expecting to find a small market, but instead, at the end of the main road, there was an enormous store, big enough to fit everyone in town. And in front, next to the entrance, was an incomprehensible thing: a pay phone. "Come," Josie said, gathering coins. They set up in front of the booth, Paul and Ana and Follow, watching the locals come and go into the store, restocking their barbecues and picnics. Josie's stomach leapt. She had been living for weeks utterly removed from her Ohio life, from Carl, Florida, lawsuits, possible police pursuit.

"Ready?" she asked her children.

"For what?" Paul asked.

"Nothing," Josie said, realizing she was asking herself, and knowing the answer was *God, no*. She dialed the number without thinking. A distant tinny ring came through the line.

"Hello?" Sunny's chandelier voice.

"Sunny, it's me," Josie said, and looked down to Ana, whose eyes opened wide. Josie's eyes filled.

"Oh Josie honey," Sunny said, "where are you now? I talked to Sam. She said you left without saying goodbye."

Josie pictured Sunny in her house, the same house, sitting in her dining room, where she liked to take phone calls as she watched hummingbirds alight on the feeder she'd installed.

Josie did a messy job of describing something of their trip since seeing Sam. It seemed years since they were in Homer.

"I always wanted to go up there," Sunny said. "Too old now."

"Shush," Josie said.

"Carl called," Sunny said, and seemed to be waiting for some expression of shock, but Josie couldn't breathe or muster words. Given Sunny's age, Josie wondered: Could she have given Josie's location away?

"What'd you tell him?" Josie asked.

"Oh, I didn't answer. I didn't call back. Should I?"

"No, no. Please don't. I'll call him."

Ana was reaching for the phone, and Josie relinquished it. "Hi," she said. "This is Ana." For a minute Ana held the phone close to her face, nodding occasionally. She tended to forget the listener couldn't see her, and thought facial signals would suffice. Losing interest, she handed the phone back to Josie.

"Josie," Sunny said. Her voice had dropped an octave. "Did you know she died?"

"Who died?"

"Evelyn Sandalwood."

Josie did not know.

"It was just five days ago," Sunny said. "She was undergoing some procedure related to the cancer."

Josie said nothing.

"You didn't know—oh god, that's what I figured. Josie?"

"I'm fine," she said, but heard a hoarse tremble in her voice.

"Helen took the liberty of calling your attorney. Apparently nothing's changed. But you probably could have assumed that."

Josie had no idea what to say. She looked around her, to the tops of her children's heads. Ana was stroking Follow's tail, while Paul was watching one of the parade floats, now disassembled, drive home.

"All that struggle, it meant nothing," Sunny said. "She gets nothing from it all. She's dead. You get nothing. It's senseless. But Josie."

"Yes?" Josie said.

"They did not defeat you."

Josie knew this. "I know," she said, then felt a surge of strength. What she was feeling was not defeat, but triumph. She was thinking: Evelyn, I flew north of your rage. She thought of Evelyn's son-in-law, the lawyers, all their devious eyes, and she thought, *I flew north of your anger. I flew away and felt none of it. I was gone. I am gone.*

"You've had plenty of reasons to doubt," Sunny said.

But Josie did not feel doubtful. She felt invincible. She felt like continuing. She needed nothing she did not have there with her. She had Sunny's voice, she had Ana, she had Paul. She told Sunny that she loved her, that she would call again soon, but she wasn't sure when that would be. She had planned to call Carl, too, but now she felt that could wait. Enough news from home for today.

"Gotta leave him outside," the checkout woman said. She'd seen the kids and Follow all this time, and when they tried to enter with the dog, the woman was ready.

"It's a she," Ana told her, but the woman did not care.

They tied Follow to a pole outside. "We'll be quick," Paul told Follow, who was dancing around in a way that implied they would return to find that she'd peed or defecated on the sidewalk. Josie made a mental note to buy plastic bags.

"Bright," Ana said, and the three of them spent a full minute standing in the doorway, the store seeming an acre wide, two dozen rows of food stocked seven feet high. It had only been a few weeks since they'd been in a store like this, but it seemed like years. The customers were the same people she'd seen at the parade and the park, denim and baseball hats, but now Josie felt foreign among them. Under these lights, amid all this abundance, everything so clean, the antiseptic floors and blue-white lights, she was uncomfortable.

"Can we use the real bathroom?" Paul asked.

"If you can find it," Josie said, and Ana went with him.

Josie grabbed a cart and went about quickly loading into it everything they needed—rice, beans, cans of soup and corn. Evelyn Sandalwood was dead. She thought of the funeral, all that anger. Sunny had sounded so old. What was she now? Seventy-five. Seventy-six. Josie would need to see her soon. Oh god, she thought, thinking of Sunny older still, unable to care for herself. What would happen then? Some combination of all the young women she'd helped would come to her aid. Josie would need to see her. Josie would be there for her. Oh god, she thought. She missed Sunny desperately at that moment. She wanted to call her again, see her immediately. But then her mind reversed itself, insisting that she needed to keep moving. That she was healthier here, that she and her children were growing far beyond what she could have imagined a month ago. Did that mean they could never return to their former lives? No decisions were necessary now, she knew. Right now they would get food, and would return to the cabin, and then what?

Paul and Ana emerged from the bathroom. They filled the cart with bread, canned juice, regular milk, powdered milk, cereal, granola, vegetables, an array of meats, and brought it all to the woman who had barred Follow's entry.

"Can we go see her?" Paul asked.

"Stay on the sidewalk," Josie said.

Before she was finished paying, though—$188, a crime, a travesty—they were back. "There's a lady there," Paul said.

"Mean one," Ana said.

Josie paid, left the bags inside and followed the kids outside. Standing over Follow, holding the dog's leash, was a large woman with black hair streaked in blue. "This is my dog," she said.

"Excuse me?" Josie said.

"Where'd you take her from? Do I need to call the police?" The woman was wearing a puffy vest and jeans, and had already taken out her phone. Paul's eyes were wet. Seeing his state, Ana began to cry, the tears like tiny plastic jewels tumbling down her face.

Josie explained that Follow had been all the way over the ridge, in the mine, at least two miles from town, that the dog had been scared and desperate. "Your dog followed my children home," she said. "We fed her and took care of her."

"No one lives there," the woman said, meaning the mine. "I think I need to call the sheriff."

"We're house-sitting," Josie said, already feeling the need to leave this conversation, this woman, her posture aggressive, her eyes wild with indignation. Paul and Ana were standing behind Josie now, hiding. Josie knew the dog was lost—the woman was clearly the owner—and the town was small, and this woman likely knew everyone in it. "We saved this dog," Josie said. "My kids rescued her."

The woman leaned back and crossed her arms, nodding

and smiling, as if she'd heard this hustle before. It was all Josie could do not to say *You don't deserve this dog* or *Go to hell* but she knew they needed to get away, to evaporate. "Let's go," she said, and hustled her weeping children back into the store, where they gathered their bags and went out the rear exit.

"It's okay," Josie said as they walked to the trailhead, knowing it was not okay. Paul shuffled behind Josie and Ana, sighing, his shoulders collapsed. "She's got a good home," Josie said over her shoulder, knowing that was not true, either. In an effort to cheer up her brother, Ana was walking with her hands down her pants.

"Hands in my pants!" she roared, and Paul rolled his eyes.

They were almost at the trailhead when Josie realized they couldn't go there, either. Not in the light of day. The chances were remote, but the woman who owned Follow might have reported that a woman with two children had found her dog there, might be squatting out there, were likely to steal other animals and care for them.

"Hold on," she said, and looked around her. There was the RV park ahead, a woman working on a satellite dish installed on her roof. There was a seaplane flying low over a row of pines. And beyond the trees, there was the Yukon. "Let's go there. Picnic."

They settled at the bend of the river, Ana finding a sharp stick and wetting its tip in the water. She brought the point to her nose.

"Smells clean," she said.

They ate sullenly and watched an unmanned dinghy pass, taken downstream by the current. Josie thought of Evelyn, wanting to conjure some sadness for her death, but felt only the waste of it all, the misplaced rage, the inevitability of victims begetting victims.

"Getting darker," Paul said, pointing to the leaking light.

"Let's hustle," Josie said. She was carrying the groceries in six plastic bags, three dangling from each hand. Paul and Ana had pleaded to carry their share, but she knew they would relinquish them in minutes, so she balanced the weight and they walked swiftly.

"Too dark," Ana said.

By the time they arrived, night had come on, and the RVs in the park were bathed in moonlight. It was a quarter-moon, tinged with orange and pink, and not bright enough to guide them.

"Sorry," Josie said.

There was one store open nearby, a gas station they'd passed that looked to have a convenience store attached, so she brought the kids along the frontage road and under the bright lights and into the store. She had eight dollars left with her, and held out hope that the store would have some smaller model of light, the kind of thing attached to a keychain.

They had no such thing. She sent Paul all over the store to no avail. They had one flashlight for sale, a forty-five-dollar machine that seemed capable of signaling planes and ships.

"You have just a regular flashlight?" she asked the woman behind the counter.

"Sorry," she said. "We have candles, though. You lose power?"

Apparently there had been some power outages related to the wildfires, and the store had had to stock up on candles. They'd sold out three times in the last month, the clerk explained. And so Josie left the gas station with a twelve-pack of candles, each with a tin rim to catch the wax, and a pack of matches. With these they would make their way through the forest and over the ridge and back to their cabin.

"We get our own?" Paul asked.

Josie was sure that the only way she could manage to get her children aboard for this task, walking through a black forest at nine o'clock with only candles to guide their way, would be to allow each of them to hold their own.

"Yes," she said, as if it had been the plan all along. Then, realizing that with her hands full of grocery bags she wouldn't be able to hold a candle at all, she delivered the coup de grace. "You two will have to light our path. I can't do it."

It sounded more dramatic than she'd intended, but they took the bait. They made their way down the road and at the RV park they ducked across the frontage road and into the darkness. The candles gave them a circle of light that allowed them to see one another, their shirts ghostly white. But the short reach of the candlelight meant that all around them was still darker. All along the walk, trees arrived in front of Josie's view with alarming suddenness. She could only keep faith that they were on the right path, that the path did not split or detour, and that because it was inclining slightly all the way, they were making their way up the hillside and over the ridge.

"Smell's getting worse," Paul said. He was right. The wildfire's acrid air seemed to be stronger, denser.

Tomorrow she would return to work with Cooper. She smiled to herself, disbelieving that she'd made a proposal like that to a stranger. He had agreed, and now her head was full of ideas, elaborations and reversals. The show about *Grenada*? Would that be the first thing to explore? Or *Disappointed: The Musical*? Or something encompassing all of Alaska. *Alaska!* No, without the exclamation point, because this was not a demonstrative place, no, it was a place of tension, of uncertainty, a state on fire. Alaska with a colon. *Alaska:* Yes. The show would start with Stan. Stan and his wife, awash in white carpet, closing the door on Josie and her children, the Chateau in motion. Josie thought briefly of *Starlight Express,* the actors on roller skates—that kind of debacle could be avoided. There would be Norwegians, and naked showering nymphs, magicians from Luxembourg. The zip code guy? He'd tip the show, obliterate all else, as he did on the cruise ship. You could get Jim in there, Grenada. You'd have to have Kyle and Angie. Guns everywhere.

"Mom?" Paul asked. "Has anyone ever done this before?"

Paul asked this question every so often, when they were

in new situations, when something seemed wrong. He'd asked it once when he peed in his pants at school. Has anyone ever done that before? he wanted to know. There was comfort in precedent. Happens every day, Josie had said then. Now she said, "Walk in the dark? Every night, Paul, someone is walking in the dark."

For a moment it seemed Josie's wording had made it worse, conjuring an army of stealthy night strollers, but Paul seemed satisfied, and Josie returned to her show. Could it be that there would be periodic shots in the theater? The actors would sing, the orchestra would play, but every few minutes a rifle shot, the pop of a handgun, would break open the air, and there would be little to no attention paid to it. Who was shot? Was it real? The play would go on. Josie thought she would try that the next day with Cooper's group—some kind of arrhythmic interruption that might mean death but would not stop the music. The crazed music—for it had to sound like organized lunacy—would always go on, loud and ceaseless.

"Champagne on my shoulders!" Ana yelled.

Then: "Stab stab stab!"

And: "PBS kids dot com!"

Josie laughed, and Paul laughed, and they both knew that by her getting a laugh, Ana would not stop until forced to. Encouraged, she sang louder. "Cham*pagne*! On my *shoul*-ders!" Where could she have heard these things? But then again, Ana was tuned to a different galactic frequency, and there was no telling what signals she was picking up. Josie had no choice but to allow Ana's babbling nonsense; she needed both kids to be happily distracted from the fact that they were walking without the dog they had in the morning, over a mountain in the dark holding disintegrating candles.

"Mine's almost done," Paul said, and they stopped so Josie could transfer the flames from the gnarled and spent candles to the pristine new ones, and the kids seemed similarly re-energized with the new candles. Josie chose not to think about the possibility that they would be attacked by bears, wolves or coyotes. She had seen signs warning of the presence of all of these animals nearby, but she guessed, without any evidence to support her thesis, that the candles would ward them off.

So there would be periodic gunshots. Mortar fire. Thunder but no rain. There would be horns, and strings, but the woodwinds would dominate. The clarinets—and flutes! They sound innocent but always signal deviance. They would underline the madness. The air would be full of smoke. At times the audience would barely be able to see the action, and everyone, especially the Alaskans, would wonder why Alaska, the last frontier, pure and undiminished, ragged and filthy, endless, independent but then wholly dependent, which had sent billions of gallons of oil through a pipeline to be burned and sent into the atmosphere, was now on fire. And so there would be tragedy, too.

"There it is!" Paul yelled. On the opposite side of the ridge, the rusted roof of the mine was visible, just a slant of black against the sky, and Josie had the strange sensation of being home. The abandoned mining town was now their home. The path was illuminated by the partial moon and the kids could find their way.

"Wait," Josie said, and scanned the area for cars. She half-expected a police car to be waiting. But there was no one. They were still alone, and her heart swelled.

"Can we run?" Paul asked.

Ana looked to him, as if unsure if she could support this suggestion. Then she nodded vigorously, kicking herself for doubting any radical act, especially one involving running.

"Just to the cabin," Josie said, and enjoyed saying that. The kids ran ahead, down a dark path, toward the amber light.

Could you have animals in the show? she wondered. Wolves and bears. A bighorn sheep. An eagle dropping it a thousand feet to a silent death. Cruel logical murder in the wild. More gunshots. Someone would die but no one would care. The fires would burn. That could be part of the soundtrack—the slow hushing crackle of the fires. Sirens. She couldn't help picturing the curtain call: cops, prisoners, firefighters. Evaders and crusaders. The fires, on stage, would rage behind them, pushing them to the edge. Finally the actors would leap into the audience, flee for the doors. More gunshots, real or unreal, no one would know, as everyone left the theater and ran into the night. When they left the theater, they'd forget where they'd come from.

Josie unlocked the front door, let the kids in and turned the light switch on. Nothing happened. She tried again, nothing.

They entered the cabin by candlelight, trying anything electric, and found that something had happened: the power was out. She opened the fridge, feeling its fleeting cold, threw their groceries in, and closed it, wondering what among the things they'd just bought would go bad by morning.

"Is this okay?" Ana asked.

Josie turned to find her face, orange in the candlelight, her eyes shining. What Ana meant was: Should the lights really be on? Did someone turn off the lights because we shouldn't be here? Should we be in Alaska, in an abandoned mine, alone, in this home that isn't ours? What does it mean that it's dark here, and we have only candles, and we just crossed a mountain to get here, and were not harmed by beast or man? How is this all allowed?

"It's fine," Josie said.

They lit more candles and brushed their teeth, and Josie read them C. S. Lewis from a copy they found in a bathroom drawer, and in the flickering candlelight, while reading *Prince Caspian,* Josie felt that they were living a life that had kinship with the heroes of these books. They had only walked two miles through the dark, through a forest and over a ridge to their home in a twice-abandoned mining town, but she felt there was not so great a difference between what she and her children were capable of and what these other protagonists had done. Courage was the beginning, being unafraid, moving ahead, through small hardships, not turning back. Courage was simply a form of moving forward.

XXI.

COOPER LIVED IN A REAL HOUSE, a red-brick ranch
with a black roof, which was surprising, though Josie didn't
know why. He'd told her he lived there in town, and he'd
been wearing clean clothes when she'd met him, so did she
really think he lived in a tent? Something about the hootenanny had her thinking of hoboes.

Josie and the kids had walked over the mountain trail
and into town, and Cooper opened the door before she rang
the bell. "Right on time," he said. He'd told her to come
at eleven, with the rest of the players trickling in after
noon.

The kids entered the house reluctantly, but then Ana
ran to the back porch, where she'd spotted an ancient hobby
horse on wheels. Paul walked in slowly, looking around as if
this might be his future home.

"I made some lemonade," Cooper said. "The kids can
drink it out there if they want," he said, indicating the
backyard, where Ana was already testing the horse for weak

points. There were a handful of other playthings strewn about the porch, all of them weather-worn and missing key parts. "Or they could stay and watch."

Ana was already outside and couldn't hear him. But Paul stayed by Josie's side as Cooper led them into a wide living room, most of it dark but for a cone of light in the center, coming from a bright round skylight. There were Persian rugs overlapping each other, a pair of drama masks, happy and sad, over the fireplace. Josie complimented the house, which was cave-like and clean. Cooper sat on a leather ottoman and gathered his guitar on his thigh.

"I figured we could start alone," he said. "Just to get your bearings. Or for me to get mine."

"And the rest of them? They're all okay with a checkup?" Josie tried to conjure what tools she'd be able to muster and sterilize. She'd have to bend a paperclip. "And these guys are professionals or . . . ?" She wasn't quite sure why she asked. She knew they weren't a band of professional musicians, playing parades and parks in Alaska.

No, no, Cooper said. They all had full-time jobs, or as close to full-time as anyone had in the town. A couple were seasonal oil workers, one was in commercial fishing, another had retired as a lumberjack. "Suki's the drummer. She waits tables at Spinelli's. And Cindy's the new mailperson around here. She's the singer," Cooper said, and it was clear that there was something about Cindy—was she beautiful? Were she and Cooper involved? "We just found out a few weeks ago she could sing. She wasn't at the parade."

Josie didn't know what to do with herself. Stand? Sit? She sat on the arm of the couch.

"So guitar?" he asked. "I play piano, trumpet . . ."

"Guitar is fine," Josie said.

"You have in mind a song, or—" he asked. "I assume you have lyrics already."

Josie didn't have any words at all in mind. She had only the thousand notions from the night before.

"Maybe you could start with some lower chords," Josie said. "It was when you were strumming yesterday, at the end of that last song, that I started thinking about this."

Cooper tried a few chords, and then strummed one that sounded right.

"What's that?" Josie asked.

"G."

"Just G? Not flat or sharp or anything?"

"Just G. You want me to keep going?"

"I should be writing this down," Josie said.

"I'll remember," Cooper said, then went to the kitchen and came back with a legal pad and a pencil. Paul was sitting close to Josie, silent and seeming to understand what was happening. She knew the important thing, now, was to act normal, in command—to avoid this being some pivotal moment where he realized his mother had left the rational world.

"Can you write for me?" she asked Paul.

He took the pad eagerly.

"Write down G," she said, but he already had. He

underlined it for her, and looked up at her, now involved, no longer concerned.

Josie asked Cooper for other chords that were low like G. He played two more, named them A and C, and Paul wrote them down.

"You have a piano here?" Josie asked.

Cooper smiled, and Paul reached across her lap to point at a small piano in the corner. Josie glanced out the back window, and saw no sign of Ana.

"Can you go check on her?" she asked Paul.

"No," he said. Josie was stunned into silence. "I want to stay," he said, his tone softening. "I want to hear."

Ana reappeared from the side of the house, carrying the disembodied antlers of a deer. She seemed to be speaking to them, or to herself, animated but stern.

"Okay," Josie said. She turned to Cooper. "While you strum the G, could I play with the piano?"

"Of course," he said, and Paul wrote, "Mom on piano:"

She hit a key, and it sounded tinny and wrong. She moved twenty keys down, and that was all wrong, too. She found a spot in between and hit a note. It sounded like a bell. It sounded like Sunny. She hit it again.

"That's nice," Cooper said.

"What was it?" Josie asked.

"B-sharp."

Paul wrote that down, and Josie had a thought, too soon to articulate. What she couldn't say at that moment was that this sound from the piano was what should be her voice. In her head Josie heard this strumming, his low strumming, then heard a bell-clear voice, high in pitch but strong, lyrical but determined, and this voice was both hers and Sunny's.

"Is that the note you want?" Cooper asked. "Any others?"

She tried some of the keys nearby, but none sounded as certain as that first one.

"Can you strum that G again?" she asked, and he did. "Now can you vary between G and F and D? Make some kind of song out of it?"

Cooper played the chords, and they sounded right for a moment, until he began filling the transitions with some kind of extra flourishes.

"No, no, not those," Josie said, and mimicked what he'd been doing. He laughed, stopped, and returned to the regular rhythm he'd begun before. Paul was busy writing.

"Good, good," she said, and returned her attention to the piano. She played her B-sharp, and then leaped a foot over and found another note she liked.

"What's that?" she asked.

"F-sharp," he said.

Now she alternated between the two notes, the sound like a bad man walking up a set of very high steps. Her eyes welled and her breathing grew shallow, but her fingers continued, now with more force. It sounded like it happened that way. That's the way it sounded, she thought, but she didn't know what the music was describing, what exactly it was recounting.

"Should I keep going?" Cooper asked.

"Yes!" she said, not looking up. She saw only the keys in front of her, and she made the footstep sounds louder, then softer, faster and then slower. She paused, continued. It was exactly right, she thought, though she never wanted to hear it again.

"I'm going to check on Ana," Josie said, and walked outside. She needed a break. It was too much. From the back porch she saw Ana in the shallow woods, holding the antlers on her head.

"You good?" Josie asked.

"I'm looking for a frog friend," Ana said.

"Makes sense," Josie said, and returned. Paul was scribbling furiously on his pad, as if to avoid eye contact with the two new women in the room.

"Couple new arrivals," Cooper said.

One was introduced as Cindy, the singer. She was a blond, cherub-faced woman of about thirty, wearing a tanktop and the grey and blue pants of a mailperson. The other was Suki, Asian, lithe, muscular, in a fleece vest and shorts. The two of them were setting up Suki's drumset.

"So you're a dentist?" Cindy asked. "I haven't had a checkup in a few years. Am I doomed?"

"I think you'll be fine," Josie said. "We'll make sure afterward."

"After what, exactly?" Suki asked. "Coop says you're a composer?"

Josie looked over to Cooper, whose face betrayed no

strategy. But Josie figured there was no harm in a reach of confidence.

"Amateur," Josie said.

"We're all amateurs," Cindy said.

Cooper was looking at his phone. "The rest of the guys are coming in one van. But it'll be a little while. Should we get started?"

Josie sat on the edge of the couch, her back straight, her hands raised a bit, indicating the position of a conductor.

"We're improvising," Cooper said to Cindy and Suki. "Just stay loose." He began with G, and instantly Josie felt more sure. This chord seemed right and it gave her strength. It sounded as sturdy as the earth beneath them.

"Just tell Cindy when you want her to sing," he said.

"Thank you," Josie said. "Now vary between that and the F. You decide how."

And so he strummed the F, then the G, and Josie looked over to Cindy, whose face was teetering between enthralled and afraid.

"Ready?" Josie asked.

Cindy nodded.

"Hit the B-sharp," Josie said.

"Just the note? Any words?"

"Anything. Sounds or words," Josie said.

Cindy sang a quick succession of notes, something like fa-la-la-la-la, and it was wrong. Josie grimaced, and Cindy saw her grimace, and stopped. "No?"

"Your voice is beautiful," she said. "Maybe a little lower?

And when you sing, it doesn't have to be pretty. It could be Ya! Ya-ya-ya! Yaaaah-ya-ya! Or calling out to someone, someone about to cross the street in traffic."

Cindy tried it and again it was wrong. She was tentative. She was mimicking Josie and it sounded false.

"Make any words you want," Josie said. "But urgent."

All the while, Cooper had been strumming loudly, and with more force. She nodded to him. *Good, good.*

Cindy's eyes showed she was thinking of words to say, words that would fit the urgency, and the syllables, and the staccato pattern Josie gave her. She seemed to settle on something, and closed her eyes, and when Cooper hit a transition, the beginning of something, her eyes opened again, and now she was possessed.

"Now! Now no! No no no! Now now no!"

She was singing these words at a volume just below yelling, and it was wonderful. Josie forgot to breathe. Cindy's eyes were open to the wall, avoiding Josie and Cooper. Cooper was looking at Cindy anew, and was nodding in approval. Finally she looked to Josie, needing to know if she should continue, and Josie nodded vigorously, because she loved Cindy very deeply now, because she was vocalizing the music inside of her. Paul had stopped writing.

"Okay, ready?" Josie said to Suki.

Suki raised her sticks.

"You have a sound in your head, Josie?" Cooper asked.

There was indeed something in her head, Josie told Cooper and Suki, and to describe it Josie made a rolling sound with her lips, a rolling bumping sound like heavy rain on a hollow porch. Suki tried to replicate the sound and succeeded immediately. It sounded very much like, and better than, the sound in her mind, and Josie asked her to continue making that sound, with any of the drums she had before her, as if there were a storm overhead, and the rain and sleet were coming in heavy waves. Suki began again, and now the storm did come in waves, heavier, then lighter, faster then slower, but always it was the same storm, the heavy rain and sleet on the hollow porch. Suki was the storm outside and Cooper was a pair of great wings flapping inside a house pelted by steady rain. Josie didn't know where she'd heard this sound, but it sounded to her like some home she'd once had. Where had she lived with a porch like this? With a roof like this, with the rain and sleet in the darkness?

Josie waved to Cindy that she could join in again.

"Now now no! Now no no no! Now no no no no! Now now no!" Cindy sang, venom at the end of every line. Suki kept the tumbling coming, fast and slow, and Cooper strummed his low chords, the volume filling the dark room. Cindy continued, "Now now no! Now no no no! Now now no no!" adding one long "Nooooooo" that lasted as long as she had breath. It wavered wonderfully at the end, and it sounded so much like Josie's teens, those forgotten years, and her twenties, a whole decade of wretched, regretful self-inflicted pain contained in that long *Nooooo*. Josie threw her head back and stared at the ceiling, spent.

"That was cool," Cooper said.

Josie nodded seriously, inwardly blooming, so happy about his respect for what they were doing, as if he actually believed that the process had precedent and worth.

The door opened. Josie turned to find a man, tall and familiar. He was one of the musicians from yesterday's circle. He was carrying a cello.

"Frank," Cooper said, and walked to the cellist. He was wearing a fur-lined corduroy coat, far too warm for the weather, grey flannel pants and rubber boots. He and Cooper exchanged a few private words by the door, and Cooper went quickly to the kitchen to retrieve a pair of chairs, which he placed in the living room.

Frank approached Josie, extending his hand. His face seemed conflicted with itself—his face was long, jowls falling into his collar, but his eyes were small and bright.

There was a knock on the door, and another face appeared, a grey-haired man Josie didn't remember, carrying a guitar, and a half-dozen more people immediately behind him. Two carried guitars, one a trombone, another a trumpet. The last in was an older woman with a violin. "Word got around," she said, and closed the door.

"Getting weird out there," Frank the cellist said, indicating the world outside, as he brought a chair from the kitchen and positioned himself near Cooper. "The winds are heading this way," he said.

Josie wasn't sure what that meant, but assumed this was a kind of shorthand for locals, that this meant something to them.

"So get set up," Cooper told everyone. "We already got a good start. Everyone know Josie? This is Josie," he said, and the musicians, crowding together in a two-ring circle, nodded respectfully to her.

Paul was writing feverishly. Josie peeked over his shoulder to see he was naming every instrument and some description of the person playing it: *Old lady, red shirt, dirty hands.*

Josie saw something outside and had an idea. "Can I move that in here?" she asked Cooper, but didn't wait for an answer. She walked out to the back deck, the sky yellowing and wind gusting, took his weight lifting bench and carried it inside. Cooper held up his hands in surrender, and Josie carried the bench past him and set it in the middle of the carpet, between him and Suki. As the musicians warmed up and tuned, Josie lay down on it, her eyes to the ceiling, and it felt right.

"Everyone ready?" Cooper asked. "Start with the same thing?" he asked Josie.

"Actually," she said, "can we start with the trumpet?"

The trumpeter, a portly man of about fifty, with a buttoned-up shirt and glasses, put on a comical air of self-importance, straightening himself in his chair.

"Your name?" she asked.

"Lionel," he said.

"Something a little vaudeville, a little tragic, Lionel," Josie said to the ceiling, and Lionel began, and it was better than Josie could have imagined. It was like so many of those old records they had in that Rosemont house, that sad old trumpet sounding like decay, like adults who let themselves regret and wallow. There was a sound like this in just about every musical she could remember. But why?

"Now the cello?" Josie said, knowing the sadness would be multiplied. It felt so good to hear this, she thought, knowing it was just for them, heard only by the people in this room. She looked around, seeing the musicians nodding, their heads tilted, some with eyes closed.

"A little snare?" Josie said.

Suki began, a slow march, and the three of them, being musicians, unfairly blessed with the power to weave together instantaneously, created what sounded like a real song, a slinky and seductive tune, that might announce the arrival of a femme fatale. Josie closed her eyes, and in a flash remembered a time when her mother appeared at the top of the stairs wearing an antique mink coat—something she'd gotten from her own mother. She'd sashayed down the stairs to some old song, her eyes encircled in heavy eyeliner. Josie had been twelve, maybe, and it had thrilled and confused her to see her mother this way, a sexual being, capable of theatrics and artifice. Josie had been at the bottom of the stairs, with her father. Holding his hand! She remembered this now, how strange it was to hold his hand at age twelve, but she had done that, hadn't she? They had stood at the bottom of the stairs, and at her mother's behest they'd put on a record. What was that record? And they had watched as she vamped down the steps, a nurse wearing furs and makeup, her hair curled and shiny.

"Josie?" It was Cooper. "Anyone else?" he asked.

Josie sat up, finding the faces of the other ten musicians, everyone at the ready. "Sorry," she said. She looked over to Paul, whose eyes seemed on the verge of worry. "I think we're ready for everyone now."

"Continue from where we were?" Cooper asked.

"No," Josie said. "Something different. Let's start with your G. A faster tempo now. Just strum, the G and D and F, but faster."

Cooper began, and she swirled her arm, telling him faster. He sped up, and the sound overwhelmed the room. She pointed to Suki now, who began a slow rumble, a self-serious rhythm.

"Now you," Josie said, pointing to Frank. He began to play, and after just one stroke of his bow across the human curves of the instrument, Josie stopped breathing. The cello was a voice. More than any other instrument, the cello was a human's voice. A dying man, a dying woman. Josie's eyes quickly filled, and Frank noticed, and seemed ready to pause, but she gestured to him, insisting he continue. She pointed to Cindy, who began singing, but now at a lower register, responding to the cello in a way Josie didn't expect but felt was correct, or correct enough for now. Suki, unasked, grew louder, and Josie liked that, and Frank grew louder, too, slicing his cello, vacillating between a few notes, Josie had no idea what notes, what chords, but they sounded like every disappointment, speaking for her terrible love of her poison-ous past, every bit of it tasting bitter but filling her with a dark intoxicating fluid. The cello was the steady downward pull of lost time.

From behind her a violin leaped in, and she turned to find the older woman, now with her eyes closed, glasses atop her head. She was playing something different, though, a jauntier tune, and Josie nodded vigorously. It was time. She pointed to the violinist and smiled.

"Everyone like that!" she yelled over it all.

And now, one by one, the musicians joined in. The guitars doubled the sound and doubled it again. The trombone gave it the lumbering sound of everyday, the trumpet gave it the sun, the bursts of irrational joy—trumpets were the sound of laughter, Josie knew now—and on top of it all, the oboe and clarinet provided the madness. The woodwinds sounded like the insane, like loons and coyotes, a fighter plane twirling down from the sky to its doom, like a row of Rockettes. Now Ana appeared in the doorway, her antlers at her side.

"Come," Josie yelled, and extended her arms.

Ana didn't walk to her, but instead began sneaking over, the antlers held on her head, as if she were a deer trying to enter the room unnoticed. The musicians smiled, their eyes crinkling, and Ana fed on it. Josie was sure she was on the verge of exploding.

She was right. Ana dropped the antlers and raised her arms, as if drawing more power from every corner of the room. Now she sprinted in place. She turned on one foot, then the other. She danced with shocking rhythm and funk, shaking and twisting and periodically kicking one foot toward a musician—giving each of them, Frank and Lionel and everyone else, a kick of salute, never actually touching—a theatrical kick of fraternity and communal insanity. A kick for *you*! she was saying, and then would turn to kick another. A kick for *you, too*!

The musicians could barely keep it together. She was a star, a natural being of the theater, meant to exaggerate and eviscerate the attempted dignities of being human. Animals! her body was saying. *You are animals. I am an animal. It is good to be an animal!* She kicked high in Paul's direction, then kicked again, this time knocking the legal pad from his hands. Delighted, she pulled him to the carpet, to dance with her. Not knowing how to keep up, first he simply lifted her into the air, and she went with it, raising her hands to the sky like a figure skater raised high by her partner. But she wanted down, and Paul lowered her, and now she circled him, and he followed suit, and they circled each other, growling and pawing, and finally just leaping straight up, again and again, urging each other higher. All the while the music grew louder, Cooper strumming with what seemed to be double the volume and depth. The pace was growing quicker, more urgent and frenetic, and Josie looked around to find that the musicians had left their own moorings. They were all on their feet, dancing, high-stepping, kicking, following Ana's lead. Two were on the ground, their legs pedaling upward. The trumpeter was in the kitchen, playing into the fridge, and it sounded marvelous. It was all a maniacal wall of cross-cutting sounds, all of it separately desperate and tragic underneath but on top of it all, there was a lunatic spiraling, all of it sounding exactly like but completely different from any of the sounds she'd heard in her head for so many years, when she thought she had some music in her. She lay back down, luxuriating in the sounds, thinking she could stay here, not just at Cooper's, but in this town, too. She could be a dentist again, as Cooper suggested, and every week could come to Cooper's house like this, could further articulate this chaos inside her, could clean their teeth, and in exchange there would be this kind of release.

But now there was a new sound. Josie sat up, annoyed. It was an artificial sound, a man-made sound of panic. Sirens. They wove slowly into the music. And one by one the musicians stopped to listen, and phones began to ring, and it was all over.

XXII.

JOSIE STEPPED THROUGH the front door, feeling dazed and sated, the light an assault to all senses, and saw a pair of fire trucks speed by, sirens screaming. She turned around to find Cooper on his cellphone. Frank hustled by, squeezing past her and out the door. "Fire's coming this way. They're evacuating. Told you."

The rest of the musicians followed, and spread all over the lawn, going in all directions, carrying their horns and guitars. Paul and Ana appeared in the doorway.

"We have to go," Josie said.

But she didn't know where. She didn't know where the fire was coming from. She assumed from the south, where the closest fire had been, but what did that mean for the cabin, the Chateau?

A woman in an orange vest was running down the street. "Mandatory evacuation," she called out. She was out of breath.

Suki emerged from the house and breezed past her. "Bye Josie," she said. Cindy followed her, going the opposite way. "Bye Joze," she said. Josie said goodbye and turned to the woman in orange.

"Where's it coming from?" Josie asked her.

"South," the woman heaved, and pointed.

Josie followed her finger to the mountains. The sky was white, choked with smoke. "How close is it?" she asked.

"Close. You have to go north. There are buses if you need them. They're headed to Morristown. Leaving in twenty minutes."

"Do you know if it's already at the silver mine?" Josie asked, but the woman waved her off, and continued down the street. She was some kind of volunteer, knocking on doors.

"Where's the fire, Mom?" Paul asked.

Sirens vandalized the air.

"Let me think," Josie said.

The fire trucks were heading out of town, going south, while families with cars were already speeding north.

"Come inside," Josie said, and hustled her kids into Cooper's house. He was on the phone again. He turned to Josie. "Half hour, tops. I'd take you but I don't have room."

"What do you know about the silver mine?" she asked.

"Nothing," he said. "What silver mine?"

She took him aside, out of the kids' earshot. She told him about staying at the Peterssen Mine, over the hills, that they had all their belongings there, all their money and an RV, that it was their only way out of town. "You think we can get there in time?" she asked.

He looked at her like she'd lost her mind.

"Just get on a bus," he said.

"What about our stuff?" Paul whispered to Josie. Cooper had packed two backpacks for them, full of food and water, flashlights and batteries, and sent them down the road to the elementary school parking lot, where the buses were assembled. Most were empty—most of the people in town had their own cars and trucks.

Josie raised her hands in the air, with a magician's flair, and stepped onto the bus. Paul and Ana followed, and aboard they found only five seats taken, by two elderly couples and one teenager traveling alone. They sat down, Josie looked into the hills, where there was a wall of green and grey smoke, wondering if the fire had already taken the cabin, or would ever take it. She'd asked everyone she knew, and no one had any idea.

"Mom, really," Paul whispered. He needed clarity.

Josie knew she should be reassuring her children about their prospects, but she was too stunned to put on a front. She pictured the cabin on fire, all their drawings on fire, all the games on fire, Candyland on fire, the children's swords and bows and arrows, all the food they'd just bought. She thought of the Chateau. They had not left much there, a few items of clothing, and would not miss any of it. But it would surely be gone—if the fire came to that valley it would burn quickly and hot. There were too many trees, everything so dry, and no one there to fight off the flames.

And then she saw it. A bright yellow glow from behind the hills, as if an oblong sun was quickly rising. But it was no sun, it was the fire, and she knew it meant it had over-taken the valley of the mine. Black smoke billowed upward, and she guessed one of the machines had been engulfed, the sudden burning of some kind of fuel. The Chateau. It had to be, its tank full of gas. She thought of Stan, and how she would tell Stan, standing on his white carpet, that the Chateau was no more. Knowing Stan, he'd make a profit on it.

Then she thought of the velvet bag. All the money they had left. She had about eighty dollars with her.

"Good thing we were here," Paul said, and Josie realized the truth of it. If they hadn't come to town, if she hadn't made her attempts at music in Cooper's home, they would have been at the mine that day. Alone, without a soul know-ing they were there.

"Everyone ready?" the driver asked.

The bus sputtered awake and pointed itself north.

"Are you done with that?" Paul asked.

Josie looked over to him. He'd moved himself to the next seat over, like some independent fellow traveler. Ana was lying on the floor, gnawing on Josie's leg, waiting to be told to stop.

"With the music?" Josie asked, and Paul closed his eyes. *Of course the music,* his placid face said.

Wasn't she on the verge of some great discovery—if not one meant for the world at least a private revelation, bringing forth the music within her? Josie watched the scenery pass, the fire trucks heading the other way, toward the trouble, and she realized, with some surprise, that the music she needed to hear, that she'd just heard, that she had brought forth, had swum in, she needed no more of it. Not right now at least. Cooper would not understand this. You're onto something, he might say. Or would he say that? She was probably not onto something. She was more likely a woman, temporarily insane, who had been conjuring dissonant madness from a group of pliable musicians wanting free dental care. But what about staying in that town, Cooper's town, and weaving herself into it, becoming their new dentist, their resident eccentric, amateur composer, part of the musicians' world, raising her children there? No. Or not yet. She was free of it. She was free of so many things, the fear of Carl, the ghost of Evelyn. She would not ever feel free of Jeremy, but two out of three was a start. She was no longer fleeing anything. But that didn't mean she wanted to be kept, handled, cared for.

"I don't know," she told Paul.

She could not promise that she would not do it again. She had no idea. She needed no more music, but needed to do something else, and to see something else, and she needed to make her children braver and stronger by moving. She could make no promises about what she would want to do or see in the future, and she hoped her children would forgive her for this lack of certainty, this never-settled question in their lives, a limitless sky that had the power to make them fearless, utterly indomitable, or cripple them with fear.

They drove for hours, over streams and through wide expanses of taiga, the sky ahead a velvet blue. Cooper had said he would meet Josie and her kids, and as the scenery passed, she became unsure this was something she wanted. She was not sure she could trust her state of mind, but after twenty minutes of riding away, she felt a familiar exhilaration, the breathless freedom of having left trouble behind. It was not unlike the feeling she'd had when she left Ohio, and when they'd landed in Alaska. Now the Chateau was gone, the cabin was gone, they were free from everything again. They knew no one on the bus, and were headed to a place where they knew not a soul.

By the time they pulled into a wide parking lot loud with police lights and emergency vehicles, Ana was asleep on Josie's lap and Paul had moved to another seat, two rows up. This was new: until even just a few weeks ago, he never would have ceded the position of human pillow; he certainly wouldn't be so far away from the sleeping Ana, when at any moment she might need his help. Now, though, he was looking out the window, taking in the bright parking lot scene, the police lights, the dozens of volunteers in orange and yellow rushing to and fro.

"Inside the school there," the driver said.

Josie woke up Ana, and she led her and Paul off the bus. Paul was carrying one of the backpacks and Josie had the other.

The school was a low-slung brick building, the front double doors opened wide, a woman sitting at a folding table inside.

"Hi there," the woman said, her voice quiet and kind, as if she knew of the sleeping horror inside of them and didn't want to wake it.

Josie gave the woman their names, and the woman directed them into the gym, where enormous lights illuminated, in discrete sections, every service available—first aid, bedding, food. At the window where the high school normally served lunch, a variety of fresh food was being spooned onto plates. Half the gym was a grid of cots that had been neatly arranged, though most were empty. A computer-printed sign advertised the services of a registered nurse. She stood by the sign, a young man lying on a cot next to her with no discernible injuries; he was leaning over the side, reading a comic book.

On the gym's stage, a trio of kids, all under six, chased a fourth child, a yellow-haired girl wearing a cape. "Are you sheltering here tonight?" a voice asked.

Josie turned to find a man in all black, a priest or pastor.

"I don't know. I guess so," she said.

Josie and Paul and Ana devoured spaghetti and broccoli, watermelon and chocolate cake. They hadn't eaten, she realized, most of the day. "Are we going to school here?" Ana asked, her teeth brown with frosting. Paul smiled and shook his head.

"No, sweetie," Josie said. "We're just staying here a night or two." But she had no idea what they would do next.

She listened to snippets of conversations between the volunteers in the gym. Most of the evacuees in the gym were from Morristown or other nearby towns. Only a few outbuildings had burned there so far, she learned. An army of firefighters were working valiantly, aided by a favorable wind that had slowed the progress of the burn.

When she brought their finished plates back to the cafeteria window, Josie noticed that a woman in a black uniform, a kind of fire information officer, had just pinned up a new map of the scope of the burn. Josie scanned it for Morristown and found it, an almost imperceptible rectangle just next to a hulking red mass, the area of the fire, the color and shape of an oversized heart. On the border between the red and the white she found, in tiny type, the words Peterssen Mine, nearly obscured by an X written in red ballpoint.

Josie returned to the trio of cots she and the kids had arranged. They had pushed them together to make one loosely connected mattress. Paul and Ana were playing Go Fish with a new deck of cards.

"Someone gave us these," Paul explained.

Josie sat on the edge of the bed, then dropped to the pillow. She looked to the ceiling, thirty feet up, a mess of ropes and beams and banners reminding visitors of the school's better seasons.

At nine o'clock most of the gym's lights went off with a loud crack and sigh, leaving one bright cone in each corner. Ana wanted to continue to play cards, but Paul told her they should be quiet and still, so as not to disturb the rest of the people trying to sleep.

"You guys have everything you need?" a voice asked.

Josie looked up and squinted, adjusting her eyes to the dark. It was a man, an older man with a sweep of grey hair across his eyes. He looked familiar. Josie thought of home, someone from Ohio. No. Then she realized it was the firefighter she'd met before—it seemed like months ago—the gentle-eyed man who had come upon her when the inmates had changed her tire.

"We do," she told him, and realized he didn't recognize her. Why he was here, checking up on evacuees, was unclear. She didn't want to distract him from his work, or get into a conversation about just what she'd been doing then, on that road, or what she was doing now, hundreds of miles north, in this shelter. She wouldn't be able to explain it if she tried.

"Rain's coming." These were the first words Josie heard in the morning. It was dawn, and already the gym was bustling with volunteers loudly preparing breakfast. "This afternoon," the voice said. It was coming from outside the gym, this booming voice with this significant news. Ana had woken up with the noise, but Paul slept on. Josie led Ana silently off the mattress and into the lobby, looking for the booming voice, but he had disappeared. Still, throughout the school hallways there was talk that the worst had come and gone, that the weeks ahead would bring more rain, more cold, a wet autumn that would end the fires and purify.

They walked outside to find the sky was still the same, white and yellow and smelling acrid. Josie stepped farther into the parking lot and now saw, coming from the north, a wall of dark clouds. Back inside, Josie peeked into the gym to see if Paul was awake, but he was still splayed on the bed, his mouth open, as if astonished by rest.

When she turned around, Ana was not at her side. Josie looked through the lobby, and heard some small voices coming from another hallway. She turned the corner to find Ana at the drinking fountain with another child, this one smaller. At first glance it looked like Ana was being Ana, pouring water from the fountain onto the head of this other child, a tow-headed boy of about four.

Josie was about to tell Ana to stop when she realized that Ana was feeding water to the child. Ana had directed the child to turn the faucet on, and while the water flowed, Ana reached up, her tiny hands making a tiny bowl, and she was bringing this water to the child, most of it landing on their shirts but enough finding its way to the blond child's mouth.

Josie walked to them, and Ana looked up at her, worried, knowing she would need to explain.

"It's okay," Josie said.

"He couldn't reach," Ana said.

"I know. It's fine. Let's clean up, though."

And so the three of them found paper towels in the bathroom and cleaned the water from the floor. The boy's mother arrived as they were finishing and took the boy back to the gym. Josie and Ana stood in front in the hallway, next to the school's darkened trophy case.

"Do we have to sleep here again?" Ana asked.

Josie didn't know.

"I don't want to," Ana said.

"I don't, either," Josie said, realizing this was the first candid conversation she'd had with Ana in months, maybe ever. Usually she was strategizing how to tell Ana something, avoid telling her something, parsing and obfuscating in order to get a civilized result. Now she looked into Ana's eyes, knowing that her daughter was different, she had evolved, and she saw, too, that Ana knew. She knew that she had shed one shape and was taking on another.

"We only have eighty-eight dollars," Josie said, looking not at Ana now but at the portrait of some champion athlete from the early nineties, a girl who was probably now Josie's age.

"Eighty-eight?" Ana said. "That's a lot!"

*　*　*

Paul slept through a loud breakfast, and through the activation of the loudspeakers above, which announced a series of developments, the imminent arrival of other evacuees, and more news about the rain coming from the north. When he finally woke, there was a smattering of applause from the volunteers. A grandmotherly woman brought him a bowl of homemade oatmeal, which he ate greedily as she watched.

"Well, you're safe now," she said to Josie and her kids, as if concluding a conversation about their prior worries. "And at noon we're having an activity for all the evacuees. All the families will be invited to participate in a crafting workshop, and afterward to talk about their feelings. It'll be very therapeutic. But fun, too!"

Josie smiled, and the woman left to pick up the bowls left in various parts of the gym by the dozen or so children now running roughshod through it. The gym had gotten more crowded in the last hour, it seemed, and smelled of too many humans without access to showers, too many humans sleeping in old clothes in close proximity.

Staying here another hour suddenly seemed painful—another night altogether impossible. Josie tidied up their beds and took their two backpacks, and led Paul and Ana out of the school. She had no plan in mind, but wanted to see what options there were in town. Eighty-eight dollars would buy them one day of lodging and food at a real motel.

Now a woman was approaching. "Ma'am, I forgot to ask before"—Josie couldn't place if she'd ever met this woman, but had to assume she had—"whether or not you have access to a phone. So many evacuees either left theirs behind or can't get coverage. But we have landlines here. You can call long-distance, whatever."

Josie told the woman she didn't in fact have phone access, and she and Ana were led to the principal's office in the school. On the counter where tardy slips were usually handed out, there was a phone at the ready.

"I'll give you some privacy," the woman said.

Josie dialed, got a wrong number and dialed again.

He answered.

"Carl?"

"Who is this?"

"It's Josie."

"Oh hey. Where are you? How are the kids?"

His voice was upbeat, casual.

"You don't know where we are?"

"I know you're in Alaska. Sam told me. But where?"

"You *do* know. You sent a guy after me."

"Wait. What?"

"Didn't you serve me papers?" she asked.

"Serve you papers? What for?"

His voice was so bright and amused that she had to realign everything she expected to say.

"Someone served me papers," she said, her mind racing through just who it could have been. Evelyn?

"What kind of papers?" Carl asked.

"I don't know. I never touched them. I took off."

Carl laughed out loud. It was a big belly laugh, the laugh of a contented man. Josie heard a distant squeal through the line, the sound of a gentle crashing wave. Was he on a beach? He probably was on a beach. "Oh wait. Your lawyer buddy called me, looking for you," he said. "Maybe that could have something to do with it."

"Elias? What did he say?"

"He said he wanted to give you a heads-up. I called you a few times about it. You probably didn't bring your phone. Am I right?"

"I didn't want you tracking me."

Again Carl laughed, but this time there was something hurt and uncertain in his mirth. "Anyway, remember the power company you sued? Well, they countersued all the lead plaintiffs. Elias said it was a standard scare tactic, said he'd handle it."

Josie's heart spun. She hadn't thought of that lawsuit in weeks.

"So the kids? They're good?" Carl asked, switching back to a tone of brightness and levity. Was he drunk, too? Who was this happy carefree man?

"They're good. Sorry about Florida," she said.

"It's okay. I understand. It probably sounded like a weird request. But the kids should meet Teresa at some point. They'll like her, I think. She's a child psychologist. You know that?"

Josie did not know that. But now her interest in Carl made sense.

"So you guys are in Alaska!" Carl let out a loud exhalation that admitted his own foibles and forgave Josie's dramatics. She was still squaring all this: Carl had not gone after her in any way—he was not following her, suing her, nothing. Instead, it was a power company. They'd sent some random server to scare her.

"From the news, it looks like the whole state is on fire," Carl said.

"We actually just fled one," Josie said. "We're in a shelter." She recounted the day, the school she was calling from. She looked around her, remembering she was in a principal's office. A sign on the wall said I'M A PRINCIPAL. WHAT'S *YOUR* SUPERPOWER?

"And you're okay?" he asked.

"We're fine."

"Okay. Stay safe. Give a shout when you get back."

She hung up and left the office, realizing Carl hadn't asked to speak to the kids. He hadn't asked when they were coming home. Even the idea of seeing his children, bringing them to Florida to present them to Teresa and her family, that Goebbelsian photo-op, was a casual notion, not a big deal either way. His interest in them came and went, like his passion for economic equality or triathlons. But he was harmless. This was so crucial and freeing to know.

* * *

"Let's get out a little," Josie said. She was standing over the cot where Paul and Ana were playing cards.

"Go where?" Ana asked.

Josie shrugged. "The river?"

This town was about the size of Cooper's, and they meandered through it, noticing that it was largely empty. Most of the residents were either helping at the high school, Josie figured, or had left the state for less flammable lands. They passed a truck repair operation, a real estate office, a frame shop, all closed, and found themselves at the Yukon, gray and moving slowly. They sat down, Josie suddenly feeling too tired to move. She lay back, staring into the white sky, and could feel the sun beyond it, still oddly warm.

"This one's heavy," Paul said, and a loud thunk followed.

Her children, stripped of all possessions, were throwing stones into the river. The clicking as they sifted for the right one, an almost imperceptible wind as they threw the stone high, the bass note as each hit the water.

"You want me to put one on your foot? It's hot from the sun." It was Ana, standing above her.

"Okay," Josie said, her eyes closed. She felt the hot weight of a large rock placed on her instep. It felt wonderful. She murmured her approval.

"You want another?" Ana asked, and Josie said she did.

Ana placed another rock, a lighter one, on Josie's stomach, and Josie felt the heat of it through her shirt. Choosing to keep her eyes closed, she allowed Ana, and soon Paul, to cover her with stones. There were a dozen on her chest and stomach, and a key few in her lap, feeling very right, and finally a large flat stone on her forehead, smaller, rounder stones covering each cheek. The warmth of these stones! It slowed her breathing. She couldn't move. Covered like this, minutes were days, and she heard the voices of her children as they tried to find more places to cover their mother, their voices delighted though nervous at the edges. What were they seeing? Their mother covered in stones, so far from home.

Josie allowed herself a moment of doubt. There was a possibility, she admitted, that she and her children should not have come to this state on fire. But the doubt did not last. Instead, at this moment, she thought she was right about everything.

That we can leave.

That we have a right to leave.

That very often we must leave.

That only having left could she and her children achieve something like sublimity, that without movement there is no struggle, and without struggle there is no purpose, and without purpose there is nothing at all. She wanted to tell every mother, every father: There is meaning in motion.

As the sun fingerpainted lurid colors on her eyelids, Josie felt a surge of belonging. She had love for everyone. She knew it wouldn't last, this outpouring of gratitude and forgiveness, so she named names: She loved Jeremy, and Sam, and Raj, and Deena, and Charlie from the cruise ship, and

Grenada Jim, and Carl, of course Sunny, and had something like love for Evelyn, whose dying filled her with rage, and Josie knew rage, and so she loved Evelyn. With a shudder she knew she loved her parents, too, and that she wanted to tell them this, and felt she must tell them this, that it was time to tell them that she knew them to be no better and no worse than herself.

"We're taking them off now," Paul said. There was a tone of finality in his voice, hinting at his growing discomfort with his mother covered in stones. When Josie's chest was free from the weight, she sat up and her children looked at her quizzically, as if they expected her to have become someone else. But she was only their mother, sitting up in the bright sun. They continued to remove the stones from her lap and legs.

"How heavy do you think this is?" Paul asked. He put one of the rocks in her hand. It was warm.

"Was that on my chest?" she asked.

"Yes," he said.

"Maybe a pound?" she said.

Paul made a disappointed sound.

"Maybe two, three pounds?" she tried. His face brightened slightly, but then soured again as he stared at the rock.

"Ten pounds, easily," she said.

"Ten pounds!" Paul said to Ana, who was duly impressed.

Ana removed a rock from Josie's thigh and put it in her hand. "How much is this?"

This one was lighter than Paul's, and Paul knew this, but he and Josie exchanged a look. "This one's about the same," she said. "Ten pounds. Maybe more."

Ana's eyes sparkled, and Josie assumed Ana would keep the rock in some coveted place, but instead Ana turned and threw it into the river in a reckless diagonal. "See ya, sucker!" she roared.

They continued to remove the stones, and each time, they asked Josie how much she thought each weighed, before dispatching that stone into the river. Ana threw hers with cruel send-offs, usually repeating Josie's measurements before casting them at violent trajectories. Each time a stone was removed, Josie felt closer to levitation. They were just stones, and she was only sitting by a lake shushing the jagged shore, but each time her children lifted one she let out a tiny gasp, and her body felt closer to release.

"Look, Mom," Ana said, and finally Josie stood up. Ana was pointing to a spot in the woods behind them. It seemed to be a simple trailhead sign, a standing map, but on it were colorful sagging orbs.

"Balloons!" Ana said, and ran to the sign.

"Trailhead," Paul said, following her.

The sign, decades-old, depicted a path that wound through a valley, along a narrow river, on a steady upward trajectory until it reached a mountain lake. If there had ever been any indication of distance or scale on the map, it had been worn away by weather, but Josie figured it couldn't be more than a mile or two, and the elevation no more than three thousand feet.

"I've always wanted to see a mountain lake," she said.

"Me too," Paul said, staring with great seriousness at the map.

Paul had never said anything to Josie about a mountain lake, about knowing what one was, or wanting to see one. But Paul did not, could not, lie, and Josie had no choice but to believe that this, along with his knowing he could marry a girl named Helena, was a secret and real desire, and that from him there would be far more unspoken wants and needs in the future, and that she would be privy to so few of them, and she would have to accept this.

"So should we go?" he asked.

"What's a mountain lake?" Ana asked.

XXIII.

THEY HAD ONE APPLE, a bag of unpeeled carrots, a bottle of orange Gatorade, a bag of crackers, half a pack of Starburst candy and a bottle of water, two-thirds full. The kids were wearing jeans and T-shirts. The temperature was in the sixties. Josie felt good about their chances to make it to the lake and back to town in time for lunch.

"Paul," she said, knowing she was about to delight him, "can you make a copy of that map?" His eyes took on the spark of duty as she handed him a pen and, from her wallet, the back of a grocery store receipt. His rendering was clear enough, and included most of the information on the sign's map, which is to say not a great deal. There was a long winding trail, and an oval lake, and next to it a tiny rectangle, which Josie assumed was some kind of picnic area, maybe a shelter of some kind. It looked less like a modern Forest Service map and more like the sort of thing an illiterate bandit would have drawn while drunk on hard cider.

But when they got to the trail Josie saw that it was wide and well marked, and for all she knew there were souvenirs and snack shops along the way. They began. They walked into a copse of birches spaced in an orderly fashion, the light on the forest floor dappled and the air cool. Ahead they saw a yellow stripe, the size of a hand, on the trunk of a tree, and Josie laughed, knowing this trail would be easy; someone had marked it every hundred yards. They looked at Paul's map and it told them nothing new. The lake was up ahead—still seeming no more than an hour's walk.

"A bridge," Paul said, and pointed to where a log, halved lengthwise, had been laid across a tiny ravine leading to the river. Covering a narrow creek of shallow water moving slowly, the bridge was rudimentary and slick with moss, but Paul and Ana insisted on walking across it without her help. It was only a few feet down, so even if they fell in they couldn't possibly be hurt. Josie allowed them to cross, and then they wanted to do it again, so they went back and did it again.

They walked along the river for a time, an hour or more, the heat of the day peaking, Paul and Ana starting to wilt and then the path turned inward and toward the hills, and they walked in shadow. Ahead, the path seemed to run directly into a boulder the size of an ancient barn. They followed the path all the way to the boulder, which up close looked more like a granite wall. They looked left and right and saw no yellow markers.

"I think we're supposed to go through it," Paul said. He seemed utterly serious, until a tiny smirk overtook the left side of his mouth.

"Look. Yellow," Ana said.

Josie and Paul turned to see that Ana had found a tiny yellow stripe on a tree high on the hill overlooking the river. There was a narrow thread of trail leading up to and around the boulder, and they took it, all three of them, Josie and Paul and Ana, having the distinct sense that without Ana they would not have seen what now seemed like an obvious path upward and over. In half an hour they climbed the path, using tree roots for footing, until they'd reached the top and they could see a clearing ahead.

"Might be the lake," Paul said.

Josie looked at her watch. It was just after noon. If they were indeed at the lake, even if they made it there, turned around and walked quickly, they'd be back in town by two. They reached the top of the ridge, but there was no lake, only remnants of, or the origins of, a shallow stream pooling. Around them was a wide meadow dotted with wildflowers of violet and yellow.

"Is that the lake?" Ana asked.

"It's not the lake," Paul said, then turned to Josie. "Is it?"

"No," Josie said.

This was the kind of setting, tucked into the curve of a mountain, where she expected to find it, and now they had walked so far and climbed over the ridge, and found something else, some swampy stream—it was a cruel thing.

"Okay," she said. "Let's think." And she contemplated the time, and their place on this trail, halfway up a mountain far larger than she'd imagined. It had taken them hours to get this far. There was time to go farther, reach the lake and turn back, she thought, though she had the tangible sensation she was making the wrong decision. She was afraid to look at Paul, for fear his eyes would judge her.

Ana pointed to the sky. "Look, Mom," she said. A great dark cloud had come from behind the mountain. The moment they saw it, they heard thunder. It was a loud clearing of the throat that filled the valley, an introduction to calamity.

"Is that coming toward us?" Paul asked.

"Will there be lightning?" Ana asked.

The thunder came again, this time louder. Josie looked up to find that the cloud had moved closer, casting half the mountainside in grim shadow. And they were standing near the shallow stream.

"I don't know," Josie said. Realizing they were standing by a stream, she tried to remember the workings of lightning and water. Was the water a conductor or a deterrent? There seemed to be no good choices around her. Lightning was coming. Likely rain, too. If they stayed out in the open, they would get soaked.

"Should we go there?" Ana asked, pointing to a forest ahead. It seemed to be about an eighth of a mile across the upward-sloping meadow, a distance not daunting, but then again all distances so far had been warped. Everything that had seemed within reach was in fact twice as far and took three times as long.

"The lightning goes after the trees, right?" Paul asked.

"I don't know," Josie said. How could she not know? Stay away from water or go toward water? Into the trees or away from the trees?

Then again, they hadn't seen lightning yet, so she held out hope that they could make it to the forest before the real storm came, if it came at all. The forest seemed the safest option. They could rest there, stay dry.

"Let's run," Josie said.

Paul and Ana's eyes spoke of their exhaustion, but this was quickly replaced by the spark of a necessary task.

"We're going to run to that bunch of trees, okay?" Josie said.

They nodded. Ana positioned herself in a sprinter's start.

"Ready?" Josie asked. "Let's go."

They took off, away from the water and across the flow-ered meadow, not caring what colors they crushed underfoot.

"Yes!" Ana roared behind her.

Josie turned and saw Ana's tiny feet fly over rocks and bramble, her big orange head leaping like a candle carried by a rabbit. She watched Paul's face, set with purpose. The trees were only a few hundred yards away now. They would make it. When they were near the first great pines, Josie felt silly, having made this more dramatic than it needed to be. After all, they were simply outside, running in a developing storm. She didn't want her children to be afraid of the rain, or the thunder, or lightning, even if, given their altitude, the storm might be coming from a perilously close distance. Before the forest there was an array of small jagged boulders, and among them Josie stopped, allowing Paul and Ana to pass her, smiling as she watched them fly by her, pumping their arms, both of them grinning wildly.

"Good, good!" Josie roared, almost jubilant.

A screaming crack ripped open the sky above. The world went white and Josie's back seized as if whipped. In front of her, Paul and Ana were frozen in the white light for a few long seconds, photographed in mid-stride. She had the momentary thought that they had been struck, that this was what it was to be struck by lightning, that her children were being eliminated from the world. But the light turned off, the world returned to color, and her children continued moving, continued living, and the flash was followed by a thunderclap so loud she stopped and threw herself to the ground.

"Get down!" she yelled to Paul and Ana. "And come here."

Paul and Ana crawled to her, and she draped herself over the two of them. They stayed low for a minute as the sky growled and panted, as if impatiently looking for Josie and her children.

"I'm scared," Ana said. "Will the lightning hit us?"

"No," Paul said firmly. "Not while we're low like this. Make yourself small," he said, and Ana shrunk, holding her knees with her arms.

"Good," he said.

"Okay. We're going to run again," Josie said. "Just to the trees." She looked up, seeing they were no more than a hundred yards away from the next forest.

"Ready?" she asked.

Paul and Ana nodded, ready to push off and run. Josie paused a moment longer than she had planned, and she had no reason why. For a fleeting moment she looked into the forest, and ran her eyes up the length of the tallest tree, wondering briefly if it was true that the lightning would strike the tallest object in any field.

"Are we going?" Paul asked.

And then the world tore open. A sickening light filled the forest and a blue-white bolt split the tree, the one she'd just been contemplating, a quick ax driven down its spine.

"Shit," Josie said.

"Mom, will it get us now?" Ana asked.

Josie said no, it wouldn't get them. That last strike was the closest the lightning would come, she told them, though she had no reason to believe this was true. If anything, the lightning was getting closer each time. It seemed to be acting with intent.

They waited, watching the charred remains of the split tree smolder, a narrow plume of grey smoke spreading upward. The thunder roared again, sounding like a tank moving across the roof of the sky. Josie ran all available options through her mind. They could stay where they were, but they'd get soaked. The rain would come soon, she was sure, and the sun would set, and the dark would be absolute. They would be wet and cold and unable to find their way back. They had to continue, now. She could see the trail winding up the next mile or so, interrupted by small stands of trees. They would have to sprint between them between lightning strikes.

"We're going to that next forest," she told her children. "It's just a few hundred yards." But the path there was wide open, unprotected, and while they ran across the expanse they would be easy targets for whatever malevolent force was patrolling their progress.

"No, Mama," Ana said. "No, please."

Paul explained that the lightning had just struck the trees, so why would they go where the lightning had just struck?

"It won't strike there again," she said, not believing herself. "And it's going to rain soon, okay? We have to move." She had some irrational hope that there was something, some human structure, even a discarded tent, at the lake. "One, two, three," she said, and they ran again, their shoulders hunched, their heads fearing reprisal from above.

The first raindrops fell on their sprinting forms as they found the shelter of the trees. They passed the tree that had been struck, smelling its charred wood, the scent strangely clean, and continued until the forest thickened, dark with low boughs. Josie stopped and Paul and Ana gathered around her, and the three of them, out of breath, sat down against the wide trunk of an ancient pine.

"Can't we just stay here?" Ana asked, and Josie thought

it very possible they could stay there, at least for a spell, in hopes the storm might pass. As she was contemplating this, though, the rain came heavier and a gust of cold wind shot through the trees. The temperature seemed to drop twenty degrees, and the rain drenched them in seconds. She looked down at Ana, who was wearing a short-sleeved shirt. Her eyes were wide and her teeth began chattering. No, Josie thought. No. Only one option. She took off her own shirt. "Let me put this on you," she told Ana, and Ana gave her a horrified look.

"Put it on," Josie said firmly.

Ana threw the shirt over her head and it draped awkwardly over her torso and rested across her knees.

"You're going in just that?" Paul asked, nodding toward Josie's white bra, a utilitarian style with a tiny fringe of lace.

"I'm fine," Josie said, mistaking his statement for one of concern. He was embarrassed for her, she realized. He didn't want his mother running across a mountain trail in a bra.

"Let me see that map," Josie said, asking Paul for the hand-drawn rendering he'd made when they'd begun. Josie wasn't sure what she expected to find on it, but she had begun to think their forward push was ill-advised. They were heading further into the storm, into territory they knew nothing about, but if they turned back, no matter how long it took or how wet and cold they got, they could be sure to find the town. Paul hesitated for a moment, then a grave look overtook his face. He pulled the paper from his pocket, unfolded it and hovered over it, protecting it from the rain.

Above, two jets collided. There could be no other explanation. Josie had never heard thunder so loud. The raindrops grew still bigger. Her children, already soaked, somehow grew wetter, colder. Josie estimated the temperature was in the high fifties and would drop ten degrees in the next hour.

Now she looked at the map, and though it was as rudimentary as the one he'd copied it from, showing only a meandering trail leading to an oval lake, there was that tidy rectangle next to the oval. It had to be some kind of structure, she thought. Even an outhouse would be life-saving.

"You're sure about this?" she asked, pointing to his drawing.

"What?" Paul said. "That? It was on the original map."

"Okay," she said. "You're sure?"

"I'm sure," he said.

She knew her son would have taken the task of map-drawing with the utmost seriousness, and now, if he was right, the box on the hand-drawn map might save them. It was far closer than going back to the trailhead—miles closer. It was just around a wide bend in the trail.

"You guys rested?" she asked.

Neither child answered.

"We have to run again," she said. "We have to run until we get to the lake and the shelter. Do you understand? We'll go in stages. We'll run from point to point and we'll rest when you need to rest. Okay?"

Above, a planet popped like a balloon.

"Can you guys be brave?" Josie asked.

Paul and Ana did not hesitate. They nodded vigorously, wanting to be brave, knowing there was no choice but to be brave, that there was nothing greater than being brave. Josie knew, then, that better than searching for a person of courage—she'd been on this search for years, dear god—better and possibly easier than searching for such people in the extant world was to *create* them. She didn't need to find humans of integrity and courage. She needed to *make* them.

A private smile had overtaken Ana's face.

"What?" Josie asked.

"I can't say it," Ana said.

"Say it. Doesn't matter."

"It's a bad word I think," Ana said.

"It's okay."

"Shitstorm," Ana said, and Paul laughed, his ice-priest eyes smiling, lit from within.

"It *is* a shitstorm," Josie said. "This is a shitstorm. Are you ready to run through this shitstorm?"

They grinned and took off again. They ran through the stand of trees and when the trees ended and the trail was exposed for another hundred yards, they saw another yellow marker and scrambled to it. The rocks on the path were wet now, and Ana slipped on one, and went down, gashing her leg against the scree. Lightning lit the world in slashing blue light but Josie didn't pause. She picked up Ana in mid-stride and carried her chest to chest until they reached the next small forest.

By the time she was able to put Ana down, Josie's

back had shifted. Something was very wrong. She couldn't breathe. She set Ana down and lay on her side, trying to find a workable way to bring air into her body. A slipped disc. A punctured lung. Broken rib. Anything was possible.

"What happened?" Paul asked.

Josie couldn't speak. She raised a finger to ask for time. Now both children were staring at her, Ana with her mother's wet shirt draped over her like a smock. Josie looked up into the treetops, the black fir silhouettes against the sky, angry and grey like an ocean storm.

Josie slowly regained her breath and when she was able to sit up again, she found that Paul had torn a strip from the bottom of her shirt, the shirt now worn by Ana, and had used the strip to tie Ana's leg with a makeshift bandage. It looked like something you'd find on a WWI battlefield, but Ana was caressing it, humbled by its grandeur. An oval of blood emerged from within and Ana's eyes widened.

Josie looked up the trail and thought she could see, just beyond one more stripe of trees and over a low ridge, the clearing where the lake and shelter might be. She stood, very much afraid she might not have the strength, or that the act of standing would make whatever had happened to her far worse. Though she was wrecked, and now noticed that her legs were bleeding in a dozen places, she could breathe and was reasonably sure she could run again.

"She can't run," Paul said, indicating Ana.

"Is that true?" Josie asked her. Ana's eyes welled up and her chin quivered. Josie looked down to see that Ana couldn't put weight on her right foot. Josie examined the leg up and down and felt no fracture, but when she put the lightest pressure on the bandage Ana wailed. "You twisted it. Nothing broken," Josie said, and now Ana's eyes flooded. "Okay. Wrap yourself around me," Josie told her, "like a monkey."

Ana threw her arms around her, burying her tiny shoulder in Josie's neck. When Josie stood again, now carrying forty extra pounds, her back roared in protest.

"Ready, Paul?" she said.

"Just to the next trees?" he asked.

Ahead lay a few hundred yards of dirt and scree cutting across open valley, utterly vulnerable.

"Exactly," she said. "You run and I'll be right behind you. Don't stop until you get there."

"Now?" Paul asked.

"Now," Josie said.

They ran, and Josie ran with one arm draped around Ana's bottom, her other arm feeling her way forward, ready to break their fall. She expected to fall. She'd never run carrying Ana like this, on a wet path strewn with loose rocks like this, with pain like this. Every step sent a sharp stab of steely light through Josie's spine and down her leg. Ana's weight was exacerbating whatever it was Josie had done to her back, but she couldn't slow down on the open ground. She had to catch up with Paul, who was suddenly moving with effortless speed and agility. Josie watched him leap and land, thrilling in his agility and courage.

As if to punish her for her moment of pride, the sky ripped open, end to end. Paul fell to the ground, and Josie dropped to her knee. No earthquake, no tornado could be that loud. Josie had lived almost four decades and had never heard a storm like this, had never known a sky this punitive.

They rose and ran again and made it to the next forest. Josie followed Paul to a spot against a dead pine trunk. They sat side by side like soldiers in a foxhole, heaving. Ana was still attached to Josie's torso, her matted head in Josie's neck.

"You cold?" Paul asked her, nodding at Josie's bra, her mottled skin.

"I'm fine," Josie said. She was soaked with cold rain, and the cold wind was cutting through her as they rested, but she had felt warm while running. The pain, though, overwhelmed her senses.

"We're beating this," Josie said. "You see that, right?"

Paul nodded, serious in his acknowledgment, as if his mother was confirming something he'd begun to suspect and had hoped was true. They were moving, fully inhabiting the beautiful machinery of their physical selves, and they were outwitting the unthinking brute power of the storm.

"We just have to get around that bend, I think," Josie said, pointing ahead. Paul took out his map, and pointed to a wide arc his pen-drawn path made just before it reached the lake.

"I think we're close," he said.

A different kind of thunder overtook the air. It was as loud as the sky-cracking they'd heard before but this was coming from up the trail. It was more gradual, a growing roar, sounding like rocks, a thousand rocks moving together.

Josie stood and looked up the bend of the trail. She saw nothing. Then a wave of dust came from behind a bulge in the cliffside. She had never heard or seen an avalanche but she knew this was an avalanche, not a thousand feet ahead. After the strangely orderly roar of it ended, the valley was quiet, as if resting after its exertion. Josie had no idea what to do. To retreat was impossible for all the reasons she'd arrived at earlier—the kids would suffer, it was too cold, they'd be soaked and frozen. But to go *toward* the avalanche?

"Was it, Mom?" Paul asked.

"What?" Josie asked.

Paul gave Josie a wide-eyed look, indicating that he didn't want to say the word "avalanche" in front of Ana.

"I think so," Josie said.

In a rush, the rain seemed to double in volume. Each drop was heavy, distinct. Josie knew they had to move. She made a plan to make their way to the blind bend of the trail and at least peer around the corner, to see what had happened, if there was still a path to follow. Again she picked up Ana, whose grip around her neck was somehow tighter than before, painful but necessary, and she set off. She led this time, with Paul just behind.

Far before the bend, they could see the evidence of the avalanche. A rough grey diagonal of rocks and scree obliterated the trail and had settled onto the valley floor hundreds of feet below. Josie looked up to the cliff face, looking for some clue about its intentions. Beyond the fallen rocks she could see the path as it continued to what seemed like a clearing. Somehow she and Paul and Ana would have to climb over the fallen rock for fifty yards or so and join the trail again, all the while facing the possibility that the rock would move again, that their traversing it would send it all downhill.

Some impulse in her told her to do this quickly, to avoid rumination. "Let's go," she said. Her back wailed again, but she crawled up on the settled rocks, finding it almost impossible to gain traction. She raised a foot, put her body's weight over it, and immediately her foot slipped, and she went down. Ana flew off and onto the dusty stones. Josie's hands braced her fall but her forehead had struck a high-standing stone. The pain was quick and severe but Josie knew the injury was not great.

"You okay?" Paul asked. He had appeared next to Josie and Ana, and given his light weight, he was able to move quickly atop the scree without sinking into it.

Ana nodded and Josie said she was fine.

"There's some blood on your face," Paul said to Josie. "Not that much."

Josie had no hands free to wipe it. And she knew that to make it across Ana would have to crawl on her own.

"Follow Paul," she said, and Ana made no protest.

Favoring her unbandaged leg, Ana moved nimbly over the mass of loose rock, and Josie did her best to follow. She tried to make herself lighter, more agile.

"Wait!" she yelled. The children were far ahead of her, finding this too easy.

Josie was crawling, slipping, her limbs dropping through the surface as they would through newly fallen snow.

An idea occurred to her and she acted on it, knowing she had no choice but to try anything. She turned onto her back and pushed herself with her feet, like a mechanic under a car. The scree scraped her back, her exposed neck and the back of her head, but it worked. Her hands and legs had been concentrating too much weight on the loose rock and causing her to fall through it. But her back, acting like a snowshoe, was spreading her weight, and she moved this way across the expanse of fallen rock, as her children watched and eventually encouraged her.

"Almost there," Paul said.

"Almost there," Ana repeated.

Josie had a strong sense that this image would stay with them, the picture of their mother backstroking across an avalanche in the middle of an Alaskan electrical storm. Josie snorted, and she laughed a loud laugh as the rain fell heavily upon her.

When she was across, her children were waiting, Ana standing on one leg, holding her brother's shoulder for support. Paul's legs were raw and bleeding, his hands white with torn skin and the dust of the stones he'd crawled across. Ana's legs and hands were similarly aggrieved, and at some point she'd acquired a cut on her temple, a finger-sized red slash. Above, the thunder cracked again, as loud as any thunder had ever been since the birth of creation, and Josie laughed out loud again. "It never ends, right?" she said. "One thing after another." Ana and Paul smiled but seemed unsure exactly what their mother was talking about, and Josie was happy that the subtext of her statement had been lost on them.

"Okay, ready?" she asked. She turned, expecting nothing, but now, on the other side of the avalanche she could see it, the bright blue lake, no bigger than a swimming pool. Josie laughed again. "Oh god," she said, "look at it. It's so small. All this way for that!"

"But it's so blue," Paul said. "And look."

Josie had been searching for the shelter the map had promised but Paul had found it first. It was more than a shelter. It was a sturdy cabin made of logs and bricks, the straight line of its chimney standing like a beacon. On its door there was the same sagging trio of balloons they'd seen on the trailhead sign.

Josie didn't need to tell her children what to do. They had already begun running, Ana somehow strong again, and Paul sprinting ahead, knowing his sister would be fine, and Josie walked behind them, her shoulders shuddering with cold and a kind of tearless weeping.

When she made it to the cabin she saw the sign over the porch. "Welcome Stromberg Family Reunion," it said. She opened the door to find Paul and Ana, soaked by rain and streaked in blood, standing amid what seemed to be a surprise party. There were balloons, streamers, a table overflowing with juices and sodas, chips, fruit and a glorious chocolate cake under a plastic canopy. All around the cabin were framed photos from every era, most in black and white, all neatly labeled. The Strombergs through time. Josie could only assume that some intrepid member of the family had been to this cabin days ago, had set all this up for the family reunion, and then, for whatever reason, fire or unrelated trag-edies, had canceled it all, leaving the cabin and all its bounty to another, smaller, family: Josie, Paul and Ana, so tired.

"Who are the Strombergs?" Paul asked.

"Today we are the Strombergs," Josie said.

There was enough firewood for three winters, and there was plenty of water, so Josie started a fire, and they took off their clothes and cleaned themselves and sat naked under a vast wool blanket as their filthy clothes dried before the fire. They ate and drank whatever they wanted in no par-ticular order, and were soon sated and though their muscles ached and wounds roared for attention, they would not sleep for many hours. Every part of their being was awake. Their minds were screaming in triumph, their arms and legs wanted more challenge, more conquest, more glory.

"That was good, right?" Paul said.

He didn't wait for an answer. He stared into the fire, his face aglow and seeming far younger than it was—perhaps reborn. His ice-priest eyes had found a new and untroubled happiness. He knew it was good.

Josie found herself smiling, knowing they had done what they could with what they had, and they had found joy and purpose in every footstep. They had made hysterical music and they had faced formidable obstacles in this world and had laughed and had triumphed and had bled freely but were now naked together and warm, and the fire before them would not die. Josie looked at the bright flaming faces of her children and knew this was exactly who and where they were supposed to be.

XXIV.

But then there is tomorrow.

ACKNOWLEDGMENTS

Thank you first to Jenny Jackson, calm soul, sensitive reader and blessedly relentless champion of this book. Thank you to Sonny Mehta, Andy Hughes, Paul Bogaards, Emma Dries and all at Knopf. Thank you Em-J Staples, constant friend, tenacious editor and proud Illinoisian. Thank you Andrew, Luke, Sarah and all the unwavering advocates at the Wylie Agency. Thank you to Cressida Leyshon and Deborah Treisman, for their faith in, and astute editing of, this book's first excerpted incarnation. Thank you Alison and Katya, heroes and Homerites. Thank you careful readers Nyuol Tong, Peter Ferry, Christian Keifer, Curtis Sittenfeld, Sally Willcox, Clara Sankey, Tish Scola, Tom Barbash, Ayelet Waldman, Carrie Clements and Jesse Nathan. Thank you patient musicians Thao Nguyen, Alexi Glickman and Jon Walters. Thank you Terry Wit, Deb Klein and Kim Jaime. Thank you philosopher-dentists Tim Sheehan, Larry Blank and Raymond Katz. Thank you Alaska for persisting. Thank you V, A and B for existing.